WIELDING A RED SWORD

By Piers Anthony
Published by Ballantine Books

Book Four

**INCARNATIONS
OF IMMORTALITY**

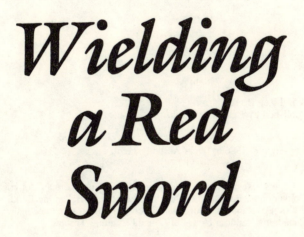

*Wielding
a Red
Sword*

PIERS ANTHONY

A DEL REY BOOK

BALLANTINE BOOKS • NEW YORK

A Del Rey Book
Published by Ballantine Books

Library of Congress Cataloging-in-Publication Data

Anthony, Piers.
  Wielding a red sword.

  (Incarnations of immortality ; bk. 4)
  "A Del Rey book."
  I. Title. II. Series: Anthony, Piers. Incarnations
of immortality ; bk. 4.
PS3551.N73W48 1986   813'.54   86-7900
ISBN 0-345-32220-7

Manufactured in the United States of America

First Edition: October 1986

10 9 8 7 6 5 4 3 2 1

CONTENTS

—1—

MIME

It was a traveling show, the kind that drifted from village to village, performing for thrown rupees. There was a chained dragon who would snort smoke and sometimes fire when its keeper signaled, a harpy in a cage who flapped her wings and spat curses at the audience, and a mermaid in a tank who would, for a suitable fee, bring her head out of the water to kiss a spectator. Standard stuff, hardly impressive, but fun for the children. The dragon was old and flabby, the harpy was ugly, and the mermaid, though pretty enough, evidently spoke no local dialect. But at least this show was convenient and cheap, and the crowd was thick.

The man who watched was undistinguished. He was slightly below average height, wore a faded gray shawl, and he kept his mouth shut. He had evidently suffered some abrasion of the face, for it was to an extent swathed in dirty bandages, so that only his eyes, nose, and mouth were exposed. He had the mark of the Sudra caste, though he could have been taken for an Aryan in race. Since none of the twice-born would mix voluntarily with the more lowly merchants and laborers of the once-born, his identity had to be taken at face value.

Of course, caste had been legally abolished in most of the kingdoms of India. But what was legal did not necessarily align with what was actual. One had only to watch the reaction of anyone who inadvertently brushed by a Pariah to understand that!

Now the main show developed. A stage magician performed sundry acts of illusion, causing the faces of demons to manifest in smoke and a flock of birds to startle out of his hat. One of the birds let a dropping fall on the head of a spectator, who complained loudly, whereupon the magician gestured and changed the bird into a shining gold coin, which tumbled to the ground and rolled. The spectator pounced on the coin—but it converted to a venomous snake that hissed and struck at him, while the other spectators laughed. Good magic!

Then there was an exotic dancer, who undulated in the company of a giant python. Her performance was partly artistic and mostly erotic, and the percentage of men in the throng increased. Then the python opened its mouth and took in her left hand. The dance continued, and the reptile swallowed her arm and then her head, and finally the rest of her body. There was strong applause as her two kicking feet disappeared into the maw and the snake slithered heavily back into its curtained cage.

Now a startlingly lovely young woman took her place on the small stage. Her skin was so pale as to be almost white, and her hair was the color of honey. She had a little harp and she set herself and began to play and sing. The song was in English, a language generally but not universally understood in this region. This was a novelty, and the audience was quiet.

The song and music spread out to captivate the listeners. There was a special quality to it that caught them up, even those who could not follow the words. It was as if a mighty orchestra were playing and a chorus of deific beings singing—yet there was only the one woman and her instrument. This was a phenomenon beyond what had been presented before, and all stood entranced.

When the song was done, there was a hush. Then the rupees began flying, landing at the woman's feet, fairly burying them in metallic brightness. All that the audience had came forth, begging for another song.

The woman smiled and sang again, and it was as before: every person within range was transported. Even the old ones were rapt. Now those of the Vaishya caste, the husbandmen and merchants, entered the throng, heedless of propriety, listening. When the second song was done, the shower of money from these higher-class listeners overwhelmed the prior contributions. Applause enough!

The Sudra man stood transfixed, even after the woman had taken up her harp and retired to her wagon and the next show had come on. Jostled by his neighbors, he recovered enough to walk away, his gaze almost vacant. He had evidently been smitten and hardly knew how to cope with it.

He found his way to a wall that offered some slight seclusion and leaned against it. Then he reached into an inner pocket and brought out a ring in the form of a coiled little snake. He set this ring on his smallest finger and brought it covertly to his bandaged face.

"She?" he whispered in English.

The snake-ring came alive and squeezed his finger once.

The man removed the ring from his finger and returned it to his hidden pocket. He paused, considering. How was he to approach this lovely and talented woman, and how would she receive him? He could get more specific advice from the ring, but he preferred to work it out for himself, as his possession of the ring could identify his nature if it were seen by others.

In the end, he waited till dusk, when the throng dissipated and the traveling show was closing up for the night. He approached the covered wagon he had seen the woman with the harp enter. He stood by it and clapped his hands, gently, so as to attract attention without generating too much of it.

The woman appeared. "Yes?" she inquired. Now her lovely fair hair was bound in a heavy kerchief, and she wore a functional skirt and jacket, but her beauty overcame these restrictions.

The man opened his mouth, but did not speak. He gestured helplessly.

"I am sorry," the woman said. "I can see that you have been injured, but I do not speak the local dialect. Do you know English?"

The man tried again. His mouth worked, and finally the sounds came out. "Ah—ah—ah—I do," he said.

She glanced sharply at him, tilting her head. "You are shy?" she inquired. "There is no need to be. What is it that you wish?"

–3–

The man struggled again to speak. "N–n–n–not sh–sh–shy," he said. "I st–st–stu–stu–stutter."

She did not even smile. "Come inside," she said.

He followed her into the wagon. Inside, the space was tight, but well organized; there was room for two to sit facing each other, and this they did.

"I do not know you," the woman said. "I have not before talked directly with a person with your problem. Forgive me if I am clumsy; I don't quite know how to help you."

Again the man tried. It took time for him to get the words out, but the woman was patient and did not try to interrupt or to fill in the words for him. Digested, what he said was this: "I need help to leave the Kingdom."

"But if you have committed some crime, and are fugitive from justice, I shall not help you," the woman said.

He asserted that he was not a criminal; he just had need to depart anonymously.

"Forgive me again," she said, "but I must ask you to touch my harp. This will advise me whether what you say is true."

He touched her harp. Nothing happened.

She smiled. "Thank you. Now let us be introduced. I am Orb Kaftan of Ireland, and I sing for my supper. My harp is a gift of the Mountain King and it will not suffer the touch of a dishonest person. I am sorry I had to doubt you before."

"I—must not tell you my identity," the man said haltingly. "I am not injured; I wear the bandage to conceal my face."

"Ah—a political refugee?"

"Approximately." His stutter was diminishing as her warm attention helped him, but that word remained a considerable challenge.

"May I see your face?"

He unwound the bandage. His face was clear and handsome, almost aristocratic. "But I must not show it openly," he said.

"I think we might help you, but I am not sure you would like the manner," Orb said. "We always have need of inexpensive labor, tending the animals, cleaning the cages, menial chores. I think you are of higher birth than that."

"I am. I will do the work."

"Perhaps we can improve upon your camouflage," she said. "Let me fetch you a mask."

She set him up with a clown-mask. She assured him that it would not seem unusual, as long as he remained with the group, as most of the members had more than one task, doubling as entertainers and workers.

And so he joined the group and shoveled dragon manure and cleaned the harpy cage and fed fish to the mermaid. He was paid only with food, a bunk in a wagon, and his right to be anonymous.

The group moved slowly from village to village, on wagons hauled by rented elephants, and put on its show at every stop.

After several days, the man approached Orb again. "I think I could perform," he explained haltingly.

"But everybody laughs at the clowns!" she protested.

"They laugh *with* the clowns," he clarified. "And I could do other things that don't require speaking. I could be a mime, a juggler, an acrobat."

"These things are not as easy as they may appear," she protested.

"But I have some natural ability and some training," he said. "My mouth may be handicapped, but not my body."

"Well, if you're sure, I can take you to the tour master," she said doubtfully. "But he is an exacting man."

"Take me to him."

She did. The tour master was large and fat and, when he wasn't playing to a crowd, he tended to scowl. "Show your stuff or get out," he said gruffly.

The clown did a front-flip in the air, then stood on his hands, then flipped back to his feet.

"So-so," the master said, unimpressed. "Can you do it on a high platform?"

The clown nodded. There was no platform handy, so he scrambled lithely up a tree and took his stance on a horizontal branch. He repeated his flip and handstand, then swung himself down, around, and back to the top of the branch.

The master became more interested. "No fear of heights, eh? What else can you do?"

"He says he can juggle," Orb explained.

"Jugglers are a dime a dozen. He'd have to be something special."

The clown pointed to a collection of knives, used by a sometime knife-thrower. Then, with permission, he took five, tossed them up singly, and juggled them. The blades flashed as they twisted in the air, but no knife dropped to the ground.

"What else?" the master asked, impressed.

The clown had evidently prepared for this. He went into a mime act, doing a clever imitation of a warrior whose sword kept getting in his way. He had no costume and no sword, but it came across clearly. When he managed to spear his own foot, the master smiled. When he tried to sheathe the blade rapidly and passed it through his crotch instead, the master laughed.

"You got it, mime! Work up a complete act; I'll put you on pay. We'll call you—um, let's see." The master stroked his chin. "The Mime. No, Mym. Mym the Mime! You've got a talent, boy. Wish I'd known before."

And so he joined the paid performers, leaving the dragon dung behind. "I had no idea!" Orb told him warmly. "You are a very talented person, Mym."

It was merely coordination and training, he informed her, as much by gesture as by words, for he did not like to embarrass them both by constant stammering. Orb was always understanding, but still it represented an imposition, and the last thing he wanted to do was burden a woman as lovely, inside and out, as she.

But her interest in him had been aroused, and his ascension to performer status brought them into closer natural association. Though the group was casteless—which made it technically Pariah—it did have its own type of stratification, with the master at the top, the performers next, and the menials at the bottom. Orb, as the main attraction, was second only to the master in importance—but as Mym refined his act and the flow of rupees increased, his status ascended correspondingly. At first the others had been condescending or diffident, because of his speech impediment and his inexperience, but no one laughed at him, because all were outcasts in their own fashions. The mahout who tended the lead elephant had a clubfoot, and the dragon-trainer was an alcoholic—the dragon liked the smell of alcohol—and the cook was so grossly fat that he expected in due course to assume performer status as a freak. None of them were inclined to laugh at something as minor as stuttering.

In fact, Mym discovered that the group was a kind of family; it looked out for its own, and he had become a part of it. This became clear one day when they were setting up for a show in a village not far south of Ahmadabad, the giant capital of Gujarat. He was helping the exotic dancer, Pythia, prepare for her act. She had to strip and spread a special protective grease over all her body, so that the digestive acids of the python would not damage her skin. She had a magic pill she would gulp just before the snake swallowed her head that enabled her to stop breathing for twenty minutes or so; that and the salve enabled her to perform her act once each day. But the girl who normally helped her and who reached into the python's open mouth to haul her out by the feet when the act was over, had run away with a handsome drifter, and a replacement had not yet been recruited. So Mym, whose act was done before hers, helped her with the preparation and the conclusion.

He was spreading the salve on her body, making sure to catch every spot, when they were interrupted by a party of armed, uniformed officers of the Gujarat law-enforcement staff. "Stand where you are, masked man!" one snapped at Mym, holding his sword ready. "Identify yourself."

Mym, of course, was unable to respond, in part because of the stutter. Had they found him? He had thought he was free . . .

The dancer, knowing his problem, faced the troops. Her breasts shone with grease and became more pronounced as she inhaled. "This is a private dressing room!" she protested in the local dialect.

The chief officer contemplated her assets. "This is Kingdom business, woman," he said gruffly. "We are in pursuit of a party of thuggees. They may have passed this way—and this man is masked."

"This man is my assistant!" she exclaimed, taking a really significant breath. "He is no thuggee! He has been with me all day!" She shook herself, and all three officers struggled not to gape. "He wears a mask so the fumes of the python won't hurt his face.'' She snapped her fingers, and the great snoozing snake woke and lifted its snout, hissing.

The men backed away. "To be sure," the leader said. "If you speak for him—"

"Of course I speak for him!" she said. "I couldn't function without him."

They departed, and Mym relaxed. He resumed spreading the salve. "Certainly I spoke for you," Pythia said. "I didn't even have to lie, really, but I would have. I know you're no thuggee, and whatever you did do to make you hide is no business of mine. We cover our own, here."

He continued with the salve, not trying to speak.

"You do a good job," she added reflectively. "Your hands are clever. You get me covered much faster and better than I could do myself, even in the easy places. That girl I had before never was much good; she'd tickle me in one place and skimp on another."

Which meant that she had been at risk for burns from the stomach acids. Mym knew she didn't like that!

"Do you know why I asked for you to help me?" Pythia continued. "It wasn't because you are good. It was because I can get any ten men to do this, but their hands would be sweating hot and their eyes would be hotter. I don't like having a man do it—never since one got carried away two years ago and tried to rape me." She smiled reflectively. "The only reason he missed was because the salve made me too slippery to hold. Actually, I'd have given it to him, if he'd asked; I can take a man or leave him, anytime. What's a little thing inside me for a minute, compared to what *I* go inside of for my act? But I don't like to be forced. So I told the master, and he made a eunuch of that man. I was the lead act, then, you see. Don't misunderstand; I'm not jealous of Orb. I'm in this for the money, and she brings in three times as much as we ever had before, and the master is generous when the takings are good. And you, too—you're bringing it in nicely, too, and that's so much the better. But that's what I'm saying; when you're with us, we take care of you, and you take care of us. The master took you on because Orb asked him to— and now he'd do anything you asked, too, because you're good for the show, Mym, you really are. But I asked for you because

I knew you could handle me without making a move." She meant the handling physically—his hands rubbing salve into every part of her, public and private.

He was finished, now, and her act was almost due. She turned to speak directly to him, as she slipped into her scant costume. "I know you get hard when you stroke me; any man who's a man does. When he doesn't, I'll know it's time for me to retire. But you wouldn't try to force me, because you're the most disciplined man I ever met—yes, you are, even if you try not to show it!— and because, even if you weren't, you're in love with Orb and you wouldn't touch another woman if you thought there was any chance at all you might one day touch her, because you know she's a one-man woman and expects the same in return. So I'm safe with you, Mym. *That's* why."

Mym stood there, chagrined. Had it been so obvious?

She answered, not needing the question. "No, you hide it well. But Orb—what I can do to a man by showing my body, she can do just by being herself. I'm dried fish; she's caviar. So I knew what to look for."

She stepped toward the stage, bringing the python along with her, but paused once more. "And you know, you just might," she said, winked, and went on out.

If Pythia understood him that well, then perhaps she also understood Orb. If she thought he had a chance . . .

He watched the dance and consummation, half-dazed. But he snapped out of it as the python slithered back, bearing its burden, because he had to get Pythia out before she suffocated. The trained snake opened its mouth, which had been defanged, and Mym reached in and caught the dancer's bare feet. He hauled, and the greased body slid out. The skimpy dress had already dissolved away, leaving nothing to impede the motion. Of course this would never have worked with an ordinary python or a fully clothed and ungreased woman, but that didn't matter; it was a decent show, and as long as it never played twice at the same place, the seeming horror of it remained.

He got her clear and hosed her down, getting the acids away. The salve combined with the acid, so that both were neutralized, but, as long as she remained inside the snake, more acids were forming, so it was important to get the refuse off. After the hosing, he set her up, took a clean cloth to her face, cleaned her closed eyes and mouth carefully, then did the same for her genital region. Then he snapped his fingers at her ear, waking her from her trance.

She shuddered, then resumed her breathing. Her eyes opened. "You do such a good job," she said. "With you, there's never any smarting, no bad patches. I'm completely clean." She leaned forward and kissed him. She put her arms around his neck, set her face into his shoulder, and sobbed for a moment. Then she lifted her face. "Thank you. I am back from the abyss. This, too, is very fast with you."

Mym nodded. The act, spectacular as it was, was not accomplished without cost. Pythia risked death, and the trance that stopped her breathing was halfway to death; though she had been through it many times, each time she knew it could be the last, and each successful recovery was a profound relief. Most others, even in the group, were not aware of the full nature of the experience she undertook.

"Should you ever need me, you won't even need to ask," she said. "You are the best of men, Mym."

Had his heart not already been committed, he would have taken her up on that. Yet Pythia's acceptance of him was only a manifestation of the acceptance of the group. He felt as good as he could remember.

It was the monsoon season, and daily the winds and showers intensified. The master had a spell to ward off rain during the actual show, but it was too valuable to waste during travel, when there was no money to be reaped. The dragon did not like getting wet, but was too big to cover, so he was increasingly surly. Mym had a good way with the animals, so had to be out cajoling the monster forward, getting soaked himself.

Then one of the wheels on the mermaid's wagon got mired in mud, and all other hands were committed, so Mym went to take care of that. He used a pole to lever it out, but got thoroughly muddied in the process. When the wagon was finally clear, the others were far ahead.

The mermaid poked her head out of her tank. Naturally the rain didn't bother her. "Come, ride with me, Mym," she called.

Startled, he looked at her. He hadn't realized that she spoke English. Normally she didn't speak at all, because it was difficult to do when her lungs were full of water. But she could drain it from her gills and breathe air when she chose, as she was an amphibian.

She patted the side of the tank. "Here," she said, smiling. "You must be tired; you deserve a rest."

He *was* tired, as well as being soaked and dirty. He climbed up on the wagon, holding onto the edge of the tank. The mermaid clicked to the mahout, and the mahout urged the elephant forward. The wagon began to gain on the others.

Mym's hands were occupied, holding on as the wagon bumped along, but the mermaid's hands were free. She took hold of his head and turned it to please her. Then she kissed him. "My thanks for your service, sir," she said. "Should you ever require something novel—"

He blushed, and she laughed. "I'm only teasing, maybe. But you are a good man."

Finally the wagon caught up to the others, and he dropped off, for his help was needed elsewhere. But his mind was whirling, for this was the second time an attractive woman had made him an offer. He had no prejudice against halflings, and the mermaid had known this; had his situation been otherwise, he would have been interested. But what intrigued him most was the evident fact that he had sex appeal for these women. He had known many women before—more than he cared to count—but had never considered himself attractive in that sense. The others had been made available to him because of his position; he had assumed that they would not have offered so from their own personal choice. But here in the group, women were making themselves available by choice. True, he had done them favors of a sort; but he had not acted with the thought of such reward. Their interest had to be genuine, and that flattered him in a profound manner. Perhaps his stutter was not the barrier he had supposed. If so, this group had already given him more than refuge.

They came into Ahmadabad, a sprawling city of more than a million inhabitants. Here they expected to have large and generous crowds, for the city folk were more sophisticated than the villagers and more interested in oddities. Indeed, their first show was a great success, and the master was so pleased that he issued bonus payments to the performers.

Naturally Orb, typical of her gender in certain respects, wanted to go shopping. The master could not deny her, but insisted that she have some protection. "Thieves are thick in cities," he muttered.

"Mym can come with me," Orb said brightly.

The master scowled, but evidently remembered the way Mym had juggled knives. "But stay out of trouble," he admonished. "I don't like risking two star performers together."

So Mym went shopping with Orb, glad for the opportunity to be with her, however slight the occasion. He wore a nondescript tunic and an artificial beard that completely changed his appearance. Still, it was risky for him—but perhaps no more so than performing in this city as a mime.

Orb was delighted with the wares set forth in the open market. She went from stall to stall, exclaiming at the bright woven materials and pretty baubles, choosing first one and then another.

But Mym was nervous. He felt a motion in his inner pocket, so he quietly put his hand in, found the snake-ring, and put his finger through it. "T-t-t-trouble?" he murmured, as if to himself.

The ring squeezed once.

That was all he needed. He tried to draw Orb aside to warn her; but she was distracted by her shopping, and his effort to speak was inhibited by the stutter, so that he could not get through to her.

He sighed to himself. His hand remained in the pocket, out of sight. *Accident?* he thought at the ring, but it squeezed twice. *Malice?* That brought a single squeeze. *Robbery?* Three squeezes. *And rape?* he thought, and got a single squeeze. *And murder?* One squeeze. *The thuggees?* One squeeze.

Now he tried again to warn Orb. He caught her arm and squeezed, somewhat harder than would ordinarily have been necessary. She paused, looking at him, realizing that something was amiss. He made a motion with his head, signaling toward the region from which they had come.

"Time to go home?" she asked, and he nodded affirmatively.

"Very well," she said. "Just let me find one more thing."

He tried to signal no, but she didn't understand. Rather than make a scene, he waited, though the ring was pulsing warning.

Orb completed her purchase, and they started back. Mym guided her along a route they had not taken before, hoping to give the thuggees the slip, but soon he saw the subtle pursuit developing. They were watching, closing in—three, four, five of them. They wanted the money the woman evidently had to spend and her body, and they were not the type to leave witnesses behind. The Kingdom had made an effort to eliminate the criminal class, now called the thuggees, though these were not actually connected to the original guild of assassins. They were just common cutthroats, always on the prowl for vulnerable wealth, not trained killers but dangerous when they banded together.

Mym's teeth bared in an unconscious snarl. He hated the thuggees, of whatever stripe! But he had not brought a weapon, for complex reasons that now seemed invalid, and the fact that Orb was the obvious target made it worse. Alone, he could have given them the slip, but there was no way she could do that. This was going to be ugly.

What way? he demanded of the ring in his pocket. Then he ran through a mental list of alternatives, beginning with straight flight and ending with mayhem. The ring squeezed at mayhem.

Where? he thought next.

The ring signaled as they passed a deserted alley. This was the best place to meet the thuggees.

Mym did not question this; he trusted the ring. He took Orb by the elbow and guided her into it.

The thuggees were jubilant at this break. This was exactly what they wanted—the prey secluded, so that the dirty work could be done without witnesses. Killing could be accomplished quickly, but it took longer to rape a living woman—and it wasn't any fun when she was dead—because they had to take turns. Here in the alley, setting two of their number as guards for the occasion—

They closed, one of them blocking off the far exit, the other four advancing from behind.

Mym took Orb to a niche between buildings, where some dilapidated crates were piled. "Hide!" he directed, his stutter not manifesting during his distraction. Seeing the tough-looking men, she obeyed, frightened.

Now Mym stood before the crates, holding a board with a nail protruding, facing the thuggees.

The five closed in. As one, they laughed, pointing at his inadequate weapon. They were armed with knives of various descriptions, and their leader had a short sword.

Mym bit his tongue, deliberately. In a moment he tasted the blood. His eyes glazed, his breathing quickened, and his dark skin paled.

"Hey, he's freezing!" one of the thuggees exclaimed, in the native tongue.

"Trying to imitate a berserker," another said, unconcerned.

The blood in Mym's mouth continued to flow. His body began to shake. The breath whistled out through drawn lips.

"Well, I'll berserk him!" the leader said, stepping forward and raising his sword. "He's shaking in his boots!"

A thin line of reddish froth appeared at Mym's mouth.

"Hey, I don't know—" another thuggee began, worried.

Then Mym moved. The board dropped.

The leader saw no more than a blur, before his sword was expertly wrenched from his grasp. Then that sword whirled demonically, slicing at the thuggee to the right. A line appeared at his neck, below the left ear, and he collapsed. The sword lifted and came down on the head of the thuggee farthest to the left, splitting his face open from forehead to nose.

The leader, disarmed, gaped. "He *is*—" he began. Then the sword whistled across with such force that his head lifted from his neck and tumbled to the ground before the body fell.

The two remaining thuggees tried to turn and run, but one was caught by a thrust to the bowel, and the other, starting away, got the point of the sword through his skull from the rear. The tip of the point showed through at the front as he fell.

Mym glanced back at the crates, where Orb still hid. He pondered a moment, then reached for his ring again. *Can she handle this?*

The ring squeezed twice.

Best way to get her through? He ran through several notions in his mind and stopped when the ring squeezed once. He had his plan.

Mym drew out a silk handkerchief he normally used in his mime act. He went to the woman. Orb's head was ducked down, and she was shivering, evidently afraid of the violence and of what was about to happen to him and to her.

"V-v-v-v-veil," he got out, giving her the handkerchief.

She glanced up. "You mean—to hide my face? That won't fool the robbers!"

She did not know they were dead. "Qu-qu-quickly," he said. "Ey-ey-eyes too."

Frightened and mystified, she tied the handkerchief across her face, covering even her eyes. Then he urged her up and out of the crates and guided her from the alley.

Once they were clear of it, he removed the veil. "But why didn't they follow?" she asked, perplexed anew.

He shrugged, allowing her to think that the matter was too complicated for an immediate stuttering explanation. They hurried on back to the group's camp.

There was an ugly taste in Mym's mouth, and not from the blood he had invoked. He had deceived Orb, and he did not like that one bit. But he believed the ring; she was not ready for the truth. He had done what was necessary to save her life; that knowledge had to suffice.

– 2 –

PRINCE

They returned safely, and Orb secluded herself in her wagon to recover from the shock of the near escape. Mym got busy on routine tasks, helping organize for the evening's show.

They had several shows at different sites in Ahmadabad, because in this city a few blocks put them into an entirely new neighborhood, generating a fresh audience. The take was excellent, and news of Orb's singing spread so that the master received an invitation to do a private showing for a noble. Stunned, the master accepted.

All were delighted—except Mym. He went privately to the master. "Sir, I cannot perform before nobility," he said, though not nearly as smoothly as rendered.

The master heaved his paunch about and focused directly on Mym. "Do you know, I had a visit from the police," he said. "There has been a particularly bad bunch of thuggees operating in this region, leaving a messy trail of dead. Some officers even checked this group, a while back, but of course we harbored no thuggees."

Mym nodded, knowing what was coming. How much had the master pieced together?

"It seems that a beautiful woman had an encounter with them

recently, but she managed to escape," the master continued. "The police realized from the description that she was from our group, so they came to inquire. Indeed it was our Orb, and she confirmed that the encounter had taken place. Five brutish men, armed with knives and a sword. But it seems that you managed to dissuade them and escape unharmed."

Mym nodded again, for once glad that he was unable to speak with facility.

"The five were found slaughtered in an alley. The pattern of their bodies is typical of that left by a berserker warrior. You know—the kind who tastes blood and goes crazy."

Mym shrugged.

"But something doesn't match," the master said. "A true berserker would have slaughtered the woman too, then gone out through the city and killed and killed until overwhelmed by a force of twenty armed, trained men. This did not happen."

Mym waited.

"Orb reports that you had her don your handkerchief to hide her face and that you led her out of that alley. She doesn't know how you persuaded the thuggees not to follow. There was no one else—just you."

Again Mym shrugged.

"Now I never heard of a temporary berserker," the master said. "Obviously you are not one; you weren't even armed. So I must assume that either a berserker happened upon the premises at that moment, destroyed the thuggees, and expired from a lucky return-thrust before he got to you—which makes no sense, as no other body was found—or that a highly trained warrior who hated thuggees did the deed."

He had obviously caught on. Mym's hand went to his inner pocket, and his finger found the ring. *Lost?* he thought.

The ring squeezed twice.

"You are very handy with knives," the master was saying. "But I have never seen you juggle anything except weapons. This suggests that you were never an entertainer before. You merely have learned to handle weapons with an extraordinary facility. I can think of only one class of person who would have access to training like that—a noble."

Still Mym waited.

"And now you tell me you cannot perform before a noble. Because you would be recognized?"

Mym nodded.

"Well, let me tell you something about concealment," the master said briskly. "The best concealment is that which the observer never suspects. That is the secret of the legerdemain I practice. Misdirection. The very last place any noble would expect a noble to be hiding would be onstage before other nobles. I want you to do your act; I guarantee you will be secure from discovery."

Mym shook his head negatively.

"Ah, but there is the stutter," the master said, as if just remembering it. "Now it occurs to me that that might indeed be an identifying trait. I have no deep knowledge of the nobility here; I travel too much to keep current. I have heard of no stuttering noble, but that may be just my ignorance. Suppose we were to add some words to your mime act? Under your mask and makeup, no one can see your mouth move. If at key points a voice-mimic behind the stage were to throw his voice, so that it seemed to emanate from you . . .?"

Mym, vastly relieved, reached out and clasped his hand.

"But though there is no need for me to know details that do not concern me," the matter concluded, "I think there is one who must be advised. I would not have her hurt for all the world, and nobles are notoriously casual about romantic liaisons. I think, before things proceed further—"

Mym nodded affirmatively. It was indeed time.

They talked, as the caravan waited out one of the monsoon downpours north of Ahmadabad. It was pleasant in Orb's wagon as the sound of the rain beat loud, for her covering did not leak the way some of the others did. First she told him her history, for she wanted him to know about her. She had been born in Ireland twenty years before and raised with a kind of sister she called Luna. Mym wasn't quite clear on the relationship, but it seemed that Orb's parents were Luna's grandparents, and that the two girls seemed very like twins. Luna painted with a magical brush she had received from the Mountain King, and Orb sang with the harp from the same source. It was the golden harp that extended her power, so that the audience could experience it.

Her father had had the same talent, but it only manifested when he was touching the person to whom he sang.

But what was she doing here in India? Mym wanted to know. For it was obvious that she could enchant audiences anywhere in the world and had no need to wander in such uncivilized reaches as these.

Well, she was looking for a song, she explained. It was titled the Llano, and it was the most marvelous song ever to be sung on Earth, but it was highly elusive. For one thing, it was very challenging to sing, so that only a few people in each generation could perform it successfully. She thought she might be able to sing it well enough and wanted to try. For another thing, it was said to be the most compellingly lovely song that the human voice was capable of rendering, and that intrigued her too. But mainly, she believed that her destiny lay with the song, for whoever traced it to its source would discover the avenue to a wholly new fulfillment. Orb, dissatisfied with her mundane existence, sought that fulfillment.

"I have heard of it," Mym said haltingly. And he explained how the manifestation of the Llano had been said to accomplish miraculous things. Once a young woman had loved a great warrior, but she was of lesser birth, and the warrior was not aware of her. So one day she sang him a segment of the Llano, and he was instantly captivated and loved her from that moment.

Orb adored the story. "Of course it couldn't happen in real life," she said regretfully.

"It could happen," he assured her.

She looked at him, understanding. "I—but of course you're not a prince." She was trying to mitigate the possible cruelty of the situation. "Not that that matters, Mym. I—have been growing very fond of you. Even—"

He cut her off before she could say anything she might prefer to retract later. "I-I-I-I—" But the stutter overcame him completely; he could not get the words out.

Orb put her hand on his. "It doesn't matter, Mym."

He shook his head. It *did* matter! But he couldn't say it.

Then she brightened. "I have heard that sometimes—Mym, can you sing?"

"S-s-s-sing?" he asked blankly.

"It invokes a different portion of the brain, as I understand it. So some stutterers can sing clearly, even though they can't talk. Come, try it; sing with me." And she launched into one of her Irish songs: "O Danny boy, the pipes, the pipes are calling, / From glen to glen, and down the mountain side."

Doubtfully, he joined her: "And from the trees, the leaves, the leaves are falling, /'Tis you, 'tis you must go and I must bide."

They both paused, astonished. He had not only managed to sing it without stuttering, he had sung it clearly and well.

"You could make it as a singer!" she exclaimed.

"I-I-I-I could!" he agreed, awed.

"No—sing it," she urged him. "You don't need a song; just hold the note, any note."

"I can!" he sang in a level note.

"Now you can say anything you want to!" she exclaimed. "Oh, Mym, I'm so pleased!" And she flung her arms about his neck and kissed him.

He let her do it, but did not respond. First he had to acquaint her with his own history, and he wasn't sure she would be pleased.

"I am not what I seem," he sang on a single note, reveling in this sudden new ability while he dreaded what he had to say. "I *am* a prince."

Orb sobered rapidly. "Go on," she said with sudden reserve.

In singsong, he did. He was the second son of the Rajah of Gujarat and had been raised in a palace, his every whim obliged. His older brother was slated to become the new Rajah when their aging father died. Mym's real name was a complex construction that translated, loosely, as "Pride of the Kingdom." Of course, he explained ruefully, he had been named before it was realized that he had a speech impediment. He was of course no pride, and the name had become an irony, one that he never used. His confinement to the palace had been as much to conceal him from public awareness as to cater to his needs, for indeed his father was ashamed of him.

But a prince remained a prince, and care was taken to bring him to the necessary level in every princely art. For if anything should happen to his brother, before there were issue, Mym would, to the consternation of all who were in the know, still assume the throne. How he could do this, when he could not even give a cohesive directive, no one dared speculate. It was vital that his brother be married early, so as to alleviate the possibility of disaster.

His brother had married early—but both his wife and his leading concubine had proved to be infertile. This was an embarrassment of another nature. They were maneuvering to obtain a fertile wife, but such matters were complex. Meanwhile, Mym— and the kingdom—remained at risk.

Mym had finally had enough of this. He did not want to assume the throne any more than his father wanted him to. He wanted only one thing—to be able to talk normally. But neither magic nor science had been able to help him; stuttering simply wasn't properly understood. So he had run away.

It was perhaps a signal of the family's degree of concern, he sang wryly, that his escape had been accomplished so readily. It was true that he was an accomplished infiltrator, who could slide past guards as if almost invisible—that was one of the talents useful to a Rajah, when rebellion threatened—but he was aware that only the most cursory attempt had been made to locate him. The truth was that his family knew that it would be better off without him. With luck, his older brother would carry the line on through, and the stutterer could be expunged from the records.

And so he had slipped about and spent his money cautiously, learning how to merge with the population and get along without having to speak. For a time, the challenge of surviving had kept him occupied, but then the tedium had begun to encroach. Skulking around the streets of Ahmadabad had not been much more rewarding than being waited on as a prince. He had not dared show his princely skills, lest he betray his nature, and he lacked nonprincely skills. He had ranged beyond the city, seeking what he could not define. A magic charm had helped guide him and keep him from serious mischief.

Until he had seen and heard Orb sing and play. Then all the rest had faded away, becoming unimportant, and he had known the face and form of his ideal. And so he had come to her, revealing to her his handicap at the outset so that she would not be deceived, and had taken service with the group.

Orb, amazed at first, was evidently acclimatizing as his narrative continued. "So you *are* a prince," she said.

-21-

"Not by choice," he sang. "I desire nothing more than to remain here and be with you."

"But I am not a regular part of this tour," she protested. "I joined at Calcutta and will leave at Karachi, in Sind, where a ship will take me elsewhere in the world. It is the song I seek, the Llano."

"Then I would go with you and be your bodyguard," he sang.

That reminded her. "Those thuggees—as a prince you must hate them."

"They are a bane to our fair kingdom," he agreed. "They are vermin, to be exterminated wherever found. Most particularly when they threaten a woman like you."

"You—trained in weapons. You can juggle five knives in the air without cutting yourself. Surely, then, you could—"

This was the other thing he had dreaded to tell her. "I could kill them," he agreed. "And I did—and blindfolded you so that you would not see their bodies."

Her face stiffened, and she turned away. He got up and went outside, knowing that the thing he had feared had come to pass. Orb was a lovely and somewhat innocent woman; she was revolted by physical violence. She was not temperamentally equipped to understand why or how a prince would master the secret art of controlled berserkery, the ability to kill swiftly without losing his sanity. Yet the master had been right—he had had to tell her, before she began to share the emotion he had for her. There was no way he could bear to hurt her—and if her interest in him hurt her, then it had to be abolished.

But two days later Orb approached him. "I apologize for my reaction," she said. "I realize that if you had not acted as you did, those thuggees would have killed you—and me—and then gone on to do the same to other innocent people. They did have to be destroyed. I—I simply have a problem adjusting to—to this sort of thing. I know you are not a violent man, Mym. I know you did what was necessary. I remember that you tried to get me away from harm before the thuggees showed, and I delayed to make another purchase, so it was really my fault, too. Will you forgive me my ignorance?"

"Forgiven!" he sang in a faint monotone, greatly relieved.

She came close, evidently intending to kiss him. But he shied away, for they were in the open. "People are watching!" he sang.

"Let them watch!" she exclaimed. She flung her arms about him and kissed him most soundly.

For a moment he savored the sheer delight of the experience, for she was all he had ever dreamed of. Then he broke somewhat. "I am a prince," he reminded her. He knew that was no recommendation for her; she did not really believe in royalty.

"I think I loved you before I knew," she replied. "I feared you were a criminal or a renegade, so I fought against it, but really I *knew* you were not. You are a remarkable man, who has been taunted by circumstance, and now that I understand you better, I do want to be with you. I would remain here in India, if I had to—"

"No, no!" he sang. "You must continue your quest for Llano! I would not deny you your dream!"

"But I think I have found my dream in you," she said.

"Only part of it, only part," he demurred. "And that part you can have without sacrificing the other. I will go with you, wherever your quest leads."

She smiled. "You are truly the most wonderful of men." Then she kissed him again.

Naturally the news was spread throughout the group before their dialogue was done. "I am sorry to lose you," Pythia said as he prepared her for the evening show.

"But I will continue helping you!" he protested in his new singsong.

"The master has already scheduled a replacement," she said. "Your belongings are being moved to Orb's wagon. It is not meet for you to handle me after today."

"But I am not—"

"Oh yes you are," she said, smiling. "The mermaid is threshing the water angrily with her tail; she had hoped you would work it out with Orb at a sufficiently later date."

He had to laugh. "Thank her for me," he sang. "You and she have done more for me than perhaps you realize."

"Oh, we realize," she said. Then it was time for her act.

That night he spent in Orb's wagon. Contrary to the popular impression, they did not make love; it was enough simply to talk, getting to know each other in pleasant new detail. When at last they slept, they slept embraced, but that was all—and more than sufficient. The very touch of her caused him almost to vibrate with melody. What made it even more delightful was his realization that she reacted similarly to him. The love of the ideal woman—for the first time, his awareness of his handicap became secondary. It had helped bring him to this, and he would not have had it otherwise.

On another night they did make love. It was the first time for her, for she was truly a chaste woman. He had explained that aspect of the life of a prince, fearing that this would dismay her, but she only said: "You never loved before." And that was true and it made the rest as inconsequential as his stutter had become.

In fact, his thorough experience enabled him to do the most that he could for her, so that there were no awkward confusions or embarrassments or discomforts. "But all of this, with any other woman, would not compare to the merest touch of your hand," he told her sincerely.

"What, even the most beautiful of women?" she inquired archly.

"You are that."

She laughed. "How can you know?"

"I *do* know. The most beautiful concubines of all the kingdom were culled for my pleasure in the palace."

She sighed, not perturbed. "I realize this is true. It is surely a rare compliment."

"They might as well have been oxen," he sang.

"So I am the best of all the oxen you have known?"

"They were beautiful women!" he repeated quickly, and they both laughed.

So it continued, for the long months of the monsoon, as the group wended its slow way northwest toward Sind. Geography hardly mattered to Mym; his delight was wherever Orb was. She had a rare talent in her singing, but even that no longer mattered; he cared nothing for talent, only for her.

They crossed the Indus, taking a slow ferry, and did their show for the folk of another language. It didn't matter; the appeal of the show was universal.

But still Orb did not discover the thing she looked for, the

Llano. This did not frustrate her; she was content to seek it in this fashion for a lifetime, with Mym beside her.

But as they reached the outskirts of Karachi, an armed, mounted party descended on the group. The march came to an abrupt halt. The cavalrymen wore the livery of Gujarat, and this was beyond the territory of that kingdom, but the group was in no position to protest.

An officer consulted with the master, then strode directly to Orb's wagon. "Prince, we have come for you," he called.

So they had known all along where to find him! Mym was dismayed but not really surprised. Probably that business with the thuggees had given them the hint, and they had simply kept track of the touring group thereafter. But why were they acting now?

There was no way to avoid them; they had the group surrounded, and they were alert. They were also first-class cavalry; he knew which was which. He stepped down out of the wagon. "What is your business?" he sang.

The officer did a double-take. Evidently he had not been advised of this detail. Mym wore the whiteface makeup that he used for more than the mime act, and of course they had expected him to stutter.

But in a moment the officer recovered. "The Prince, your brother, is dead," he said formally. "Pride of the Kingdom, you are now the Designated Heir." He made a formal token bow. "You will return with this honor guard to the captital, where the Rajah awaits you."

Disaster! Mym had never been close to his brother, indeed, hardly knew him, but this sudden death was a shock to all the family, himself included. His elevation to Designated Heir was a worse shock. "H-h-how did he d-d-d-die?" he stammered, forgetting to singsong.

"Sir, he died in battle against Rajasthan, honorably."

"But we are not at war with Rajasthan!" Mym protested in singsong.

"It was a routine incursion."

Just a border skirmish—and naturally his bold brother had gone out personally and gotten himself killed and brought this mischief on them all.

Orb came out. "You must go," she said. "Your Kingdom needs you."

"Damn my Kingdom!" he sang.

"I will go with you, my love."

"No," the officer said firmly. "The Prince alone must come. He will marry a princess of the Rajah's choosing."

"N-n-n-never!" Mym cried.

"We are instructed to pay the woman an adequate sum," the officer said. "She will not be in want. But she is not to see the Prince again, by order of the Rajah."

"An adequate sum!" Orb exclaimed indignantly.

"It is here," the officer said, proffering her a small package.

They were quite serious. Mym knew that there was no way to talk them out of this; the Rajah's word was absolute. He bit his tongue.

Orb, bemused, accepted the package, but did not look at it.

"You will be given a few minutes to make your parting with the woman," the officer said. "You will not need to take any belongings, Prince; we shall provide you with suitable raiment."

The blood flowed in Mym's mouth. His skin paled. Tiny bubbles appeared at his lips.

The officer kneeled before him, proffering the hilt of his sword. "If it pleases you, Prince, strike off my head first, and any others you wish. We shall not take arms against our leader. But you will return to the Kingdom."

"Mym!" Orb screamed, understanding. "They are only doing their duty! You must go with them!"

He paused. She was correct—but even if she had been in error, he realized that he would not expose her to this. She was not a creature of mayhem.

He turned his head and spat out the blood. Then he took the officer's sword, reversed it, and handed it back. "A moment," he said, in this instance not stuttering.

"As my lord wishes," the officer said, seemingly unruffled. He sheathed the sword.

Mym turned to Orb. "I will return to you," he sang. "After I persuade my father that I will not serve. Until that time, I give you this." He brought out the ring that was shaped like a little snake.

"But what is it?" she asked, her eyes glistening with tears.

"It is a royal charm. Wear it, and it will answer any question. One squeeze means yes, two mean no, and three mean it can not answer in that fashion. It will also protect you, if you ask it to."

"Protect me?"

He put the ring on his own finger. *Demonstrate*, he thought.

The little snake came to life. It slithered into his palm; then, as he brought it to Orb's hand, across to hers. It reared up momentarily, issuing a tiny hiss, then coiled around one of her fingers and went metallic again.

"You mean—it bites?" she asked, amazed.

"Deadly," he sang. "But only on command. This you can always trust. Wear it and be secure."

"Until you return," she said.

He nodded. Then he took her in his arms and kissed her deeply. Some of his makeup smeared on her face, but that didn't matter. She was too lovely for any smear to alter.

He stepped to the officer. "Now I will go with you," he sang.

They brought up a fine horse, and Mym mounted. He paused to wave to Orb and to the others who had befriended him. Then he rode out.

– 3 –

PRINCESS

The Rajah was older than Mym remembered him. Of course, Mym
had been no closer to his father than to his brother; it was not
the royal way. He had encountered the man, physically, perhaps
no more than a dozen times in his life, and most of those during
his childhood, before his mother had had the bad judgment to
bear a daughter and had been divorced and dismissed from palace
life. Mym had had no close family life thereafter, and realized
now that this had been a considerable part of what he had sought
and found in Orb—true love and closeness between individuals.
He was not about to give it up.

Still, the sight of his father was something of a shock. It was
not just that the man was old, but that he was both grand and ill.
He was elegantly robed, of course, which was his normal state,
with golden embroidery and a necklace of bright rubies, but his
bearing was a thing beyond dress. The Rajah could have been
naked and still radiated authority. His illness showed in the sal-
lowness of his complexion and the hollowness of his cheeks. Obviously magic had buttressed his health, but there were limits even
to magic, and the man was inevitably descending toward his release of this body. No wonder he was concerned about the state
of his Heir.

"It is necessary for the Heir to have an heir," the Rajah said. "You will be betrothed to a princess of the royal house of Maharastra, a politically suitable alliance. We are now negotiating the dowry."

"Sire, I will not be betrothed," Mym sang.

The Rajah gazed at him, nodding. "So it is true. The wench taught you another mode of speech. This is an improvement, though still not ideal."

"The wench," Mym sang between his teeth, "is the only one I will marry."

The Rajah considered. "Do your duty by the princess, and in due course you may recover the wench as a concubine."

Mym turned his head and spat.

The courtiers jumped, and a royal guard went so far as to touch his sword, but the Rajah did not react. After a moment he made a tiny gesture with one hand, dismissing his son.

Mym bowed and backed away, departing the Presence. It had not been a very positive encounter.

He was put under house arrest at an attractive palace on the outskirts of Ahmadabad. Naturally he was not tortured or imprisoned or coerced by magical means; he was the Heir. But neither was he given his freedom. He knew he would be freed the moment he gave his word to cooperate, but he would not give that word. The word of a sovereign was inviolate and never given insincerely. So he languished in total comfort, provided with gourmet meals, phenomenal entertainment, and expert instruction in any art that might interest him.

Two weeks into his confinement, he tried to escape. He was unsuccessful, as he had known he would be; he was merely testing the defenses. In the past, his father had not cared about his whereabouts; now the Rajah did care, and that made all the difference. Mym could not escape.

After the first month, an ambassador from the Rajah came to pose the question: would he now consent to the betrothal? Mym turned his head again and spat, and the ambassador departed.

But the Rajah's wish was not lightly scorned. Two days later a beautiful concubine was ushered into the palace. Her hair was lustrous midnight, and gems sparkled in it like stars. "The Rajah bids me be yours," she said.

"You will never be mine," Mym sang curtly.

Her lovely face stiffened. The palace guards hustled her away.

One hour later the chief of the palace guards approached. "Prince Heir, the Rajah bids you witness what we have done."

Curious, Mym accompanied the man to the front gate of the palace. There, mounted on a tall spike, was the head of the concubine. The gems still sparkled in her hair.

A month later another concubine arrived. This one was a creature of the northlands, with bright blue eyes and hair like finely wrought silver, bound about by threads of gold. "The Rajah bids me be yours," she said.

Mym hesitated. He realized that this was a game in which his father's resources of persuasion dwarfed his own powers of rejection. At best, his adamance could lead to a chain of lovely heads upon the spikes of the front gate; at worst, the Rajah would obtain and present Orb herself in this manner.

"Remain," he told her curtly. "I will summon you at need."

That sufficed for the moment. But when the week expired, and he had not made use of her, this woman's head abruptly appeared beside the first, on the gate.

The third month another concubine arrived. Her hair was the color of burnished copper and buckled in place by combs of fine green jadeite, and her eyes mirrored the jadeite in hue.

Mym closed his eyes. *Forgive me, Orb!* he prayed. *I can not be the murderer of these lovely women. They are too much like you.*

Then he took the hand of the concubine, and brought her to his bed, and dispatched her maidenhead that hour.

In this manner did the Rajah slowly bend his son to his will. But still Mym refused to agree to the betrothal. His body was captive, but his heart remained his own, pledged to Orb.

Two years later the Rajah himself came to the palace. The ravages of his illness had intensified, but his will had not abated. "If you care not for your own interest," the Rajah said, "consider that of your Kingdom. I will pass within three years, and our enemies conspire against us, but the Heir is not ready. Your presence, and the alliance with Maharastra, can secure our frontier against serious incursion. This is necessary for the welfare of all citizens of Gujarat.''

''Adopt a worthier heir,'' Mym sang. ''Let me rejoin my beloved.''

''The Princess of Maharastra is beautiful and accomplished, completely worthy of any man. Accept the betrothal and all else is yours.''

''I will not marry any woman but my beloved. Release me and all else is yours.''

''Fairness is a virtue, even in a prince,'' the Rajah responded. ''Spend one month with the princess at the Honeymoon Castle. If, thereafter, you still decline to betroth her, I will grant you your freedom.''

Victory, so suddenly! ''Agreed,'' Mym said. What was one month's temptation, compared to the two years he had survived?

The Honeymoon Castle was situated in remote mountains. It was a phenomenally attractive estate, with sculptured hedges, gardens of infinite color, picturesque architecture, and every likely luxury. No grounds-crew maintained it; an enduring spell kept it in perfect condition, with an ideal climate independent of what existed beyond. Favored nobles were granted weekends here when they married, and the Rajah himself retired here when in need of restoration. But for one full month it was to be Mym's residence.

Of course a person could get bored with even the most wonderful accommodations, in the absence of human company. That was why there were always two people here—and only two. For the most remarkable property of the Honeymoon Castle was the magic it performed on the minds of those who came into its ambiance.

The emotion and conscious thoughts of any person here expanded, in a fashion, beyond his body, and became manifest to any other person present. There were no secrets of feeling, here. That was why it was so potent for those who were freshly in love—and why it was no place for those who were no longer in love.

However, Mym was forewarned and prepared. He had never

before been to the Honeymoon Castle, but he doubted that its magic could shake his enduring love for Orb. If there were any question, his close contact with what might well turn out to be a simpering, spoiled southern princess would eliminate it. He had in Orb a standard of excellence that no other woman could match. What was her name? He had almost forgotten it already!

Rapture of Malachite—that was it, as though there could be delight in cold green stone. It was surely as ironic a designation as his own, Pride of the Kingdom. No, he knew he would emerge from this encounter victorious and be free at last to rejoin his only true love.

He stood alone at the landing patio, awaiting the arrival of the princess' carpet. There were no servants, of course; no other minds could be permitted to snoop on the naked thoughts and feelings of royalty. The two of them would be truly alone for the duration, until the carpets returned in a month to pick them up.

It arrived on schedule, first a speck above the mountain pass in the distance, then a floating shape, flat below, lumpy above. Finally it coasted in for the landing, a broad carpet bearing a cushioned, curtained cage.

It settled gently to the tiles. The cage opened, and the princess stepped out.

Mym stood in the shadow of the gate and gazed at her, this nemesis of his love that he had never seen before.

The Princess Rapture of Malachite of Maharastra was a spectacular figure of a woman. She wore a belted robe that caressed a figure reminiscent of an hourglass, with a sash of shining pale gold mesh, and buttons that were deep red rubies. Her hair was a lustrous flowing river of blue-black that whorled and swirled its way down about her shoulders and framed her face most prettily. Her eyes were like those of oxen of the lowland breed, great and dark and liquid. Her tiny ears showed at the edge of her coursing hair like shells at the fringe of a lake, sparkling iridescently. Her mouth was a perfect dainty crimson bow, too delicate for anything approaching a coarse word. Her breasts beneath the robe were like twin fawns, firm and perfectly rounded, surely as soft to the touch as man's desire could wish. Her hips—

She turned to face him. *Stay your lascivious thoughts, ruffian!*

she thought fiercely at him. *Have you forgotten already where you are?*

Indeed, he had, for the moment! Her amazing beauty had smitten him unprepared, disrupting his anger at her presence before it could be fairly settled. Now he felt himself blushing, and that infuriated him—and made his face burn more hotly.

She laughed, satisfied to be one up on him. He had broadcast his impressions as openly as any schoolboy might have, while she had maintained her reserve.

But now she sobered. "Know, O Prince of Gujarat, that this union is no more my wish than yours," she said clearly, and now her emotion came at him, controlled anger. "I love another and will always love him; but for the will of my father, I would be with him this moment and forever. You are but an obstacle in my way, and we shall pass this trial most readily if you keep your body and your mind well clear of mine."

Mym could hardly believe it. "You are against this betrothal?" he sang. "That I did not know."

"There is surely much you do not know, Prince of the tongue-tied. And much you had best never learn. Now come into the open so I can see the image of my enemy."

Embarrassed anew, Mym stepped out into the light.

Why, he is a handsome man, she thought with surprise.

That is immaterial, he responded in the same manner, and now it was her turn to blush. She had been caught the same way. It was one thing to know that their thoughts would be completely open to each other, and quite another to experience the reality.

"True, Pride of the Kingdom," she replied, and that set him back again. Even as it happened, he kept forgetting!

Choose what quarters you prefer, he thought quickly, to cover up whatever else he might otherwise think. *I shall take quarters on the opposite side.*

"There is nowhere on the premises that we can avoid each other's minds," she said. "Only mental discipline will suffice."

That will suffice, he agreed grimly.

So they selected suites on opposite sides of the castle. But that proved to be impractical, because there was neither food nor water in the suites; they had to emerge to obtain these things. There was a kitchen section, stocked with all manner of delicacies, but it was so constructed as to require the simultaneous action of two parties. One person had to hold open the pantry door, while the other reached for the food; it could not otherwise be obtained. It spoiled rapidly outside the magic pantry, so that it was not feasible to cooperate for one big raid; two people had to be present for every fresh meal.

The water was even more of a problem. It issued from an old-fashioned pump with a long red handle. One person had to pump, while the other held the cup in place; there was no other way. Each served the other for a cupful—but even this evaporated the moment it was taken from the dining chamber. They were stuck together for meals.

That was the least of it. "But I want to wash!" the Princess said annoyed.

Mym pondered. "I could pump while you sat under the spout," he sang.

She turned on him a withering look. "Or I could pump while *you* sat under it."

He appreciated the problem. *Believe me, Rapture, I have no desire to gawk at your fair flesh,* he thought.

"You lie, Pride," she gritted.

True, he realized. He did not love her and had no wish to be corrupted by her, but he was a man and enjoyed the sight of voluptuous female flesh wherever it occurred—and hers was as voluptuous as such flesh came. He was a voyeur at heart.

"And I have no wish to corrupt you," she retorted.

You lie, he thought back at her, for beneath her overt anger at the situation was a covert pleasure at his assessment of her body. She was a true woman, subject to fits of vanity; she wanted to be almost irresistibly appealing to all men, while obliging only that one she chose, at her convenience.

Damn you! she thought, and her sudden rage was like a crack of thunder.

He smiled, somewhat bitterly. *This is the nature of this castle,* he reminded her. *To force us together, to set up feedback. To make me desire you, and you to appreciate that desire, until we both are lost in mutual admiration.*

"But we are royalty, not animals," she pointed out. "We have no need to succumb slavishly to feedback."

He decided to change the subject, for it was treacherous. They *were* disciplined human beings, and she was evidently as dedicated to her other love as he was to his—a trait he admired in her—

"Watch your thought!" she snapped.

So it behooved them to cooperate to avoid the obvious temptations. He must *not* look at her flesh, or think any appreciative thoughts about it, no matter how luscious—

Animal! He wasn't sure whether that was her savage thought or his. This business was trickier than he had anticipated!

"True," she agreed.

"I will turn my back and pump while you wash," he sang, having a bright notion. "Then you can do the same for me. We need never gaze upon each other's flesh."

She considered. She didn't like it—her feeling was consistent with her thought—but saw no better alternative. "Let's experiment. You pump while facing away, and I will wash my hands."

"A-a-a-agreed," he stuttered, then cursed himself for forgetting to sing.

"Prince, we can surely discover significant things to detest in each other," she said, sympathetic. "We need not be ashamed of that which we have no power over. Speak as you will; it is not an issue between us."

She forgave him his stuttering! Mym was for the moment overwhelmed by a surge of gratitude. So few of either sex ever bothered to understand—

Stop that! she thought fiercely. *I don't want your feeling!*

She was trying to do the proper thing, which was to maintain her alienation from him. He understood perfectly and was trying to do the same himself. But her compassion for his handicap cut through to his deepest self-image; he could mask but never quite abolish his gratitude.

"Oh, pump the pump!" she cried in frustration, struggling with imperfect success to stave off that gratitude.

He turned about, reaching behind him to grasp the handle, awkwardly. His gaze fell on the wall he now faced.

It was a wall-sized mirror.

Mym sighed. The builder of Honeymoon Castle seemed to have thought of everything. Well, he could simply close his eyes.

"Better a blindfold," she said.

They tried that. He draped a blanket over his head and pumped, while she set about her business.

"Oh!" she exclaimed abruptly.

Cold water, no doubt. He kept pumping—but now his thoughts focused determinedly on speculations about what flesh the flowing water must be touching to evoke such reaction. He tried to divert his mind, but there was no way now not to think about what he shouldn't. Clear water, glistening breasts—

"Oh, this is worse than just plain looking would be!" she exclaimed in frustration. "Take off that blanket!"

But I'm trying to control my—

She reached across and tore off the blanket. Mym blinked. There before him was a bare bosom every bit as grand as the one he had been trying not to imagine.

"Might as well get this over with," she muttered, her spoken words almost blotted out by the underlying anger she broadcast. She stripped the rest of the way, while Mym, bemused, watched, ashamed for the admiration he was unable to suppress. She was indeed the perfect woman.

In due course she finished and dried and dressed. "Now it is your turn," she said ferociously.

Mym quailed. Fair was fair—but naturally he had suffered the masculine reaction; if he stripped, this would be all too evident.

Rapture blushed. "Some other time," she decided, and fled.

Of course his thought has been about as revealing as his body would have been. He blushed himself; he had not meant or wanted to expose her to that. She was a fine, discreet woman, who had probably never seen a man in—

Enough! her thought came, undiminished in intensity despite the distance she had put between them.

At that he had to laugh, ruefully. The Castle was making fools of them both.

Rapture reappeared. She was trying to maintain her anger, but the perverse humor of it was spreading to her. "We must escape this castle!" she exclaimed.

"Y-y-yes!" he agreed fervently.

"Y-y-yes," she echoed, and she was not mocking him.

But neither of them had much of an idea how to do it. The

estate was girt by a high enchanted wall that could not be scaled, with a lake on the back; the only approach was by magic carpet, and they had none. They agreed to ponder during the night and compare notes in the morning.

They got through the evening meal, and then Rapture shut her eyes and pumped while Mym washed. If she peeked it didn't matter, for she could not help but read his physical state through his mind. She merely flushed and continued pumping, while he counted numbers backwards constantly to drown out what he could of his own thoughts. He was glad when it was over.

They separated, each going to the appropriate suite. But Mym had hardly entered his when her scream resounded through his mind. He charged to her section, threw open the curtain—naturally there were no doors—and found her standing with her delicate fist in her mouth.

"Something was there!" she cried.

From her mind he got the image—some shadowy, skeletal, demonic figure that had sought to sneak up on her, but retreated when she turned to look.

"But there are no other people or creatures on the premises," Mym reminded her. "We would intercept their thoughts."

"I *saw* it," she insisted, and he knew she had—or believed she had.

Which left open the possibility of something other than a person or a creature, he realized. Was this Castle haunted by demons?

"Demons!" she exclaimed, horrified.

But why would there be anything like that in a castle intended for lovers?

"To ensure that they are together," she said.

And that, of course, was it. Those who insisted on sleeping apart would discover company of an unpleasantly alien nature. Rapture was obviously extremely ill at ease; he felt it throughout her mind. What were they to do?

"I will ignore it," she said bravely. But though she intended to make the effort, he read her deep fear of the demonic. She would not be able to sleep.

It was a man's business to protect a woman from whatever threats existed, in whatever way he could. Mym knew that his sword would not be effective against a demon—but that was not the point. *I will stand guard,* he thought.

"I couldn't ask you to do that!" she protested. "We must sleep apart!" But she wished he *would* do that, for she was genuinely afraid.

I will sleep by the door, he decided, amending his notion. *That will be no hardship.*

Her relief was manifest. "I wish I could thank you, Prince Pride," she said.

They both knew why she could not. "I prefer Mym," he sang.

"Mym—the name they gave you at the sideshow," she said, reading the context. "Where you met the woman you love."

Where I was happy, he agreed.

She retired to her large, soft bed of feather pillows and colorful quilts, and he settled down in the doorway and slept in the way a warrior did, alert for any intrusion. They left the lamp on, so that nothing could enter unseen.

In a moment he jerked awake. A horrendous demon was tiptoeing toward the bed. Rapture turned and saw it, and screamed.

Mym leaped up, his sword whipping from its sheath—but the demon charged through a wall, making no sound, and disappeared.

He turned back to the bed, where Rapture was shaking with reaction. Her emotion was a tangled mass of loathing, fear, and shame, for she knew she was imposing on Mym despite her resolve to cause him no more trouble.

He went to her, sat on the bed, and took her into his arms. *It is the nature of the innocent to be afraid of evil,* he thought soothingly. He felt no fear himself, of course, merely disgust that he could have allowed an intrusion of this nature. He had been on guard, had he not?

She sobbed into his shoulder. Then, buoyed by his lack of fear, she calmed. "I—I apologize for my weakness, that so inconveniences you," she said. "I never meant—"

I know. The Castle made deception impossible; she was not practicing any artifice in her fear, and he practiced none in his lack of it. They had been trained for different things.

"But this is exactly what the Castle means to do!" she said. "To force us into each other's arms—"

"There is no love in it," he said. "I would hold a frightened child so."

That abashed her further, yet she could not deny it. "If child I must be, then so let it be," she said. "My weakness and my humiliation are laid open to you, and I deserve your contempt."

You showed no contempt when I stuttered, he reminded her.

"But you couldn't help that!"

"And you can not help this."

She paused, considering. "I showed none because I felt none," she said slowly. "But had I felt it, I would have changed my opinion by now. You are a brave man and a kind one."

I am a Prince. I am what I am trained to be.

The bravery, yes, she thought back at him. *The kindness, no.*

The best ruler tempers justice with mercy, he thought, echoing what he had been trained.

But with you the mercy is stronger than it should be.

This was true, he realized. He had mastered the physical abilities required of his office, but not the emotional ones. Had he possessed proper discipline, he would not have been swayed by the fate of the concubines he rejected or by the subservience of the cavalry officer who had come to bring him back. He was weak—and his father the Rajah had played upon that weakness with an expert touch.

"Oh, Mym!" she cried, reading his mind. "I did not know!"

It was not your business to know. Was not similar pressure put on you to come here?

"Not exactly. My father simply shipped me here. I had no choice."

Being a woman, he agreed. *A prince must accede; a princess must obey.*

"Physically," she agreed. "But my heart is my own."

Or his whom you love.

"Yes," she agreed. But now another aspect of her embarrassment was spread out involuntarily for his perception—she had no other love. The man she had been interested in was not the equal of Mym and no prince; that interest had evaporated like vapor in the past few hours. She had resisted coming here simply because she did not like being played like a pawn, assigned to a man for the sake of a political liaison. She was no concubine!

I never thought of you as a concubine! he thought.

"Oh, I wish I could keep my thoughts to myself!" she wailed. "All my secrets are leaking from me!"

Your secrets become you, he responded.

"I would rather lie naked to your gaze!"

She had already stood naked to it when she washed. But he understood exactly what she meant. A woman, more than a man, was a creature of dainty privacies, of hidden places, and it was cruel to expose these.

"Thank you," she said.

Lie here. Sleep. I will remain alert.

"It is our separation that emboldens the demon," she said. "Keep your arms about me and sleep yourself; the demon will not come."

Surely true. This intricate, so-personal net of the Castle annoyed him, but he saw no way to break out of it. They lay down together, she in her negligee, he in his dayrobe, with his sword on.

Tomorrow we shall flee this place, he thought with determination.

"Tomorrow," she agreed. Then, slowly, they slept.

—4—

STORM

In the morning they got up, and Mym faced away while Rapture changed into fresh apparel; then they went to his suite, where she faced away while he changed. But it hardly mattered; the enforced openness of their minds and feelings made physical concealment pointless.

They had breakfast. Then they took a walk by the placid lake.

Mym stood at the shore and removed his clothing. *Two times two is four,* he thought intensely. *Two times four is eight.* It pretty well drowned out whatever else he might have been thinking.

Rapture looked askance, then nodded. She was bright enough. *Two times three is six,* she thought as she removed her own dress. *Two times six is twelve.*

Their two sets of computations tended to interfere with each other, making concentration difficult. They simply started over, when an error was made.

Naked, they entered the water and swam for the far shore. Mym had not dared to ask directly whether Rapture swam, for that would have betrayed his intent. It was evident that she did indeed swim well; in fact she was especially lovely as she stroked along beside him. He remembered the mermaid in the tank—but Rapture was far prettier than the halfling had been.

Two times twenty-four is forty-eight! Rapture thought emphatically, reminding him to keep his mind on his own computations. Half-guiltily, he did.

In that manner they crossed the lake, making excellent progress. But as the farther shore approached, there was a swirling in the water around them, and small fish of many hues glided by in schools.

Then four fish poked their snouts up in front, chanting: "If your father knew, he would fall into a deadly rage!"

Rapture gulped a mouthful of water and spluttered. For a moment she thrashed inelegantly, before recovering her equilibrium. "My father!" she exclaimed, upset.

Mym was treading water, making sure she was all right before resuming the swim. The speaking of the fish had been a shock, but this was evidently a harmless manifestation. He glanced back—and saw a huge fin cutting the water toward them.

Now he felt dread, for he was weaponless and ill-equipped to defend himself in the water. Rapture, of course, was even more vulnerable. She screamed.

The fin circled and cut between them and the shore ahead. There it remained, awaiting them.

Mym considered. The talking fish had made it clear that their attempt to escape had not gone unnoticed, and the fin suggested rather strongly that it would not go unpunished. He sighed.

He pointed back to the Castle. They began to swim back the way they had come—and the fin did not follow.

They spent the rest of the day touring the lovely gardens and alcoves of the premises, remaining close together, and it was pleasant enough. The Castle did not threaten them as long as they tried neither to escape it nor to separate from each other. But this proximity continually caused Mym's thought to dwell on the obvious virtues of the Princess, and she felt flattered, though she tried to fight it, and this feeling came back to Mym, encouraging further thoughts.

They sat in a pretty stone patio, sharing the feeling of captivity. "What are we going to do, Mym?" Rapture asked. "You know where this is leading."

"I know," he sang. "But perhaps if we knew each other better, the result would not be what is intended."

"It would not?" She was perplexed.

"Every person has faults. My impediment of speech is obvious. You have been gracious, but I think you would tire of it soon enough."

"Then stop singing and speak!" she exclaimed, understanding immediately.

"Y-y-y-yes," he stuttered.

"And if you understood my faults better," she said, "you would surely find me less interesting."

"W-w-w-what f-f-f—?" But his thought had been clear long before the word could get out.

She felt pensive. "I had hoped to conceal—but of course that's foolish. I have three great faults, and the first is quite as obvious as yours."

He gazed at her, baffled. "It is n-n-n-not ap-ap—"

"It *is* apparent," she said. "I was a terrible disappointment to my father, because I was born a—" Here she balked, but her thought came through.

A girl! he thought. *But that's no fault!*

"It is if a male heir is needed," she said grimly.

"I w-w-would n-n-not c-c-c-call—"

"Then you are more generous than my father," she said.

He would not have had her otherwise! He could not imagine this absolutely lovely woman as a male. What a sad commentary on the state of contemporary values that such a creature should consider her gender to be a fault!

"You're not cooperating, you know," she said.

He made a mental laugh. *I hate the situation, but I cannot hate you, Rapture of Malachite. There is no fault in you I have yet seen, other than the fact that you are slated to replace the woman I love.*

"And none in you, Mym," she said.

In the evening the demon showed again, terrifying Rapture. Mym was perplexed; by day she was a self-reliant woman, competent in whatever way required, yet by night she was helpless.

"It is true," she confessed. "I am, as I said, a woman; I have no strength to stand up to malice or ugliness. From my childhood, I have been terrified of demons. I deeply regret being this burden to you."

There was indeed, he realized, some fault in being female. No man he knew of would have permitted anything like a demon to dismay him. But of course men were trained to fight. Women were trained to be dependent. It was still not truly a fault, but rather an aspect of the cultural expectation.

And if women were destined to be vulnerable, so were men destined to protect them. He lay on her bed with her, as before, and put his arms about her, and slept.

His dreams had always been chaotic, but this time they were more so. He dreamed he was holding a beautiful woman and knew that the dream was true. He dreamed that he rejected her—and saw her head mounted upon a spike.

He woke to the sound of screaming. The demon was leaning over them, leering, reaching out. Mym grasped his sword—but the demon faded back and away.

It was Rapture who had screamed. She had read his dream, and felt the spike.

We have to get out of here! he thought, and she agreed.

Next day they explored the premises more thoroughly—and found a brass ring set in the ground in the corner of a chamber seldom used. Mym wedged it up, and it was the handle of a metal slab, and beneath the slab was a deep hole. Stone steps descended, curving out of sight.

Rapture fetched a lamp, and they descended. The steps ended somewhere under the wall, and a squared passage led onward beyond the wall. This was a secret tunnel, a possible escape!

The air became cool, and the walls clammy. Rapture shrank away from contact, but stayed close beside him. They did not bother with the mental sums this time, as it was evident that they had not concealed the prior day's escape attempt. At least this time they were on their feet, and Mym had his sword.

They came to a chamber wherein were several stone altars, and on each altar was an object. The first had a bright gold ring, the second a burnished copper lamp, and the third a calf molded from gold.

Rapture, always intrigued by jewelry, paused to pick up the ring. She tried it on one finger, and then another, but it fit none of them, so she put it back.

Mym picked up the lamp, to see whether it would serve better than the one they had, but it had no fuel. It was merely a decoration, of no practical use. *I wonder whether I should rub it?* he thought.

"Or make a wish on the ring," Rapture added.

They considered, then decided that these artifacts were likely to be traps for the unwary. What horror might be invoked, if they tried to summon the powers of ring or lamp? Better to pass quietly by.

But as they passed the gold calf, it lifted its head and said: "If your father knew, he would slaughter a woman an hour!"

Mym jumped, appalled. That spoke to his own weakness, his dislike of unnecessary killing.

Then there was a sound from the tunnel ahead, a series of thuds that jarred the chamber, as of some creature striding toward them. Mym drew his sword—and there was a horrendous roar, and a blast of smoke came from the tunnel.

"That's a dragon!" Rapture squeaked. "You can't fight that!"

Surely not. The fire it breathed would burn them both to death before the thing came close enough to be stabbed.

Mym sighed, again. "We must retreat," he sang, and set the example, turning and walking back the way they had come. Rapture followed close behind, carrying the original lamp. The dragon did not pursue.

Back in the castle proper, they talked again, and Rapture confessed her second great fault. She had, once in her childhood, permitted a man to touch her. She had found her way out into the city, sneaking away while her nurse was preoccupied, and did not yet realize that all children were not princesses, or that there were different castes. She had come upon a laborer and touched his hand to get his attention. Then her nurse had caught up with her.

The man had been an Untouchable—one of the casteless. There had been a serious row, and she had been subjected to a horrendous series of cleansings and ablutions to purify her from that hideous touch. The laborer, of course, had been summarily executed, and his family clubbed to death. But what she remembered most was the rage of her towering father: TWICE YOU HAVE FAILED ME!

And Mym suffered another vision of a lovely head set on a spike. *No!* he thought. *You did not know! You meant no harm!*

"That hardly mattered," she said. "Ignorance is no valid excuse." But emotion surged up within her bosom because of his supporting thought, and she had to fight it back down, for it was not what they sought.

They spent the night together as before. This time Mym dreamed that he held her in his arms, as he was doing in reality, but the dream continued farther. He kissed her, and then he began to undress her, and her flesh was warm and silken-smooth, and he sought to possess her—

And wrenched himself awake. Reality had been mirroring his dream, and her body was open to his touch.

Why did you not stop me? he demanded.

"I tried—but couldn't," she whispered.

I never forced a woman in my life!

"Couldn't—make myself protest," she confessed.

We must escape this place!

"Of course," she agreed.

But it was several more days before they discovered another way to make the attempt. High in the Castle, on a turret, birds of every description landed to take the pure water offered there. On occasion a very large bird came—a roc.

"That bird could carry us over the wall," Mym sang.

"But wouldn't it consume us?"

"Not if we let it know our nature. Man-eating rocs have been hunted to extinction; only safe ones remain."

And so they climbed the myriad stairs to the high turret and brought there a large bag fashioned of net. When the roc came, they stood in the net, and Mym hurled the tie-rope out to snag in a claw. The startled bird took off with a great downdraft of air and hauled the bag up with it. They dangled precariously below, airborne.

The roc climbed rapidly to the clouds. As they approached a cloud bank, a great face formed, and wintry air whooshed out of the mouth-hole. "If your fathers knew, they would blame each other," the cloud thundered. "Their Kingdoms would go to war, decimate each other, and become so weakened that the alien Mongul horde would sweep down, enslave both, and use their fair young women to satisfy the lusts of prize bulls and their men as flesh for dogs. Furthermore—''

"Enough!" Rapture screamed, voicing Mym's thought. "Roc, set us down!"

The big bird obligingly descended and settled back on the turret, where they cut away the net and retreated. They had failed again.

"Tonight," Rapture said with grim determination, "and every night following, we must sleep apart."

"But the demon—" he sang.

"I fear the demon now less than I fear what will happen if we are together. I am weak, and you are merciful; we are at the limit of our resistance."

And this was true. Surely the demon would not actually hurt her; it existed only to frighten her into obeying the design of the Castle.

Rapture retired alone, but her fear spread throughout the Castle. Mym remained in his own suite, determined not to go to her unless she called. It was difficult.

Yet what were they fighting? he asked himself. Their physical contact was urging them on to sexual fulfillment—but that was not the same as love. He had sex with concubines; he loved Orb. Wouldn't it be easier to treat Rapture as—

No. She was, as she had said at the outset, no concubine. She was a Princess. She was not to be used and set aside.

He thought about Orb— but now she seemed far away. Of course he loved only her—yet the cutting edge seemed to have been blunted. This Castle was working its sinister magic despite all he could do!

It was not that Rapture was unworthy. She was, objectively, the equal of Orb. She was a Princess, as Orb was not, but Orb was self-assured, as Rapture was not. Orb could stand alone by day and by night; Rapture was forever vulnerable. That was a mark against her. What man wanted a totally dependent woman?

He became aware of something else. He focused on it, and realized that it was Rapture's suppressed thought. She was trying to shield it, to prevent him from reading it—and that made him curious.

THREE TIMES YOU HAVE FAILED ME!

Mym saw another head upon a spike, and this time there was no doubt about its identity. It was Rapture's.

He leaped up and charged to her suite. She was there, sitting naked on the bed, a knife at her breast. Now the muffled thought was clear to him. She was about to kill herself!

"No!" he cried. "You must not!" He ran across and grabbed her hand just as the sharp point touched her flesh. A streak appeared, as she fought to complete the act.

He forced her arm away, outward, but she clung to the knife with the strength of desperation. "Three times I have failed!" she cried.

They fell to the bed, his left arm against her right, fighting for the knife. His face banged into her bosom, and he tasted the blood.

Then a storm formed within him, as the blood brought on the berserker madness, bereft of his conscious control. He squeezed her wrist, causing the knife to fall away, and clutched her to him as the storm hurled them both into a chaos of passion.

The madness spread to her own being, for they were inextricably linked in emotion as well as body. Her lips drew back from her pearly teeth and her eyes slitted. Something like the whine of a chained killer-animal sounded in her throat. Her jaws parted, and those strong teeth snapped at his shoulder. In a moment she had drawn his blood and tasted it. Reddish froth bubbled between her teeth.

Then the storm intensified in their minds as their bodies strove against each other. Never before had Mym fought another berserker. Her strength and speed matched his, and her rage matched his. Whirling funnels developed, gouging out segments of the atmosphere, their ferocious winds screaming like banshees. His funnel advanced on hers, and hers met it eagerly, and the two danced about each other, seeking devastation.

Then the two aspects of the storm charged together, while his teeth and hers attacked their physical targets. Their snarling mouths met and struggled for purchase, but could find none. Locked together, tooth against tooth, nullified, they paused. Now their tongues sought battle, wrestling against each other. The two storm-funnels merged, and their winds formed into an overlapping pattern, doubling the force.

The coursing winds expanded, forming a larger funnel, a larger eye, bringing a new kind of order to the chaos of the storm. Steadily the air became organized into a huge circular pattern, savage in its force. And steadily their mouths, gnashing against each other, modified into a different kind of contact.

In this whirling intensity and stasis the thoughts that were the most focused aspects of their feelings and experience were stripped of their clothing of qualification, and stretched out in full view before being dissipated. *I expected a tough, callous, overbearing brute, who would ravish my body but never touch my soul*, she thought involuntarily.

And I expected a cold, aloof woman who would never risk her heart, he tought.

Their lips were softening into a sustained, deep kiss.

Or an inconsequential courtier type, of no practical use, perhaps more interested in young boys than in genuine women.

Or a seductress, set to vamp any man regardless of his merit— a concubine in the likeness of a princess.

The kiss intensified, and their bodies slowly relaxed against each other.

But I found a decent and caring man, who tried to treat me with courtesy, though he loved elsewhere.

And I found a woman who was competent and beautiful by day and vulnerable by night.

I could have despised the brute or ignored the courtier.

I could have ignored the aloof or used the seductress.

And so she had discovered in him a man she could genuinely respect. But because of that, she did not wish to corrupt him. He had another love; she would not attempt to interfere with that, despite her mandate from her father. But her good intention was subverted by her female nature. When he protected her at night, she came to appreciate him more than she wished. Unable to prevent the development of what she strove to avoid, she had finally set out to solve the problem in the only way possible.

That is why I have to die, her thought concluded. *It is the only decent thing to do. I could not face my father, after failing him for the third time, but I could not allow myself to corrupt you.*

And he had discovered in her a woman the equal of the one he loved, and one he might have loved had he met her first. But because he did love another, he had no right to compromise this one. He had exerted his discipline to act with propriety, despite the devices of the Castle. When she had required protection at night, he had done what was required—and no more.

But I could not allow you to die, his thought concluded. *That was no decent thing to do.*

And so their dilemma was upon them, for both knew that if she did not die, she would corrupt him. The ambience of the Castle made that inevitable.

He did not like that term, "corrupt."

And even if you did not love elsewhere, I would not be worthy of you, she thought. *The one you love is strong, while I am weak.*

She is strong, while you are weak, he agreed.

Therefore I must be sacrificed, that you may return to her.

But Orb, he realized, could survive without him—because she was strong. A woman like her could have any man she chose. She had blessed him with her love and done more for him than any woman before had done—but she did not truly need him. While Rapture could not, at this stage, survive without him.

So let me die! she pleaded.

Rapture loved him; this could no longer be concealed. So she chose to die, solving her problem and his. She had never sought the selfish way that would bring her the praise of her grim father; she had never tried to capture him, despite her emotion and her need of him.

He considered her, while their bodies remained locked in the kiss and their emotions swirled in a monstrous pattern about them. Rapture was the perfect woman, except for her single great weakness, her dependence on him. She was terrified of being alone. Yet she had had the courage to do what she felt necessary—to abolish her own life, to free him. This had been no pretense, no play for sympathy; she had made her decision and sought to implement it. He was assured of this, for no false thoughts were possible here. The courage she lacked for herself, she had risen to in her effort to protect him.

It is already too late, he realized.

I would be dead now, if you had not prevented me! You would have been safe from corruption.

I prevented it because I was already corrupted. Then he laughed, mentally, at the irony of the term.

Even now, let me go and you will be free! she persisted.

How can I be free by letting you die—when I love you?

Like startled birds, her thoughts and emotions swirled, finding no anchorage. *But I am weak where she is strong!*

Therefore you need me more than she does. No woman ever truly needed me before.

But this made no sense, she protested. No one would choose another to love because of a weakness!

No woman would, he agreed. *But a man—desires a dependent woman.* Whatever he might say to the contrary. A man wanted his woman all to himself. It wasn't nice, it wasn't generous, but that was what he most truly desired—when his illusions were stripped away. A lovely, talented, and completely dependent woman.

And while her confusion swirled about them, he shifted his body, encountering no resistance, and took her in the manner they both desired. The storm intensified, obliterating all else, carrying them both into the rapture of their passion, the physical expression of their love.

Then they emerged into the center of the storm—and it was completely calm, a region very like nirvana. For a thousand years they floated there, gently sharing their unbound love. The intense ecstasy of the breakthrough had become the enduring pleasure of complete acceptance, physical, emotional, and mental, and the latter was more wonderful than the former. Then it was morning.

They spent the remainder of the month as true honeymooners, going hand in hand by day, sharing a bed by night. They shared thoughts, coming to know all the details of each other's existences. They agreed that they would be married as soon as was feasible, but would keep company in the interim. It had been a desperation measure of the two Rajahs, sending them unwed to the Honeymoon Castle, because of course it guaranteed that the bride would not be virginal—but this was, after all, the twentieth century, and the rulers of nations did what they deemed expedient, regardless of the ancient proprieties. A contraceptive spell would keep Rapture from becoming prematurely pregnant; that would suffice.

"But Orb," she inquired, concerned. "What of her?"

"I gave her my magic serpent-ring," he sang. "It always informs its user of the truth, if asked. I have no doubt she knew of my defection long before I did. She had only to ask it 'Will Mym return?' and it would squeeze twice. Two years have passed; she may already have found another man. I sincerely regret putting her through this business, but she knows that I loved her when I was taken from her, that I intended to return to her, but was prevented."

"By another love," Rapture said pensively.

"That I would prefer to spare her—but surely she knew it also, if she wanted to. My respect and feeling for her has not really been changed; it has merely been superseded. But I think it will be best if I do not see her again."

"Perhaps I should see her, to explain—"

"No. She knows—if she wants to. We must leave her to her own life, which will surely be a rich one. With the ring, she may be able to find the Llano, the song she sought; that much, at least, I may have done for her."

"If you are sure—"

"You fought to protect her, to avoid diverting my love from her," he reminded her. "You meant to kill yourself. But it happened anyway, because you are what you are, and I am what I am, and the Castle is what it is. We have a new reality, and I would not change it now if I had the power."

"Still I feel guilt—"

"And I feel it when you feel it. But I think it will pass."

And by the time the month was done, it had passed.

– 5 –

SWORD

A single carpet arrived, but it was capacious enough to support them both. They boarded, drew closed the curtain, and made love again while it carried them back to one Kingdom or the other.

It turned out to be Gujarat, and the Rajah was waiting.

Mym got out and held out his hand to assist Rapture. She had had to reassemble herself rather hastily, but looked stunning nevertheless.

"Sire, I accept this woman, the Princess Rapture of Malachite, as my betrothed," Mym sang formally. "She alone will I marry."

The Rajah nodded witih glacial satisfaction. "It shall be arranged."

The arrangements proceeded. In the interim, Rapture was an honored guest at the Rajah's palace at Ahmadabad. Nominally she slept alone; in practice she joined Mym. Of course the palace staff knew, and therefore so did the Rajah; it hardly mattered, since this was exactly the commitment the Rajah wanted. The two Kingdoms were now engaged in the complex negotiations for the precise size and nature of the dowry, but it was certain that in the end a suitable contract of marriage would be drawn up. In the interim, Gujarat and Maharastra were allied, and this well served the political interests of both.

Mym plunged into the business of the Kingdom, for with his commitment to the betrothal had come his participation in contemporary matters. He would be the next Rajah and he had only three years to gain some solid experience. He talked in singsong, to avoid the stutter, and if any person thought that was funny, that person concealed his opinion most carefully, for the Rajah had issued a notice that any person caught making light of any other person's manner of speaking would be summarily beheaded. On the first day Mym had gone out, a man had laughed at a comment made by another, probably on some unrelated subject; the cavalrymen had charged into the crowd, knocking down those who failed to scurry clear, and lopped off the laugher's head— and that of his companion for good measure. Now no one found any subject the slightest bit humorous while Prince Pride was in the area.

Gujarat was not in ideal shape. There was a great deal of poverty, and some starvation in the nether castes. The problems were dual: a bad drought in the central region that had disrupted the rice harvest; and overpopulation along the coast. It would have been difficult to feed all those people if the harvest had been good; as it was, it was impossible.

Mym floated his royal carpet to the most distressed region. There he saw people spread out on the ground, having no place to go and no ability to work. Officers of the Kingdom were dispensing soup, but it was thin and insufficient; it only extended lives, without reversing their course. The distribution was being done in a fair and orderly manner; there simply was not enough soup to do the job.

Mym thought of the two years he had spent confined to the palace. He had been served the rarest delicacies, which he had not appreciated, and all his servants and concubines had been excellently fed. Now he cursed himself for his selfish neglect of the Kingdom, where the present situation had been developing. Had he done his duty earlier and been on the job where he belonged, he might well have been able to accomplish some amelioration of misery. How many good citizens had starved to death, while Mym had taunted his father with his refusal to do his duty?

As he stood surveying the ugly situation, he saw a figure walking among the dying. He signaled a minister, who hurried forward. "Who is that man?" Mym inquired.

The minister looked, but was baffled. "Prince, whom do you mean? I see none but the dying on their pallets."

"That man in the ebony-black cape," Mym sang.

The minister gazed again, his brow furrowed. "I see no such man."

Mym had had enough of this. He strode forward, the minister scurrying after him. He approached the caped figure, who was leaning over one of the pallets. "You!" he called in his fashion. "Identify yourself!"

The figure ignored him. Angry at this contempt, Mym confronted him face to face. "Speak, or suffer the consequence!" he sang.

Slowly the figure raised his head. Under the cowl, the face took form. It was emaciated beyond belief, a virtual skull, the eyes sunken and the teeth protruding. "You perceive me?" the strange man asked.

Mym was taken aback. This was obviously no ordinary person! "Of course I see you! I want to know who you are and what business you have here!"

The hollow eyes seemed to focus more specifically on him. The mouth-orifice opened. "I am Famine."

"Famine!" Mym exclaimed. "What kind of a name is that?"

"The name of my office."

"Office?" Mym demanded. He turned to the minister. "What do you know of this?"

The minister looked distinctly uncomfortable. "Prince Heir, certainly there is famine. This is why we are here. I confess I do not understand your reference to an office."

"The office this man who calls himself Famine refers to!" Mym sang angrily.

The discomfort intensified. "My Lord, I see no man."

"Th-th-this one h-here!" Mym exclaimed, forgetting to sing. He reached out to touch the gaunt finger, not caring that the man was probably casteless.

His hand passed through the figure, encountering no resistance.

Mym paused, taking stock. "You are an apparition?" he asked Famine.

"I am the Incarnation of Famine, the associate of War, on a temporary mission for Death," the figure said.

"And no one else can see you?"

"I do not know why *you* can see me," Famine confessed. "Normally no mortal can perceive an Incarnation, unless he has intimate business with that Incarnation."

"Well, I am concerned about the starvation occurring here," Mym sang. "I need to ascertain the extent of the problem and decide how best to alleviate it. Do you have advice on that?"

"Feed your people," Famine said, with a grisly grin.

"*How?* We have neither food nor sufficient distribution facilities."

"I do not give advice; I merely invoke the consequence."

"Well, put me through to your superior, then," Mym sang, angrily, while the minister backed surreptitiously away, deeming him crazy.

Famine made some kind of magical gesture, "I have summoned Thanatos," he said. Then he faded, until there was nothing to see.

Mym glanced about and saw the minister retreating. "Hold!" he snapped, and the minister, still greatly ill at ease, paused. "I have just spoken with the Incarnation of Famine and am about to speak with the Incarnation of Death. You will remain."

"As my lord wishes," the minister said nervously. It was evident that he would have preferred to be anywhere but here.

There was a flurry in the sky, and a figure appeared. Quickly it approached. It was a beautiful pale horse, galloping through the air without benefit of wings, bearing a cloaked rider. The horse drew to a halt before Mym, snorting vapor, and the rider dismounted.

If Famine had been gaunt, Thanatos was completely skeletal. His bone-fingered hand extended. "Greetings, Prince," the skull-face said.

Mym took the hand. The bones were bare but firm. "Greetings, Thanatos. Um—would it be too much to ask that you make yourself visible to the minister, here? He thinks I'm hallucinating."

Thanatos turned to the minister. "Greetings, Minister," he said.

The minister's mouth sagged open. "G-G-Gre—" he began.

"Try singing it," Mym suggested in singsong.

Thanatos faced again toward Mym. "My associate asked me to speak with you."

"I am concerned with the suffering here," Mym sang. "I want to alleviate it, but am bound about by circumstances I can not adequately control. I thought that, since you have an interest in this matter, you might proffer advice."

Thanatos lifted his skeletal wrist and touched a heavy watch there. Abruptly the scene froze. The minister's look of shock remained unchanging on his face; the clouds in the sky stopped moving. Smoke from a distant fire became stationary. Nothing moved, except for Thanatos, Mym, and the great pale horse.

"The fact that you are able to perceive Incarnations suggests that you relate to us," Thanatos said. "Therefore I will explore this matter. Chronos will know." He touched his watch again—and suddenly a figure cloaked in white stood with them, holding up a large, glowing hourglass.

"Yes, Thanatos," the new figure said. He appeared to be a normal man. "And Mars. Good to encounter you both again."

"Mars?" Mym asked.

"Mars?" Thanatos echoed, seeming equally perplexed.

"Oh, hasn't he taken office yet?" Chronos asked. "I regret my slip. I travel in the opposite direction, you know. I will erase the episode."

"No!" Mym cried, in his stress not stuttering. "Ignorance has brought enough mischief already! I will keep the secret, if that's what it is. What has Mars to do with this?"

Chronos exchanged a glance with Thanatos, then shrugged. "Your problem here is war. War diverts necessary resources wastefully, so that food is destroyed instead of feeding the hungry. To alleviate misery like this, you must first abolish war. Since you are to become Mars, the Incarnation of War, you should be in a position to deal with this."

"I—become Mars?" Mym asked, dumbfounded. "But I have a Kingdom to run, a bride to marry!"

"Well, I suppose you could turn the office down," Chronos said. "Nothing is fixed, and certainly the reality I remember can become another reality. But if you are serious about alleviating suffering in the world—"

Mym looked out over the pallets, each bearing a starving person—men, women and children. "I must stop this!" he said.

"Then the opportunity will be yours," Chronos said. "I am glad that the future is not to change in this respect; I have enjoyed working with you and will be sorry to see you depart—though of course that is not the way you perceive it."

"You—live backwards?" Mym asked, returning to his singsong as the stutter threatened. "From the future to the past?"

"True. You would think that after a decade or two, I would remember that things are opposite for the rest of you—but every so often I slip." He turned to Thanatos. "Just how long ago was the change in the Mars office made? I have been absorbed by other matters and entirely overlooked the event."

"It hasn't happened yet," Thanatos said.

Chronos grimaced. "There I go again! Of course you have not yet seen the change. I've been jumping about so much, including an interaction with Mars, here, that—" He shook his head. "What was the reason you summoned me?"

"I believe you have answered the question already," Thanatos said. "I was curious why this mortal could perceive Incarnations. Since you advise us that he is to become one, this becomes clear."

"Glad to have been of help in that case." The hourglass brightened, and Chronos disappeared.

"If he lives backwards," Mym asked, "why aren't his words backwards?"

"He controls time," Thanatos explained. "He simply reverses it for himself, so as to align with our frame, for a short period. But as you saw, these constant reversals can lead to confusion at times. He's a good man and an effective Incarnation, but Fate is the only one of us who really understands him. Now if your question has been answered—"

"Wait! No! It hasn't!" Mym sang. "I don't know anything about becoming the Incarnation of War some time in the future! I only want to alleviate the suffering I see here and now!"

"You are taking the short view," Thanatos cautioned him. "When you become Mars, as Chronos said, you will be in a position to accomplish the alleviation you seek."

"But that won't help these starving folk now!"

Thanatos nodded. "True. In the interest of good relations be-

tween Incarnations, I will summon one who may help you now."
He faced into the sky. "Gaea—will you answer?"

"Gaea?" Mym asked. All of this was highly confusing.

The air seemed to be thickening about them. Thin mist formed.
It became fog, then a smokelike formation that coalesced into a
vaguely human shape. The details clarified into those of a large,
solid woman dressed in green. "Thanatos," she answered.

"This man, at the moment mortal, is to assume the office of
Mars at a later date," Thanatos said. "Chronos mentioned it. But
right now, there is a concern about the folk here who are
starving."

Gaea considered Mym. "In that case, it behooves me to
oblige him. I can improve the local climate, so that the crops
flourish—"

"That would require at least a season," Mym sang. "These
here will all be dead by then."

She considered. "Then I will provide manna."

She stretched out her arms, became fog, and dissipated.
"Manna?" Mym sang, even more perplexed than he had been.

"Gaea's ways can be strange," Thanatos said.

The thinning fog settled to the ground and coalesced. Mym
stooped and scooped up a bit of the residue on a finger. He put
it to his mouth, tasting it. "Manna?" he repeated.

"Perhaps the concept is not in your legends," Thanatos said.
"In the Judeo-Christian mythos, it is a nutritious substance that
appears on the ground. I suspect it is some kind of rapidly re-
producing fungus."

"Food," Mym breathed, understanding.

"I suspect you owe Gaea a favor," Thanatos murmured. Then
he mounted his pale horse, touched his watch, and rode off into
the sky.

The scene returned to life. "Set men to collecting the manna,"
Mym sang to the minister. The man did not even try to argue; he
got on it, evidently understanding very little of this development.

In this manner a number of starving people were fed. The
manna came every day and fed them all, and no one quite understood this phenomenon, except perhaps Mym himself. But he had
a number of serious questions about the larger picture. He—to
become the Incarnation of War? Not if he could help it! He had

business to complete as a mortal. Yet the plight of the starving people had touched him deeply, and if there were some way to eliminate this kind of misery in the future—

Time passed, and no further supernatural manifestations occurred. He began to believe that his encounter with Famine, Death, Time, and Nature had been a hallucination, and the manna a coincidence. Rapture of Malachite remained loving and dependent, and he took hold of the reins of government with increasing competence as his direct experience grew. The Rajah sent him on missions to other nations and to other parts of the world, so that he could work on the broader scale to benefit his Kingdom.

He discovered himself to be surprisingly effective at this type of endeavor. He took Rapture with him to speak for him, literally. She was beautiful, so that none of the old men who ran the other nations objected to her presence, and she was trained in all the graces of royalty, so that the old men's wives found her compatible. But mainly, she understood Mym; he could convey his meaning to her by a few gestures and facial expressions and some faintly hummed words, and she would translate these to exquisitely rendered English. Since international dialogues often required the intercession of translators, no one found it remarkable that this handsome young prince of a nation of India used one, and some did not even realize that it was because of his stutter, not his ignorance of the language, that this was so.

But Gujarat's most pressing need was for modernization, and for that it required money. This meant a loan from Uncle Sugar to the West.

Mym pondered the matter. He realized that even Uncle Sugar expected some minimal quid pro quo. What did a poverty-stricken, backward kingdom like Gujarat have to offer in return for money?

Mym came to a conclusion. He took Rapture and went to brace the Rajah. "My beloved says he can get a loan of one billion dollars from the West," she announced brightly.

The Rajah almost did a double-take. He had evidently not appreciated just how well Mym and Rapture worked together. Normally women did not speak on matters of government, as they were, in the Rajah's view, incompetent for such matters. But after all the effort he had gone to gain Mym's agreement to the betrothal, he was glad to tolerate Rapture in whatever manner she manifested. "And how should this miracle be achieved?" he asked.

She glanced at Mym, who hummed, "Base."

"There is a military base that—" she began.

"Absolutely not!" the Rajah stormed. "We have never tolerated foreign military equipment on our terrain!"

Mym was already signaling and humming to her. "Oh, honored father-in-law-to-be," Rapture said dulcetly, flashing a winning smile at him. "My beloved well understands that. But this is the modern day, and the modern world is not a thing we can safely ignore. It would be better to accept the base and let them hire our people at their ludicrously high wages, and we can have our spies there to report on their secrets. It would represent a simple way to watch them."

The Rajah paused, considering. It was more than the logic that impressed him, Mym knew; it was the manner that Rapture converted Mym to a brilliant negotiator. Of course most of the words were her own, based on the discussion Mym had had with her beforehand; but because they were nominally from him, he had the credit. Mym's handicap of speech had been a sore trial to the Rajah's pride, and this apparent eloquence had to be deeply satisfying to him. "Still, the base would represent an aggravation to Uncle Vinegar to the north—"

Mym hummed and gestured. "Which may be no bad thing, Oh great Rajah," Rapture said, sending him a smile to melt ice. "It will help establish Gujarat's independence from the influence of that power."

"But—"

Mym hummed again. Rapture leaned forward persuasively. The Rajah was an old, old hand at women, but even his eyes glinted a smidgeon as they took in her décolletage. He recognized the finest vintage when he saw it. "And since Uncle Sugar will be obliged to grant us a loan of one billion dollars for the privilege of establishing that base, our independence will be further enhanced," she said.

The Rajah shook his head. He sighed. "Do it, then," he grumbled. "A prince must be allowed to make his own mistakes."

Mym knew that the Rajah would never have agreed, had it not been for Rapture. The old man was not getting soft; he simply realized that the logic was good enough to stand and that if this was the way Mym and Rapture could operate in the West, they would almost certainly get that loan. More than anything else, the Rajah wanted a truly effective leader of his own blood to succeed him, and Mym had just demonstrated how that could be.

They took a royal carpet to the outdated airport and caught one of the few international flights to the West. Magic was fine for local transport, but science prevailed on the global scale. Rapture was a little awed by the huge airplane with its blazing jet engines, but she liked the plush first-class seats and the petite uniformed stewardesses. "We should have them on the carpets," she murmured.

"They're better than eunuchs," Mym sang agreement.

The airplane angled up, up, far into the sky, above the clouds. "But why doesn't the air get thin?" Rapture inquired, worried. "I never was able to take a carpet this high without suffocating, and it got cold, too."

"Pressured cabin," he advised her.

"Isn't science wonderful!"

In due course they reached the fabulous West. Their plane landed at Washington, and they were met by a high-level functionary with a limousine. They were set up in a fine hotel, where every room had scientifically heated water, electrical lights, and color television sets. Rapture just shook her head in wonder. She knew what these things were, of course, for her kingdom was not entirely backward, but had never seen them so freely bestowed on the populace.

They met the President of Uncle-Sugar-land and made their presentation. After he and his Cabinet Ministers had gazed at Rapture, they agreed that this was the diplomatic thing to do; they really needed that base, and it was only neighborly to make the loan. Of course they preferred that the loan be spent on goods produced by the loaning nation . . .

Rapture agreed, turning on one of her winter-banishing smiles. Of course there were complications to be handled, but the understanding had been reached. Mym placed orders for modern scientific fertilizer, harvesting machinery, and trucks to haul the produce to market, and the industrialists of the West were pleased. The modernization of Gujarat was proceeding.

Meanwhile, the complex negotiations for Rapture's dowry were nearing completion, and the royal marriage was almost ready to be scheduled, two years after the month in Honeymoon Castle. "Soon you will be mine!" Mym sang.

"I have always been yours," she replied. "Soon we can conceive the Heir."

But the ways of fate and politics were treacherous. The world nearly always had war somewhere, ranging from global conflicts that spread across entire continents to tiny brushfires in isolated spots. At the moment everything was quiet except for Gujarat's smoldering border war with the eastern neighbor, Rajasthan. This expended resources that Mym preferred to use for agriculture, so that he could see to the abolition of starvation in his Kingdom, so he turned his attention to it. He took Rapture to Delhi and met with the high Ministers of Rajasthan.

The negotiation proved effective, for Mym and Rapture were by now a highly polished team. Indeed, the Ministers seemed hardly to realize that Mym was not the one speaking, so effectively did Rapture translate for him. They arranged to establish a demilitarized zone and to allow unarmed peasants to cross the border freely for purposes of trade and fraternization. Many of the peasants of that region were of the same ethnic tribe, and the war had been a special hardship to them; they would be glad to cooperate. The two Kingdoms exchanged lavish gifts, and peace was declared.

Thanks to Mym's effort, the last festering spot of war in the world had been extinguished. There was a great celebration, and a special holiday was declared. But in this, ironically, was the seed of Mym's destruction.

The Rajah of Rajasthan was so impressed with Mym's demeanor and skill as a negotiator that he decided to cement the new order with a marriage alliance. This was to be expected; and, indeed, the Rajah had a serviceable son, and Mym's sister was of nuptial age now and would make a suitable wife, provided the nuisance of a proper dowry could be negotiated.

But the Rajah did not want just a royal marriage; he wanted Mym himself. "My son, while adequate in all necessary matters, lacks the particular genius you possess," he explained. "I want *you* in charge when I assume another incarnation." For of course people did not really die in India; they merely cast off worn bodies and reincarnated in new ones, better or worse as their prior lives justified.

Mym, appalled, could not even stutter. "But Prince Pride is betrothed to me!" Rapture protested.

"Set it aside," the Rajah declared. "My son will marry you. But my daughter must wed Price Pride of Gujarat."

Mym opened his mouth. "We shall consider your generous offer," Rapture said quickly, and urged him out of the hall.

In private, Mym was shaking. "I can't marry her!" he sang in agitation. "I love you!"

"And I love you," she returned. "But we can not throw the Rajah's offer in his face. Rajasthan is a good, strong Kingdom; we dare not aggravate it so soon after making peace. We must return to our Kingdoms and consider how to turn this down without bad feeling."

She was right, of course. They returned to Ahmadabad and presented the situation to the Rajah of Gujarat.

"An alliance with Rajasthan?" he asked. "Wonderful! It shall be arranged forthwith!"

"But I am to marry Rapture!" Mym protested in singsong.

"Do not be concerned. I hereby null the betrothal; she shall be free for Rajasthan's prince."

"But I *want* to marry her!" Mym sang.

The Rajah squinted at him. "Since when did your desire have anything to do with it?" he inquired.

"But when I resisted Rapture, you sent me to the Honeymoon Castle with her!"

"You shall go again with the Princess of Rajasthan. This is a better alliance than the one with Maharastra."

Mym realized that it was useless to argue; his father's decision had been made. Almost steaming with chagrin and fury, he retreated.

They sent a message to Rapture's father. His reaction was opposite to that of Mym's father. "We have negotiated the dowry! It is too late to null the betrothal! It must be consummated!"

But Mym's father was adamant. The new bethrothal would

stand. Mym was abruptly confined to his palace, and Rapture was shipped back to Maharastra.

The Rajah of Maharastra, furious at this open snub, declared war on Gujarat.

Mym, alone except for the guards and servants and concubines, strode wrathfully around the palace. His impotent rage floated about him like a foul cloud. He absolutely refused to be cheated of Rapture—but he knew of no way to avoid it. His father might be dying and getting senile, but while he lived, he ruled, and Mym was subject to his will. He would shortly find himself back at Honeymoon Castle, with a new princess, and if he did not come to love her, he would be forced to marry her anyway.

He faced the great front window overlooking the entrance. Guards marched there, ensuring that no one passed by without authorization. Mym bit his tongue.

His body made a slight anticipatory shiver as he tasted the blood. He would not be confined here much longer!

But as his berserker rage developed, something strange happened. Outside, in the night sky above the lighted court, a glowing object approached.

Mym stared at it. It was a great red sword, angled up at a forty-five degree angle, floating unsupported. The blade was shining steel, and Mym somehow knew that nothing that sharp edge touched could remain whole. This was a magic instrument.

Still his rage governed him. Refusing to be distracted longer by the manifestation, he got ready to move.

The red sword swung in toward him. It passed through the glass of the window without breaking it.

Mym swung to face it, ready to destroy whatever came against him, whether natural or supernatural. Red froth bubbled between his lips.

The sword came to a halt immediately before him. Its glow increased. It was challenging him!

"Then damned be you!" he cried, spewing bloody spittle, his stutter absent in his rage. He reached out and grasped the hilt of the sword.

The glow of the sword magnified. Now it surrounded Mym, lighting the room. But greater than the physical glow was the emotional glow, for suddenly his awareness of himself was far more intense that he had ever before experienced. He felt strong, invulnerable, omnipotent. Strange power surged through him. His berserker rage was suspended by the wonder of this new power. What was happening?

There was the suggestion of a whisper of a sound. Mym turned, and saw a thin mist forming. It coalesced into a cloud, from which the figure of a mature women shaped. Her eyes were as blue as the summer sky, and her hair was vaguely green.

"Gaea!" he exclaimed, recognizing the manner of the Incarnation of Nature.

"You have now assumed the office of the Incarnation of War, known as Mars, Aries, or whatever you prefer, as Chronos advised," she said, coming clear. "I thought it best to be on hand, in case you had a question."

Now he remembered. Chronos, living backwards, had indeed said it; Mym had somehow let his awareness slide.

"B-b-but—" he started, then shifted to singsong: "But I don't want to be the Incarnation of War! I only want to marry Rapture!"

"Of course," she agreed noncommittally. "But you stand in need of information. You don't have to accept the office; if you simply renounce the Red Sword and turn it loose, it will seek the second most qualified applicant, and you will remain mortal. I am here to help you decide."

Mym remembered how she had brought the manna for his starving people. Gaea had extraordinary power. "I am grateful for that."

"You see, the Incarnation of War exists only as long as war exists," she said. "Wherever war is being fought, there Mars goes to supervise. There must be some order in the world, after all. On those rare occasions when there is no war, Mars dissipates, and his soul travels to Heaven or Hell, as the case may be, according to its balance of good or evil. Recently war ended, and so your predecessor vacated the office and the Red Sword was retired. But now war is resuming, so the need for the office has been restored, and the Sword is seeking the appropriate officer. It can not be just any person; only one who is proficient in weapons and martial arts and in the strategies and management of war is eligible. In addition, he must desire the position; that is, he must be the most warlike of all those eligible in the region of the resumed war.''

"But I do not desire—"

"The desire for war is defined by the emotion of the candidate," she explained. "The one with the most pervasive anger. That anger attracts the Red Sword as a magnet attracts iron. The Sword can not be in error about that."

No, it had not been in error. There was no rage like that of a berserker, even a controlled one like Mym. So the Red Sword of War had sought him out.

"But you say I can decline," he sang. "So I can remain mortal and marry Rapture."

"You may decline," she agreed. "But if you remain mortal, I doubt that you will wed Rapture. You will be subject to the conditions of your situation and will be required to marry the Princess of Rajasthan unless you suicide first. On the other hand, if you accept the office, you will wield considerable power. You will be in a position to take Rapture, if that is your desire."

"But she will remain mortal!"

"True. But she may join you, and her life will not be shortened. She would have to leave her kingdom, but if she chose to join you—"

"She would choose to," he sang with certainty.

"Then it seems you have nothing to lose by accepting the proffered office," she said. "However, I am obliged to warn you of one significant contraindication."

"The catch," he sang.

"The catch," she agreed. "It seems that Satan has his evil hand in this. He had a grudge against the former Mars and wanted him to be replaced. Thus Satan worked assiduously in what was, for him, an unusual cause—that of peace on Earth. He succeeded, for a moment—and that retired Mars. Now Satan surely believes that the new Incarnation will be easier to manage, because of his lack of experience."

"I have no truck with Satan!" Mym sang. "I hardly believe in him! I am Hindu!"

"Nominally," she said. "As a prince, you are naturally skeptical about religion."

To that he had to agree. In his private heart, he subscribed to no religion. Thus it seemed that his rage had been the determining factor, not his belief in any particular supernatural framework.

"Now, with that warning, you may decide," Gaea said. "If you fear the mischief of Satan—"

"Fornicate Satan!" he sang. "If I can have Rapture by assuming the office of the Incarnation of War, then I shall assume it!"

"It had occurred to me that you might feel that way," Gaea said. "Welcome, then, to our number, Mars."

And he knew that his commitment had been made.

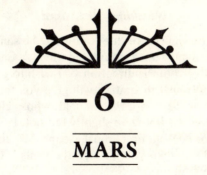

-6-

MARS

"First you must know how to travel," Gaea said. "You have a fine horse named Werre, but he's mainly for formal occasions. Or you can discorporate, but that has risks. For now, the key is the Sword. There are several modes of its operation, but all are governed by your will. If you choose to appear at the most intense war currently being waged, you simply give it its head and it will take you there, instantly. The Sword likes violence. If you want to go home—that is, to your castle in Purgatory—you give it the mental command *home*."

"Purgatory?" Mym sang.

"A Western concept, a kind of crude, structured nirvana. It may be easiest to think of it as an island in the sky, a place in the clouds, invisible to mortal folk, but real to immortals. The place where those souls who have not made the decision whether to go to Heaven or to Hell pause. A place of indecision, or of decision, however you see it."

"Reincarnation is more expedient," Mym sang.

"We Occidentals are not as sophisticated about the larger scale as are you Orientals," Gaea murmured, smiling. But he was sure that this benign green woman was as sophisticated as any living person.

"I think first I want to rescue Rapture," he sang.

"For that, you must use the directed travel," Gaea said. "Simply point the Sword in the direction you wish to go and will it to proceed. A little experimentation will give you the feel of it."

Mym looked at the sword he still held, whose glow had diminished to a dull red, as if it were slightly red-hot. He was acquiring more respect for it. "But first I must escape the palace," he sang.

"The Sword will take you through the walls," Gaea said.

"That's what I'm afraid of!"

She smiled. "An Incarnation is only as solid as he chooses to be. You will pass through without disruption."

Cautiously he pointed the Sword at an interior wall, so that he would not find himself abruptly in mid-air outside, two stories up. *Forward!* he thought. *Slowly.*

The sword moved—and he moved with it. There was no sensation; he remained standing, but traveling, as if on a moving carpet or one of those scientific airplanes. Surprised, he lifted the Sword slightly, so that it angled up—and found himself sliding upward at that angle, his feet leaving the floor. Hastily he angled it level again—and sailed through the wall.

There was a moment of darkness; then he emerged from the other side of the stone. Now he was floating slowly across the next chamber, half a meter above the floor.

He realized that he didn't have to worry about being outside at a height; the Sword made him independent of support. He could fly, literally, without effort or discomfort.

Gaea appeared in the new chamber, in the form of coalescing mist. "Shall we proceed to Maharastra?" the mist inquired.

Mym was getting to like the Sword very well. "But suppose I drop it?" he asked, still not quite certain about venturing high and far.

"Try it here," she suggested.

He let go of the Sword. It remained floating in the air—and so did he. "But I'm not touching it!" he sang.

"The Red Sword is yours until you renounce it," Gaea said. "This is not a matter of physical contact. You could give it to another person, even a mortal, and it would still be attuned to you. You can sheathe it and orient it mentally, and it will not change physically, but will act as you will. It is a symbol as much as an object, and its powers are great.''

Evidently so. Mym took hold of the sword and sheathed it in the great, ornate scabbard that he abruptly discovered at his hip—and remained floating. ''Then let's go!'' he sang.

In his mind he aimed the Sword up, at a thirty degree angle, and south. He willed a swift passage.

He got it. He shot upward at the angle, passing right through the building and into the nocturnal sky. The process was exhilarating. Up, up he sailed, feeling no wind, no change of temperature. The magic of the Sword kept him secure.

''But you must guide it, when the destination is not familiar to it,'' a cloud said.

Mym experienced *deja vu.* ''Were you at the Honeymoon Castle?'' he sang.

''Not specifically,'' another cloud replied. ''I am in all things, but I don't interfere where I don't need to.''

''A cloud talked to me, there,'' he sang.

''They do, on occasion,'' the cloud he was now passing agreed. ''You may wish to steer inland.''

He looked down and discovered that he was high over the surging Indian Ocean. He directed the Sword southeast, and his direction of travel changed accordingly.

He accelerated, and the sea and dark shore moved by at a phenomenal pace, but still Mym himself stood casually upright, feeling no wind resistance. Though it was dark, he was able to see around him; either his night vision was sufficient, or the Sword was lending him enhanced powers of observation. He flew in toward the giant city of Bombay, where he knew Rapture had been sent.

Lights shone all across the city, and the palace was brightest of all. Mym had no trouble reaching it. He simply flew in through a stone wall and landed lightly on an upper floor.

But the palace was huge, and there were many chambers and suites. How could he locate Rapture, without causing a stir while he searched?

Gaea's mist appeared, like vapor condensing. ''Use the Sword again,'' she advised. ''I understand that it can tune in on the identity of any person and enable you to share that person's awareness. It is one-way; the subject is not aware of you. But it can be quite useful on occasion."

"Tune in—on Rapture?" he sang. "But her privacy—I don't like to—"

"You have changed since the Honeymoon Castle. This, however, need not be that intimate. Merely avail yourself of her perceptions, to identify her location; then go to it."

Oh. Mym touched the Sword. *Rapture of Malachite, Princess of Maharastra*, he thought.

Nothing happened.

"Titles mean nothing to it," Gaea advised him gently. "It perceives only the essence."

Mym tried again. This time he thought of the woman he loved.

He found himself looking at an ornate feminine dagger.

He blinked—and he was still standing in the chamber, his finger touching the Red Sword.

It had been Rapture's dagger he had seen.

She was contemplating suicide.

He looked again, this time tuning in on the peripheral aspects of her vision. She was in her private bedroom, alone—but where was that? He was not familiar with the layout of this palace; that room could be anywhere.

Then her gaze wandered vacantly to the mirror, and he saw her forlorn reflection. Her lustrous tresses had dimmed, and her green-malachite eyes were rimmed in red. She was so lost without him! She had been dependent on her father and now she was dependent on Mym; stripped of that support, she was collapsing into herself. He had loved her because of that fundamental vulnerability; she truly did need him.

Behind her reflected face, a portion of a window showed, and beyond it was a fragment of green. She had set a green handkerchief at the sill, perhaps to dry after being soaked with her tears. That was so like her!

He grasped the Sword. *Out* he directed.

He sailed out through the wall and around the palace. There in an upper window on the north side was a speck of green. He homed in on it, then passed in through the window to land on the floor. "Rapture," he sang.

She jumped, spun about, recognized him, and collapsed.

He jumped forward and caught her as she fell. "Beloved!" he said, not stuttering for the moment. He held her, kissed her, and held her some more, and in a moment she revived.

"Beloved!" she echoed.

"I have come to claim you," he sang. "But there is much to explain."

"Just hold me," she breathed. "I—without you, I—"

"I saw the dagger," he sang. "No need for that now."

Then, holding her, he sang his explanation: his assumption of the office of the Incarnation of War, by grasping the great Red Sword; the new powers and responsibilities that provided him; and his ability to take her with him—if she chose to come.

"Take me with you!" she cried without reservation.

"But it will mean a complete change in your life," he warned. "You would not be a princess any more."

She just looked at him, and he knew that nothing else mattered to her except being with him.

"Well, let's see how well we can travel together, then," he sang. He touched the Sword.

"A consideration," a wisp of mist said, forming in the room.

Rapture jumped again, but Mym reassured her. "That is Gaea, the Incarnation of Nature," he sang. "She is helping me get started. She showed me how to reach you."

"If you take her away without explanation," Gaea said, "her father will assume that she has come to some foul end and he will blame your Kingdom, Prince, with which he is at war. That would lead to much mischief that I think you would prefer to avoid."

"I would prefer to stop this idiotic war entirely, by marrying Rapture!" Mym sang. "But my father—"

"Perhaps we can achieve your desire, with a little effort," Gaea said. "All that is needed is the apparent acquiescence of the principals. What would make your marriage to the Prince of Rajasthan acceptable to your father, Rapture?"

"I would not marry—" Rapture began angrily, but Gaea held up a finger, and the Princess was silenced. Mym suspected that more magic was involved. "A reduced dowry," Rapture said, after a pause.

Gaea turned to Mym. "And if you acceded to marriage with

the Princess of Rajasthan, proffering the acceptance of a reduced dowry if the same were accepted for your former betrothed?"

Mym was beginning to comprehend. "I am sure the Rajah of Rajasthan would be amenable to that; he expects to pay an exorbitant dowry. But certainly I'm not going to—"

"Would one of your handmaidens like to take your place?" Gaea asked Rapture.

Rapture smiled. "Any handmaiden would like to take the place of any princess! But—"

"Summon one you feel is worthy, who would be able to act your part, if she had the appearance and opportunity."

"That would be the one who doubles for me on boring parades." Rapture said. "But up close, she does not resemble me very well."

"Bring her here."

Rapture reached out and drew on a tassled cord. In moments a young woman appeared at the door. "Bit-of-Honey, there is a task we may require of you," she said. "Listen to this woman."

Gaea, who was now completely solid, addressed the young woman. "The Princess Rapture of Malachite must go away. But she wishes to appear to remain. If you will consent, I shall fashion you to the likeness of the Princess, and you shall take her place."

Bit-of-Honey shrugged. "I have done so before."

Gaea smiled. "For the rest of your life."

The girl's eyes widened. "But she is to marry the Prince of—" Her gaze flicked to Mym "*Was* to marry—"

"She is now to marry the Prince of Rajasthan," Gaea said. "But she loves the Prince of Gujarat, so she is going away with him. She would like you to assume her identity and marry the Prince of Rajasthan. Are you willing to do that?"

"But I am only a common girl!" Bit-of-Honey protested.

"You will be the Princess—if you are willing to give up your present life in favor of that one, and keep the secret."

"But—the Prince—I could never be more than a concubine to—"

Gaea touched her, and the girl's protestations abated. "You can be what you choose to be. I will provide you with the voice and the appearance; you must provide the will and the action. But you must choose now."

The girl looked wildly at Rapture. "Oh, Mistress, I would never betray you, but this—"

"Do it," Rapture said. "You know I have no life without Prince Pride of the Kingdom. You are welcome to the Prince of Rajasthan."

"To be a princess . . ." the girl breathed, beginning to believe.

Gaea touched her again—and her appearance dissolved and changed and became that of Rapture. Even her clothing conformed. "Speak," Gaea said.

"What shall I say?" the pseudo-Rapture asked. She sounded exactly like Rapture.

"You know what to do," Gaea said. "If you slip or falter, it will be over."

The woman looked in the mirror at herself, amazed. Then her shoulders straightened. "I will not falter," she said.

"But what of *my* disappearance?" Mym sang.

"We shall take care of you now," Gaea said. "Will yourself back to the place where the Sword came to you; it is familiar with that site. Make sure you have a good grip on Rapture."

Mym touched the sword with his left hand and put his right arm about Rapture's slender waist. *To the place of our meeting*, he thought.

And they were there.

Gaea's cloud formed. However she traveled, it wasn't the same way Mars did. "Now we need a young man to assume your identity," she said.

Mym considered. "I had a sparring partner of royal birth, for my weapons training," he sang. "He knows the ways of princes, and he likes wealth and power. I believe he could and would play the part."

They summoned the man; after a dialogue similar to the one that had occurred in Bombay, the man assumed the likeness of Mym, and was afflicted with his stutter—but was happy to marry the Princess of Rajasthan and carry the privileges and responsibilities of the position.

Now they were free to depart the mortal realm.

"The staff of your castle will assist you hereafter," Gaea said. "I shall encounter you in the line of business. I wish you well."

"I thank you for the invaluable help you have provided me," Mym sang. "I hope I shall not disappoint you in the office."

"Only if you allow yourself to be deceived by Satan," she said, and dissolved into vapor.

Mym put his arm around Rapture, touched the Red Sword, and willed them to his castle home in Purgatory.

He found himself in the entrance-foyer of a castle as seemingly solid as any he had encountered. Huge gray stones rose up to an enormous height. He tapped one and found it solid. "If this is a castle in the sky, it is nevertheless quite substantial," he sang.

There was a stir within the castle. Several gaunt figures came to the foyer. Rapture shrank away from them.

Mym recognized one in a black cloak. "Famine!" he sang.

Famine nodded. "And you are Mars," he replied.

Mym turned to the others. "And you are—?"

"Conquest," a big, hearty man in a white cloak said. He smiled, and his teeth showed like polished white ivory.

"Slaughter," the one in the blood-red cloak said. There were ragged slashes across his face that dripped fresh blood. Rapture shuddered and averted her gaze.

"Pestilence," said the one in the dirt-brown cloak. His face was a squirming mass of maggots. Rapture screamed and shrank away.

"My companion is distraught," Mym sang. "Do not take offense."

"Offense?" Pestilence asked, a maggot spraying out as he pronounced the *S*. "I am flattered!"

They passed on into the castle proper. The castle staff was lined up, ready for inspection by the new master.

"Do you know how to serve royalty?" Mym sang.

"We do," the head butler replied.

"Then see to the needs of the Lady Rapture," Mym sang. "And provide me with a person who can tell me what I need to know."

The butler snapped his fingers. Immediately two maids stepped up to Rapture. "We shall see you to your suite," one said. "There is a bath waiting and a change of dress."

Rapture hesitated, glancing at Mym. She didn't want to be separated from him in this strange place.

"Did you meet the lesser Incarnations?" the other maid asked. "Aren't they simply awful? I had bad dreams for days after I saw Slaughter, and as for Pestilence—!"

Rapture turned her gaze to the maid, discovering companionship. She relaxed. These people might be all right after all. She went with them.

"These are marvelously accommodating personnel," Mym remarked.

"This is our station in the Afterlife," the head butler said. "To know and serve your needs. The Lady Rapture will be made at ease."

"Afterlife?" Mym sang.

"We are not among the living," the butler said.

"But you seem quite solid."

"Here in Purgatory, sir, everything seems solid, but only you and the Lady Rapture have physical substance beyond these environs. The rest of us—and the castle too—are only solid in a qualified sense."

"I have some difficulty accepting this."

"We are as pictures on a sheet of paper. When you confine yourself to that frame of reference, the pictures are sufficient. But when you exert yourself in the three-dimensional frame, we no longer have relevance. You have mortal substance that we lack."

"Purgatory—is a picture on a sheet of paper?"

"In a manner of speaking. A facet of existence limited to a plane. From the surface of the Earth, mortals see right through that plane. But when you come to it, you join it and interact with us in what may seem to be a normal manner."

"I can't believe that you don't really exist!"

"We exist, sir. But only in a limited sense. Heaven and Hell are similarly limited; only mortals have the full range of experience."

"Isn't this horribly restrictive? Don't you feel imprisoned?"

"This is eternity. Though we lack the freedom to affect our destinies that mortals possess, we are freed from the concern about pain and termination that they suffer from. We comprehend the shape of our existence. Our reality is as if it were stretched out in an infinitely narrow but infinitely long path, unlike that of mortals."

"To be a butler—for eternity? No reincarnation?"

"Not for eternity. Only for a few centuries, until the inevitable shift of the ratio of good and evil in us permits departure to Heaven and everlasting peace."

"A few centuries!"

"It is worth it, sir. We have only to do our jobs—and these are not unpleasant jobs. It would be my pleasure to serve you even if my destination were not dependent on it."

Mym would not have been satisfied with such a situation—but of course he was a mortal—or was he? "What is my status, now? Will I age and die in this office?"

"By no means, sir. You will remain fixed as you are now, for your full term, which will terminate only when war on Earth abates. You are an Incarnation of Immortality—a temporary immortal."

"Who else is in this situation?"

"There are five, or perhaps seven, major Incarnations. Death, Time, Fate, War, and Nature, in addition to Good and Evil. There are a greater number of lesser Incarnations, such as the associates of War whom you met in the foyer. But the only ones you need be concerned about are the major ones, who will generally co-operate with you."

"Generally?"

"God, the Incarnation of Good, does not involve Himself with mortal matters, in accordance to the Covenant. Mortals must choose their own denouements. Therefore He will neither help nor hinder you, though He does watch you."

Mym was glad that he had picked up a smattering of Western mythology; otherwise this would have been very confusing. "What of the Incarnation of Evil?"

"He is Satan, and because he is evil, he freely violates the Covenant. He will seek to do mischief, turning your efforts to his designs. He wishes to gain power by acquiring a greater number of souls than God possesses."

This aligned with the warning Gaea had given him. Satan would cause trouble. "But how can he do this, if I am alert against it?"

"Satan is devious, and the master of misdirection. It is customary for him to, if you will pardon the crudity of the expression, work over new Incarnations. You will be a target, sir."

"It is true that Satan conspired to eliminate my predecessor?"

"It is true, sir."

"What did the former Mars do to arouse Satan's wrath?"

"He supervised a challenge that the present Fate made to Satan, ensuring that it was fairly conducted. This enabled Fate to balk Satan's design."

"But that's unreasonable!" Mym sang. "A fair contest—"

"Satan is not a reasonable entity, sir. He is interested only in his own design."

"And Mars—surely he was not helpless in his own defense?"

"He tolerated the ploy."

"Why would he do that, knowing that this would be to Satan's advantage and that he himself would perish?"

"He did not perish. He went to Heaven. That is a consummation devoutly to be desired. The cessation of war had been his most devout wish."

"But that's a conflict of interest! If he abolishes his job—"

"Not if one's wish is to go to Heaven, sir."

Mym considered that. "So Mars wanted to go to Heaven and could only get there by having his job end in a positive manner—so Satan facilitated that, and it behooved Mars to cooperate."

"Exactly, sir."

"But now Satan has a new and inexperienced Mars to, as you put it, work over."

"Exactly, sir."

"And I will not get to Heaven unless I succeed in abolishing war."

"Admirably phrased, sir."

"There's only one catch."

"Sir?"

"I don't want to go to Heaven."

"Sir?" The butler was visibly startled.

"I am a Hindu. Not a good one, obviously—but my desire is not for Heaven but for nirvana."

The butler made a *moue*. "Then it would seem that Satan does not have the inducement to proffer you that he proffered to your predecessor.''

"Correct."

"This should be a most interesting encounter, sir."

Mym smiled. "Let's hope so."

– 7 –

BATTLE

The next day, as Mym perceived it, he received news of a battle that required his attention. He had spent a pleasant night with Rapture in the excellently appointed castle; they had made love and talked and watched the scientific television, which by coincidence was concerned with news of the recent change in office-holders for the Incarnation of War and seemed to be quite current. Rapture had perked up to hear herself mentioned as the mortal consort of the Incarnation and to see herself smiling prettily for the camera, though there had been no such interview. But in the morning that same television set turned itself on with the announcement of the battle, and Mym had to rouse himself for his new duty.

"But what of me?" Rapture cried. "I cannot go to battle with you, yet I fear to remain here alone."

Mym began to perceive a disadvantage of complete dependence in a woman. "Let me investigate," he sang.

He went into the elaborate lavatory, then snapped his fingers. Immediately the head butler appeared. The man did not enter; he just appeared. Now that Mym understood his nature, he was not surprised. "The Lady Rapture is concerned about being alone in this strange place," he sang.

"Conduct her to the East Wing," the butler recommended.

Mym wasn't sure how this would help, but he had already seen the competence of the staff here, so he didn't argue.

After his toilet, which included the donning of a shining golden cloak of office, he emerged to rejoin Rapture. She had meanwhile been attended to; now she was stunningly lovely in a silken outfit of malachite green, with the lovely polished stones set in her hair. Princess indeed!

"After we eat, I must show you the East Wing," Mym sang.

She raised a fine dark eyebrow.

"You have already explored the castle?"

"The butler told me you would like it."

In due course they repaired to that Wing—and Rapture gasped with delight. It was very like the palace she had used on Earth, with glass windows and fountains and associated gardens filled with familiar plants. A high canopy even protected it from the torrential rains of the monsoon. In a lower reach a tame elephant waited.

"I must go to work," Mym sang.

She hardly heard him. "Oh, how delightful!" she exclaimed, walking through the Wing, gazing at the lovely statuary.

Mym decided to depart; she would not miss him for some time.

Now he went to the front foyer. There were his associates, Conquest, Slaughter, Famine, and Pestilence, in their colored cloaks. "You know the way?" he inquired.

"Our steeds know the way," Conquest said.

Steeds. He hadn't thought of that, but of course they should be mounted. Gaea had told him that he had a horse—what was its name?—Werre. He went on out, and there in front were five excellent horses. There was no difficulty judging which one belonged to which rider, for they were color coded.

"Werre," Mym sang, and one came immediately to him. He mounted the great golden palomino and knew from the outset that this was a steed such as man dreamed of. The animal was powerful and supple and responded to his cues so readily that he could virtually guide it with a thought. This stallion was like an extension of himself.

The others were mounted and drew up beside him. Conquest was on an albino stallion, with totally white hide and blazing red eyes. Slaughter was on the red one, the color so intense it was almost gore. Famine was on the black animal, whose body glistened in such a way as to make the gloss seem like a skeletal outline. Pestilence rode the dirty brown horse, with patches of discolor that made it look diseased, though it was healthy. Mym remembered, now, that four grim horsemen were traditionally associated with War, but he wasn't sure that these were the particular four he remembered. It hardly mattered; Purgatory and the Incarnations evidently had their own rules.

They rode out across the cloudscape, and the steeds did know the way. They galloped to the sudden edge and leaped over into the sky below, landing on air, and charged swiftly across the seeming map of the globe far beneath. The colored capes fluttered in the wind. In short order they had come to India, where they descended, touching the ground at last at the eastern edge.

Mym surveyed the region—and discovered that he was familiar with it. This was the border between Gujarat and Maharastra! This battle was to be fought between his own Kingdom and that of Rapture.

But he had arranged with Gaea to eliminate that quarrel. His double was to marry the Rajasthan Princess, and Rapture's double to marry the Rajasthan Prince, unifying the three Kingdoms by alliances. How could they be fighting now?

When he thought about it, he knew how. This was only one day after those rearrangements had been made. The news had not yet gotten out to the battlefield, where the two armies were preparing to clash. With modern scientific communications systems the word should have been virtually instant—but the bureaucracy remained as ponderous as ever. The notice was probably still sitting among the papers on the desk of a minor functionary, waiting for disposition. Meanwhile this completely pointless battle was about to happen.

He had to stop it, of course. Mym was not one to be squeamish about necessary bloodshed; he was, after all, a prince. Or had been . . . But this was not only unnecessary, it was disastrous; neither Kingdom could afford to throw away its resources like this.

Already the two armies were spread out on the battlefield, their cavalry, archers, elephants, and foot soldiers ranged like chess pieces, ready to play their roles. The forces were about even, so the skill of the generals would count for the victory—except that there could be no victory, in this wrongheaded match.

How was he to stop this folly? He had no idea.

"Famine," he called, and the black figure moved close. "This battle is not supposed to occur. How do I stop it?"

"*Stop* it?" Famine asked, his deathly gaunt face showing dismay. "We do not stop conflict, we reap it!"

And what a grim reaping that could be! "Nevertheless," Mym sang, "this conflict must be stopped before it starts. If I am truly the Incarnation of War, surely I have the power both to generate and to dissipate conflict."

Famine issued a ghastly sigh. "You do, Mars. But it is a sad day when your power is exerted to—"

"Never mind that!" Mym sang angrily. "How do I exert my power?"

"Why, there are several ways. You can enter the mind of a pivotal participant and change it, or you can freeze the entire battle in place—"

"If I freeze it, what happens when I unfreeze it?"

"Then it resumes exactly as before."

"How do I enter the mind of a pivotal participant, and how do I know which one is pivotal?"

Famine considered. "That's really not my department. I deal with my clients after the combat has ravaged the land and wiped out most of the food supply. I've never been sure exactly how Mars selects his key figures."

If Famine didn't know, the others probably wouldn't know either. He would just have to work it out by himself.

He guided his golden horse toward the banners of the Gujarat army. If he could manifest and be recognized by the general there, he might be able to cause that army to decline battle.

He approached, and no one reacted. That was right—no one could see an Incarnation, ordinarily. He rode right up to the front line and through it, and the horse's gleaming hooves made no contact with the mundane objects. It was as if the artifacts of the world were ghosts. Or he was.

He came to the general's tent. He saw immediately that this was a man he knew only by name; he had never encountered him personally before. This one had a reputation as a competent work-horse, one who had no special flair or elegance, but who followed orders and got the job done.

The general should recognize Mym, if he manifested. But how did he do that? Mym himself had seen the Incarnations before becoming one himself, but no one else had, until Gaea manifested to Rapture. Gaea knew how to do that, but Mym didn't.

But he could enter the General's being and change his mind, according to Famine. That should be just as good. If he could just figure out how.

Well, maybe if he simply overlapped the General, so that his mind occupied the same space as the General's mind . . .

He tried it. He dismounted and stepped into the General—

And found himself in a maelstrom of impressions and thoughts and emotions. He could not make head or tail of it all; indeed, he was getting nauseous, as from motion sickness.

He ripped himself out. Now he was standing before the General, who seemed to be unaffected. But Mym himself felt dizzy. Surely this was not the way it was supposed to be!

But the battle would not wait forever. Mym tried again. This time he kept a firm mental grip on himself as he phased in to the General's space. He realized that what he was encountering was the confusion of an unfamiliar system. The General's mind differed from his own; there were different memories, different habit patterns, and a different outlook. Recognizing that, Mym was able to keep better equilibrium. He phased in more accurately, so that his own eye-nerve impulses were not trying to read the General's ear-nerve impulses. He got the senses aligned and felt only slightly motion-sick.

Now he could tune in on what the General was perceiving and understand it. It was not a perfect alignment, because the General's senses were of slightly different strengths than Mym's own and so tended to feel slightly wrong. But that was minor.

His major problem was the General's thoughts. It was evident that the General's brain was wired differently from Mym's, and the resulting patterns were alien. He could not make sense of them.

Well, yes he could. The wiring might differ, but the end results were similar. He did not need to use the General's wiring to grasp the General's conclusions. He simply needed to tune in on those conclusions. And then impose his own.

He tried. CALL OFF BATTLE, he thought strongly.

"What?" the General asked, pausing in his contemplation of the map of the battle site.

The other officers looked at him, perplexed. None of them had spoken.

The General shook his head, concluding that it had been an errant thought. Every person had doubts on occasion. "Proceed with the battle plan as outlined," he said gruffly.

Mym realized that this was not the way either. He had projected his thought into the General's consciousness, but it had not been supported by any apparent logic, so the General had dismissed it. He would have to develop a more comprehensive approach, to actually convince the General that the new thought made sense. That would take time. For one thing, he would need to learn more about the General's frames of reference, so as to devise an approach that would make sense to the man.

But he didn't have time. The cavalry was already moving out. The battle was being joined.

Mym gave up in disgust. He exited the General. It felt like shedding an uncomfortable yoke. He much preferred his own identity!

He mounted his horse, who had waited patiently for his return, and galloped over and through the people to the center of the battlefield. The Maharastra cavalry was meeting the charge with one of its own—plus another element. A unit of trained griffins led the way, spreading their wings and launching themselves at the opposing line. That could be disaster for the Gujarat cavalrymen!

But the Gujarats were prepared. Precision catapults had been set up, and these now opened fire on the griffins, the object being to knock them out of the air. There was a raucous squawk as a missile scored glancingly on one, and a griffin spun to the ground with a broken wing. But the fight had not gone out of the creature; it laid about itself with beak and claws, and gore flew as it scored.

In moments the other griffins swooped down on the line, and the carnage was multiplied. "Great!" the Incarnation of Slaughter cried, riding near. "Mix it up! Tear those guts! Spatter that blood! Spread that gore!"

Meanwhile, the Incarnation of Conquest was urging on the two main armies. "Victory!" he cried to both. "Take no prisoners!"

And with that the efforts of the armies increased, and the combat became savage. Mym was disgusted. It was all so pointless!

But he had failed to stop it. What was he to do now?

Well, he could try a more direct method. He rode to the center of the carnage, climbed a hill of air to gain elevation, and grasped his Red Sword. Maybe it would enable him to manifest. He drew it and held it high, willing himself to be apparent.

And—it worked! The Sword *was* the key! He knew he was visible, because the bowmen at the rear lines were staring at him. They had never before seen a man and horse in mid-air.

Now was his chance. He would tell them all to stop fighting, until they could receive the notice that explained why.

He took a deep breath. "S-s-s-s-s—" he stuttered.

Damn! He took another breath. "Stop the battle!" he sang.

There was a moment of amazed silence. Then someone laughed. They could not believe that this noble, golden figure could utter such obvious nonsense.

"It's a trick!" an officer cried. "Shoot it down!"

Then the archers of both sides went back into action, firing their shafts at him. Mym remained frozen, furious at himself for not being able to address them effectively.

The arrows struck him and the horse and bounced off harmlessly. He never even felt them; it seemed he was invulnerable to mortal weapons.

But he didn't like being a target. He sheathed the Sword—and evidently faded out of sight, for the archers blinked and stopped firing. The officers rubbed their eyes.

Yet Mym could still see himself and his steed quite clearly. He also saw the other Incarnations. Conquest and Slaughter were exhorting the troops to greater efforts; Famine and Pestilence were watching from the sideline, rubbing their hands in anticipation of their turn to come, as supplies were depleted and hunger and disease ran their course.

A number of arrows had been in flight when he faded out of mortal view. These now passed entirely through him and the horse, without deviating at all. That was another evidence of his change; he truly had become unsolid, as far as mortals were concerned.

Could he become solid while remaining invisible? Curious, despite the tragedy around him, he touched the Sword and willed himself to be tangible but imperceptible.

One more arrow was coming. It struck the side of the horse and dropped to the ground, broken. But the archers weren't watching. That was answer enough.

But the battle continued. It remained as much folly as before, and he still had to stop it. What else could he do?

Famine had mentioned that Mars could freeze the action. Indeed, the Incarnation of Death had done that when Mym had first encountered him, and surely Chronos, the Incarnation of Time, could do it too.

He touched the Sword again. *Freeze action* he thought.

Just like that, it froze. The armies below him became like statuary, the men and animals stilled in mid-motion, the sounds of battle abated, and the clouds of dust and smoke halted in place. The few arrows that were in flight hovered in air.

But the other Incarnations were not affected. Slaughter looked up from his grisly work, gore dripping from his fingers. "Something come up, Mars?" he called.

"Yes," Mym returned shortly. But what was he to do next? He knew he couldn't keep the tableau frozen indefinitely—and the moment he abated it, the carnage would resume.

Unless he could do something to stop the battle, before allowing the action to resume. *He* was not frozen. He could go to the capitals, find where the message of termination of the war was stalled, and facilitate its delivery.

Was the rest of the world frozen too? He doubted it. But how far did the effect extend?

There was one way to find out. "I have an errand," he told the other Incarnations. "See that the freeze remains until I return."

"It is your prerogative," Conquest said, grimacing. Obviously he felt this was foolishness.

Mym urged his horse upward and forward, into the sky to the north. They galloped away from the battle site. Soon he saw people moving again and confirmed that the freeze applied only to the battle. Good enough; he didn't want to interfere with the rest of the world, just to abate the pointless bloodshed.

He come to Ahmadabad and descended to the Rajah's palace. He passed through the wall, horse and all, and approached his father's private chambers. No one saw him.

Then he paused. He had thought to manifest and inquire about the order canceling the war—but though the personnel might recognize him, they would be confused because his real self, as far as they knew, was the double Gaea had fashioned to take his place. How could there be two of him? It would not be wise to interfere with that.

Well, then, he could act through himself. He galloped his horse to the other palace for an interview with his double. The young man was no longer confined, but had seen no need to depart the palace while the arrangements for his journey to the Honeymoon Castle were being made.

Honeymoon Castle? But there the man's thoughts would be completely open to his betrothed! That would give away his true identity and quite possibly provoke a new war. "Oh, Gaea," he sang under his breath. "You overlooked one vital detail!"

Mist formed before him. "Foolish man," it breathed. "I shaped his mind as well as his body. He knows his identity, but his thoughts there will only be those of the Prince."

He stopped, there in the hall, the servants brushing through his substance without ever being aware of his presence or that of the horse. "You can do that?" he asked, amazed.

"I am Nature," the mist whispered—and dissipated.

If the powers of Mars were as he had discovered, what then of the powers of Gaea? He could only glimpse them peripherally, but he found himself awed.

He resumed his ride, entered the suite of his double, and made himself tangible. "How goes it, Prince Pride?" he sang.

The new Prince looked up, only mildly surprised. "I look upon a life that is more wonderful than any I imagined," he replied in a similar singsong. "I have seen a painting of the Princess I am to marry, and she is lovely."

Mym had seen the picture and regarded the Princess as relatively plain. But perhaps Gaea had dabbled in that aspect of the man too, so that he was entirely content with his lot. Gaea's favors were subtle but solid. No doubt her anger could be similarly devastating!

"I have a problem," Mym said. "As you know, I am now the Incarnation of War. There is a battle going on between Gujarat and Maharastra that should not be occurring. The order to halt hostilities seems to have gotten lost in transit. I need to obtain that order and get it to the front—but I do not want to seem to duplicate myself when I get it. So—"

"I will get it for you," the new Prince Pride said, understanding immediately. "Naturally I don't want lives expended uselessly any more than you do; I will have to manage this Kingdom all too soon."

He was taking hold very nicely, despite his lack of prior training for the position he had assumed. Gaea's work again, surely.

The new Prince Pride took a carpet immediately to the Rajah's palace, while Mym paced him invisibly on the horse. The trip was swift, as neither had to wait on traffic below, and in a few minutes they were there. Then Prince Pride asked for a copy of the order requiring the cessation of hostilities and took it with him. The moment he was alone, he held it in the air, and Mym materialized enough to grasp it. "Thank you, Prince," he said. "May you have a long and happy life."

He galloped back to the battle site, where things remained frozen. He brought the order to a messenger boy, put it in his hand, and phased in to his mind. No thought was proceeding, because of the freeze, but Mym projected strongly: URGENT MESSAGE FOR GENERAL.

Then he sat back on the horse, touched the Sword, and willed the release of the stasis.

The scene reanimated. The troops resumed killing each other; blood resumed flowing, and arrows completed their flights. The messenger boy looked startled, evidently not remembering how he had come to possess the urgent message, but knowing his duty. He rushed it to the General.

The General perused it. He sighed. "Peace has been declared," he said, disgusted. "Cease hostilities. Send a mission under flag of truce to the enemy to acquaint them with this news."

It took a while to sort it out, but in due course the armies disengaged. The battle was over, and not too many men had been killed.

But if he had handled the matter more expeditiously, there would have been no carnage at all. Mym knew he had a lot yet to learn about the performance of his office.

He gathered up his minions and returned to his castle in Purgatory. Conquest, Slaughter, Famine, and Pestilence went their ways, disappointed. They would have only a slim harvest from this day's work.

Rapture met him at the front foyer. "Oh, beloved, I missed you so!" she exclaimed. "Why did you have to be gone so long?"

"I have an office to serve," he sang.

"To supervise violence and rapine?" she asked. "It would be better if you stayed here!"

"To stop a battle between the armies of your Kingdom and mine," he informed her gently. "Peace has been declared, but the news had not reached the front. I was fortunate to get it stopped before things had proceeded too far."

"Maharastra—and Gujarat—were fighting?" she asked, appalled.

"Because of us," he agreed. "We refused to marry the Princess and Prince of Rajasthan, so our Kingdoms went to war with each other."

"But actual combat? I hadn't realized!"

"I stopped it. That was my business today."

"But people died, before—?"

"Some died, yes. It was complicated to—"

"Oh!" she exclaimed. "I never wanted people to die because of us! If I had realized—"

"There was no way to—" he sang.

But she turned away from him, part of her horror extending to him.

Disgusted, he left her. It seemed they were having their first quarrel.

He cleaned up, for though he had had very little contact with mortal things, he had been under some pressure and had sweated under his golden cloak. He changed to informal garb, then went to Rapture's quarters.

She met him in the hall and flung her arms about him and sobbed. He tried to speak, but she stifled that with a kiss.

It seemed that their quarrel was over.

Then they talked, and he learned what was really upsetting her. It seemed that the butler had explained it to her during the day.

This was Purgatory. No mortals resided here. This was not discrimination, but the simple fact that mortals were of a far more complex physical composition, possessing three physical dimensions instead of two. This was not a precise analogy, but the butler had made it simple to understand. Mortals could visit, when sponsored by an Incarnation, but could not remain.

"But you have been here a full night and day!" Mym sang, protesting.

"Yes, and I am starving," she responded.

"But there is plenty to eat!"

"For you. Not for me. Not for a mortal."

"You're *my* mortal!" he sang angrily. "They *will* feed you!"

She shook her head. "They *have* fed me, Mym. But this is Purgatory food. It looks and tastes real, it feels real—but it has nourishment only for ghosts. A mortal requires a thousand times the substance found in this food. What I have eaten here has been illusion, for me. I have been existing on my own bodily resources. This is easy to do, for a short period, when the stomach seems full—but can not be maintained."

He stared at her. "Purgatory food—can't feed you," he repeated.

"Mym, I must return to the mortal realm, if I am to eat."

He was appalled. "No wonder you were upset! It's so nice here, and now—"

"Now I must leave. I can visit only a few hours at a time, before hunger and thirst—oh, I feel that thirst, now!"

Mym shook his head. "Rapture, I never knew about this! I never would have brought you here, if—"

His distress seemed to ameliorate hers. "I have only to find a mortal home. I can be here each day when you return. I can spend the nights with you. It can be very much the same; I can be gone only when you are gone."

"But I have no idea where you can go!" he sang. "It can't be Bombay—"

"The butler says he can arrange something, and I'm sure he can. But—it must be soon, because—"

"Because you are wasting away!" he finished. "Oh, my beloved—"

"It will be all right," she said, though he knew she was deeply distressed. She had wanted so much to be with him always and now she could not.

They went immediately to the butler, who explained that there were those mortals who cooperated in special matters like this and maintained a system of hostels for displaced associates of Purgatory. They were discreet and understanding. "In fact you can stay with Thanatos' consort, Luna Kaftan," he said. "She is in mortal politics, but because of Thanatos, she understands perfectly. You will be fully comfortable with her."

And so it was arranged for Rapture to stay with Luna, who lived in Kilvarough. Thanatos himself came to escort them down. Rapture almost fainted when she saw the skull-face, but then Thanatos drew back his hood to reveal an ordinary human face, reassuring her. It was all right—for now.

— 8 —

SATAN

Other nights, Rapture would come to stay with him in the Castle of War. But this night she was back on Earth, for she had a day's eating to catch up on and needed to acclimatize. Mym had known the instant he met Luna, who seemed oddly familiar, that she would take good care of Rapture; she was a beautiful, brown-haired, occidental woman, whose house was filled with artistry and guarded by griffins. It was no palace, but it was the kind of place the Princess could feel at home in.

So Mym slept alone—and discovered that, though Rapture might be dependent on him, he had become dependent on her, too. He had grown accustomed to sleeping beside a loving woman and felt ill at ease by himself.

In fact, he was unable to sleep. After more than an hour of restless turnings, he sat up and looked for something to read. There was nothing; evidently his predecessor had not been a literary man.

He got up and donned slippers and night robe and walked out into the dusky hall. The castle staff had retired; all was quiet. Did the spirits of Purgatory require sleep? Perhaps so, if they required food. As he was coming to understand it, the lives—the after-lives—of these people were similar to those of mortal folk, but more diffuse and extended. If they did not eat, they would not starve—not within a century or so—for they could not die; they were already dead. But they would become uncomfortable. Likewise, probably, with sleep. So let them sleep; it did help differentiate the days, which surely were dull enough. Purgatory was not supposed to be torture, as he perceived this Western mythology; it was merely a state of indecision, a working-off of the debts of an imperfectly lived life. Westerners had no second chance by way of reincarnation to expiate their faults; they had to get it straight in just one life and then pay the consequence in the long stretch of eternity thereafter. He did not envy them their system.

But, of course, he was part of it, now. He should have been a better Hindu, so as not to stray into this inferior framework. This was really his own next incarnation, the Incarnation of War in an alien framework, and now he was bound by its laws. Punishment enough!

Yet reward enough, too, for it had solved the problem of his voided betrothal to Rapture and the war between their two Kingdoms. Had this office not come to him when it had, he would have faced disaster. So fate had not been cruel to him; it had been kind. Most kind.

Also, he rather fancied the challenge of this new position. He had made mistakes on his first day—but what person didn't, when learning the job? He now had a far better notion how to proceed and expected to do better on his next battle. The powers of his office were phenomenal and could be a great force for good when properly applied.

He came to the garden region that had so enraptured Rapture. Now it was dark; the cycles of Purgatory mirrored those of mortal Earth. The exotic plants seemed larger, the shadowed statues more alive, somehow. He walked on through it; it was indeed a lovely region, the kind that a woman could spend much time appreciating. It seemed almost natural—as if crafted by the forces of nature, rather than those of man.

The clouds parted to allow a shaft of moonlight down, and the leaves and statues turned silvery. A gentle breeze wafted through, stirring the trees. The smell of the wild came through more clearly, luring him on. The path twisted about, taking him past increasingly intriguing exhibits.

He paused to examine one statue more carefully. It was a representation of two figures, male and female, both naked, locked in close embrace. In fact they were engaged in the act of physical love. Such representations were common enough in India, but this one was unusually specific. The figures almost seemed to move.

In fact, they *were* moving. Mym thought he was being deceived by the play of moonlight, but now he heard the sounds of their exertions. The figures were alive!

Impossible. Statues did not come to life!

Yet there was definite sound and movement, as the act progressed. Mym inspected the representation closely, and finally touched the shoulder of the man. It was cold stone. So this was some kind of mechanical device, simulating human mating. Interesting.

He moved on. The breeze picked up, ruffling his hair. The moonlight brightened. The trees were larger and prettier, and the smell of their naturalness intensified. Now there was sod underfoot, slightly springy.

He turned to look back, but could not see the castle; he seemed to be in a forest. That didn't bother him; he was pleased with the extent and verisimilitude of this garden. No wonder Rapture had been delighted!

He came to another statue—and this one was larger, more animated, and more intimate than the first. These could have been real people, and their technique was quite interesting.

The man turned his head and saw Mym. "Ah, the master of the castle arrives," he said.

Startled, Mym stepped back. It talked!

The woman disengaged and sat on the pedestal, dangling her long, bare legs over its edge. She was extremely full-breasted and full-hipped, but slender in other respects. "Come, join me," she invited Mym, opening her arms.

A concubine? "Who are you?" Mym demanded. Then he paused, surprised, for he had spoken without stuttering.

"I am Satan, the Incarnation of Evil," the man said. "This is one of My innumerable consorts, each of whom is more luscious and tractable than the last.''

''Satan?'' Mym repeated, again amazed at his lack of stutter. ''Here in my castle?''

''Not precisely your castle, Mars,'' Satan said. ''You have wandered from your garden into a section of My realm, where reality is more intriguing. But have no concern; you are welcome here. I have wanted to interview you.''

''Aren't you the occidental figure of evil?'' Mym asked. ''I have been warned to be wary of you.''

''Indeed I am, and indeed you have,'' Satan agreed expansively. ''My name is Nefarious—and rightly so.''

This was not precisely the approach Mym had anticipated. He had been led to expect a creature with hooves, tail, and horns, who breathed fire. This man was none of these. He seemed entirely human, even to the act he had been performing with the woman. ''Why have you chosen to contact me?'' he asked, once again marveling at his lack of a stutter.

''Why, isn't it the neighborly thing to do?'' Satan asked. ''It is no easy thing to step abruptly into the office of an Incarnation, and it behooves others of us to facilitate your adaptation in whatever ways we can.''

Mym shrugged. ''I appreciate that effort. But other accounts indicate that you bear mostly malice to others. As the Incarnation of Evil, this makes sense. So you should be trying to make this more difficult for me.''

Satan grinned in disarming fashion, and the woman smiled. ''This shows the importance of personal contact. As you can see, I am not as intractable as others may depict Me. Come, let us converse.'' He jumped off the pedestal, not at all concerned about his nakedness, and the woman followed. She was robustly constructed, and her breasts bounced magnificently as she landed. What a concubine she would make!

As they walked, the welkin brightened, not from any dawn but from a surrounding luminescence. The trees glowed, and the ground, and even the three people, as if animated from within. This provided a preternatural clarity of vision, for there were no obstructive shadows. The garden was almost ecstatically beautiful, a true paradise.

The woman took his arm. Mym glanced at her, surprised. The enhancement of vision applied to her, too, and made of her physical form a thing of perfect splendor. She smiled at him.

"You like Lilith?" Satan inquired. "She was the model for all the statuary, and she will gladly pose for you, in any manner you desire. She has more experience than any mortal woman."

So she was of the spirit world; he should have realized. "Thank you; I already have a woman."

"But not a suitable concubine, here in Purgatory," Satan said. "A man of your stature needs more than one woman."

"True," Mym said. "But a prince does not take a used woman."

"Readily fixed," Satan said. He snapped his fingers, and Lilith vanished. Satan snapped again, and a new woman appeared. This one was just as lusciously constructed, but possessed a greater innocence of demeanor. "Lila, here, has never been touched by man."

Lila smiled at Mym. She was every bit as pretty as the concubines the Rajah had provided.

Still Mym had a doubt. "But I don't know how Rapture would feel about a spirit concubine."

"Well, you can ask her," Satan said. "Lila will be available whenever you wish." He waved one hand negligently, and Lila vanished. "How did you like your first day's work?"

"It sufficed," Mym said guardedly.

"I understand that you had the privilege of supervising a battle in your own bailiwick."

"I was trying to end it!" Mym exclaimed.

"*End* it? Whatever for?"

"Because it was pointless. There was no need for men to die on that field; peace had been declared."

Satan smiled. "Now I can see how that might be construed as an embarrassment. Still, a good battle is a good battle, whatever the circumstances. Why didn't you simply enjoy it?"

"Enjoy it!" Mym cried. "Outrageous!"

"How so, Prince? War is an honorable pursuit, and there is much challenge and glory to be had in battle."

"That is the kind of remark I should expect from Siva," Mym

muttered. "War is the root of endless evil. Slaughter, Famine, and Pestilence ride right with me when I go out."

"Siva—your God of Destruction," Satan said. "I like that. But consider where the world would be if there were no war. We know that mortals have faults; they are dissatisfied with their lots, whatever their lots may be, so they seek to better those lots at the expense of their neighbors. Men take advantage of each other, they steal from each other, they enslave each other and will not give over; whole societies have been enslaved by other societies, or by their own repressive leadership, and suffering is endemic. I know these things, for I receive the souls that are degraded and finally damned by such circumstances. Human beings are not fair to each other; each wants more than his fair share and will take it if he has the power. What mechanism exists to restore fairness to humanity? Reason? Man is not a rational animal, no matter what he chooses to call himself. He remains governed by his selfish emotions. He uses reason only as a means to an end—the end of self-aggrandizement. When reason suggests he is wrong, he dispenses with it and keeps his ill-gotten gains. No, Prince— in the end, there is only one answer, and that is to restore fairness by force. That is what we call war."

"But war does not restore fairness!" Mym protested, taken aback by this rationale. "It is noted in the spread of unfairness!"

"Only if abused," Satan said smoothly. "That is why there is an Incarnation of War—to see that it is correctly used."

Mym thought of his day's work. "I did not handle it well today."

"You will improve with experience, of course. We all do. No blame attaches to you for that."

"I would prefer to abolish all war, so that no battles needed managing."

"Then you would be neglecting your office. Some war is necessary. It is like burning off a fallow field, to clear it of a tangle of brush and to fertilize it with ashes, so as to facilitate new growth. The process of burning may seem violent, but it is in fact quite beneficial. Likewise one must not be deterred by the seeming violence of war; it is but a means to a necessary end."

"Some means are not justified, and war—"

"Or like the surgeon's knife, that cuts away cancerous growth.

It is true that some healthy flesh must be touched, but this is a small sacrifice in view of the advantage to be obtained."

"But war is not surgery," Mym protested. "It is butchery! I saw the carnage, today, when—"

"Anything can be harmful, if it is allowed to proceed uncontrolled. Fire is an excellent example; it can be man's greatest enemy or his greatest friend. One simply needs to learn how to manage it. Likewise the process of cutting; what is butchery in the bad form remains excision in the good form. It is not the agent that is to be condemned, but the abuse, as I said before."

There was an insidious logic here that Mym distrusted. "I would prefer to abolish war entirely."

"You can not," Satan said. "Nor would you want to, if you truly understood it."

"But you will explain my abilities and motives to me," Mym said sourly.

"Naturally. As I said, it behooves one Incarnation to assist another. You can not abolish war entirely, because it is not a cause; it is a symptom, the tangible manifestation of a more fundamental malady. Only by dealing with that underlying problem can you hope to eliminate war. As it is, all you can do is fan it into greater activity or damp it down, shaping it somewhat to your design."

Mym remembered the extreme difficulty he had had in turning off the battle between Gujarat and Maharastra; certainly there had seemed to be an imperative to combat that defied common sense. "And what is this underlying problem that I would not want to abolish if I could?"

"It is the nature of man," Satan said. "Man is not a perfect creature; were he so, there would be no need of Heaven or Hell, of God or Me. Man is a composite of good and evil, and the whole of his existence as a mortal being is designed to determine the extent of those elements within him, so that he can be classified and sent to his appropriate locale in the Afterlife. Naturally his mortal span is rife with tensions and disturbance; it is good and evil that are tugging him this way and that. When men band together in the larger societies they call nations or kingdoms, those larger units assume the attributes of the individuals of which they are composed. There is a fabric of social tension, a pattern of complex and subtle pressures. Inevitably these mount until they manifest in overt war, the most drastic form of competition. You could not stifle that without stifling the society's most effective mode of expression. If all such interaction could be truly suppressed, man would never be properly defined, and there would be no point in mortality. So it is not your position, as the Incarnation of War, to prevent war; instead you want to shape and guide this visible aspect of social stress and use it to reduce social inequities and facilitate the emergence of more effective leadership. You want to fashion war into the truly useful tool for redress of inequity that it can and should be."

Mym did not trust Satan, but this was a most compelling rationale. "I'll think about it," he said grudgingly.

"Of course you will, Mars; that is your office. I am satisfied to have helped clarify it for you."

"To be sure." The ease with which he spoke reminded Mym of another question: "How is it that I am not stuttering, now?"

"You are visiting an aspect of My domain," Satan explained. "This place is not governed by natural laws, but by My laws. I see no need for a person of your status to be afflicted with an impediment of speech; therefore there is none."

"But I have stuttered all through life, and in Purgatory too!" Mym protested.

"That is the difference between life and Purgatory and My realm," Satan said. "There is much I can offer you, and not merely suitable concubines."

"Offer me—in exchange for what?"

"Merely amicable relations," Satan said blithely. "Bring Rapture here tomorrow, and I will show her also what is available. She will be delighted."

"She needs no demons for amorous companionship!"

Satan laughed. "Of course not, Mars! What she craves is nourishing food—without having to travel all the way to Earth for it every day, depriving you of her company."

"You have mortally nourishing food?" Mym asked, abruptly interested. "Here?"

For answer, Satan waved a hand. A table appeared, heavily laden with a sumptuous repast.

"But the food of Purgatory looks and tastes real," Mym said. "How can we tell whether your food is solid?"

"By eating it," Satan said. "The truth will become apparent soon enough."

Mym nodded. Satan seemed to have little reason to deceive him on this score. His offerings were attractive. Pleasant surroundings, the abolition of the stutter, and a way for Rapture to remain with him. If this were truly for the sake of neighborliness, Mym was amenable.

He turned about and made his way back toward the castle. The shrubbery became more normal, and the statuary became stone; it was like moving from the supernatural to the natural.

As he entered the castle, he tried an experiment. "H-h-h-hello," he said to himself. Yes, the stutter was back.

In the morning he touched the Sword and willed himself to travel to Luna's mortal residence, where Rapture was staying. One moment he was standing in the castle; the next he was at the entrance to the house. It was a trifle unsettling to travel so far so readily, but he liked it well enough. He knocked on the door.

Rapture herself opened it, expecting him. She threw herself into his arms. "Oh, it is wonderful here!" she cried. "I missed you so much!"

Luna stood beyond. Mym caught her eye, over Rapture's shoulder, and she nodded knowingly. "It is the way of woman," she said. "To suffer pleasure and pain together."

"I will bring her back soon," Mym sang. Then he touched the Sword, and he and Rapture stood in the castle.

Rapture disengaged and started for the bedroom, but he restrained her. "Contrary to appearances," he sang, "there is sometimes more on a man's mind than that. I want to show you something."

Perplexed, she accompanied him to the garden. They walked down the path and into the extension of Satan's realm.

"But this wasn't here yesterday!" Rapture exclaimed. "There was a wall, the far end of—"

"True," he said. "But this is special."

"It must be! These plants are—" She paused. "Did you say something?"

"Not a thing," he said.

"You did!" she exclaimed. "You didn't stutter!"

"I told you this was special."

"But a moment ago—why did you sing, if you have conquered the stutter?"

"I haven't conquered the stutter. This is a gift of this garden. Here I can speak normally, nowhere else."

"Here? What *is* this place?"

Satan appeared, with Lila at his side. This time both were clothed. "It is an extension of My domain," he said grandly. "I thought you would like it."

Rapture turned to Mym. "Who is he?"

"Rapture, meet Satan," Mym said. "The occidental equivalent of Siva."

"Siva!" she cried, retreating.

"And Satan, meet Rapture of Malachite, my betrothed," Mym concluded.

Satan bowed. "My pleasure, lovely mortal woman."

"But Siva—God of Destruction and of—"

"Of sex," Satan finished. "Which brings us to Lila, here, a demoness of My realm. It occurred to Me that your betrothed is short of concubines, here in Purgatory, and if you approve, Lila will be happy to serve."

Rapture did a rapid reassessment. Western nations had different and peculiar standards, but in India the Rajahs and noblemen were expected to have plenty of concubines, who were subservient to the wife. It would be a sorry Rajah who lacked concubines, and his wife would suffer loss of status, too. People would think he was impotent. On the other hand, this was not India, and it was a trifle early for Mym to be needing a regular concubine; it would be better for Rapture to get gravid with a son first. Thereafter, it was a relief for her husband to have plenty of concubines; it provided the wife more time to herself. But Rapture was a dependent person, who didn't want to be left to herself too much.

"Let's let that wait a few months," Rapture decided.

"By all means," Satan said. He gestured negligently, and Lila vanished; only a faint puff of smoke remained where she had been.

Mym made no comment, but he was privately relieved. Concubines still made him remember his father's lesson in obedience: they tended to find their heads on spikes when declined. Since Rapture had turned this one down—or at least postponed her— he didn't have to worry about that this time. Also, he was far from ready to trade Rapture off for other women in his bed; he loved her and wanted to make the most of her while the emotion remained high. Evidently she felt the same, and that pleased him deeply.

Now the table laden with food reappeared. "This is a feast for you, honored Lady," Satan said grandly.

"But I can't live on—" she protested.

"Satan says that you can be sustained on this food," Mym said. "Just as I can talk here without stuttering."

Slowly, she smiled. "Then I can remain here with you, always!" she exclaimed.

They fell to, and the food was excellent. But privately Mym had a reservation. Satan was doing him favors here, and he did not trust this occidental version of savage Siva not to make some inconvenient claim on him at some later date. But as long as Rapture was happy, he would not interfere.

Later, alone again, he pondered further. He knew that Satan was tempting him, offering gifts it was difficult indeed to decline. He distrusted this; but, when the alternative was to be without Rapture or to have her unhappy, what choice did he have? So he knew he would not interfere with this offering, but he knew he had to some minor degree compromised himself. How could he ensure that no offering of Satan's subverted his ability to perform his office?

He wandered the bare halls of the Castle of War, nominally exploring its reaches, but actually exploring his own disquiet. Mym was a prince; he had received expert training in the administrative as well as the physical aspects of government. He knew he was treading on treacherous ground, and he wanted to find some way to improve his position without sacrificing anything he valued. It was not necessary for him to turn down Satan's offerings; it was only necessary for him to shield himself from subversion by them. If he could do that, Satan would not have the leverage he thought he had. But since Satan could withdraw the benefits of the garden at any time, any overt denial would be costly.

Perhaps he should simply inform Satan that he refused to be influenced by any such gifts, so that Satan was wasting his effort. That would be the honest course, and it was important to be honest, because Satan was the Father of Lies. Any lie would be playing into Satan's hands. But if he told the truth, and Satan still thought the gifts would subvert him—

Mym came to a chamber he had not seen before. He had been following an unfamiliar hall, and it had terminated in a flight of stairs that evidently mounted a turret, and here was a closed wooden door. Curious, Mym pushed at it with his hand, but it would not budge. He was sure the chamber beyond was not intended to be barred to the master of the castle; it had to be sealed against intrusion by the servants or visitors. Why?

He explored the door, tapping it here and there. It was solid. There was a large keyhole—but he had no key.

He touched the Red Sword. He could hack through the door— but he didn't want to do that, for that would be admitting some kind of defeat. Or he could render himself into ghost status, and walk through it—but again, that implied defeat. He should be able to obtain access legitimately, without special measures.

He touched the Sword again, considering. Then, abruptly, he snapped his fingers. He drew the Sword and willed it to change its form to that of a key.

The Sword shimmered and changed. Now a large key was in Mym's hand. He inserted this into the keyhole, and turned it. If he had guessed correctly, this should be the right key. The tumblers clicked, and the lock gave way. Victory!

He opened the door and entered the chamber. It contained only a table, and on the table was a book. Mym crossed over and picked up the book.

The volume had symbols on the cover and symbols inside. Mym recognized these as Chinese or Japanese, but could not read them. Then, as he watched, the symbols shimmered, as the Sword had, and became words, identifying the book. Its title was *Go Rin No Sho*. But he still couldn't read it.

Then the words shimmered and became English: *Five Rings— A Book*. The volume had finally zeroed in on a language he could use.

Mym had seen this book before; he had read it years ago. It was a very well known reference for Kendo, or the Way of the Sword, and was studied by serious martial artists everywhere. It seemed that the prior Mars had valued it too; evidently the man had come here often to review it, for the volume was well-thumbed.

He opened it randomly, and read a passage. *In strategy make the gaze broad. Learn to see to the sides without shifting the eyeballs. Use this gaze always, whether in battle or in ordinary life.*

Interesting. Mym had forgotten this—or perhaps he had understood it on another level before. Of course it was literal—but it was also figurative. A warrior did not want to give away the focus of his attention by shifting his eyes about; he needed to take in everything while looking at nothing, to spy the enemy to the side, without seeming to, so that the enemy would not have the advantage of surprise he thought he had. That much was literal. But also in the mind—a person should grasp concepts without seeming to and fathom deceptions while focusing on ordinary matters—just as he was tyring to do with Satan.

He flipped randomly again, and read another passage. *Become the enemy. Merge with the enemy's situation. In this manner you will gain understanding to prevail over him.*

Again, that seemed both literal and figurative. If a warrior considered his enemy's situation, really getting into it, he could more readily fathom that enemy's likely reactions. That could be a valuable tool for victory. But, in the more subtle interpersonal relations, it was just as useful. Satan was not threatening him physically; Satan was trying to modify his attitude. If he could just comprehend Satan's motive, he could judge it and work out an effective counter.

Mym closed the book. He was impressed. If two random glances offered this much insight, what would the entire volume provide? The random passages had not given him answers, but had suggested alternate ways of considering the problem. He felt that his awareness had been broadened already.

Mym sat at the table and commenced reading the volume from the beginning. Though he had read it before, this time it was as if he had an entirely new text, because he was absorbing it on a different level.

— 9 —

LACHESIS

A few days later another battle was shaping up, and the grim horsemen gathered again at the front of the castle. Rapture shuddered as she saw them in their impressive white, red, black, and brown cloaks, their matching horses stamping their hooves and snorting with eagerness.

"*Must* you associate with those ruffians?" she asked. "I realize that you have a job to do, exactly as you would have had as a Rajah, but these casteless creatures—!"

"I fear I must," he sang. "I did not choose them, but I did choose to assume the office of War, and they are the handmaidens of war."

She laughed, somewhat hysterically. "Handmaidens!"

"But I will try my best to minimize the conflict I supervise today," he continued. "War may be inevitable, but it doesn't have to be totally destructive, if properly managed. Then those subsidiary Incarnations will not have much benefit from it."

She had to be mollified. "Return as soon as you can, my beloved. I don't like being here without you."

"Well, you can return to Luna's house in the mortal realm," he reminded her. "Or you can go to the garden and have something to eat."

"You would have to take me to Luna's house, and, anyway, she's busy. She's nice and always polite, but she is engaged in local politics, and I don't like to take up her time. But the garden . . ." She trailed off.

"I'm sure nothing there can hurt you," he sang. "I wouldn't trust Satan unduly, but he is currying my favor and he knows that what pleases you is likely to please me. You could go and talk to Lila, to see whether she is worthwhile."

Rapture brightened. "Yes, I must find out how well she sews and weaves, and whether she dances."

Mym smiled inwardly. What a neat solution to her problem! Concubines did a lot of sewing and weaving in their off hours, supervised by the wife. Sometimes the Kingdoms of modern India had contests between the harems of their ranking nobles to see which produced the finest tapestries, and great honor accrued to the wives who organized the winning shows. It was said that the wives were more interested in the harems than the husbands were, though there was a snide side to that remark.

But this exchange reminded him of Satan's influence on his present existence. Satan was helping to make Rapture happy and Satan could help to make her unhappy. That remained awkward.

He had read *Five Rings*, and it had provided him with much upon which to cogitate. But he had not yet digested it sufficiently to apply it to Satan.

The heart of the book, as he now understood it, was the five great rings, which equated on one level to the five elements: Ground, Water, Fire, Wind, and Void. None of these were simple concepts, and complete understanding would require long experience and contemplation. But it was as if it were a chart for his future understanding. Once he comprehended the full nature of each of the rings, he should possess sufficient understanding of the universe to know his true course. He intended to work on it.

He donned his golden cloak, mounted his palomino, and rode out with the others. This time they descended on the border between two so-called Middle-Eastern nations, whose long-dragged-out war had broken out again after the breakdown of a truce. Persia was preparing a massive assault on the entrenchments of Babylonia, and the scale was far larger than that of

Gujarat and Maharastra had been. There was no single spot that Mym could settle on for effective supervision; there were thousands of troops deployed along a front hundreds of kilometers long.

Last time, he had sought to enter the mind of a general and had made little progress. This time he wanted to act with better effect. He had to gain a proper understanding of what was going on here. Then he could devise some strategy to diminish the wastefulness of it. Perhaps it would be better to phase in to the situation of one of the common troops.

"When is Persia's attack scheduled to be launched?" Mym inquired of Conquest, whose business it was to know such details.

"Not for several hours yet," the white-caped warrior replied. "That will give us opportunity to plan for the greatest harvest."

"Then I shall make my own investigation during that period," Mym sang. "See that nothing starts prematurely."

Conquest nodded. War's word was law to those others, for he was the primary Incarnation here.

He rode to the lines of Babylonia first. He saw in a moment that the defenses were formidable. Behind towering masses of barbed wire there were extensive mine fields, and beyond these were concrete abutments and hardened emplacements for machine guns. Any human attack on these fortifications would commence at the cost of many, many lives. If it broke through, only a small fraction of the attacking troops would survive.

Obviously the Persian military command was aware of this. What kind of an attack did it contemplate? There had to be something special.

Mym rode to the other side. None of the mortals saw him or his horse, of course. He rode through the barbed wire without being touched and into the Persian formation. There were only a few armed men at the front; the majority were in special camps, getting ready for the assault.

Who would be best to identify with for the ground-level survey? Mym pondered momentarily and decided on a random sampling. He would enter the camp, count off heads, and take the tenth soldier he found.

He found a large, crude temporary barracks building. He rode through the wall. There were the troops, massed for a preparatory

briefing. Mym counted heads, identified the tenth, and dismounted. "Be near when I need you," he directed the horse.
Then he strode to the soldier he had identified, stood before him,
and backed into the man. In a moment he overlapped him and
felt the confusion of double identity.

Slowly his eyes caught the focus, and his ears became those
of his host. The sensations of the body became his own. He was
still himself, but also, gradually, the soldier. He concentrated
solely on tuning in, on aligning the sensations of the mortal body
with his own, so that his identification clarified. This took some
time; while it occurred, the body was going about its own business, but this was a necessary delay. For one thing, the body used
an alien language; the only way that Mym could understand it
was to orient on the meaning as registered by the brain, rather
than the actual sounds of it. He made steady progress in this, but
the process could not be rushed.

The first significant thing he realized was that this body was
young. This was no man; this was a boy of about eleven! Yet he
was definitely a soldier; he had the military garb and a rifle and
he had been drilled in its use. He was now being exhorted to go
into battle for the honor of his country. It was, the instructor was
assuring him and the other boys of this command, a great honor
to fight for one's country and a greater honor to die for it in this
Holy War. He must go out and destroy the infidel enemy!

A child, Mym thought. They were all children, some younger
than this one. All garbed in ill-fitting military uniforms, bearing
archaic rifles with limited ammunition, and steeped with the
ferver of fanaticism.

He thought of the formidable Babylonian emplacements he had
viewed. These children would be crucified against those defenses!
He probed in the mind for some comprehension of what lay ahead,
but none of that information had been provided. This young boy
was very like an occidental cow in the corral, moving with the
herd toward the slaughterhouse. Cows were never treated in that
barbaric fashion in India, of course.

It seemed that Persia, having largely exhausted its experienced
adult personnel, was now throwing the lives of its children into
the breach. They would die like flies—but perhaps they would

force an opening in the enemy line that the experienced troops could then exploit.

It made sense on one level. It was pointless to throw away seasoned troops on an impossible assault and leave the children to carry the major part of the action. Better to confine the heavy losses to those who were least trained, then use the effective troops where and when they could count.

But Mym was sickened by this tactic. What barbarism threw away the hope of its future, its children, in such manner?

But he drew on his own memory to fill in more of the picture. This war had started when Babylonia, perceiving an opportunity to take advantage of its weakened neighbor, had invaded, seeking to add territory and acquire important seaports. Babylonia had acted with complete indifference to international law, grabbing at anything it supposed wasn't nailed down. Persia had fought doggedly back with inadequate personnel and resources and turned the tide, driving the invader back out of its territory. Naturally the losses had been substantial. Had Persia confined itself to conventional recruitment, it would not have had the personnel to do the job. So it had reached into its reserves—the reserves of its future—in order to guarantee that there would *be* a future for its national identity. Outsiders like Mym might condemn such desperation—but what would he have done, as the leader of Gujarat, if his Kingdom had found itself in a similar situation? Some evils were simply not to be tolerated, and among these was capitulation to brutal conquest.

He explored the attitude of the boy and found some justification there. The internecine war, dragging on as it had, had decimated the population of the region. The boy's family had been ruined by the passage of the troops, both directions; the crop had been destroyed, the father drafted and killed, the brothers driven away, the mother forced to work at starvation wages in a failing effort to sustain her remaining family, one sister raped and killed at age twelve, and the other simply stabbed by the bayonet of an enemy soldier when she screamed in fear and protest. This boy, eleven, had joined his nation's military service in order to get money for his mother, who was working herself to death; this removed from her the burden of sustaining him and made it possible for her to buy some additional food and pay rent in a temporary camp for refugees. This boy had taken the part of a man during desperate times—as had the other boys of this unit. If he died in battle, a death benefit would accrue to his mother; if he survived, he could continue contributing to her support. He was proud to do this— and Mym was forced to echo this pride. Given the situation of this region, the boy had done what he had to do, with honor and courage that would have befitted a man of any age.

No, Mym could not condemn that. Neither could he condemn the nation of Persia for using boys of this age; there was almost nothing else they could be used for, in this place and this time, and using them made it possible for them to serve both themselves and their nation. If this boy were discharged at this moment from this service, it would not be a victory for what was right and good; it would be disaster.

Mym found himself both glad and sad that he had chosen to share this young soldier's experience. How true it was—a man had to walk a distance in the shoes of another to understand the other's situation.

Now he understood enough of the local situation; he could withdraw from this host and return to his own form to supervise the coming battle. But now he knew this boy—and he found he could not simply desert him at this stage. He knew that the boy was headed straight for death—and not an honorable, hard-fought death. For a slaughter.

He had to do something. But what? This war had been grinding on, with brief intermissions, such as the one that helped eliminate Mym's predecessor, for years. Its momentum was inexorable, and the damage it had already done was staggering. Even if he managed to abolish it this moment, the carnage it had wrought would remain.

Mym struggled with this, as the preparation for the onslaught proceeded. Could he remove this boy from the locale, at least saving his life? But that would cause him to be branded a deserter—and how would the lad fare then? Looking into the boy's mind, Mym saw that this was no solution; the boy had to be allowed to complete his mission in whatever manner he could.

Could he manage to get this battle called off? Not by any action of this boy; he had chosen the wrong host for that. Now it was too late to phase in to another; the boy's unit was being marched directly to the front. The attack would commence within the hour.

There was nothing Mym could do—yet still he did not leave the boy. He had to find some way!

The unit formed at the top of a small hill. Other units formed to either side. There were thousands of youths in this action! Most of them would be dead an hour from now—and what would they have accomplished?

The order to attack was given. Bravely, the boy charged over the brim of the hill and down toward the enemy line. His associates ran beside him, their faces grim, but also charged with the unholy joy of the mission: they were engaging in the Holy War! They were half-drunk with the glory of this combat as harangued into them by the instructors. Theirs, as the words of another culture had phrased it, not to reason why, theirs but to do and die.

For moments there was nothing from the enemy. Then the big guns fired. Shells detonated in the midst of the charging line. The Babylonians had this section zeroed in, awaiting this very charge. One went off not far from Mym, and he felt the blast of it. He turned his head to look and saw something flying at him. It landed before him—a human arm, severed at the shoulder.

Now, suddenly, the truth hit home to the boy. *This was a death-field!* Whether he lived or died had no relation to his personal merit. It was random. If a shell landed on him, he was gone; if it didn't, he was free to keep running. Nobody cared. There was nothing he could do to save himself; it all depended on the shells.

The boy froze. He *was* a boy; he had not been hardened to the reality of his own complete impotence. He had thought that somehow things would turn out all right, if he just did the best he could and obeyed orders. Now he knew that was not true. The realization paralyzed him.

The sounds of the slaughter became loud in the boy's ears. Not all of the victims of the shells were dead, but many were dying. Scattered anguished exclamations projected from the over-all noise. "My foot—it's hanging by a flap of skin!" "I can't *see*! My eyes—my eyes are all blood!" "Where did those intestines come from? Allah preserve me—they're *mine*!" "My friend— his shoulder is gone—and half his head." The boys, stunned, simply did not know what to make of the horrendous carnage;

they were reacting like sightseers, in these first moments of horror. But very soon they would get down to the serious business of bleeding to death. The charge had been broken, but still the shells came.

Mym, with his training in the military arts and his experience as a commander, automatically analyzed the pattern of the detonating shells. There were five big guns oriented on this region, and they were firing sequentially so that it was possible to judge the approximate locations of the forthcoming blasts. One was due for this spot in a few seconds.

Mym extended his will and took over the boy's paralyzed muscles. He had not realized he could do this; perhaps he could not, had the boy been operative, but under this immediate pressure, he did. He plunged directly forward, getting as far away from the critical location as he could.

The shell landed behind him. The blast of it half lifted him, throwing him forward.

In that moment he spied an Incarnation. He knew it was one, because he saw a large spider slide in from some celestially anchored thread and convert to a middle-aged woman whose eyes were fixed on him.

He willed the Sword to still the scene. The action of the battle froze, with boys locked in place in mid-stride, and pieces of boys paused in mid-air.

"Mars, whatever are you doing?" the woman demanded.

"Who are you?" he demanded in return, using his necessary singsong.

"I am Lachesis."

"Ah, Lakshmi, Goddess of Fortune," he agreed.

"What?"

He smiled. "There seem to be parallels between your mythology and ours. I recognize your nature."

"But I am only one aspect of three," she said, nonplused. She wavered and was replaced by a beautiful young oriental woman, then by an old negroid woman. Then she was back to her original form.

"Yes, Lakshmi has an aspect for each of Vishnu's incarnations, to be his consort in each. When she manifests with only two of her four arms, she is the most beautiful of women."

The lovely oriental reappeared, intrigued. "Oh?"

Then the original Lachesis reasserted herself. "Stop this nonsense! I'm not part of your pantheon! I am the Incarnation of Fate, whose threads govern the lives of mortals."

"Those lives are ending," Mym pointed out. "No one can govern them now."

"*All* human events are arranged by Fate," Lachesis said firmly. "Like the tide, I will have my way."

The tide. Something connected in Mym's mind. "W-Water!" he exclaimed.

"What?"

"In the organization of the book, *Five Rings,* one of the five major strategies is based on water. But we five Incarnations may relate to this framework. War is Fire; Fate is Water."

"Perhaps," she said, nonplused. "I will debate theology with you some other time. Right now I must have an answer. Just what do you think you're doing here?"

Mym was still a bit bemused by this abrupt encounter with the occidental Fate with the spider web. "I am trying to manage this battle," he sang.

"By using *children?*"

"One must work with the resources one has," he sang uncomfortably. "I don't like this, but it seems to be necessary."

"I have very little concern for what you may consider to be necessary," Lachesis said severely. He could see that, though she was past her physical prime, she had the underlying structure of a supremely beautiful woman. It would have been interesting to have seen her in her youth. "You are using children in war and, while I recognize that you have certain prerogatives, this use is not something I am prepared to tolerate."

Mym did not like the use of children in war himself, but this put him on the defensive. "Exactly what business is this of yours, Fate?" he demanded.

"It is my business to handle the Threads of Life, Mars," she repeated with some asperity. "In my several Aspects, I spin them, I measure them, and I cut them to proper length. When you put them into a suicidal war and kill them off wholesale, you are disrupting the pattern I am setting up. I can not sit idly in my Abode while you shear off those early threads!"

There was something about Lachesis that seemed familiar, though he could not identify it. He was sure he had not encountered her before. He had been bothered the same way about Luna. "But war is my business, and these are soldiers."

"*Lives* are my business, and these are *children!*"

"Why didn't you route these young threads elsewhere, then?" he demanded, still bothered by the feeling that he should know her from somewhere. "This situation was in the making long before I assumed this office. I don't like it, but I must make the best of it. I see no better way than to complete this battle and try to send the survivors home with honor."

"With honor!" she exclaimed, outraged. "What honor is there in pointless death?"

"This boy I am studying now is earning his own support and that of his mother in the only way available to him," Mym sang. "He is serving his nation. There is no other way for him. He must do what he has to do, or worse evil will befall him and his companions. I regret this situation deeply, but if this battle could be made to disappear, it would not bring back this boy's father or his brothers, or provide food or shelter for him. I am trying to discover how to minimize the ill effect of this battle and this war, but the situation is complex, and simplistic protests by the uniformed will not accomplish anything useful."

"Simplistic protests!" she exclaimed furiously. Now, in her wrath, she seemed more than ever familiar. Her fair hair, the bones of her face . . . "Uninformed?! You can't talk to me like that! I am Fate!"

"I don't care if you're Devi herself! This is *my* business."

"I don't have to put up with this," she said. She shimmered, became the large spider, and disappeared.

Mym was about to free the stasis and permit the battle to resume, when Lachesis reappeared. This time she had a woman with her.

Mym stared. It was Rapture!

Rapture stared about her, appalled. "The blood!" she cried. "Where am I?"

"You are on the site of Mars' business," Lachesis said. "I thought you'd like to join him at work."

"She doesn't belong here!" Mym cried.

"Oh?" Fate inquired. "She is a mortal, and the thread of her life is subject to my manipulation. I thought it appropriate to allow her to participate in your activity. When this battle of children resumes, she will be among them."

Mym was stricken. Rapture would be killed in short order, and, even if he managed to rescue her from the carnage, her mind would be profoundly affected. "Take her back!" he cried.

"Are you ready to deal, Mars?" Lachesis demanded sternly.

This was coercion, but he was vulnerable to it. "Yes," he sang grimly.

Fate shimmered, changed, and vanished with Rapture. In a moment she reappeared, alone. "I arranged for a similar scene to appear on the television program she was watching," she said. "Later, she will believe that it was only a bad daydream sponsored by that program." Her gaze oriented on him. "Now I expect you to abate this war forthwith, so as to give me opportunity to route the children out of it."

"I would prefer to have the children out of it!" he exclaimed. "But I haven't found any way!"

"Then we shall *find* a way," she said. "Right now."

"These children are here because Persia needs them for its war effort," he said.

"I really don't see the point in war, anyway."

"It is a product of the natural tensions and inequities of society," he explained. "Without war, there would be no redress for certain wrongs. War is only harmful when it is poorly managed."

"Oh, pooh!" she snorted. "That sounds like something Satan would say."

That set Mym back. Satan *had* said it. "Have you any strategy in mind to alleviate this battle or this war?"

"Surely it is the result of some misunderstanding," she said. "If we can ascertain what that misunderstanding is, and clarify it, the need for combat should be eliminated. What started it?"

"Babylonia's misunderstanding about Persia's ability and will to defend its territory," Mym sang grimly.

She frowned. "Babylonia is a bit out of my regular territory; but from all I understand, it is no shining example of decency. But then, neither is Persia. It was an awful mess, extricating the captive threads of over a hundred western hostages from that country. A pox on both their houses.''

"Why are you so eager to save their children, then?''

"I could say that it is because some of those children are mine, holding western beliefs in their secret hearts. That, certainly, is what first alerted me to this problem and brought me here. But once I saw the full horror of it, I knew I had to act to protect *all* those children; I don't care what their beliefs are. They don't deserve to die in a stupid war fashioned by fanatic adults. I don't care how complicated it is, those children have to be saved.''

Mym discovered that he was coming to like this woman's attitude. He had never had much to do with children, but certainly they represented any nation's hope for the future. "I agree that the children are not responsible for this war,'' he sang. "I would prefer to see those who cause wars have to serve on the front lines.''

Lachesis laughed. And suddenly he placed that nagging recognition: he had known someone who laughed like that! "*That* would end this war in a hurry, wouldn't it!''

"Are you from Ireland?'' Mym asked.

She glanced at him, surprised. "This Aspect is. Of course, now I serve a wider clientele. Why do you ask?''

"I knew a woman from Ireland, a beautiful and good woman, and your hair, your face—I think in youth you must have looked very much like her.''

"I have come to distrust coincidence, since assuming this office,'' she said. "Did Satan have a hand in your ascension?''

"He helped eliminate the former Mars, if that's what you mean. But he didn't have any hand in my actual selection.''

"Are you sure? Why were you ready for this office, at the appropriate time?''

"I had been denied my fiancée, owing to an abrupt change of political circumstance, and—'' He broke off. "Does Satan dabble in politics?''

"Does a fish breathe water?'' She fixed her gaze intently on him. "That woman you knew—did she sing?''

Mym spread his hands. "I never heard more beautiful music. She had a little harp—''

"Orb!''

"Orb," he agreed. "You know her?"

"I am her mother."

Mym was stunned. Now the hair, features, accent, and laugh all came clear—like mother, like daughter. But what an amazing coincidence, that he should encounter the mother of his former lover!

Coincidence? "You said you distrust coincidence," he sang. "Because you arrange much of what to mortals appears to be coincidence. Do others do the same?"

"They shouldn't, but one does."

"Satan."

"Satan," she agreed. "I very much think he has been interfering again. What reason could he have had to want you in this office?"

"Apart from my inexperience that he might take advantage of, I can think of none."

"But you know my daughter."

"I *loved* your daughter. But circumstances forced our separation, and now I love Rapture. This was no design of mine, or fault in Orb; it—" He shrugged. "It happened."

"And Orb loved you?"

"Yes. But she knew why I had to leave her, and I think by now she has made her own life. She was—is a wonderful person."

"Is it possible that Satan was jealous of you?"

Mym broke into a stuttering laugh. "For what possible reason?"

"Because my daughter loved you."

That sobered him. "Satan—has an interest in Orb?"

Lachesis pursed her lips. "Possibly, in his devious fashion. Satan—well, he once expressed interest in me, when I was young and attractive. I was said by some to be the most beautiful woman of my generation, and males are attracted to that sort of thing. Orb is not far off that standard and she inherited that phenomenal musical talent from her father's side of the family. Satan tried to prevent her from getting her harp, and her cousin Luna from—"

"Luna!"

"My granddaughter."

"Your—! But—"

She smiled. "I bore Luna's father in my youth, and Orb later. It is complicated. We raised the two girls together, and they were like sisters. Now—"

"But Luna does not resemble Orb! Both are beautiful women, but the manner, the bones, the hair—" But he knew as he spoke that the two did resemble each other, and that was the undefined thing he had been aware of in Luna.

"Luna dyed her hair brown and adopted different ways. That, too, is complicated to explain. At any rate, Luna is slated to balk Satan's grand design to assume greater power on Earth, and Satan has been laboring mightily to eliminate her. But she is protected by Thanatos, so he must be roundabout. Orb, however, is not so protected, so he may have mischief in mind for her, to put pressure on me and on Luna. And—I dislike saying this—he may have a certain personal interest in Orb, because it seems he is partial to that type of woman. That might be a ruse, of course. At any rate, if any of this conjecture of mine is true, Satan might resent whatever man Orb took an interest in and act to eliminate that man."

Mym was appalled. "Could—could Satan arrange to have a prince killed?"

"Surely so. Satan can arrange evil for any person not protected by another Incarnation."

"It was my brother's untimely death that caused my separation from Orb," Mym sang, shaking with shock and anger. "He was to be Rajah: when he died, I had to assume that office. So I was denied Orb and given Rapture, against my will. The circumstances of my love for—"

"No mystery," Lachesis said. "Rapture is lovely."

"And you were going to kill her!" he sang, suddenly enraged at her.

"No. It was a bluff to make my point."

"You made it! I would not allow Rapture to be hurt."

"And Orb—if Satan threatened her, now—?"

Mym spread his hands. "I did not lose my feeling for her, when I came to love Rapture. I—would be vulnerable."

"Well, don't worry. I am watching Orb's thread. Satan can not interfere directly with it without alerting me, and if I can't protect her, the other Incarnations will help me. Satan knows that. I suspect that it was the other way around; he was trying to use you to hurt her. I wasn't watching your thread, and certainly not your brother's thread."

"And Satan was pretending to be my friend!" Mym gritted.

"He does that. Never trust him; he always has some devious scheme brewing."

"But—once he had taken me away from Orb—why would he try to separate me also from Rapture?"

"To make you angry enough to qualify for the office of the Incarnation of War?"

"But why would he want me in that office? I could not do him much mischief before, but now—" Mym considered, and realized that he didn't know how he might harm Satan. "Surely I am, or will be, more of a threat to him now, as an Incarnation."

"One would think so. But of course you weren't supposed to know about his machinations in your life—if, indeed, we have conjectured correctly. Only our meeting here has clarified that."

"He had to know I would in time recognize the mother of the woman I once loved!"

She sighed. "Yes, I suppose so. I suspect that we have not yet properly fathomed Satan's mischief. We must be alert for it. Satan never exerts himself without bad reason." She smiled briefly. "But we have drifted from the topic. How can we abate this battle or this war?"

"By putting the one who started it on the front line," Mym sang. "We had agreed on that."

She considered. "I had thought we were joking. But now I wonder. Why *not* put that man here?"

"Because it would be murder. You don't approve of that."

"And you do?"

"I would call it an execution. If the life of that one guilty man could cause the lives of the remaining children to be spared, I would gladly destroy him."

She grimaced. "Then I leave it in your hands." She converted to her spider form and vanished.

So quickly! Yet they had come to an agreement, and if she, like many of her sex, lacked the stomach for what was necessary, it made sense to leave it in the hands of one who could handle it.

Mym withdrew from the boy and mounted his horse, leaving the battle frozen. They galloped across the terrain of Babylonia, seeking the palace of the ruler of the nation. This took time—but it didn't matter, for the battle was not operative. Mym located the man and, without ceremony, set a hand on his shoulder. This brought the man into Mym's magic frame; he disappeared from the eyes of mortals and was carried through the air, through the walls, and into the sky.

Mym set him down on the battlefield, directly in the path of the boy he had inhabited before. Then he released the stasis.

The battle resumed. The pieces of bodies completed their flights through the air and socked into the ground. The boy, boosted by the blast behind him, stumbled, caught his balance—and spied the gesticulating enemy before him.

The boy reacted automatically. He stopped, raised his rifle, sighted, and fired.

Whether his bullet scored was doubtful; good marksmanship was unlikely in such circumstance. But his action alerted the other boys of this region. They stopped, raised their rifles, and fired. Several bullets tore into the man, and he screamed and fell.

The boys charged up, saw the man's face, and exclaimed with amazement. They had seen that face before; it had been on posters used for hate training. They cried the name.

A Persian officer spied the commotion and chanced his hide by coming to investigate. He, too recognized the casualty. He gave orders, and the boys took hold of the corpse and dragged it back up the hill. The body was heavy, but there were many hands; few were slow to realize that this detail was taking them away from the worst danger. The battle, such as it was, dissolved.

Mym watched from his steed, invisibly. He saw them get the body into a bunker. He saw the boy he had occupied identified as the soldier who had killed this horrendous enemy. The boy was an instant hero, given a commendation and sent to the rear to report to higher authorities. He would be safe—and neither he nor his mother would suffer further privation.

Persia had said, publicly and often, that it would carry on the war until this enemy leader was deposed. Suddenly the man was dead. The stated reason for the war had been eliminated. The attack was called off, and a *de facto* truce developed.

No more children would die for a while. Perhaps the war would now be allowed to end, and the recovery could begin.

Mym wasn't sure what the final judgment might be on his method of stopping this war, but he was satisfied. He had not only accomplished his objective, he had learned another way to make his position effective.

– 10 –

THANATOS

Concerned by what Fate had told him of Satan's designs, Mym tried to talk to Rapture about it that night. "I think you would be better off with Luna in the mortal realm," he sang. "Since you can still readily spend the nights with me, here, the separation is really not that onerous."

"With the cousin of the woman you loved before me?" she inquired bittersweetly.

Ouch! "Who informed you of that?"

"Lila, of course."

"Lila—the creature of Satan."

"She's an interesting woman. She will make you an excellent concubine."

"I'm not so sure I want a demoness for a concubine. She surely serves the interests of Satan before mine."

"You don't like the notion of any woman serving any interest before yours?"

This was not the type of question Rapture had asked before this. Mym wasn't sure he liked the change. "I don't like the notion of being that close to a creature provided by the Incarnation of Evil."

"Oh, pooh!" she said. "Lila isn't evil! She's an educated woman."

"What is she doing in Hell, then?"

"She says it was a bum rap."

"A what?"

"A bum rap. A false charge. A misunderstanding. Before she realized, she was in Hell and couldn't get out. So she makes the best of it."

"It still sounds suspicious to me. She's a demoness."

"Oh, don't be such a fuddy-duddy!"

"A what?"

"An old-fashioned bore."

"It sounds like reduplicating echoism to me. This occidental slang does not become you, Rapture. Don't forget you are a princess."

"*Was* a princess. Now I'm a woman. And so is Lila. Oh, the things I am learning from her!"

"Like what, apart from gossip and slang?"

"Like this," she said, and kissed him in a fashion that made his skin heat.

"You're coming on like a concubine!" he protested.

"I'm coming on like a woman who is learning what it's all about."

"A princess does not need to know what it's all about!"

"But a woman does. Lila is certainly right about that."

"I really think you would be better off with Luna Kaftan."

"Luna is a fine woman, and I like her—but now that I know how similar she is to your former love, I prefer to keep my distance from her—and your distance too. It's enough trouble adapting to this new lifestyle without having to worry about what's going on in your mind."

He found that concern singularly difficult to address. He felt no romantic attraction for Luna, but it was true that his new knowledge of her relation to Orb worked a subtle effect on him. Where was Orb now? How had she fared, after he had deserted her? Had the ring enabled her to cope adequately? She had been a western woman, and he had loved her; now Rapture was assuming some western attributes, and he did not find them appealing in her. Perhaps there was justice in her disinclination to remain with Luna.

"Well, perhaps you could stay with another mortal woman," he suggested.

"Why? I like it here. The food is good, the grounds are beautiful, and Lila is a fine companion. Soon she is going to take me to visit Hell."

"To visit Hell!" he exclaimed in singsong, almost choking. "I don't want you going near that place!"

"You prefer that I sit in the castle all day, sewing handkerchiefs?"

He sighed. It was true that there was not a lot for her to do here in Purgatory. "Perhaps you could find something to do in the mortal realm to keep you busy. I'm sure Luna would—"

"Her, again. She seems much on your mind."

Unfortunately true, after the dialogue with Fate. He had never expected to be thrown into the company of Orb's close relatives. But because he had known Orb well, he trusted those relatives. And he wanted to get Rapture away from the insidious influence of Satan. "I just feel that Satan means to do you some mischief, and it would devastate me to have that happen."

She softened. "That's an unprincely thing to say. Why don't you just order me to do what you wish?"

"Because I love you."

"You know that's a decadent Western concept." But she could not suppress her pleasure. "I will seek some mortal employment."

"That pleases me."

Then they made love, and all was good.

The next situation requiring the personal attention of Mars was in Latin America. Conquest, Slaughter, Famine and Pestilence were eager to get to work, but Mym lacked proper enthusiasm. Increasingly he was wondering whether he was the proper man for this office. He had been trained for command and for war, but he took no special joy in it, especially not in pointless bloodshed. He would prefer to abolish war. But there was the conflict of interest, because, if he succeeded, he would lose the office— and where would he be then? Locked into this alien Afterlife, his mortal life completed. What chance at the ultimate relief of nirvana would he have then?

He had learned that new Incarnations had a period of apprenticeship or trial, after which they could voluntarily give up the offices. Perhaps it would be best for him to do that—to step down when that chance came. Would that return him to mortal status? He suspected so. But what offered then? Would he have to resume his position as Heir-Prince to Gujarat, displacing the man he had established in his place and marrying the Princess of Rajasthan? That would be horrible!

Suppose he could step into the mortal world in some other capacity? Become a new person in the occidental world? That had its appeal. But what would he do? He was trained to be a prince, and that was not a preferred employment in the west. Also, he was a stutterer. He had made it on singsong well enough, but that was in large part because he had held positions of extreme power, both as Prince and as the Incarnation of War. Others did not laugh at the powerful; they accommodated their idiosyncrasies. But if he tried to assume an *un*powerful position—

No, he would have to make do with the situation he had, try to be the best Mars he could be and, if he succeeded in abolishing war, to retire to whatever the Afterlife offered. This was not a bad existence, really. He could emulate Musashi, author of *Five Rings,* learning to prevail through humility and hard work.

That book spelled out the Way to learn the author's strategy very simply and directly, in the section on the Ground: to think honestly; to train, to learn every art and know the Ways of all professions; to distinguish between gain and loss, develop intuitive judgment, perceiving what could not be seen; to pay attention even to trifles, and to do nothing that was of no use; in sum, to be honest and perceptive and purposeful throughout life. So easy to read and to agree with, but sometimes so hard to honor! How would Musashi have handled the situation with Rapture?

Mym sighed. As far as he could tell, the great Japanese Samurai had never married or formed any significant relation with a woman. Perhaps he had been most practical of all in that!

They arrived at the site. It was a jungle. Lush tropical growth spread all about. "What's the situation?" Mym asked.

"Muddled," Conquest replied. "This is a guerrilla war, festering for a number of years. I was surprised when it died down at the time of your ascension, because the underlying causes had not changed."

"Satan had a hand in that," Mym sang. "He didn't like my predecessor."

"True. But Satan's grudges are legion."

"So we don't really know how things are faring, here, because guerrilla warfare is not open and measurable," Mym said. "We only know that there will be bloodshed, much of it by innocents."

"Yeah!" Slaughter said raptly.

"But there is a strong indication that something of extreme significance is about to occur at this site," Conquest said. "That's why this action requires our personal supervision."

"I should have known there would be more to it than mere routine destruction and killing," Mym sang sourly. "Just what kind of development is this?"

"We don't know," Pestilence said. "But I feel it in my flesh, so it must relate to me."

Mym looked at him. The figure's flesh writhed with maggots and mold and leggy things; and when he moved, flies buzzed up. If a man was known by the company he kept, Mym thought, he would have preferred other company.

Again he thought of the Book of the Ground, in *Five Rings*. Pestilence was like a rotting segment of ground! But this was an erroneous association, for Musashi did not talk of decay, but of the importance of basic organization and proper timing in all things, the groundwork for success, and of ascertaining the reality, so as to have one thing but to know ten thousand things. Knowledge—there was a prime key. The warrior who knew all things did not waste his effort on what was of no use.

Information! That was the first requirement here—to perceive that which could not presently be seen.

"I will investigate," Mym decided. He dismounted and looked about. What should he look for? He didn't want to identify with another eleven-year-old boy!

"There is a government outpost there," Conquest said, pointing.

"That will do." Mym strode toward the building. As he came near, four men emerged. They were rough-looking types, wearing unkempt uniforms, carrying sidearms and knives. Mym paced himself to overlap the evident leader and phased in.

Again he suffered disorientation, but he was getting the hang of this and soon he was using the soldier's perceptions. This man was reasonably well fed and healthy, but dirty and dissatisfied. He had little formal education and owed his position of limited leadership to his muscle and general insensitivity to the plight of others. Mym did not like him at all, but stayed with him because it would have been too much of an investment in time and energy to phase in to another body. This overlapping was not pleasant for him, but it seemed to be the best way to get a real feel for the situation. If a person wanted to know how to deal with worms, there was nothing like being a worm for a while!

This squad was on a mission. The host was barely literate in Spanish, his native language, but one of his henchmen could read well. "It's the farm across the stream, there," the man said. "We'll have to watch it; he's got dogs."

"We know how to deal with dogs," the host said, and the others laughed coarsely.

They trekked to a small wooden bridge across the river. Two emaciated children were sitting there. They stretched out their thin arms in a gesture of supplication as the party approached. "Candy?" the little boy begged in Spanish. Mym could understand this language now, because he was tuning into the sense of it as rendered by the host's brain.

"Get out of our way!" a henchman grunted. He lifted his boot, set it against the boy's shoulder, and shoved. With a scream the boy tumbled backward into the river.

"Death Squad!" the little girl cried, struggling to her feet. "Bad men!" She started to run away.

"Don't let her go!" the host cried. "Can't have her telling anyone we were here."

A henchman strode after the girl and caught her. He hauled her back by one spindly arm. "What do we do with her?"

"Kill her," the host said.

"But she's just a kid," the henchman protested.

"She's a *witness*," the host clarified.

"But we can't just—"

"Where are your guts?" the host demanded. "We've got a job

to do.'' He drew his knife. ''We don't want noise. I'll show you how to make it quiet.''

He took hold of the girl's straggly hair, hauled her head up, and brought the knife to her exposed throat.

Mym acted. He exerted his will and paralyzed the man's arms. The little girl dropped from the slackening grasp and lay on the ground, unmoving. She had fainted.

''See? No noise,'' Mym forced the man's vocal apparatus to say. It was difficult, because Mym had to focus the thought without language, forcing it through the brain so that it came out in the proper words.

''No noise,'' the henchman echoed, relieved. ''For a minute I thought you were going to kill her!''

Mym eased up on his control. The host found himself in the awkward position of having done a senseless thing by his definition. He had indeed intended to kill the child. Now he had to explain his action.

It was easier for him to pretend that things had gone as planned. ''Now you know,'' he said gruffly and turned and moved on across the bridge.

Mym had navigated that crisis. But had he done it by proper planning and decision or by simply muddling through? He still had a lot to learn of the Way of Strategy!

They proceeded on toward the farm. Mym now knew that this was a killer group that went surreptitiously to murder individuals who opposed the policies of this nation's government; he had read about these during his military studies. Thousands or tens of thousands had been killed in this manner—but instead of securing the government's power, this had generated a backlash that had become a full-fledged guerrilla revolution. This government was at war with its own people and would have fallen long ago if not generously supported by powerful outside interests.

Mym had no sympathy with terrorism, whether practiced by the government or against it. If this was the way this government operated, his sympathies were with the opposition.

But it was not his job to dictate the political system of a nation or the manner it maintained its base of power. It was his job to supervise the violence that resulted.

Well, perhaps he could redefine his job. He had succeeded in drastically changing the configuration of the war between Babylonia and Persia; was there a way to eliminate these Death Squads here?

Aside from arranging another elimination of a head of state, he wasn't sure how. And when he started practicing assassination himself, how did that differ from what the Death Squads were doing? It was no easy decision.

Now the men were near the farmhouses. The dogs spotted them and charged. A henchman tossed down bits of meat that he removed from a special package. The dogs, poorly trained, paused to snap up the meat—and in moments they were writhing on the ground. The bait was poisoned, of course.

"He's supposed to be alone today," the literate henchman said. "His wife's off at the big celebration." Mym wasn't able to grasp the exact nature of the celebration; it was tied in too closely with cultural values that did not align with his own.

"We'll play it safe, anyway," the host said. "We'll surround the house. I'll challenge him from the front; you be ready to catch him when he tries to sneak out the back."

They deployed accordingly. But as the host came to the front, the figure of a woman appeared in the doorway.

The host cursed under his breath. Mym read his thought: the intelligence had been wrong. The wife was home. Now it would be messy, and they would have to kill her too. They would charge extra for that.

The woman disappeared inside the house, slamming the door. The host charged, knowing that time was now of the essence. He would have to catch and kill the woman, because his weak-kneed cohorts wouldn't want to do it. He couldn't have her escaping and bearing the report of the identity of the killers; that would embarrass the employer, who preferred anonymity.

He lifted his boot and kicked at the flimsy door. It crashed inward. He stepped over it and into the house. There was the woman, speaking into a telephone.

A telephone! There was another vital detail the intelligence report had overlooked! If he had known about that, he would have taken time to cut the wires before approaching the house. It was a nuisance, but had to be done. Now it was too late; she had already made the call.

He strode across and swept the phone out of her hand. The woman screamed and spun away from him. He caught at her, getting hold of her shawl. It came free, and he threw it down and grabbed again, this time catching her blouse. That tore as she fought to escape, exposing her haltered bosom. Evidently she had been less formally garbed and donned her blouse over the halter when she heard activity near the house.

The host paused. This was a well-shaped woman! Of course he had to kill her—but it would be a shame to let a form like that go to waste. The henchman would catch the escaping man; he could spare a few minutes.

He got both hands on her and bore her back against the wall. She screamed, so he knocked her in the face. Blood welled at her lips, but the scream cut off.

He caught at the halter and yanked. The thing was sturdier than it looked; instead of coming away it stretched out and down, baring one of her breasts. The sexual passion of the host was magnified by this sight. He stared at the breast, then reached for it.

Mym, bemused at the proceedings, had failed to act in time to abate the host's violence. Now he exerted himself, fighting to control the sudden lust of the man. But though he had been successful in saving the girl-child, he was now up against a greater determination. The host had not really wanted to kill the child, but had intended to do it as a necessary thing; in contrast, he was inflamed by desire to possess this woman before he killed her. Perhaps with more experience, Mym could have assumed control. As it was, he could not. While he tried, the host opened his own clothing and brought his body up against that of the woman.

Mym gave up the struggle and withdrew. He had possessed a hundred different and lovely young women in his life as a prince, but had raped none. He refused to share a body engaged in such an act.

Now he stood beside the man and woman, watching the commencement of the rape. He was angry.

He touched his Sword. Suddenly he was solid. He reached out and grasped the thug's collar and hauled him back. But the man was heavier than Mym, and this pull was not enough.

Mym touched his Sword again. If the instrument could make

him solid, it could make him solider! He reached out a second time, caught the collar, and made a terrific exertion.

The man was lifted back and away, and hurled at the opposite wall. He collapsed to the floor, unconscious. It was as if a giant had thrown him!

Curious despite the situation, Mym turned and struck the wall with his fist. His fist punched right through it.

He had indeed become more solid! Ordinary matter was now of a lesser density, so that his flesh had the relative mass of a sledgehammer, and his force was magnified many times. No wonder the thug had flown!

The woman was staring right through him. Mym remained invisible; she had no notion what had saved her. Then she recovered her wits and scrambled up and away, simultaneously hauling her halter back into place.

The thug had been right about one thing; she was an attractive woman. But now Mym had to attend to the other members of the Death Squad, to prevent them from killing the wealthy farmer.

He looked through the house, but saw only the woman, hiding behind the stove. The farmer must already be outside.

But when he went outside, he found the three other Squad members waiting. The farmer had not emerged.

The woman must have been alone. That intelligence was really fouled up!

Then Mym heard something. It was a kind of scuffling down the drive leading to the house. Something was coming. More killers from the government?

He summoned his horse with a thought, and the animal appeared. Mym mounted, and the horse staggered.

Oh. That extra mass. He touched the Sword and willed himself back to masslessness. The horse relaxed.

They galloped toward the new sound. In moments they spied the source and paused, astonished.

It was a troop of ghastly people shambling along. Their eyes were staring, their mouths hung open, and drool fell across their chins. Their hair was wild, their clothing haphazard. Their arms and legs moved as if operated by marionette strings, jerking up and forward and slapping down. Each one of them seemed about to collapse, but somehow did not.

These were not ordinary people! They were zombies! What were they doing here, roused from their ground?

From the ground? There was that theme again!

Mym watched as the zombie troop shuffled along toward the farmhouse. The members of the Death Squad saw them and yelled. The leader staggered out, still woozy from his fall. The zombies continued without pause.

This could not be coincidence! The woman must have summoned the zombies when she phoned. But that explained only part of the mystery of this occasion. Where had the zombies come from, and how had the woman known about them? Where was the man of the house? Why had he left his lovely wife unprotected?

Shots were fired. The zombies proceeded without pause. The Death Squad members fired again, taking better aim—but still there was no visible effect. They were baffled.

Now the woman appeared in the doorway. She yelled at the zombies and pointed to the Death Squad members.

The zombies understood. They pursued the men.

Too late, the men realized what they were up against. They tried to scramble away, but the zombies surrounded them. Dangling hands flopped against the men, and slack jaws worked. The attack was inefficient, but it was apparent that the zombies felt no pain, so that nothing the men could do to them had any effect. Each of the men was soon buried under a clumsy mass of bodies, and slobbering mouths labored to bite at living flesh.

Mym might have interfered, but found he had no inclination. He knew firsthand the evil of the Death Squad members; they were not worth saving. Also, he had no desire to make physical contact with the zombies, who were about as repulsive as creatures of human form could be. He realized now that they were not refugees from a graveyard, for none of their flesh was rotting and there was no earth on them; rather, they were like almost total idiots.

Another horse galloped down from the sky. At first Mym thought it was one of his own companions, but then he realized that the color of the horse did not match those he knew. It wasn't any color; it was pale, though the rider was caped in black. Certainly it was supernatural, however.

The horse landed and trotted to him. Now Mym saw the skull-features of Thanatos, the Incarnation of Death. "What are you doing here, Mars?" Thanatos called.

"I think I am supervising a battle," Mym returned in singsong. "Of precisely what nature, I hardly know."

"Of an illicit nature!" Thanatos said. "Those are zombies!"

"I had come to that conclusion," Mym agreed. "But they seem to be serving a good cause."

Thanatos was obviously agitated. "Do you know what a zombie is?"

"An undead," Mym replied. "We have them in India, too, though I have never seen them fight a battle before."

"A zombie is a living man whose soul has been removed."

"Yes, I suppose so, since life departs with the soul. If the mortal body does not lie still, it is called a zombie."

"But these bodies have not been killed!" Thanatos said. "They are not on my schedule."

"They are evidently on mine," Mym sang. "They are doing a necessary job, summoned in defense of that young woman."

"You may organize a battle as you choose," Thanatos said, his bone-jaw grim. "But you may not impinge on my prerogatives. You may not interfere with the souls of mortals before their deaths."

"I don't know how these zombies came to be," Mym sang. "But if they are what it takes to set matters straight, I'm amenable."

"If you do not eliminate the zombies, I will!" Thanatos said angrily.

This sounded like a challenge, and Mym was not in the mood to be challenged on his own turf. Evidently Thanatos represented the Ground, but that did not give him leave to interfere with Fire. "Show me how to make a zombie, and perhaps I will know how to eliminate one," he sang.

"Like this!" Thanatos said, and reached his skeletal hand into Mym's body. The fingers passed right through his flesh, which wasn't surprising while he was insubstantial. But then they caught on something within him and pulled on it, and he was abruptly in mortal agony.

Thanatos had grasped his soul and was pulling it from his body!

Mym reacted involuntarily. He stepped into Thanatos, over-lapping him, and exerted his will to take over the other man's mind. That transferred some of his agony to the host—to Thanatos.

Thanatos immediately let go of Mym's soul, as now he could only hurt himself. Mym stepped out of the body.

They looked at each other. "Incarnations should not quarrel with each other," Thanatos said after a moment.

"Agreed," Mym sang. He knew he should not have reacted so imperiously and was glad to accept the truce. The Way of the Warrior was a resolute acceptance of death. Here he had Death literally before him and should have accepted Death's concern. "But if only you can draw out the soul from a living body, how did these zombies come to be? Certainly *I* did not create them."

"We had better find out."

"The young woman summoned them; perhaps she can answer."

They went to the woman, and Thanatos spoke to her. "You must inform us how the zombies came about," he said.

The woman seemed startled, as if she hadn't realized that any-one was near. She started to turn to face the cloaked figure.

"Do not look at me," Thanatos said quickly.

She hesitated, then spoke in Spanish. Mym, now disassociated from the thug host, was unable to understand it, but Thanatos did.

"I am the Incarnation of Death," Thanatos replied to her. "But I have not come for you, only to discover the truth about the zombies."

She spoke again, with some force.

"The Death Squad thug tried to rape you?" Thanatos asked. He was speaking in English, yet the woman seemed to hear him in Spanish. Mym wondered how that was accomplished, but knew that matter was not worth pursuing at the moment.

The woman spoke again.

"So you asked the guerrilla connection to send help, but you did not know the nature of what would come," Thanatos said, and the woman nodded.

"Give me that number that you called," Thanatos said.

She protested; it was a secret she could not divulge.

"Look at me, now," Thanatos said.

The woman turned to stare into his face. She quailed, then spoke a number.

"Thank you," Thanatos said. He gestured to Mym, and they went into the house.

Thanatos picked up the phone and dialed the number. When the connection was made, Thanatos turned to his fine pale horse. "Mortis, orient on that location," he said. Then he hung up the phone.

They went back outside. The zombies were still working on the thugs, and the woman was watching with a certain horrified pleasure. It was not every woman who got such a chance to see an attempted rape and murder so obnoxiously punished.

They mounted their steeds. "To that location," Thanatos told his horse.

The animal took off. Mym's own mount followed. They galloped swiftly through the air. Soon they came down in a small jungle clearing and trotted to an isolated cabin.

This was the place, all right: a number of zombies shuffled about. A trainer was instructing them, evidently teaching them how to walk without falling and how to follow a road. A truck was parked, hidden under a tree—the primary transportation for the zombies. "They drove them to the vicinity of the farm, then pointed them toward it," Mym said. "That must have been all that was necessary."

"Yes. But my concern is with the crafting of them."

They dismounted and walked to the cabin. It was closed, its windows boarded, so they walked through the wall to enter.

A man was inside, using mortar and pestle to work up a white paste. That was all.

Thanatos manifested before him. "Look at me, *Mortal*."

The man looked up—and stiffened. He recognized Death.

Thanatos questioned him, and Mym picked up the essence; the man had been seeking a better way to purify cocaine and had stumbled upon a savage variation. This product affected the subject so deeply that he passed right through a trance state into somnambulance, and could not be aroused. His body lived, but his mind was almost entirely gone.

Thus, the zombies—living people deprived of their souls, proceeding without personal volition, doomed to degenerate shortly from neglect. Hence the connection with the Incarnation of Pestilence; in days, those bodies would be riddled with disease, the prey of flies and worms.

Certainly this related to War, for these zombies were being used to oppose the Death Squads. In fact, the woman's husband, the man the Squad had come to assassinate, was involved with this project; when he had gotten news that he was to be hit, naturally he had arranged to test the zombies in action. His brave wife had remained at the house to alert him when the Squad arrived. She had been supposed to phone him and hide in the attic, but the premature break-in of the Squad leader had cut off her escape. The zombies would have wrapped things up anyway, but only Mym's intercession had spared her from rape and possibly murder before their arrival.

However, Mym realized that it was the development of the zombies that had brought him here, so perhaps that was not coincidence. Nevertheless, there was no question that it also overlapped the office of Death, since people were being killed, and in a manner that was supposed to be reserved for Thanatos. They were going to have to work this out.

Where did they get the people to de-soul by means of this drug? From captive government troops. It made perfect sense, to the guerrillas and to Mym, who had just seen how the government operated. But it didn't make sense to Thanatos. "If mortals learn how to handle souls, there will be no end of mischief," he declared. "This knowledge must be abolished."

Mym thought of the way the zombies had shuffled into battle and concluded that Thanatos was correct. Killing was bad enough, but de-souling would give unscrupulous people a motive for more of it. They would generate armies of zombies, and no person would be safe. It would transform war, making it uglier than it already was, because the killing would be done before the battles ever started.

"But how can knowledge be abolished?" he sang.

"We shall have to get help," Thanatos decided. "Chronos could do it."

Because Chronos controlled time, Mym realized. He could tilt his Hourglass and cause time to freeze, and—

No, that wouldn't work. Both Mars and Thanatos had the ability to freeze scenes—but the scenes resumed unchanged later. Chronos would have to run time actually backwards to undo the discovery of the drug. That would complicate the world in other ways. "There must be an easier way," he sang. "Maybe Gaea—"

"Yes, Gaea would be best," Thanatos agreed. "She knows how to do things with least disruption. I will summon her." He lifted the heavy black watch he carried to his face and spoke into it as if it were a microphone. "Gaea."

Mist coalesced, thickening and forming into ghostly, then solid, shape. Mym, still conscious of *Five Rings,* recognized this as the manifestation of Wind—or Air. Musashi also called it *Tradition.*

"I was waiting for your call," the voice of Gaea said, slightly before her appearance was complete.

"We have knowledge to eliminate," Thanatos said.

Gaea frowned. "To eliminate!" she exclaimed. "Since when have you become regressive? Satan thrives on ignorance."

"I shall explain," Thanatos said.

Mym heard something outside. He signaled the others that he would investigate while they clarified the issue and walked through the wall.

Military trucks were pulling up. What was this? More victims for de-souling being brought in? The Incarnations were taking action none too soon!

"The government!" the trainer of the zombies cried.

The first truck screeched to a stop, and soldiers piled out of the back. "Take them alive!" an officer called.

The trainer and the zombies fought as well as they were able, but in minutes all were captive, for the government forces were overwhelming. "Spread out!" the officer cried. Mym wasn't sure whether he was speaking English, or whether Spanish was becoming intelligible now. "Secure all property! Destroy nothing!"

They were after the secret of making zombies! They must have traced the zombie-truck back to its source and mounted a mission to capture both the site and its personnel.

Mym stepped back into the building. "The government is coming after the secret!" he exclaimed in singsong.

"Too soon!" Thanatos said. "We have not yet decided on a way to abolish it."

Gaea smiled. "Perhaps we can delay them somewhat," she said. She stepped to and through the wall. Mym and Thanatos followed.

Outside, the government troops were combing through the jungle and the clearing, hundreds strong, poking at the ground with bayonets. Before long the line would intersect the cabin. There did not seem to be any way to stop it.

"I think fire is best," Gaea said. She raised her hands, her fingers spread, and jags of electricity radiated from them. The jags touched the ground—and fire erupted. It spread between the points of its origin, formed a line, and swept toward the troops.

The soldiers were quick to realize their peril. "Fire!" they cried. "They've torched it!"

"Beat it out!" the officer cried. "Save that shack!"

But the troops were demoralized by the fire. They retreated from it.

Gaea turned about. More current flared from her hands. The cabin burst into flame.

"But the man inside!" Mym sang.

Gaea shrugged. "Rescue him, then."

Mym strode through the flames and the wall, feeling neither. The man inside was standing, alarmed. Mym caught him by the arm, then touched the Sword.

The two of them flew up, through the roof, and into the sky. The man's mouth hung open; he could not believe this was happening. Mym brought them down beside Gaea and Thanatos.

The woman turned to the man. "Who besides you knows the secret for making the drug?" she asked.

"N-no one!" the man said, his knees seeming to weaken.

A streamer of mist poured from Gaea's right hand. Snakelike, it slid toward the man's head, and into it. "No one," she repeated.

The man's expression changed. "I—have forgotten how!" he said.

"And you will never remember or rediscover it," Gaea said. "Now depart, before the troops apprehend you."

"But—but the fire—"

"Will not touch you," she finished.

The man walked, neared the line of fire that enclosed the cabin, and walked through it. He was magically protected—for the moment. Soon he was out of sight.

The officer had succeeded in restoring some discipline in the troops, and they were now attacking the fire with shovels, beating it out. A gap was forming in the fireline.

"With the material and equipment destroyed by fire and the memory of its process gone, they will not be able to fathom the secret," Gaea said. She fuzzed, became vapor, and dissipated.

Mym exchanged a glance with Thanatos. "It seems our problem has been solved," Thanatos said. "I have no further interest in the proceedings." He made a signal, and his pale horse appeared at his side.

"Wait!" Mym sang. "Your friend Luna—did you know that I once loved her cousin?"

Thanatos paused. "I did not know. I have not met her cousin, but I understand she is easy to love."

"Now I love Rapture—and I don't like the influence that Satan is having on her. I want her to be more with Luna, a better influence. But she—she fears any contact I might have with Luna, because of her similarity to Orb—"

Thanatos smiled. "I will deliver Rapture between Luna's estate and your castle," he said.

Mym grasped his bony hand. "I thank you, Thanatos! If I can ever repay the favor—"

"We Incarnations must help each other to oppose Satan," he said. "When I help you, I help myself, for now you will oppose Satan's designs on Luna."

"I will certainly do that! But what is it Satan means to do to Luna? Lachesis told me that Luna is destined to balk—"

"She is to cast a decisive vote against Satan's political power on Earth, some years hence. Satan means to remove her from political office, or in some way circumvent her, so that his will shall govern, and he shall be able to corrupt the mortal realm and gain a majority of souls for himself. This would represent his final victory over God."

"Satan can do that? Change things about on Earth to suit himself? Why doesn't God stop him?"

"The two made a Covenant of noninterference," Thanatos explained. "God is good, therefore he honors it and allows free will among the mortals, wherever it may lead. But Satan, being evil, violates it and seeks always to win more power."

Mym remembered that Gaea had said the same. Still, he found it hard to accept. "But then—what is to prevent Satan from winning?"

"The other Incarnations," Thanatos said. "And the war is now coming to you. Wage it well."

"I will try," Mym sang. "But I remain new in this office and still have much to learn."

"That is why the next battle must be yours. Satan always attacks the weakest point."

Which made sense, Mym realized. But he had little comfort in the realization. *Five Rings* recommended attacking the enemy's strongest points first—but had the author ever come up against Satan directly?

— 11 —

CHRONOS

Rapture, having made a genuine effort to find a place for herself in the mortal world, had found one. She was to be a part-time consultant on Indian Culture for the University of Kilvarough. Luna, when asked, had been of considerable help, and Rapture was pleased. She was well qualified for this position, as she spoke both English and the languages of several Indian Kingdoms and was excellently versed in the conventions and artifacts of them. The money she would earn would enable her to pay a nominal rental for her stay at Luna's house, which gave her a sense of independence that she had never enjoyed before.

Thanatos, true to his word, brought her to and from the Castle of War each day. At first she had been leery of the skeletal figure, but acquaintance with Luna had reassured her. "Zane," Luna had told her—that was the name she called Thanatos— "is not really the Grim Reaper. He is an ordinary man with a difficult job and a great deal of compassion."

Compassion. It was, in its way, a magic word. A dependent person valued that quality in others. So she came to respect Thanatos, without being any more thrilled by the nature of his employment than she was with Mym's.

And that employment was a continuing wedge between them.

Rapture did not argue the case or make demands on him, but he could feel the tension in her whenever the subject of his work came up. He learned not to tell her of the details of his day's work, because that made her uncomfortable, and she grew cold without being conscious of it. Their lovemaking became awkward. Yet what could he do? He had reservations of his own about his office, but had thrashed it out with himself and concluded that his best course was to stick with it. It was ironic that the same office that had enabled him to rescue himself and Rapture from the heartbreak that had awaited them in the mortal realm was now inexorably separating them.

There came a night when Rapture did not appear. It seemed that there was a special late seminar at the University that required her presence, so it was easier to stay over at Luna's so that she would not be late the following morning. She would see him the next evening.

This was all clear and sensible—but Mym did not like being alone at night. Out of sorts, he walked again in the garden.

There was Lila, of course. "I think you are ready for a concubine," she said. "Give me leave to enter your premises, and I will serve in any manner you desire."

Mym looked at her. She was garbed in a slightly iridescent, slightly luminescent, slightly translucent robe that enhanced a figure he knew was crafted in Hell. Her face was classic in its perfection, and her lustrous hair flowed down across her shoulders like a midnight river of silk.

But he had seen—and possessed—beautiful women before and he still distrusted the motives of the creatures of Satan. He did not want any of them having access to his Incarnation premises. "You," he said shortly, again able to speak without stuttering in this region. "You were the one who gave Rapture notions of independence!"

Lila's eyes widened innocently. "Why, we talked, and she inquired about the ways of Western women," she protested. "I told her nothing that was not true."

"Such as the relationship between Luna and Orb?"

"They are both good women."

"And you are not."

"And I am not," she agreed.

"You told Rapture that you were in Hell on a 'bum rap.' I am sure that's not true."

"She misunderstood. I was speaking of another. I am a demoness. I never had a mortal existence. But for that reason, I lack the modesty of true spirits. I can provide you with the kinkiest types of passion that a decent woman would never—"

Angry, he caught her by the arm, not certain what to do with her. She came readily in close, the musky perfume of her body manifesting. "You may hit me if you wish," she murmured. "Or whatever else may please you. Anything at all . . ."

He cast her loose. "Nothing about you pleases me!" he snapped, turned about, and stomped back toward the Castle.

"Each lie you tell," she called dulcetly after him, "brings you closer to Satan, the Father of Lies."

He ignored that gibe. But as he returned to his solitary room and tried to settle down for sleep, the barb returned to haunt him. *Five Rings* had advised him not to think dishonestly, but he *had* lied, for Lila's body, if not her nature, pleased him quite well. And actually her nature, her willingness to be with him and to serve his needs, was also quite tempting. He was not looking for a wife, just a concubine; why hadn't he taken her?

Because of what Lachesis had said about Satan. If Satan had really conspired to deprive Mym first of Orb, and then of Rapture—the second plot foiled only by Mym's accession as Mars—then Mym wanted no further association with the Incarnation of Evil. Indeed, Satan had been using his agent Lila to subvert Rapture's mind, putting female-suffrage notions in her head; he was glad he had gotten her away from Lila. Was he now to be with Lila himself? Obviously not.

Finally he slept—and dreamed that Lila had come to his bed, her flesh quivering lusciously. He woke, angry, and found himself alone. And could not get to sleep again.

The next action requiring his attention was in Cush, a kingdom in Africa. It seemed that a tribe of Nubians in its northern section were rebelling and that the government was using its troops to combat this uprising.

Of course it was more complicated than that, because Mars did not need to supervise every battle personally, any more than

Thanatos needed to supervise every death personally. It was only when something special was happening that he had to attend. Wars and battles were going on continually in scattered regions of the world; if they ever all stopped at one time, Mym would be retired.

"So what's the situation, this time?" he asked Conquest as they rode to the site.

"Interesting that you should say 'this time,'" the white-cloaked Incarnation replied. "It does seem to involve time, though we aren't sure how."

The subsidiary Incarnations never seemed to have full information; Mym realized that that was probably one reason they *were* subsidiary. It would be up to him, again, to ascertain the precise situation and decide what action should be taken. If it really involved time, he would have to consult with Chronos.

They came down to Earth and galloped across the hot terrain. The earth was sere and barren; there had been a bad drought, destroying the crops. What a time to fight a war!

They arrived at the site. The battle was about to begin; the government troops were converging on a rebel site. There were mounds and trenches around the village, so it was evidently defended. But there was no sign of anything unusual.

"I will investigate," Mym said. He dismounted and strode across to the village perimeter.

He stepped down into the first defensive emplacement he saw and phased in to the man there. The initial confusion was milder and shorter than before; he was learning how to minimize this, as he gained experience. In just a few minutes he identified reasonably well with the man and could understand what the man heard in his own language, though it was foreign to Mym himself.

This man had been a small farmer, doing not well but adequately, back in the years when the weather was better and the crops grew satisfactorily. Then the government had been taken over by the Communists and American aid had stopped and the drought had come, making it impossible to farm effectively. This man's farm had not made its quotas and had been expropriated; rather than serve as a laborer on what he had once owned, he had joined the opposition. Many others had done the same. But the same government that said it lacked the resources to hire magic for rainmaking to save the crops seemed to have plenty of resources to send troops to harass the common folk who tried to stand up for their rights.

The only weapon this man had was a spear, while the soldiers had rifles. He was hungry, while they were well fed. But he knew he was right, while they were wrong, and he had nothing left to lose. His children had starved to death, and his wife had died of dysentery. He had survived only because, as part of the rebellion, he had been a position to capture and pillage a government outpost. He had carried two pounds of grain back to his wife, only to discover that the weeks he had been in the field had been too long, and she was dead. Friends had taken care of the disposition of the body, and for that much he was grateful. He had seen what dysentery did to others—the pain, the vomiting, the blood-suffused diarrhea. The thought of seeing his wife like that, and of being unable to help her—no, it was better that he had been spared that.

But the troops that were to come at him! He would glory in *their* blood! He hoped to take several with him before he died. He knew that their bullets would make holes in his body, but he also knew that the first shot was seldom immediately fatal. He steeled himself to keep going, no matter what the pain, until he could ram his spearpoint into the eye of the enemy, and into the eye of a second if he could, and a third. Whatever he could manage before he dropped, that would be good enough. He knew that on either side of him his companions in the defense of their common soil were similarly determined. Their last supplies of food had been exhausted the day before, despite fractional rations; honorable death was all that remained.

Now the first soldier appeared, a head bobbing near the ground, coming toward him. If only he had a gun, he could put a bullet through it now, if he had a bullet. If he knew how to work a gun.

The bobbing head was joined by another and a third. They were coming rapidly; now they were almost upon the trench. The man braced himself for his final effort, offering up a prayer for the souls of his dead wife and children and for his own.

A stone flew from the right, striking the lead soldier on the shoulder. The hit was a nuisance, no more, but the soldier turned to fire at the source—and didn't watch where his feet were going.

As a result, he stumbled right into the trench, issuing a cry of dismay as he fell.

This was so unexpected that the defender did not know what to do. He squatted there, staring at the soldier. The soldier, disheveled but not hurt, hauled his face out of the dirt and brought his rifle around.

Mym acted. He lifted the spear and jammed it in the soldier's exposed ear, hard. The point broke off, for it was a flimsy, homemade weapon, but the effort sufficed; the soldier gave one hoarse scream and collapsed, blood welling out around the wound.

Mym stepped forward and caught the rifle. His experienced eye identified it as of obsolescent design, of such ancient vintage as to suggest the Czarist Empire, but serviceable nonetheless. He whipped it about and fired it at the next soldier coming at the trench, holing his heart. The soldier plunged, dead, into the trench. A third one appeared, and Mym put a bullet up his nose.

Then he stood and peered out across the field. More soldiers were coming, but the defensive farmers were giving a decent account of themselves and causing the soldiers to move with greater caution. "Take their rifles!" Mym called to the trenches to either side of him, forcing his thought through the brain and mouth of his host. "Get the ammunition from the bodies! Quickly! We can hold them off!" And he shot another soldier, by way of example.

"But we don't know how to use them!" one farmer protested.

"I have figured it out!" Mym responded. "Come singly to my trench, and I will show you. It's not hard and it's better than dying! There may be food—rations—on some of those bodies!"

Food! That thought cut through to the deepest need of the hungry farmers. One scrambled to join Mym, who got out new ammunition, set up his rifle, showed the man the trigger, and gave it to him. "Bring it back here when it's empty," he said; it was too complicated to explain the loading mechanism.

In this manner they soon formed a formidable cell of resistance that expanded as more rifles came on-line. The farmers were terrible shots, but the fact that there was return fire caused the soldiers to lose courage, and they began a disorderly retreat. The farmers were winning the day!

Then, abruptly, it happened. The battlefield froze. No one moved. Even the bullets became anchored in air.

Mym looked about with confusion. He had not stilled the battle! How had this come about?

Obviously this was the reason he had been brought here— someone else was using a supernatural method to stop the battle. And that party was the enemy, for now he saw a helicopter flying away. It was above the battlefield, evidently too high to be affected by the stasis. Perhaps it had dropped a time bomb, freezing time.

Mym phased out of his host, for he had to be able to move. He was not affected by the stasis, because he was an Incarnation, but his host was. He touched the Sword. "Chr-Chronos," he said, his stutter back now that he was using his own vocal equipment.

Chronos appeared, sailing down from the sky, holding his glowing Hourglass aloft. He landed beside Mym. "You have a problem, Mars?"

"When an aspect of death was used without Thanatos' approval, he objected," Mym sang. "Now an aspect of time is being used without my approval; is it with yours? If so, I must inquire why you choose to interfere in my business."

"I would not interfere," Chronos said somewhat stiffly. "I assumed it was your stasis. I have no memory of such violation."

"This is the first time it has happened," Mym sang.

"My memory is of your future," Chronos reminded him.

Oh. "And this has not happened henceforth? It must be a fluke."

"Hardly. The supernatural is not incurred as a fluke. Some mortal has discovered how to interfere with time." And, indeed, Chronos was angry, now.

"Can you discover who has done this and eliminate it?" Mym asked. "That way, you will have no memory of it because it never happens again."

"That will be an awful chore," Chronos grumbled. "I can deal with the discoverer of the stasis effect when I identify him, but that's a needle in a haystack."

"You can't just trace the time bomb itself back to its origin?"

"I will have to, though it's not the bomb I want, but the person behind it—and that person will be most carefully hidden. There may be deliberate false leads. They may not have expected

Chronos to be tracing it down, but their mundane security provisions will be devious enough."

Now trucks rumbled up to the battle area. These ones did not freeze; they parked and disgorged active men. These men advanced on the village defensive positions.

"Spot nullification!" Chronos exclaimed indignantly. "Another infringement!"

Now the strategy of it was clear to Mym. The government, having located a point of stiff resistance, had time-bombed it into stasis, then sent in special troops to nullify the enemy. Already the new troops were passing among the defenders, taking away their weapons, and restoring them to the government troops. It was obvious that when the battle resumed, the advantage would be all with the attackers. "That's outrageous!" Mym sang. "The defenders won't have any chance at all!"

"A minor matter," Chronos said. "What's important is their infringement of supernatural prerogatives."

"Oh, forget the prerogatives!" Mym snapped in song. "It's a clean device to conclude a battle without bloodshed. If it weren't so unfair, I would hardly be concerned."

"Well, I am not concerned with the 'fairness' of anything as appalling as physical combat," Chronos retorted. "But when mortals start interfering with—"

"I should think your effort would be better spent arranging for food for the starving," Mym sang, nettled by this slight on his office.

"Without your effort, and that of your cohorts, few would *be* starving," Chronos reminded him. "Look at Famine over there, eager to reap his bitter harvest!"

"I'm trying to reduce his business," Mym sang. "But there is starvation here because of the drought, not because of the war."

"We are drifting from the point," Chronos said. "We have a problem here."

True. Mym didn't want to argue with yet another Incarnation. "I was caught by surprise by this manifestation of the Void."

"The void?"

Mym smiled, "My predecessor left me a book, *Five Rings*, that aligns the basic concepts as Ground, Water, Fire, Wind, and the Void. I find myself thinking of them as the Incarnations, with my office being the fire of War, and yours being the void of eternity—no beginning and no end. It is the most difficult concept to grasp. I meant no offense."

Chronos returned the smile. "None taken, Mars. I like that concept. I shall have to look at that book, unless it has ceased to exist."

"Ceased to exist?"

"To you, a book may be published at a certain date, and exists thereafter. To me, that same date represents its cessation."

"Have no concern, Chronos! That book was written in 1645."

"Then it should indeed be available to me for some time yet. When I have leisure, I shall peruse it."

"You are welcome to borrow my copy."

"By the time I get to it, I suspect, I shall have to ask your predecessor."

"I'm sure he will agree." Mym considered for a moment. "I think I could do something to locate that man you want, because I can phase into minds and learn their thoughts."

Chronos brightened. "Yes, I had forgotten! If you would do that—"

"It might take a little time, no pun intended."

"I can give you time," Chronos said with a smile. "In fact, I could arrange for a shipment of grain to be delivered here, by changing the time frame."

"Then why don't I try to spot your man, while you see to the grain?" Mym sang, pleased. "We can do each other some good, which is the way it should be."

"The way it should be," Chronos agreed. "But first—" He lifted his Hourglass, and Mym saw the trickle of sand within it change color. The moving men froze, joining the already-frozen ones. There would be no action here until the Incarnations were finished.

Mym mounted his steed, and they trotted after the departed helicopter. The horse climbed the air as if it were a mountain; when they had sufficient elevation, Mym was able to see the flying machine in the distance. "Follow that scientific device," he told the horse.

Werre accelerated, churning up fleeting contrails as he galloped. Mym wondered whether any mortals were watching this part of the sky from below; what would they think of those cloud-lets? But probably the divots were no more visible than the horse and rider were. Mortals simply couldn't see the supernatural, ordinarily.

They overhauled the helicopter and entered it. Werre stood on its deck, part of him overlapping the wall. Of course it didn't matter; the horse related only casually to the mortal world. Otherwise his weight would have caused the helicopter to skew and lose altitude.

Mym sat in the pilot's lap and sank into his body, phasing in. Soon he was reading the thoughts. The man had no knowledge of the nature of the bomb he had dropped; he thought it was some kind of gas to immobilize the enemy. Where had he picked up the bomb? From a guarded military truck that had driven onto the military airport and departed forthwith.

Dead lead, there. But Mym knew how a military operation worked. There would have had to be clearance for that truck, and the officer in charge of airport security would know about that. So he disengaged from the pilot, remounted Werre, and headed for the airport.

As it happened, the security officer was on one of his frequent coffee breaks when Mym found him. That was no problem; Mym phased in and drank spiked coffee with him. He introduced the thought: What about that truck? Had the clearance been tight? Yes, it had been; that truck had come directly from the New Devices Lab, and all was in order.

And what did he really know about that Lab, Mym mused, inserting the thought. Well, not much, but its clearances were of the highest nature. The General in charge of it brooked no interference by any other department and was a very bad man to cross.

Mym got the name and address of the General and rode there. He didn't know how long this would take, and there was a fine green lawn outside the building—there might be a drought in the farmlands, but they found plenty of water for the military premises—so he turned Werre loose to graze and used the Sword to move himself inside.

The General was watching the battle. He had a closed-circuit television system, with pickups stationed beyond the freeze-zone, and was using his controls to switch from one camera to another.

Even with telephoto lenses he was having trouble getting a clear picture; nothing seemed to be happening.

Mym phased in and tuned in to the General's thoughts. The man was frustrated. Obviously the bomb was working—but why weren't the backup forces moving? They had nullifiers! Curse this inadequate equipment!

Mym had no sympathy for the man's frustration; he only wanted the source of the technological breakthrough. He shaped a thought and adapted it to the General's train of thoughts so that it seemed a natural bypath. Could there be some flaw in the system? What did he know about the designer? Could the man really be trusted? If the equipment had some secret liability—

The General was of a naturally paranoid turn of mind, so this thought took hold readily. He plunged into a review of what he knew about the somewhat oddball genuis who had abruptly come up with the time bomb, when the horrendously financed laboratories of nations far, far wealthier than Cush had been unable to make this breakthrough. The time bomb promised to be the key to suppression of the Nubian rebels now and conquest of the world tomorrow. But only if it worked perfectly. The individual who had devised it was, ironically, a Nubian himself, a refugee from the drought who had sought whatever employment he could get and turned out to be extraordinarily clever with electronics meshed with magic. No one else really understood what he was doing; indeed, the device seemed impossible on the face of it. But they had tested it on an isolated peaceful village, and it had worked: the villagers had remained in absolute stasis for six hours, then abruptly resumed activity as the effect wore off. They had been amazed at the sudden jump forward by the sun, not realizing that the world had lived through six hours in the seeming blink of an eye. Then came the companion discovery—how to protect men from the stasis. That had worked too.

But now they were using both for the first time in the field— and something was wrong. The protected troops seemed to have succumbed the same as the unprotected ones. If this were betrayal—

Mym phased out, having gotten what he wanted—the identity of the scientist who had made the breakthrough. The General had no notion of the technology; all he knew was that the devices worked—up to a point. The scientist was the real key.

The man was not in the lab today. He had been granted leave to work at home, because that was where he worked best. They had tried to keep him at the lab full time, but that had led to no accomplishments. Because the erratic genius was his, they had to let the man operate in his own fashion.

Mym went to the man's home. It was unpretentious, not even in the better section of the city.

The man looked just like an unemployed farmer. He was in patched, baggy clothes and he was asleep on his battered couch. This was the genius scientist?

Mym hesitated. Should he try to phase in to the sleeping man? He had never tried that before.

He lay on the man, sank into him, and phased in. He was getting expert at positioning himself so that all senses aligned, but still it always took a while to get the complete mind tuned in. The mind was much more than the physical brain, and the brain was no simple mass of tissue! Each brain had its own idiosyncratic patterns, no two even remotely similar in the cellular detail of the routines, and he simply had to discover the way of each one by guess and error.

And this one was different, not in configuration, but because it was asleep. Sleep was a whole new mode. Furthermore, it was dreaming. It was hard enough to adjust to the particular brain and mind, but harder yet to grasp that alternate reality that was the dream state. Some folk presumed that dreams were simply an alternate consciousness, governed by the same rules as those of the waking state, as if the person merely stopped from one room into another. It was not so!

Mym was the man—and the man was walking through a section of a park. There was an overhanging tree, its branch seeming very large and heavy. Then there was a face, the face of a woman, eclipsing the tree; in fact the tree was gone, sloughed off without further attention. The woman was the man's mother. But she was dead—and now there was a gravesite, and across it walked a bird of some sort. And now a bowl of rice, but there was not enough; the bowl was almost empty. Memory of hunger surged up—years of hunger. A dog appeared—and a stone flung out, catching the dog on the rump, and it ran away. Anger; the animal had escaped. Poor aim; the stone should have struck its head, knocking it out. Water, a large lake, remembered from long ago, a wonder re-doubled in this time of drought.

Mym realized that he was seeing the cuttings from an idling consciousness—those snippets of information and memory and feeling that bobble about just below the surface of thought, as if awaiting their opportunity to be drawn to full examination, and sometimes breaking through when the critical mind was relaxing. The conscious mind tried to make sense of these almost-random bits, forming them into dreams, but that sense was nonsense, like forming a story from random words, meaning sometimes seeming to manifest, but illusory. He could not afford to drift along with this; he had to discover how this man had made the time bomb breakthroughs.

So he inserted his own thought of the bomb and watched while it had its effect on the mélange. The bomb—a dream, in this case a dream within a dream, a memory of that. Sleep, and dream of hearing a call and walking toward it and discovering a door in the wall, one that had not been there before. Opening that door, en-tering a passage with a glow at the far end. This was working beautifully; it was a familiar memory, that played itself off when triggered. Walking toward that glow, discovering it to emanate from a book, *Success*, written in some unknown language, but in the dream he could read it as if it were his own, realizing that the pages of this book contained all that a man might need to know about improving his condition. He put his hand to the cover— and drew it away, for the cover was burning hot. Indeed, flames surrounded the volume; it was from them that the glow came. But he knew that there was no other way to read the book, and that if he did not do so now, he might never have another chance. So he nerved himself and touched the cover again, and lifted it, and the flame wrapped about his hand and burned it hideously, destroying it, but now the book was open, and there were the words that would facilitate his destiny of success. And they were the words of the formula for the time bomb.

He read them, though he was illiterate, and they burned their impressions on the inner surface of his skull, never to be forgot-ten. He retreated and in a moment he was back in his own room.

The dream faded out, and his hand was whole again, but the seared image in his skull remained.

Mym pondered, slightly shaken by the intensity of this borrowed experience. He was not illiterate; that was the farmer. But what was the true source of the information? The farmer could not have developed it from his own subconscious; the technical information was far too sophisticated.

But the formula for the time bomb was only part of it. What of the spot nullifier?

Mym nudged the sleeper toward that, and the remembered dream returned. It was similar to the first. The call came in the dream within a dream, and the door in the wall appeared. He entered and walked down the sinister passage—and his right hand became a charred mass, its malady restored. He came to the dread book, *Success,* the alien word intelligible even to the illiterate, fire reaching up from it. The right hand was useless; he had to use the left to lift the cover, and when he did that, the flame scorched it into charcoal. But the words were there, different words, and the fire of their formulation reached in through his eyeballs and singed their imprints on the interior of his skull. Now he possessed the nullifier, and the magic was complete.

He backed away and emerged again, and once more his hands were restored, and he was awake, with the letters of fire against his pulsing brain. All he had to do was repeat those twin formulas to those who could interpret and apply them, and success was his.

Mym knew that the man had done so. He now had the excellent life he had desired. Yet now that he had it, it seemed somehow inadequate. He could not tell anyone beyond the secret project of his significance, because that would make him a target for enemy agents, so he had to pretend to be no more than a simple farmer who had come into wealth. That was unsatisfying. He desired acclaim. He wanted beautiful women to seek him for his personal attributes and charm. He wanted the heads of state to consult him, to take him seriously, and to compliment him on his knowledge.

Mym recognized the problem. The farmer had been bitten by the worm of desire for fame and could not be satisfied with only part of it. He was driven to seek more than he had, more than success.

Perhaps stirred by Mym's realization, the dreamer entered a new phase. The dream within a dream formed.

"I wouldn't do that," Mym said in the dream. But the dreamer shrugged him off. The worm of ambition was too strong; its poison had spread too far. It could not be denied.

Mym withdrew himself from the dreamer. He watched as the man made walking motions with his legs, and door-opening motions with his hands. Then more walking—and the two hands curled up as if de-nerved, becoming useless claws.

There was a pause, and Mym realized why; the man was trying to figure out how to open the magic volume of Success when both his hands were useless husks. After a moment, one leg stirred; he was lifting the cover with a toe.

Mym did not stay. He could see the progression: each additional piece of information would cost a part of the body. After both feet were gone, the man would have to open the book with his teeth, and his head would be incinerated. That would be the end of him; his mundane body might seem unchanged, but his mind would be dead.

Mym summoned Werre, mounted, and returned to the site of the battle. Chronos was there, waiting for him.

"I thought you were going to go facilitate a shipment of grain!" Mym sang, half-challengingly.

"I did—last week," Chronos replied.

"But it has only been a few hours!"

"You forget my nature."

Now Mym remembered Chronos was the Incarnation of Time. Chronos could step into last week and return to the present. "Where is the shipment, then?"

Chronos sighed. "I did what I could do, but found myself balked by a greater power."

"What power is that?" Mym asked, alarmed.

"Human corruption." And Chronos explained. He had found the bottleneck, manifested, and by dint of some fast talking gotten the train moving toward its destination—only to have it held up at the next station by officials who were determined to collect a decimating tax on its wares. This was a relief train, not taxable, but they affected not to understand that, and unloaded a segment of its cargo. The same thing happened further down the line. At every stop, more was taken, until the train was empty—before reaching its destination. Corrupt officials had stolen the entire cargo. Against this, Chronos was powerless; he could manipulate time, but time was not the problem here. Human greed was. Greed had defeated Time. The grain was now being sold on the black market; none of it would reach the starving folk for whom it had been intended.

"But the government!" Mym protested. "It should be protecting the train, not robbing it!"

"When the train is destined for a segment of the country that is in rebellion against that government?" Chronos asked.

There, of course, was the underlying reason. The government would not permit a rebellious province to be fed, for that could strengthen the rebellion. So it permitted the graft while protesting innocence.

Mym clenched his fist. "There *is* justification in war!" he sang. "To abolish governments like that!"

"Perhaps so," Chronos agreed. "It is a thesis you have made to me before."

"I have?" Mym asked, startled.

Chronos smiled. "In future years, your framework." Then he frowned. "I regret I have not fulfilled my part of the bargain. Therefore if you—"

"No, you made an honest effort," Mym sang. He was learning more about the limitations of the Incarnations when meddling in human affairs. Mortals could be so determinedly short-sighted and wrong-headed! Were they really worth helping? "I have discovered the source of the technological breakthroughs on the manipulation of time—or part of it. A man had a series of visions or dreams that revealed the key formulas to him. Eliminate that man slightly before he eliminates himself, and there will be no breakthroughs."

"Not a scientist?" Chronos asked, surprised.

"Not a scientist. He dreams of a special chamber in which is a fiery book labeled *Success*, and it burns him when he takes the information."

Chronos frowned. "All in a vision? That seems familiar."

"Oh? How?"

Chronos shook his head. "I—suspect I should not burden you with my conjecture, as I am drawing on memories in your future. Let me just say that I am not sanguine about this."

Mym shrugged. Chronos' incidental revelations about the future had confused him before; probably it was indeed best to let this matter drop.

But what was he to do about the battle that remained frozen? He chewed on his lip as he looked out over it.

"Do not be concerned," Chronos said. "When I eliminate the breakthrough, none of this will have happened. You may supervise the battle as you choose."

Mym wasn't sure quite how that would work, but was willing to find out. "Very well." He described the location of the key man.

Abruptly the battle resumed—but not as it had been. This time the defending farmers were getting the best of it, and no time bomb dropped.

"You prefer this?" Chronos inquired.

Obviously the man had been at work, traveling back and forth in time. Now reality had changed, at least for this region. The breakthrough had never happened.

Mym shook his head. "I think I have had enough of battle for today—even if none of it happened. I'm going home."

"This is the way it often is in my domain," Chronos said.

Mym wondered how the man maintained his sanity. Who could guess what convolutions Chronos had endured—that never happened? He made a gesture of camaraderie and mounted Werre.

– 12 –

GAEA

Rapture was away increasingly as time passed. She was very positive about her mortal job and seemed to be doing well, but it apparently made considerable demands on her. Mym was glad that she had adjusted so well, but the frequent nights alone bothered him.

Naturally Lila was available. When he couldn't sleep, he took walks in the garden, and she was always there. Of course she was ready, willing, and able to serve as his concubine, but a complex of considerations prevented him from exercising this option. For one thing, she was from Hell, and he still distrusted the creatures of Satan on general principle. For another, he was becoming uncertain of Rapture, and that made him less rather than more inclined to use another woman. Had Rapture been solidly established and pregnant, it would have been virtually his duty to use a concubine, so as not to place demands on the bearer of his Heir; as it was, a concubine was premature. His seed needed to be saved for the Heir, rather than expended frivolously. So to use a concubine at this stage might be to suggest that he did not desire Rapture or seek an Heir, and that was not the case. Also, and this was an insidious consideration, he was not certain that Lila was a virgin. It was, of course, necessary for a man to know a number of women, as no single woman could provide essential variety, but it was important that a woman know only one man. It would demean his princely heritage if he were to consort with an unchaste woman. The creatures of Satan, by all accounts, were of questionable pedigree, and their forms here in the spirit realm were malleable, so Lila well might be a pseudovirgin.

His pride kept him from making application to the Purgatory front office for a legitimate concubine, because of the problem with Rapture. Thus he was caught without adequate service in this respect. That was what made Lila so infernally tempting, as well she knew.

"Alone yet again tonight?" she inquired dulcetly, appearing ahead of him as he passed the copulating statue. "Maybe you should bring your fiancée back here."

"Where she can be corrupted by your occidental notions of female suffrage!" Mym snapped. As always, he found pleasure in the ability to speak without stuttering, here.

"But Mym, she's a mortal," Lila said. "You brought her out of her oriental situation and planted her in the West. Things are different here. Women are supposed to have minds of their own."

"For what?" he demanded. "Rapture was already well-versed in what she needed to know."

"For pleasing a man and bearing a son," she agreed. "But what about her own fulfillment?" She stretched her arms out and up, so that her gown opened in front to reveal the perfect globes of her breasts, lifting with her motion. She was very like a statue in contour.

"That *is* her own fulfillment!" he retorted.

"Not in this hemisphere," she said, coincidentally touching one of her own. "It would be grand for a creature like me, but not for a mortal like her. She needs to assert herself, to branch out, to explore her larger potential."

"So speaks a creature of Hell."

"I may be damned, Mym, but I'm not ignorant. I have learned common sense the hard way." She bent to adjust her fastenings, in the process exposing one leg up through the plush buttock.

"Not as I see it!" he said, and strode out of the garden.

But alone in bed, he did curse himself for foolishness. Why should he allow the words of a Hell-slut to bother him? The opinions of women mattered little, and those of a pseudowoman even less. Why hadn't he simply used her for her explicit purpose and not listened to her at all? Discussion, after all, was no necessary part of sexual fulfillment.

Of course he could return to the garden and do that now or simply summon Lila here to the castle. He could do anything he wanted with her and banish her without notice. That was the obvious and sensible course. That flesh she had arranged to show him—he knew that though she was of the spirit world, that body would feel completely solid and alive. She was, indeed, designed to satisfy the lust of a man.

But that would mean a kind of capitulation, and that he could not abide. So he suffered alone. He was Mars, an Incarnation, dedicated to settling the quarrels of mortals efficiently, yet he could not settle his own.

When Rapture showed up again, the change was more apparent. She was not satisfied to remain placidly in bed; she wanted to converse about unrelated things. She was full of detail about the students she was helping to educate and their interest in the quaint customs of the Orient, where science was little practiced. She now had classes at all levels, ranging from adult to juvenile. She loved the experience of independence, of being able to make decisions based purely on her own preferences. She was developing a confidence in herself and her individual worth she had never before experienced. She was acquiring an occidental wardrobe, so that she could avoid being taken for an Indian at times when she preferred to be herself. She even wore jeans in public.

"What?" Mym demanded.

"Trousers fashioned of denim material, blue in hue," she explained. "Very convenient and comfortable for—"

"For laborers!" he exclaimed in singsong. "Not for princesses!"

"I am no longer a princess," she reminded him, quite undisturbed by the demotion.

"I have seen the occidental women in those abominations!" he sang. "Their posteriors practically rip open the fabric!"

"Yes, that is one of the appealing aspects," she agreed.

"For every passing male to see!" he concluded indignantly.

"They don't object," she pointed out. "In fact, I have received some compliments."

"You are *my* woman!" he raged. "Only I should see such detail in you!"

She laughed. "Where do you think you are, Mym? In archaic India? In the Western world, the wealth is shared."

"Are you sure you haven't been talking with the demoness?"

"Lila? No, I haven't seen her since I moved to the mortal realm. But I have been learning about the real world, Mym."

"I think you had better resign that job and return here."

"I will do no such thing!" she exclaimed. "I am supremely happy with my new life. For the first time, I feel genuinely independent and useful, and I know they need me at the museum."

"I need you *here!*"

"Oh, pooh! You have everything you need without me."

"I do not! I spend too many nights alone."

"Alone? What happened to Lila?"

"I haven't touched her."

"Whyever not, Mym? She's your concubine."

"I don't want a concubine, I want you!"

She smiled. "That's sweet. But no need to go to extremes. When I'm not here, use the damned concubine."

Mym was shocked, at her language as much as her sentiment. He wasn't certain whether she was swearing in the occidental fashion, or referring to the status of a creature of Hell, or both.

"Well, let's get this over with," Rapture said, and moved her beautiful body against him.

Get this over with? What did that imply? But he realized that further dialogue might only result in his having to spend another night alone, so he let it pass.

The business of Mars became routine. Mym remained somewhat dissatisfied with the details of it and with the passions of the lesser Incarnations he had to associate with, but he was satisfied that, to an increasing extent, he was bringing war under control and permitting it to wreak less havoc among the mortals than would have been the case without his supervision. There were indeed causes that deserved promotion and that could achieve it only by violence. War, properly managed, was certainly better than the alternatives of oppression or dispossession. But how much better it would be if the causes of war did not exist! If mortal man could simply exist in peace and harmony and plenty, requiring no Incarnation to supervise his violence.

But the mortal realm was as it was, and human nature was intractable. Therefore the various Incarnations were required, and Mym was satisfied to perform this necessary office. It was not his job that bothered him, but his home life.

That proceeded from unsatisfying to disastrous, in a single step.

Rapture appeared and dropped it on him. "Mym, I'm leaving you," she said abruptly.

"W-w-w-what?"

"I have found a nice mortal man, and I'm going to move in with him."

"Y-y-y—" Mym remembered his singsong and invoked it. "You're marrying a mortal?"

"No. I am moving in with him. If it works out, then maybe I'll marry him, but there are no commitments yet."

"But you are *my* woman!" Mym protested.

"Not any more, Mym," she said. "We have grown apart, since you became Mars; you have your life, and I have found mine. It is best that we recognize this and take proper action now."

"I won't let you go!" he protested. "I love you!"

"What will you do—make war on me?" She smiled compassionately. "Mym, you never loved me; you loved my body and my complete dependence on you. I loved your appreciation of me. But I don't love your present position, and if I am to be a sex object, I prefer to be it as an independent agent. So it is better with John than it is with you, and I am simply recognizing that fact. I hope this parting of our ways can be amicable, but amicable or not, it is occurring."

If Rapture had been dependent, she was so no more! Mym was so angry at this betrayal that he could not even speak in singsong.

"Well, farewell," she said, and turned and walked away. Now Mym saw Thanatos in the adjacent chamber, ready to convey Rapture back to the realm of the mortals. She had come only to inform Mym of her decision.

Mym tasted blood in his mouth. In his rage he had bitten his tongue. Now that blood was triggering a rage of a different nature. He would deal with this "John" of hers!

He grasped the Red Sword and willed himself to the mortal realm. He knew where Rapture worked and where she lived; from there he should be able to trace this mortal man John.

But then he paused. Was he, the Incarnation of War, to exert his power in a purely selfish, negative way? To hurt the one he loved, or had loved, or thought he had loved? How much of his ideal of peace would he be spreading that way? And this John—surely an innocent young man, for Rapture would not have told a mortal about her relation to an immortal. A man who liked Rapture very well, who probably needed her more than she needed him, and wanted to get to know her as well as he could.

Mym reversed his course. No, he had no need and no desire to hurt Rapture or her friend. He would set the example that he wished mortals would follow and accept the inevitable with what grace he could muster.

He returned to his castle and walked in the garden, severely out of sorts. It was true that he and Rapture had been growing apart, and her initiative had been valid. But he had discovered the joy of loving and being loved with Orb and rediscovered it with Rapture; he could no longer countenance being alone.

Orb. Where was she now?

Lila appeared. "So she dumped you," she said.

Damn her! Except that she was already damned. "No thanks to you, demoness," he said.

"She wasn't right for you anyway," Lila said. "Maybe she was when you were playing the Prince-Princess game among the mortals, but not for this situation. You need a woman who understands about Incarnations."

"True. I shall look for one."

She smiled, inhaling. She now wore one of her translucent outfits that were more maddeningly suggestive than full nudity would have been. "No mortal will do, Mym. You need one who is committed to the Afterlife."

"Thanatos seems to do well enough with a mortal."

"Thanatos has a quite remarkable mortal. There is not another like Luna."

"You err, demoness. There is her cousin Orb."

Lila shrugged eloquently. "That's right. You had an affair with her, didn't you! But that's long over, and you can't go back."

"I'm not so sure. I loved her before, and she loved me. I could love her again."

Lila paced in front of him, allowing her flesh to quiver provocatively. "You finished that relationship when you deserted her for another woman."

"That was not my choice!"

"Nevertheless, you left her in a rather difficult situation. You see, she was gravid."

"Gravid?"

"With child. It happens to mortals, you know."

"Pregnant? She couldn't have been!"

"Verify it in Fate's threads, Mym. She was carrying your baby girl and she bore her after you left and gave her up for adoption. That rather finished that aspect of your romance. I doubt very much that she would choose to go through that again."

"But she never said anything to me!"

"She didn't know it when you deserted her."

Mym was stricken. "If I had known!"

"Fortunately, creatures of the Afterlife don't get gravid. With them, it's all pleasure, no consequence. So why don't you become sensible and do what you have been longing to do for so long?" She shimmered, and her clothing dissolved into mist. She opened her arms. "I can be most accommodating, Mym, and I make no demands."

He looked at her. This creature of Hell seemed on the verge of victory at last. Her body was beautiful, but her nature demonic. He trusted her to serve her master, and her master was Satan.

He tasted the blood in his mouth again. This time he let the berserker reflex take over.

Abruptly he was moving. His great Red Sword was out and whistling. It lopped off her head. The head flew up, its face surprised; the body remained standing. There was no blood.

The Sword whistled back. It lopped off the upper arms and the top of the torso cleanly at the line of the breasts. The shoulders rose, and the neck and the tops of the two breasts, also bloodlessly. The nether sections of the breasts resembled two bowls filled precisely level with gray stuffing. Both sections of that bosom were expanding, for Lila had been inhaling at the moment of his attack.

Again the Sword passed through, severing the body at the slender waist. And again, at the genital region, and at the knees. Five swift cuts, and the body was tumbling in six major segments, which in turn were fragmenting as the separate arms and legs fell skew. In a moment there was simply a collection of items on the ground.

"In this manner, too, I am ready to serve you," the head said. It was lying to the side, where it had bounced and rolled. The truncated neck was up, the face inverted.

"I just want to be rid of you!" Mym gritted.

"Then stuff my parts in a trunk and ship it straight to Hell," the head said.

"I have no trunk." Mym was looking at his Sword and finding no blood on the blade. His berserker rage had faded, being replaced by bemusement. He had known that demons differed from people, but had not been quite prepared for this.

"Use the base of the statue."

Mym went to the copulating statue and hacked off its figures. The pedestal now manifested as a hollow chamber. He sheathed the Sword and wrestled this up. It was indeed about the configuration of a coffin.

He picked up a piece of torso and dumped it in the chest. The piece was like warm wax, firm but slightly soft, the flat cut side no different from the exterior. Obviously Lila had had no digestive apparatus, no circulatory system, and no respiratory system. She was simply a shape formed of pseudoflesh, a body without a person.

Yet she had walked and talked and seemed alive. She had sewn mischief with Rapture, and much of what she said made infernal sense. She was not a person, obviously—yet she was also not inanimate matter. What, then, was she?

He paused, with the upper and lower sections of a leg. He tried fitting them together. They fused, forming the full leg.

"You may put me together again if you wish," the head said. "One more section, and you will be reaching interesting territory."

Mym dropped the leg into the chest. He picked up the pieces

of the other leg, and the arms. Then he got to the section of the torso from the waist to the mid-bosom. It was amazing how full and firm those half breasts were, as far as they went.

"Or you could reassemble just that portion of me you wish to use," the head suggested.

He dumped the half bust in. "I prefer a genuine woman."

"A genuine woman would dump you in favor of a mortal man," the head retorted. "Here in the Afterlife, you need a woman of the Afterlife."

There was that insidious logic of hers. What she said made more sense than he cared to accept. He had to try to refute it. "I am not of the Afterlife; I am a mortal in temporary residence. I need a woman in similar circumstance."

"That, too, can be provided," the head said.

Mym finished dumping the rest of the body in the chest, but hesitated to pick up the head itself. So he talked to it a moment more. "How can such a thing be provided?"

"You could take up with a female Incarnation. The youngest aspect of Fate, called Clotho, is known to be obliging."

Mym visualized the young, pretty Oriental, Clotho. The notion appealed. But then he remembered the far more mature Lachesis, actually the same Incarnation in different form. Surely the minds of Fate were the same, though the body changed. In that sense, she was no better than the demoness. A young and innocent body with an experienced and cynical mind was not what a man really desired in a woman. Also, Fate surely had associations of her own and would not necessarily be eager to take up with a man like him.

"Then there's—but, of course, you wouldn't be interested in her," the head remarked.

An obvious ploy! But Mym still was not eager to pick up the talking head, so he accepted the ploy. "Who?"

"She's a damsel, a princess, locked in a castle of frozen mist, unable to escape because no one cares about her. But, of course, that's none of your business."

"Who is she?"

"Her name's Ligeia. But—"

"Why was she put there?"

"It's her penalty for the mischief she did in life."

"Oh—she's another demoness."

"No. She's a damned soul."

"There's a distinction?"

The head laughed. "Certainly there is! Demons are creatures of Hell, who serve My Lord Satan implicitly. They are constructs of ether with no living processes, exactly as you see in my flesh here. Souls are the immortal essences of mortal beings; they share the consciousness, intellects, and feelings of mortals, but no longer have mortal existence."

"Like the staff of the Castle of War," Mym agreed. "But since they *aren't* mortals, they are hopelessly committed to the Afterlife and are no better for my purpose than are you demons."

"True. But Ligeia is a special case. She was improperly damned, and if she could only get a fair hearing, she might be reclassified."

"Why can't she get a hearing?"

"A *fair* hearing. There are hearings aplenty in Hell, but they aren't fair. Every time she tries to present her case, they laugh at her. She must be pretty upset by now. I think she'd really be appreciative if someone with some power were to take up her case. But of course, if she got her fair hearing, and won reprieve, she'd only go to Heaven, so that would be the end of that. There's no point in someone like you getting involved with her."

Mym was sure by Lila's attitude that she wanted him to get involved with Ligeia, so he reacted negatively. "I agree," he said, and caught up a trailing strand of hair and lifted the head by it and swung it into the chest. "Now how do I ship this to Hell?"

"Simply address it for the destination," the head said. The words were somewhat muffled, because the face was now down.

"To Hell with you!" Mym said.

The chest and its contents exploded. A dense cloud of smoke puffed out. When it dissipated, the chest was gone.

The next call for the supervision of Mars was in Ireland. When Mym arrived with his grim entourage, he surveyed the situation in his usual fashion and learned that the Hibernian Army, a revolutionary organization, had used gene-splicing technology to develop a virus that affected only Protestants. They were about to loose a plague that would either kill or greatly debilitate those it infected. The HA would not even have to fight; they would simply take over after the plague had done its grisly work.

"Isn't this phenomenal!" the Incarnation of Pestilence exclaimed. "It has been long since I have had the opportunity to supervise a dread plague!"

"Gene-splicing," Mym murmured thoughtfully. "I have a feeling Gaea will be on this, if I don't check it with her first." He put a hold on the action, mounted Werre, and headed for the residence of the Incarnation of Nature.

But when they reached the Green Mother's estate in Purgatory, they encountered an enormous moat that shielded it from intrusion. Mym sought to have Werre simply hurdle it or trot across it, but the palomino shied away.

"What is this?" Mym asked the horse. "There is nothing in the world that you can't traverse."

But Werre simply neighed in negation. Mym remembered that this was not the world; it was Purgatory, a region of different rules. This moat might be enchanted to balk equines.

He dismounted and stepped to the bank. Immediately a weird sort of fish swam close. No, not a fish; it had the legs and lower torso of a man. But above the waistline it possessed the fins and gills of a fish, and its mouth was full of teeth.

"A manmer," Mym murmured. He had never seen one in the flesh before, but there was no mistaking the crossbreed. A merman had the top section of a man and the tail of a fish; the manmer was the opposite. While it was possible to get along with mermen and mermaids, and maidmers could be tolerably good company if one's interest was not in faces, manmers were said to have the worst elements of each species. They were brainlessly vicious, existing only to tear apart victims.

Mym made as if to touch the water with his boot, and the manmer snapped as it so violently that a spray of water and sparks went up. No question, this monster meant business.

He pondered, then touched the Sword. "Gaea," he sang.

The woman did not appear. Instead a colorful parrot flew in. "Who seeks? Who seeks?" the bird demanded.

"Mars seeks Gaea," Mym replied, annoyed.

"Prove it! Prove it!" the parrot squawked.

"You birdbrain, don't you see me?"

"I see a hundred like you every day," the parrot replied. "All fakes sent by Satan to pester my mistress."

A hundred like him a day? Suddenly Mym realized that Satan was up to more mischief, trying to infiltrate his demon minions into Nature's domain by imitating the Incarnations. No wonder Gaea had instituted defensive measures. "Go tell Gaea and she can verify for herself my validity."

"The Green Mother is busy with her own concerns; she can not waste her time exposing every imposter."

That, too, made sense. "How can I prove my identity to you, so that you will advise her of my presence?"

"Get in to see her yourself," the parrot squawked. "Only a true Incarnation can do that." And it flew away.

Mym sighed. Right when he needed to consult with Gaea, Satan had set up an interference pattern. Unfortunate timing.

Unfortunate? No, maybe Satan had planned it that way, to prevent Mym from completing the consultation, so that Gaea would not be alerted, and the plague would not be halted before it ravaged the Protestants.

That meant that it was doubly important that he get through. He was really opposing Satan, not Gaea.

But the manmer waited with eager teeth. Though Mym knew himself to be invulnerable to mortal attack, he was not at all sure about the present situation. If an immortal were invulnerable to the teeth of the manmer, the demons would be able to get through. Certainly Werre didn't trust his flesh to that water, and there was evidently a spell to prevent the horse from leaping or flying over the moat. Mym didn't care to risk his flesh that way.

Well, he could still pass. He drew the Red Sword. "I regret this, Manmer," he said. "But I'm going to have to slay you in order to pass."

But still he hesitated. Demons could wield swords, too, and would certainly be willing. Why hadn't they done so?

The more he considered, the less easy he became. Finally he picked up a loose stone and threw it across the moat.

At the far bank, the stone exploded. Something had destroyed it.

That something was apt to do the same thing to a man or a demon. Again, it wasn't worth risking. Also, he really didn't want to slay a creature, the manmer, who was only doing the job it had been assigned.

But how was he supposed to pass, if a demon could not? There had to be a way, or this was no valid test for his identity.

He considered, and decided that he would have to do some perhaps unpleasant research. He got down beside the water and, when the manmer snapped at him, he put one discorporate hand into the creature itself. Startled, the fishman paused in place, and Mym dropped the rest of his body onto it and into it. His arms aligned with the fins, his head with its head, his legs with its legs. He had phased in, physically.

He adjusted his brain, getting it aligned with the brain of the monster. He had become accomplished at this maneuver, but this was a special challenge, for this was the brain of a fish. Only the most primitive aspects of his brain could align properly; there simply was no higher center in the fish's head to match his own.

Fortunately very little identification was required. The instructions for the manmer were uppermost in its limited mind, and Mym assimilated them before he got fairly into the rest of the creature's identity.

There was a grating in the bottom of the moat. When the water turned cloudy, that grating became permeable; it was possible to swim through it. Of course Cutefoot would consume any person or creature who tried—except for the one who addressed him by his name. That one, and that one only, he would suffer to pass.

That sufficed. Mym withdrew from the manmer and splashed through the water, back to shore. It took the manmer a moment to realize that someone was there; then he acted. But Mym was already scrambling clear.

Werre was waiting for him. "Loyal steed, I must proceed alone from this point," Mym informed him. "Return to the Castle of War; I will summon you when my business here is done."

Werre neighed, wheeled about, and galloped away. That was one intelligent steed; the like hardly existed in the mortal realm. Mym realized that this was a significant part of what he liked about this office—the possession of truly competent accoutrements like the Sword and Warhorse.

Mym gazed into the moat. Yes, deep down he spied the grate;

the water was clear, so he could see it. All he had to do was wait until it clouded.

There was the sound of hooves. Mym glanced back, and saw a golden palomino approaching, bearing a golden-cloaked rider.

That was Mars! Rather, it was a demon disguised as Mars; Mym was in a position to know that it was not the genuine Incarnation. He had better get past this moat before the demon arrived.

But the water remained clear. He could not afford to enter it yet. He could stop the manmer by speaking his name, but would not be able to pass the grate. He had to wait.

Another figure galloped up, just like the first. The parrot had been correct: there were demons all over. No wonder the Green Mother had gotten fed up with it. He had to move on through, before a crowd of them gathered and made that impossible. But still the water was clear.

The first demon arrived. "Ho, miscreant!" it cried challengingly. "Dare you assume my image? Begone, imposter!"

The sheer audacity of this challenge put Mym into an instant rage. Suddenly the Red Sword was in his hand and whistling through the air. The demon-horse's head flew off, then a segment of its neck, then the top half of the rider. As with Lila, there was not blood; it was as if the sections had been fashioned separately and set together, and now were falling apart again. The demon's upper body splashed into the moat and sank.

The water swirled as the manmer went after the fragment. The vicious teeth slashed out, cutting the demon substance into lesser fragments. The action moved down as the fragments sank; the manmer meant to consume it all. The muck of the bottom was stirred up, clouding the water.

"Ho, miscreant!" the second demon challenged.

Mym looked up. The thing was charging down on him, sword swinging. Behind it, three more were coming, all identical.

Damn them! Literally! Mym lifted the Sword—and paused.

The water of the moat was cloudy.

He turned, sheathing the sword. He dived into the water. "Cutefoot!" he cried just before he splashed.

The manmer froze in place, letting him pass. He stroked down to the nether grate and through it, the bars seeming insubstantial. He passed into a submarine cave that extended forward.

There was no surface here, so he could not take a breath, but he was in no discomfort. He realized that as an Incarnation he could not drown, for he could not be killed. Breathing was now mere reflex and convenience, as was eating.

In due course, the cavern surfaced, and he emerged into the garden estate of the Green Mother. It was lovely. Shrubs and trees of every description flourished, and flowers abounded. Squirrels jumped from branch to branch, and a chipmunk nibbled at a nut atop a boulder. This would be a most pleasant place simply to remain.

But he had business. Mym forged on, following a path that led toward the center of the estate.

Soon he came to a narrowing of the way. Rocks rose up on either side, squeezing the path between them. In the center of the narrowest section stood a small lizard.

Mym paused. There was something about that little creature. It was not afraid of him, and it eyed him with a disturbing alertness. It was dull red, actually rather pretty, and reminded him of—

Of fire. This was not necessarily any lizard; it could be a salamander.

He reached to the side and found a section of an old branch. He heaved this toward the creature.

The tiny reptile leaped up to intercept the branch, biting at it. As contact was made, the wood burst into flame. It burned explosively. By the time it struck the ground, it was a mass of charcoal and ash that quickly smoldered into dust.

That was a salamander, all right. A creature who set fire to whatever it touched, other than the ground it stood on—fire that burned until only ash remained.

If he tried to pass that creature, and it bit him, he would burn similarly.

Of course he was an Incarnation, he reminded himself, immune to mortal threats. But again he remembered that this was not the mortal realm; this was Gaea's garden, where other rules governed. If this creature could prevent a demon from passing, it might as readily prevent an Incarnation too.

"But there are no demons here," he muttered in singsong.

A figure appeared behind him. "Ho, miscreant!" it cried.

"How the hell did you get here?" Mym demanded, startled and angry.

"I said the same magic word you did, so the fishman let me pass," the Mars-demon replied. "Now defend yourself, imposter!" And it charged, sword swinging.

Mym ducked. The demon stumbled over his hunched body and tumbled into the salamander.

There was a flare of flame. "Aiii! I burn!" the thing cried. Then the form became a structure of ashes and collapsed.

"One demon, returned to Hell," Mym sang. He felt no regret, knowing that these beings lacked any aspect of humanity, apart from their outer semblance.

But how foolish he had been, to utter the manmer's name in the presence of a demon. Naturally the demon had heard, copied, and gotten through.

Well, the demon was gone now. All Mym had to do was figure out how to get by the salamander.

"Ho, miscreant!"

What, another demon? Mym realized belatedly that what one could copy, another could. There could be any number of demons here in the garden, thanks to his carelessness. It was a good thing that the Green Mother had had the foresight to place a second barrier.

The demon charged. This time Mym dodged out of the way, squeezing by so that the demon found itself advancing directly on the salamander. Let the demon be destroyed the way the other was!

"So, salamander!" the demon cried. "I shall deal with you!" And it swung the blade of the red sword down.

Mym waited for the flash of fire—but it didn't come. The sharp sword cut the salamander in two. The tail twitched back and forth, while the head coughed out a spurt of fire and expired. The salamander had been slain.

This shook Mym's confidence. If a demon could kill one of the defenders of Gaea's estate, then the demons could get through, and this was no valid separation of intruders. Should he be trying to enter himself, if the Green Mother's power was so uncertain?

The demon Mars strode on along the path—and was struck by

a bolt of lightning from a hovering little cloud. Nothing was left of the creature except a whiff of sulphurous gas.

Mym was reassured. The Green Mother's defenses were tight after all! Demons could no more pass this spot than they could the moat, without the proper credentials. The salamander was only part of it.

A second salamander crept out from behind a rock. Things were back as they had been.

Mym took another stick and poked at the little creature. When it sprang and bit, igniting the stick, Mym reached down with his free hand and grabbed it. He phased himself in to it as well as he could, channeling his identity down through his own arm. He had not realized that Mars could do this until it was done—yet he realized that he must have known it in some other aspect of his being, because this would have been a suicidal gesture otherwise.

The salamander's mind was small and vicious, but again it was easy to read, because the operating instructions were uppermost. Its name was Sweetbreath, and it would not attack the one who spoke that name. When smoke clouded the region, a hole would open in the wall.

Mym phased out and dropped the salamander, stepping hastily back before it could snap at him. Then he glanced about, perceived no other demon, and fetched an armful of slightly damp leaves from the adjacent forest floor. He dumped these on the salamander's head.

Of course the creature fired the leaves. A dense cloud of smoke and steam puffed up, covering the path.

Now Mym spoke the name: "Sweetbreath."

The salamander froze in place. Mym stepped into the smoke, deliberately breathing and keeping his eyes open, and verified that he was unaffected. There were certainly compensations to being an Incarnation! His vision was impaired because of the thickness of the smoke, but there was no personal discomfort.

He felt along the wall, but found no opening. Had he misunderstood? The smoke was beginning to thin.

Then he realized that there were two walls here. He lurched across to the other, and passed through it and into the ground. Success after all!

He was in another cave, this time a dry one. He touched the

Sword, and it emitted a glow that enabled him to proceed without stumbling. The cavern wended its way through the hill and emerged at the other side.

A lovely valley opened out before him, with ornate bushes and colorful grasses. From above, the pattern of vegetation resembled a labyrinth, but there were no teeth in it, for it was easy to pass around the bushes. Here, too, it would have been pleasant to remain and relax—if he only had time.

He strode on through—but as he proceeded he discovered that the bushes were getting denser and thornier, closing off the routes around them. He had to pick out an appropriate route, and finally found himself channeled into one, that led to a central glade at the deepest crevice of the valley. Above, on the far side, stood the Green Mother's fancy tree house, not far away at all. At last!

But in the glade was a single item of standing deadwood, a petrified tree, and on a branch of that tree perched a harpy. He would have recognized her by the smell alone.

Well, challenges seemed to run in threes. He would have to phase in to her and learn the correct way past.

"Ho, miscreant!"

Another demon! "How did you get through?" Mym demanded, frustrated by this pursuit by his likenesses.

"I masked myself as a piece of stone and watched what you did," the demon said. It was evident that these creatures lacked the subtlety of their master. It didn't occur to them not to answer a direct question. "Then I did likewise. Now I shall watch you again."

"Oh, no, you shan't!" Mym returned, drawing the Sword.

The demon showed no fear. It drew its own sword, which looked identical, and met him at the edge of the glade. The two blades touched—and the demon's was cut in half. It was no more than normal demon substance, having no super-hardness.

But how, then, had the other demon slain the salamander? There had to be more to the weapon than this!

The demon leaped at him, striking with the remaining part of the sword. Mym dodged and ran his own point through the other's torso. The blade slid through and emerged on the other side, but the demon did not stop; it walked on up the Sword and struck again at Mym.

There was a clang as the demon's weapon stuck Mym's cloak and rebounded. Mym felt the impact; that sword certainly did have substance!

He twisted his own weapon about and lifted it in an upward sweep. It cut the demon in half, from the belly up through the head, but the creature did not fall. Mym brought his blade down and chopped from the side, and half of the upper torso of the demon, including its left arm, fell off, cleanly severed along horizontal and vertical lines. But the right side continued to fight.

Mym increased his effort and hacked the demon to pieces. Now at last it was finished. This business of fighting demons was strange. They seemed to feel little or no pain or fear, had no blood, and they talked and fought freely while intact. What motivated them? They could seem most human at times, yet most alien at other times.

He turned again to the harpy, who had watched this without reaction. He was sure he could deal with her—but how could he be sure that more demons weren't watching? If they could mask themselves as stones or other items, they could be all around. It would be better to wait a bit before making his move.

"How are you?" he asked the harpy.

Now she reacted. "Unsssex me here!" she exclaimed, spitting at him.

"I gather you are not very sociable," he said with a smile. He had hardly expected otherwise.

"I have given sssuck!" she screeched indignantly.

Mym still saw no other demons, so he proceeded. He picked up one of the destroyed demon's arms and tossed it to her. The harpy caught it with one claw and tore into it with her teeth; in a moment the demon-substance was being shredded. But while she was partially distracted with that morsel, Mym reached up to touch her wing, channeling his identity quickly through the connection and phasing in with her as well as he was able.

She was Lady MacBeth, and when a cloud of dust obscured the region, a hole would open in the ground. That was all; this was just another variant of the usual device.

He disengaged and picked up a larger morsel of demon. He heaved it at the harpy, but it fell low, so that she could not catch it. In a fury she flapped her wings so hard that a cloud of dust was stirred up.

Now he spoke her name: "Lady MacBeth." The harpy froze, and Mym walked into the dust and found the hole in the ground. He stepped down into it and found himself in still another cave.

This time he did not proceed forward. He turned and waited.

Sure enough, a demon followed. Mym lopped off the thing's head, then sliced up the rest of the body, until the pieces lost their animation.

Another demon appeared. Mym dispatched that one too.

He waited, but no more demons came. This, then, should be the end of them; as far as he could tell, demons were not bright creatures and acted the moment they saw reason to. Any who were able to follow should have done so by now.

He turned and went on down the passage he was in. It brought him to a nether gate. He opened this and found stairs leading up. At the top of the flight he found a green and brown room.

"Why, fancy meeting you here," Gaea said.

"The approach was more difficult than I expected," Mym said, realizing that he had at last entered her domicile.

"Those demons are a nuisance," she said. "Permit me." She gestured, and a swarm of flies seemed to issue from her hand. They buzzed about Mym and landed on his cloak.

Suddenly there were puffs of smoke all about him. "W-w-w-what?" he asked, startled.

"They are stinging the remaining demons into oblivion," Gaea explained.

Mym was dismayed. "You mean I brought some in with me?" he sang.

"Indeed," she agreed. "But I have dealt with them now."

"But then your barriers—they didn't work!"

Gaea smiled. "They worked, Mars. They showed me which of the thousands of false images was the real Mars. I have no fear of demons here; I merely dislike being deceived. I would have had no rest at all if I had watched every image; as it is, I have to watch only you. What brings you here?"

"I am supervising an engagement in which one side means to use gene-splicing to create a virus that infects only the folk of the other side. I thought you would have an interest."

Gaea pursed her lips. "Indeed I do, Mars! I thank you for bringing this to my attention!"

"Well, I have been encountering so much difficulty with the other Incarnations that I thought—"

The Green Mother smiled. "I appreciate your consideration, Mars. Certainly I could not have let such a ploy pass. I shall straighten this out for you—but in return you must give me an intimate part of yourself."

"I must give you—?" Mym sang indignantly. "I came here to—"

"Indulge me, Mars," she said.

"Oh, take what you want!" he sang angrily. He should never have expected gratitude from another Incarnation!

"In due course."

She questioned him closely, then lifted her hand to her face. She leaned forward and touched one eye with her right forefinger, and her left with her left forefinger. Two glistening tears fell to the fingers and clung there in globules. She put the globules into separate little sponges. "Take these to your battle zone," she said. "Put them together there."

"T-t-two t-t-tears?" he asked, astonished.

"Not ordinary tears, Mars. When these merge, they will form a compound that nullifies what Satan has done in Ireland. Their virus will expire and be beyond recovery. No one will die of this particular plague."

"What Satan has done?" he sang.

"Obviously Satan has been behind all the mischief you have encountered," she said. "He caused the drafting of children for battle, revealed to another party the secret substance to make zombies, sent a vision to yet another to reveal the technology of the time bomb, and gave the secret of the Protestant plague to another. He has been working you over, Mars."

Mym formed an angry fist, knowing that this was true. Why hadn't he seen it before? That vision in Cush—obviously Satanic! "D-d-d-d-damn him!" he swore.

"Which means you must deal with him directly," Gaea said. "Only then will you be free of his interference."

"I shall challenge him now!" Mym sang.

"He will not meet you on a field of your choice," she warned. "Be careful, Mars; you can nullify the Incarnation of Evil only by properly understanding him. Bide your time; you will know when your opportunity comes."

Mym knew she was right. "I shall," he sang. "Now, will I be able to leave here without going through all the challenges again?"

She laughed. "Of course, Mars! But first—" She touched him with one hand. He felt a peculiar wrenching and knew that something vital was indeed gone from him. Nature had taken her payment.

Then he stepped out of her front doorway, which was an opening in the trunk of the great tree she lived in, and saw the Castle of War just across the open valley. There were no barriers at all.

– 13 –

LIGEIA

If Mym's nocturnal restlessness had been bad before, it was worse now. He had been frustrated by Rapture's repeated absences, but had known that she would return. Now he knew she would not. His hope for future satisfaction had been negated.

He walked in the garden. There was Lila.

"Hello, Mym," she said in familiar fashion. She wore one of her slinky, form-fitting robes that seemed to reveal more of her than would have been seen if she had been nude.

"I chopped you up and sent you back to Hell!" he protested. "What are you doing here?"

"I am trying to serve your needs," she said. "You are welcome to chop me up again, if it gives you pleasure."

"I just want to be rid of you!"

"Now don't be that way, Mym. You know you can't manage without an obliging woman, and I am most obliging. You can torture me, and I won't be hurt; you can cut me in pieces, and I can be reassembled. But I really think you would prefer to love me."

"I *hate* you! You are a creature of Evil!"

"Well, then, you can hate me," she agreed, stroking her own torso suggestively. "Summon me to your bed and revile me freely while you—"

"Get out of here!" he cried, clenching his fist.

"Make me, Mym," she suggested, striking another seductive pose.

He paused. He knew that if he took hold of her, she would twine against him, trying to seduce him. If he cut her up, she would reconstitute, in due course. She was a demoness, not subject to the ordinary limitations of mortals. So he avoided those alternatives and confined himself to words. "How can you intrude here, against my will?"

"*Is* it against your will, Mym?" she inquired, taking a step toward him.

"Of course it is!"

"Do I not tempt you with my flesh and my willingness?"

"No!"

She shook her head. "Every lie you tell brings you closer to Hell, Mym. Then you will be mine indeed."

"This is my castle! You have no right to intrude!"

"This is not your castle, Mym. This is an intermediate ground, where mortals, immortals, and the damned may meet."

"This is the garden annex to the Castle of War!"

"This is an extension of your garden annex. You are no longer on your own turf, Mars. Otherwise you would not be able to speak without stuttering."

That gave him pause. It was true that only in this region could he speak normally, avoiding both singsong and stuttering. That was one of the things that attracted him to it. But such speech was a gift of Satan, and he should not allow himself to be affected by it.

This reminded him of another aspect of the region. "Rapture was able to eat, here. How was this possible, if this is merely a compromise aspect of Purgatory?"

"It extends to overlap the mortal realm," Lila explained. "The table of viands is actually at one of our mortal locations, topologically convoluted to appear local."

"So she wasn't really remaining here!" he exclaimed.

"That depends on your definition of 'here,' Mym. Reality is as one perceives it."

"Or so Satan would like to have others believe—that lies are reality, because he is the master of lies."

"Master of Illusions," she said, as if clarifying a carelessly employed term. "Once one believes an illusion, it becomes reality. If you were to accept me as a real woman—"

"I know you are not!"

"But I could make it easy to forget. For example, if I assumed another form—" she shimmered and became the likeness of Rapture.

"Get out of that form!" Mym shouted.

"Why—doesn't it appeal to you?"

"I don't want you in that form!" he could only say, not wanting to give her the satisfaction of inciting his further anger. It was evident that demons did not have human emotions, but only emulated them.

"Then I shall offer you another form." She shimmered again and assumed the likeness of Orb.

"No!" Mym cried, half in anguish.

The Orb-image shook her lovely head. "You are a challenge to please, Mym. Do you crave slightly less licit delight?" And she became the likeness of Luna.

"I don't want *any* likeness!" Mym said, appalled.

"I am sure you have noticed how attractive Thanatos' woman is," the Luna-likeness said. The insidious thing was that she also sounded exactly like Luna and had whatever mannerisms he had noted in her. "Now you can have her, without stirring up trouble with another Incarnation. You can relish her most private parts—"

"How can I be rid of you?" he demanded.

The Lila form reappeared. "Well, there are several ways, but I think two are most feasible for your situation. One is to retire to your Castle of War, where I can not intrude without your express invitation, and live alone, never emerging to this garden. I dare say that would enhance your prowess as Mars, for you would get pretty violent after a while."

She spoke truly. That was one of the things that annoyed him most. Lila always spoke the truth—the truth he did not want to hear. "And the other?"

"You could find yourself another woman. Once I see that you are fully satisfied, I will leave you alone, for there will be no hope for me."

"Demons have hope? Isn't that a mortal feeling?"

"A mortal illusion," she said, again correcting him. "But also an immortal one. There is no mortal hope like that of a damned soul who dreams of eventual release to Heaven."

"But you are not a damned soul; you are a demoness."

"True. I spoke figuratively. I exist only to corrupt you, in any form I can." She wavered again and became Lilith.

"You—are she?" Mym asked, appalled again.

"The distinction is meaningless, Mym. I am the demoness assigned to torment you into doing my Master's will. There is no individuality among demons, and form is but a convenience."

"So when Satan sent Lilith away and brought you in her place—"

"I only exchanged forms," she agreed. "It doesn't matter."

"But she was represented as an ancient succubus, the companion of evil men since time began, while you were represented as a virgin!"

"Representations are but another form of illusion. For you, I would have been a virgin."

"But that was a lie! I thought you always told the truth!"

"Truth is meaningless to a demon," she remined him. "It is only a tool to be used as convenient. But this was not a lie, for there can be neither virginity nor nonvirginity in a demoness. She has no mortal flesh. The only distinction is in your perception— as is the case with mortals, too. Virginity has always been a figment of mortal male imagination."

What bothered him most was that she was making sense. Perhaps what he deserved was a creature like her, who could meet both his physical and intellectual needs, for she was beautiful and intelligent. But that was the nature of Satan's trap.

"Then I will find myself a woman!" he said, and stomped away.

"Find Ligeia," she called after him.

He paused, then turned back. "Why do you advise me like this? Isn't this to your disadvantage?"

She was Lila again. "Mym, you are an honest man and a good man. I am only a creature of Hell. But while I am with you, I am shaped by your expectations, and I become what you would have me be, for that is the way I serve. Thus I help you in whatever way you ask."

"But I detest you! I only want to be rid of you!"

"No, You only want to be rid of the demon aspect of me. You deceive yourself when you say otherwise, and because I serve in the way you wish, I become your conscience and correct you on that. Eventually, you will accept me, as you have molded me to be."

Mym shook his head. "Woman, you are dangerous!"

"I am dangerous," she agreed. "Because once you accept me, I will subvert you, and you will serve Satan, though you deny it."

"And you claim you have no emotion?" he asked. "You do not care at all for me, you only labor to subvert me?"

"True."

"I think you are lying, Lila."

She averted her gaze, not answering. He looked closely at her and saw a tear at one eye.

He started to speak, but stopped. He reached out to her, but stopped. *Her human emotion—this was the true lie!*

And it had almost worked.

He turned away and hurried on down the garden.

The farther reaches of the garden became rougher, as he passed beyond the presentation section. Instead of trimmed hedges, there were unruly bushes, and the animated statues were replaced by irregular pylons of stone. The original pathway deteriorated into a rut, and the flowers that had bounded it now were weeds. Even the weather changed, losing its balmy glow and becoming cold and gloomy.

Mym realized that he should turn back, for this was no place for a man to be. But his cloak protected him from environmental extremes, so he suffered no physical discomfort and, of course, he didn't have to walk if he didn't want to. He could simply use the Red Sword to travel—

Or summon his good steed.

"Werre!" he called.

Immediately he heard the sound of hoofbeats. There was the horse, galloping in from the side. "How glad I am to see you!" Mym cried, hugging Werre about the neck as the animal drew up. Then he mounted. "Take me to Ligeia," he said, uncertain whether the horse would be able to respond to such a directive.

Werre took off, galloping across the wilderness landscape. Evidently he did know where it was. Soon they reached a barren plateau, a kind of snowy tundra, as desolate as Mym's romantic prospects. Werre galloped across, and ahead there came into view a sparkling palace, as pretty in its symmetry as the plain was dull.

But the palace came no nearer, though the horse was moving at a velocity no mortal steed could match. Perplexed, Mym sighted carefully at it and discovered that it was like a mirage, keeping a constant distance from them. "Whoa, Werre," he said, using the occidental term the horse preferred. "I think we have here a special effect."

He dismounted and walked toward the palace. Now he made progress; it was closer. He called to the horse, but as Werre approached him, the palace receded.

"Now that's curious," Mym said. "It is keeping its distance from you, not from me. Well, you have brought me close enough; I'll use the Sword to take me in the rest of the way. Return to the castle, Werre, and I will rejoin you later."

Obediently, the horse galloped away. Mym regretted losing him, but if this were the only way to approach this equine-shy domicile, then so be it. He touched the Sword, and in a moment he was standing at the outer wall of the palace.

The structure was larger and prettier than it had seemed from a distance. The wall was of glistening ice and towered up some ten meters before giving way to the first embrasure. Mym tried to climb it, but the ice was tractionless and he could make no headway.

He touched the Sword. "Up," he murmured.

The Sword lifted him up along the wall to the embrasure. But when he got there he discovered it was halfway illusory; invisibly transparent ice covered it, so that there was no entrance. The turrets were the same; the ice sealed everything in. This castle was tight, iced all over.

He returned to the ground and considered. Though the ice seemed transparent, diffraction increased with depth, so that the interior became opaque. But he was sure this was the right place, because Lila had described it as a castle of frozen mist, and this was that, albeit somewhat more solid than anticipated. Also,

Werre had been headed here. He needed to get in, to rescue the damsel in distress.

Mym drew the Sword. "I hate to do it," he murmured to himself. "But I'll have to cut my way into the beautiful structure."

He braced himself and swung at the wall, knowing that the Red Sword could cut through any substance, and could be damaged by none.

And almost fell on his face as the blade passed through the wall without resistance. It was mist indeed!

He recovered his balance and touched the ice again. It was absolutely solid. He knocked at it with a knuckle, and it was hard.

But then how had the Sword—?

He lifted the Sword and poked the point slowly at the wall. It sank in without contact. He moved the blade about, and it swept through the wall without affecting it. What *was* this?

He set his left hand against the cold wall, then passed the blade slowly down through it until the edge touched his hand. The Sword did not cut him, of course; the magic of his office protected him from his own weaponry. The edge nudged him and stopped.

His hand was firm against the wall, while the Sword felt nothing except his hand. To his hand, the wall was solid ice; to the Sword, it was mere mist.

How could he carve an entrance out of mist?

Mym remembered how this palace had been unapproachable by the horse. Now it was untouchable by the Sword.

He retreated a few paces, then unstrapped the harness and set the Sword and scabbard on the snow. He had no concern about losing the weapon; it would come at his beck, and no other person, mortal or immortal, could use it without his leave. It was not physical contact that bound the Sword to him, but the office.

He located a hefty stone, picked it up, and carried it to the wall. The stone weighed about four kilograms and had a ragged point at one side; it would do as a sledgehammer.

He smashed the stone into the wall. The ice cracked, sending radiating lines out in all directions. He struck again, and a chip of ice flaked off. Several more blows gouged out a small crater, then a larger one. Continuing effort broke a hole in it. He bashed away at the edges, until he was able to step through the opening and stand within the palace.

It was as lovely inside as out. There were halls and chambers and stairs, all silent and clean. Light emanated from the ceiling, resembling the Northern Lights. Carpets of ice hung on the walls, with snowflake patterns within that formed pictures of snowscapes.

He walked along those eerie halls, studying it all. Though this palace was cold and would be horrible for a normal person, he found it pleasant. But why had it been constructed? Solely to punish an errant soul? That seemed to be an awful amount of design and effort for a soul that could be made miserable by far simpler means. Yet it did seem to be the case.

He found the central chamber. There, on a kind of pedestal, was a box, formed of transparent ice, and in the box was a bed, and in the bed was a lovely young woman, protected by a coverlet of puffy white snow.

Something about this situation nagged at Mym's memory. He paused to search it out, and had it: the occidental children's story of the Slumbering Lovely. She had been enchanted to sleep for a century or so, until a prince of a later generation rescued her.

Apparently it had been a mechanism for merging two lines of royalty when one was not eligible at the appropriate time.

Well, he was, or had been a prince, and the demoness had called this one the Princess Ligeia. It seemed appropriate to rescue her. Certainly she was beautiful, and seemed to be about his own age, though of course there was no telling how long she had been here; she might be of his grandmother's generation. Did that matter? Not really; not if she had slept unaware for the intervening time, so remained young in outlook.

He touched the box, discovering that a dome of ice covered the top, sealing in the Princess. Well, he could break it so as to be able to get to her and—how were slumbering lovelies awakened? By a kiss, as he recalled. Probably a euphemism for a rather more intimate contact. He could accommodate that.

He tapped on the glassy dome. It rang, but did not break.

The girl stirred. Her eyes opened. They were green, like deep ice. She saw him. Her mouth opened, and her bosom heaved so violently that the snow blanket bounced off, but there was no sound.

"Don't worry," Mym said in English, as he doubted that this

Nordic woman spoke his native language. "I am about to rescue you."

But she sat up, throwing off the remaining cover, and kneeled on the bed opposite him. She wore a fetching pink nightie that only enhanced the delightful contours beneath. Her hair was so fair as to resemble frozen water, and her skin almost translucent. Lovely, indeed!

Her bosom heaved again and her mouth worked, but still there was no sound. Evidently the ice enclosure was a perfect sonic barrier. She seemed to be violently protesting something.

"But I'm not here to harm you," Mym shouted back. "I have come to rescue you! I am a friend." He put his mouth almost on the ice and repeated: "A FRIEND!"

But still she seemed not to understand. She shook her head violently back and forth in negation, her silken tresses flying out like fancy skirts. Her mouth formed exaggerated *O*s. She seemed to be speaking English, crying "No! No!"

Could he have encountered a captive Princess who didn't want to be rescued? A moment's consideration convinced him that that was not the case. Probably she had been tormented by demons in the forms of rescuers, much in the manner Gaea had been, so assumed that he was another such. Naturally she didn't want to be grasped by a demon.

"I'm Mars, the Incarnation of War!" he cried, mouthing the words carefully. "The *real* one!"

She seemed to understand. "Mars," she mouthed. But then she shook her head in even more violent negation. "No! No!"

Mym reconsidered. If she knew he was genuine, why did she remain negative? Had Lila deceived him about this Princess's desire to be rescued? Did Ligeia dislike him personally? Neither seemed likely. The demoness seemed never to have lied to him before, and this particular deception would be pointless. And the Princess could hardly dislike a man she didn't know. Also, her reaction did not seem to be one of dislike, but rather one of concern.

Aha! If he broke into the box, as he had the palace itself, the flying shards of ice might cut her. Also, the box might protect her from the cold, and a sudden opening might freeze her. He could not be sure that her blanket really was snow; it might have been fashioned to look that way for artistic effect. That could certainly concern her.

But he could warm her with his cloak. He demonstrated that to her, opening the cloak, showing that there was room in it for two.

She nodded, again seeming to understand. But then again she shook her head in negation.

He tapped again on the ice. It was solid, but if he broke it at the end, the shards should not reach her. She could even shield herself with her blanket.

He struck the ice harder. It rang, but did not break. The princess watched, seeming unalarmed by this. Good enough.

He found a solid ice lump and used it to bash at the box. The contact was hard, but the ice would not crack. So he returned to the entrance he had broken and picked up the sledge-rock. This would do it!

He returned, hefting the rock. Ligeia remained sitting on her bed, now passive. He slammed the rock into the ice—but this ice was harder than that of the palace wall, amazingly, and neither cracked nor flaked.

After several attempts, he realized that this was not going to do it. He could not break in this way.

Mym set down the rock and paced about the chamber, trying to think of his next step. How could he rescue a woman from an unbreakable container? There had to be a way; after all, she had been sealed into it, so unless it had been constructed around her, there was a way to get by it.

She was, he reminded himself, not a mortal person, but a damned soul. Obviously Satan intended to see that no one got her out and gave her a fair hearing. But how could physical substance imprison a bodiless spirit?

Obviously it was possible, both because she *was* captive and because the structures of the Incarnations could serve as a barrier to demons, who were evidently as versatile as spirits in physical movement. Perhaps there was some spiritual barrier that seemed solid to souls, though mortals didn't notice it. But he, as an Incarnation, should be able to pass it, and to convey her past it, when she was in contact with him. It was the physical barrier that balked him, not the spiritual one.

That being the case, how could he circumvent the physical barrier, without breaking it?

Abruptly the answer came to him. He could make himself either visible or invisible to mortals, solid or vaporous. He could do the same here.

He reached down to touch the Sword—and remembered that he had left it outside in the snow. Careless of him!

"Sword," he murmured, holding out his hand.

The great Red Sword appeared in it, scabbard and all. Then Mym willed himself insubstantial and put his hand to and through the icy cover.

Ligeia's eyes widened as she saw this. Mym extended his hand toward her, holding it open, pausing.

The Princess hesitated, then slowly extended her own little hand. The two hands touched—and passed through each other without resistance.

Here was another dilemma! Though Mym could make himself as insubstantial as a ghost, and Ligeia *was* a ghost, the two of them were not in the same frame. Maybe in the residences of the Incarnations spirits could seem as solid as mortals, but this was open territory, and such interaction was not possible. So he was physically barred when he was solid, and spiritually barred when he was insubstantial. He still could not really touch her and, therefore, could not rescue her.

Mym shook his head. Surely Satan was laughing now! What a fiendish situation! To have the damsel in distress so near to rescue, yet untouchable. Would he have to go home, leaving her unrescued?

No, he refused to do that. There had to be a way to bring her out of that box, and he intended to find that way.

He paced the floor some more, pondering. She was a spirit, a damned soul. He was a mortal, but he had a soul of his own. If he could just set his body aside for a moment, much as he had his horse and his Sword—

And there it was. As an Incarnation, he could do that, he knew. Gaea had mentioned something about the ability to discorporate. She had said there was a risk, but of course there was an element of risk in most things, sometimes directly proportional to their benefit. Whatever the risk, if this could do the job here, it should be worth it.

He sat on the floor and leaned back against the wall, so that he needed no effort for support. Then he willed himself out of his body.

And he did rise out of it, with no trouble at all. He stood, stepped forward, turned about, and saw his body propped there, unbreathing, lifeless for the moment. But it would reanimate the moment he returned to it, and the returning would be as easy as phasing in to any other body, as he had done so often before. That phasing had to be a variant of this; his physical body made impalpable, while his soul intergrated with the other.

He turned again and approached the box. The Princess's gaze passed from his body to his soul, perceiving both—and abruptly her agitation redoubled. "No! No! No!" she cried soundlessly, gesturing frantically.

"But this is the way I can rescue you," he replied. "I will just take your hand and bring you out. You will have your chance at last."

She put up her hands, spread out in a stop-stop gesture. She shook her head so violently that her hair became a whirling halo. Her whole aspect cried denial.

Mym paused, perplexed. "Are you afraid of me again? You weren't a moment ago!"

When he paused, she paused. But still she pushed him back, figuratively, with her hands. She did not want him to come to her.

"Don't you want to be rescued?" Mym asked, knowing she could not hear the words.

But it seemed that she did understand the gist. Her hands spread in a gesture of helplessness. She seemed to want to convey something to him, but lacked the means to do it.

"Then let me enter, so I can hear you," he said reasonably. "Then you can tell me. If there is good reason for me not to rescue you, then I will certainly not force it upon you. I'm only trying to help." He took another step.

Again she reacted with desperate negation. But this time he did not pause; he had to get close enough to explain his position to her, to ease her concern. Perhaps she did have reason not to be rescued; he would consider it carefully. His leading hand passed through the ice without resistance, then his arm to the shoulder. It was working.

She screamed—and as his head passed through, the tail end of that scream suddenly manifested.

He reached out and took her hand, and this time the contact was real. They were two spirits now, and felt to each other exactly the way two solid mortals would, for they were equivalently solid. "Ligeia," he said. "Please, listen to me. I shall not force anything upon you."

She burst into tears.

Mym sat on the bed and took her in his arms. She was warm and very soft; she smelled of spring flowers and new-mown hay, and her tears were wet against his shoulder. It was amazing how physical the spirit realm seemed! He patted her on the back. "There, there," he said. "It's all right, now. I have come to take you away from this."

Suddenly she raised her head and her flowing green eyes met his. "But you can't!" she exclaimed.

"I won't—if you don't want me to," he said reassuringly. "Just explain how you feel, and I will honor it."

"Oh, I tried to stop you!" she wailed. "But you wouldn't listen!"

"I couldn't hear you," he explained. "But now I can. Just tell me what—"

"Oh, you don't understand," she said. "You just don't *understand*!"

"But I'm trying to," he said reasonably.

"Oh, you poor man!" The tears resumed their flow.

"I have no problem," he protested. "Come, let's step out of here, and then we can talk."

He leaned forward, extending one hand to the ice wall of the box to get his balance. The hand banged.

He looked at it, then tried again. It banged again. The ice was now solid to him.

"But only my spirit is here!" he said, wonderingly. "I just passed through it!"

"That's what I was trying to tell you," Ligeia said. "It's one-way ice. A soul can enter, as I did, as you did—but it can't leave. We can't get out. I tried so hard to warn you!''

''Can't get out?'' he asked, bemused.

''This is Satan's trap,'' she explained. ''This is a capsule of Hell. No one can escape it, except into the rest of Hell.''

''I'm trapped in Hell?'' Suddenly Gaea's warning returned to him—Satan would not meet him in an arena of his choosing. Now he would have to meet Satan in the arena of Satan's choosing— Hell itself.

The capsule began to move. It descended through the floor, carrying the two of them with it.

They were headed for Hell proper.

– 14 –

HELL

The capsule stopped at a facility very like an airport, coming to rest beside a large glassy building. An accordion-pleated ramp extended out to touch the capsule; there was a click, and the ice dissolved at the point of contact.

"We're here," Ligeia said. "Oh, I wish—" But she didn't finish, and Mym understood why. What use were wishes in Hell?

"You knew this would happen?" Mym asked as they set foot on the walk.

"The moment I saw you," she agreed, her tears in the process of being replaced by fatalism. "Satan told me I was going for a— oh, never mind. I was a fool, yet again."

"A hearing?" Mym asked. "And instead you were bait for a trap."

She nodded grimly and preceded him to the building.

He realized that she could be lying. But what was the point? Whether demoness or genuine damned soul, she had done the job, and he had been caught. He preferred to believe that she was as much a victim of Satan's deception and cruelty as he.

Satan was waiting in the terminal. "Welcome to Hell, Mars!" he said jovially, stepping forward with his hand extended. Mym considered refusing the hand, but concluded that civility was better than antagonism, even in Hell. He shook the hand.

"I can't say I am completely pleased to be here," Mym said. "What is the point of this device?"

"Merely to get your attention, my dear associate," Satan said, smiling. "I am sure that you and I shall come to a perfect understanding."

"I hope so," Mym said. "It has been my impression that one Incarnation does not interfere with the business of another on a casual basis; there could be a consequence."

If Satan reacted to the thinly veiled threat, he gave no sign. "Incarnations should always cooperate," he agreed. "Come, share the hospitality of My domain, and we shall converse."

"If I may go, now—" Ligeia murmured.

"By no means, My dear," Satan replied. "This man is a prince; we shall not foist off on him the company of a woman beneath his station. You shall be his escort while he visits."

"But I really would prefer not to—"

"Your preference, My dear, is a matter of indifference to Me. I suggest that you put a suitably fair face on the matter."

Evidently reluctant, she nevertheless nerved herself and smiled at Mym. "It seems I must," she said. "I assure you, sir, that my reticence does not reflect on you. Are you really a prince?"

"I was, in life," Mym agreed. "That is behind me, now. Are you really a princess?"

"In life," she echoed.

"Excellent," Satan said. "The Old Smoky House has palatable fare; shall we dine there?"

"It seems we shall," Mym said. He was sure that Satan could not hold him in Hell against his will, but not sure how he was to escape it. He was still to new in this office, so did not yet know how to use his Incarnative powers to their full extent. Until he figured out his best course of action, it was best to make no dramatic and possibly pointless gestures.

Ligeia took his arm, and they followed Satan to another chamber. This was set up like a contemporary occidental restaurant, with dim lighting and soft music and elegantly garbed waiters and waitresses. It surprised Mym to see such an establishment in Hell, but obviously it belonged. He was sure that neither demons nor damned souls required food for sustenance, but if it made them more comfortable to honor the amenities of life, that was all right.

Of course, most of the souls resident in Hell probably did not actually get to eat; probably Satan tortured them by allowing them only to smell the good food.

"Shall we have steak?" Satan inquired, surveying the menu.

"The flesh of a cow?" Mym asked.

"Um, true," Satan said. "You are from India. Perhaps a nice fancy curry then?"

While they dined on curry and the other aspects of an excellent Indian meal, Satan made his pitch.

"You and I seem to have been working at cross purposes, Mars," he said. "When actually we may have a common purpose."

"I doubt that," Mym replied. "My sympathy is with the force of good, while you represent the force of evil."

"We each represent forces of expedience," Satan said. "Just as you understand that there must be violence in mortal affairs, so I understand that there must be evil. Sometimes violence abates evil; sometimes evil abates violence. But the two can go together."

Mym didn't like the sound of this, but he confined his reaction. "In what way?"

"It is My duty to harvest the souls where evil preponderates. But too many souls are shades of gray, with the good and evil so hopelessly intertwined that Thanatos himself can barely distinguish them. The situation is too complex; I wish to simplify it by generating more action."

"More violence?"

"Yes. One does not get dirty laundry clean without agitation. Since this aspect falls under your—"

"So you want me to stir up more war," Mym said.

"Yes. Not too much, just enough to enable the souls to settle out more rapidly."

"In other words, to have more people die."

"That is one way to put it. This activity would of course enhance your position."

"And yours," Mym said. "Because you would reap an earlier and greater harvest of souls. Because the stresses of war would generate famine and slaughter that would not otherwise have existed."

"Well—"

"Not interested," Mym said, rising from the table.

Satan hastened to stay with him. "Of course there could be lagniappe. For example, this borderline soul, the Princess Ligeia, could be made available to you in Purgatory."

"No!" Ligeia cried.

Satan glanced darkly at her, and she shrank back, silenced.

Now Mym looked at her. "Satan requires that you remain with us; I do not. I came to help you, not to oppress you. Certainly I would not take you to the Castle of War if you objected."

"Oh, no, Mars," she protested. "It's not that! You are a prince, and there are things that only nobility understands. I am sure you would be compatible, and I would gladly go with you, but—"

"But not at the behest of Satan, as part of a corrupt bargain," Mym concluded.

Mutely, she nodded.

Mym liked her attitude. She was correct: there was a camaraderie among those of royal status that commoners accepted but seldom truly grasped—things like the importance of appearances, the routines of palace existence, and the use of concubines. There was much that he would never have to explain to Ligeia, just as he had not to Rapture, and much that she would not have to advise him of. But more than that, it was fitting that royalty consort with royalty. This was one thing that had kept him from dealing with Lila or any other woman. He had to establish a relationship with one of his own station first; then the rest would fall into place.

Certainly Ligeia was loath to establish any relationship with him by Satan's directive. Only her father had the authority to make such a commitment for her. Or, since her father was in another realm, herself. She would make her own commitment, in her own fashion, or make none at all.

"We can arrange other habitation for you, woman," Satan said. "Your mortal rank carries no significance *here*."

"Let her be," Mym said gruffly. Satan had just demonstrated the ignorance and insensitivity of the commoner. "Isn't it enough that you hold her here illicitly, and that you used her against her will to bring me here? Why try to force further corruption on her?"

"This is my domain, Mars," Satan said evenly. "The determination of treatment is Mine. This slut is overdue for a touch of flame.''

Slut? Mym controlled his blaze of anger. There would be a reckoning for such insults in due course.

Satan raised his hand. Ligeia shrank away from him, terrified. Satan pointed, and flame appeared. The fire followed the line traced by his finger, moving toward the woman. Mym stood abruptly, flinging the chair to the rear, and stepped into the path of flame. The fire touched his cloak and turned back, unable to penetrate. ''Let her be,'' Mym repeated.

''You accept my offer?'' Satan asked. ''The woman's consent does not matter; she fears the flame and will cooperate without limit to avoid it.''

''I reject the offer,'' Mym said.

''Then you may remain the guest of this establishment indefinitely—and she will burn while you reconsider.'' Satan gestured, and a sheet of flame appeared. Ligeia whimpered.

Mym put his arm about her, enfolding her within his protective cloak. The flame leaped up about them both, harming neither. ''I believe it is time to see that this woman has a fair hearing,'' he said.

''You may not be touched,'' Satan said. ''But she is Mine. You can not hold her.'' He lifted one hand and snapped his fingers.

Huge, menacing demons appeared at the entrance to the restaurant. Some had horns and tails and snorted fire; others had huge crab claws in lieu of hands. They closed in on Mym and the girl.

''Get a good hold on her,'' Satan directed them. ''His substance is not subject to our power, but hers is. Take hold and pull; he will let her go, lest she be torn apart.''

Mym bit his tongue. He was here in spirit only, but he felt the pain and tasted the blood. ''Do not touch her,'' he warned the demons.

''No, I will go with them!'' Ligeia protested. ''It is another trap for you, Mars! Satan means to—''

Six demons pounced, converging. Two grabbed for her feet, hauling them up and apart. Two more grabbed for her hands, doing the same. One grabbed for her silver hair, pulling cruelly

on it. The sixth, slavering, opened its tusked face to take a horrendous bite of her bosom.

That sixth received Mym's fist in its teeth. The tusks broke off
and the teeth were jammed back into its throat. The demon fell,
choking on ivory. It was evident that the powers of Mars remained
with him, even in spirit form.

But the strength of the other demons was hauling the girl away
from Mym's other arm that held her about the waist. Mym realized that to deal with the demons, he would have to have both
hands free—which meant letting her go. He didn't trust that; she
could be whisked away in an instant, the moment he lost physical
contact. How would he ever locate her again in this fell region?

But even though he retained his hold on her, it was no good,
because the five demons were trying, literally, to pull her apart.
The two on her arms were bracing to haul in opposite directions,
the one on her hair was yanking so hard that her eyes were being
drawn wide open, and the two on her feet were wedging her legs
so far apart that they were spread almost a hundred and eighty
degrees.

Mym used his free fist to club one of the arm-holding demons
on the skull. The skull caved in and the demon fell. Then, moving
with the blinding rapidity available to him in the berserker state,
he swung his hand across, caught the hair of the hair-pulling
demon, and yanked the entire demon up into the air and down
against the floor, breaking its hold and body in the process.

But the three remaining demons had not left off. Taking advantage of Mym's own effort, they succeeded in getting Ligeia
free of his grasp. He leaped at one of the leg-holding demons,
grabbed one of its own legs, lifted it, braced one of his feet against
the other leg and forced a split that went into an obtuse angle
before the demon's leg broke off.

Mym whirled—and saw the two remaining demons dragging
Ligeia across the room. Rather, one was dragging, its hands
locked under her shoulders and about her bosom, while the other
was using its pincers to clasp her thighs apart while it walked into
her. In a moment its evident demon lust would—

Ligeia screamed.

Mym had never before heard a sound of that nature. It pierced
the atmosphere of Hell, like a power saw cutting through metal,

and stunned the demons. They fell away, leaving her collapsed and sobbing.

Mym was unaffected, protected by his office. So was Satan. "Now you see what she is," Satan said. "You don't want to get involved with a creature like that."

"*What* is she?" Mym demanded.

"A siren, of course. One who destroys with her voice. The secret shame of her royal family; such defects are not supposed to run in royal lines. That's what got her sent here."

Secret shame? Mym, the stutterer, understood very well about that sort of thing.

Satan shrugged. "Well, might as well wrap this up; she's of no further use to Me." He raised his hand.

Mym leaped across, again intercepting the flame with his cloak. "I don't care what she is; she's a decent soul!"

"Another reason you can't have her," Satan said. "Had she been willing to cooperate, I would have let her be with you. As it is, I shall treat her unkindly." He glanced about, noting the sprawled demons. "But first I had better gag her." He gestured, and a snake appeared, wrapped about Ligeia's head, its body wedging into her mouth so that she could not speak.

Mym realized that there was no way to protect her from Satan's direct mischief. Not here in Hell. Unless he could manage to hide her, somehow.

He took hold of the woman, heaved her up and ran out of the restaurant. Beyond it was a flat, bare plain—no place to hide!

But he was Mars, he reminded himself. He could change his aspect, and the aspect of anyone with him. Simply by touching the Red Sword.

Oops! He had left that with his body.

Still, physical separation did not cut off the Sword's attachment to him. He should be able to do the magic of the office regardless, even here in Hell. All he had to do was will it.

He rendered himself invisible. He hoped. He could still see himself and Ligeia, but—

Several more demons charged out of the restaurant. "And tear her apart!" Satan's voice came after them. "Or *you'll* be torn in her stead!"

The demons paused, peering about. They saw nothing, though

Mym and Ligeia were standing near, she with the snake still wrapped about her head. The three of them—man, woman and snake—could be perceived only by each other, for the moment.

Except Satan himself. As another Incarnation, Satan would not be subject to the illusion. Mym knew he had to get Ligeia away before Satan emerged.

He ran across the plain, carrying her, for she was not moving voluntarily. He knew why; she did not want to be either a drag or a corrupting influence on him. She was a decent girl who meant no harm, yet had been required to be the agent of much mischief. Probably she would have let the demons take her away to the torture, had one not threatened to rape her on the spot.

Suddenly the plain ended. Mym stopped abruptly. This was not a plain, it was the level top of a mesa! The drop-off was sheer and seemed to extend a kilometer. It was awesome.

The demons were spreading out, going over the entire area, searching. Satan had not yet emerged, but could do so at any moment.

Mym hurried along the brink, searching for some way down. He didn't want to have to jump. He was a soul, and Ligeia was a soul, so they couldn't be killed, but he was sure the fall would incapacitate her for a time and be extremely painful. He might suffer himself; he wasn't sure whether his office protected him from acts of sheer folly in Hell.

There was a path, a niche, a crevice leading down! Mym walked down it, getting them out of the line of sight to the restaurant. For the moment, Satan would not be able to spy them; that was all that counted.

Ligeia struggled, still unable to speak. "Don't *do* that!" Mym warned. "Look where we are!"

She craned her head to look, stiffened, and went slack. She didn't like that sort of height any better than he did.

"They've got to be here somewhere!" Satan's voice came. "If not on the mesa, then on the slope. Did you check the slope?"

Mym knew that in moments this scant path would be swarming with demons. They would not be able to see the fugitives—but would they be able to feel them? In life, Mars could make himself intangible, invisible, or both at once. But this was not life, and he feared that one spirit could not be made insubstantial to another spirit. After all, Ligeia had become tangible to him when he encountered her in spirit form in the capsule in the palace of ice. He could not afford to risk contact with a demon.

Yet the invisibility ploy was working, so maybe—

Now the silhouette of a demon showed at the rim of the mesa. The demon started down the path.

Mym looked ahead. The path wended on down and around the mountain. He had to follow it; there was nowhere else to go. He would not risk contact with any demons unless he had no other alternative.

"I'm setting you down; stay with me," he whispered to Ligeia.

She shook her head in negation, still unable to speak because of the snake.

Mym reached across and took hold of the snake. Quickly he caught its head, and squeezed it just hard enough to make the reptile realize that it was in his power. Then he unwound it, freeing the woman. "You have been very good about this, wanting to spare me further trouble," he whispered. "But now I'm *in* trouble, and so are you. Neither of us has anything to gain at this point by having the demons capture you. If you leave me now, all it could do would be to give away my location. Do you want that?"

She shook her head no.

"Then follow me," Mym said. "As long as you stay close, you will remain invisible." He turned, holding the snake with one hand, and proceeded down the path.

A short distance down, the path widened, and an overhang developed. This was a relief, because any slip would send them tumbling off the mountain. Mym saw that there was a hole in the overhang; perhaps this was the remains of an ancient cave. But the path continued on down, and the demon had been joined by others behind, so Mym didn't pause.

Then he heard something. Demons—ahead! They were coming *up* the path from below!

"We're trapped!" Ligeia moaned. "But I can scream at them—"

"And alert the whole of the rest of Hell to our location!" Mym returned. "Keep your mouth shut!" He considered momentarily. "We'll have to try that cave."

"Oh, I hate caves!" she said.

He ignored that. They moved back up the path, and to the cave. The demons above were getting close.

"I'll boost you up," he said. "Then I'll follow." He wished he had the Red Sword; with that he could have flown right off the mountain.

Well, maybe he could do that anyway. After all, if the invisibility worked—

He tried it, willing himself into the air, while Ligeia made her way cautiously up the rock. Nothing happened. Evidently he could change his appearance by himself, but had to have the Sword right with him in order to travel. Perhaps it needed to see exactly where he was going in order to operate. Or maybe he simply didn't have the right mental key for remote control. Too bad.

He boosted her by the pert bottom, and she scrambled up into the hole. "Very well—here's the snake," he said, handing up the reptile. Ligeia seemed less than eager to handle it again, but took it. Then he fitted his hands to the edges of the hole and heaved himself up. She was there to help him navigate the edge.

It was a small cave, hardly more than an etching in the mountain, but large enough to hold them comfortably. The snake settled down to the side, seeming satisfied.

The demons reached the overhang, talking gruffly among themselves. "Oh, I'm afraid!" Ligeia whispered.

Mym put his arm about her shoulders. "Remember, they can not see us. Just be quiet, and they'll pass."

She was quiet, though her body shivered. The demons tromped by from the upper path, grumbling; evidently they felt that this search was so much foolishness. Mym wondered how they could be so similar to mortals in their minor reactions, if they were soulless constructs of ether. They should have no personality, but that was obviously not the case. Perhaps demons were crafted in Satan's image, much the way man, according to the occidental mythos, was crafted in God's image. Of course that was illusory; how could such imperfection come from perfection? Man had a delusion of grandeur. Mym was glad that he did not share such confused thinking. Reincarnation made so much more sense that any sensible person should be able to understand it.

The upper demons met the lower demons. There was an outcry, and the sound of a brief skuffle; then a descending wail as one of them fell or was thrown off the ledge. Irascible creatures, demons!

Now the demons tromped back up the path. "Not on this ledge," one was muttering. "I don't care what *His Foulness* says! We'd have found them, if—"

"The cave—did you check the cave, you moron?" another demanded.

"*What* cave, imbecile?" the other asked.

"*That* cave, idiot!" the other retorted. "The one we use to entertain that demoness in our slack time."

"Oh, *that* cave," the first demon said. "Where is that demoness, now? I haven't seen her in a century."

"She's on sunside duty," the second replied. "Seducing some mortal."

"Some mortals have all the luck," the first muttered. His tusked face poked into the cave from below.

Ligeia stiffened, for the demon was staring right at them. But the creature's gaze passed through them, and it saw nothing but the cave. They truly were invisible.

Then the demon spotted the snake, which was separate from Mym, and just beyond the ambiance of his power. The demon reached for the snake, but the snake rose up hissingly and opened its jaws wide, and the demon thought the better of it. His head ducked down. "Nothing but wildlife here."

"Well, let's go back," the other demon said. "Either they fell off the mountain, or they never were on this path. I don't know why Satan's so hot to get them; they can't escape Hell anyway."

"He wants to torture the woman, rotface," the first said. "She was supposed to corrupt the Incarnation, and she tried to bug out, so she's in for it."

"Yeah, I hope Satan gives her to me to play with," the second said as they resumed their tromp up the path. "I'd bring her right back here to this cave and really work her over! Did you see those legs of hers when we held her?"

"I was *on* one of those legs, snotpuss! I saw all the way up . . ." The sound faded as they departed.

"Oh, I hate those demons!" Ligeia whispered. "All they think about is lust and torture!"

"Well, Hell is supposed to be an unpleasant place," Mym responded, "to make the damned souls regret their crimes in life."

"But I don't *belong* in Hell!" she exclaimed.

"I think we'd better wait here until the demons give up the search," Mym said. "That could be some time. Why don't you tell me how you came to be here? I came here to help you and I still hope to do so."

"You can't help me," she retorted. "I can only hurt you. You should get away from me right now."

"Why? You seem like a nice young woman, apart from your obvious virtue as a princess."

"I *am* a nice young woman, apart from that virtue. You'd probably like me if you knew me, especially since you seem to be immune to my scream. That's why you need to get away."

"Maybe I'm being dense. I don't follow the logic."

"Because that's what Satan wants!" she exclaimed. "He wants you to—to—"

"To treat you as the demons would? I wouldn't do that, Ligeia."

"To fall in love with me," she blurted.

Mym smiled. "I have been in love before and I can't say that that is a fate worse than death. They were good women, very good women. If you are a good woman—"

"Because you're an Incarnation, Satan can not hold you any longer than he can fool you, which shouldn't be long. But I'm a damned soul, and he *can* hold me; if you fall in love with me, then you won't leave without me and so you won't be able to leave at all and you'll be trapped forever in Hell and Satan'll have his way with the mortal realm!" she exploded.

So that was Satan's plot! No wonder Lila had told him of the imprisoned Princess! And was it Lila that the demons had taken to this same cave? An interesting coincidence that they should happen to mention it just when he was here to hear.

Coincidence? Deception, more likely! Wasn't it possible that Satan knew exactly where he was—and had instructed the demons to leave him here, because he was doing what Satan wanted—being with Ligeia? And Ligeia, by all the signals, was a genuinely loveable woman, no part of this plot. Had she been in on it, she should not have warned him of its nature.

Yes, this was very interesting. The demons had gotten Ligeia away from Mym and could have removed her to some far reach of Hell so that he could never have found her. But they had paused, seemingly foolishly, and threatened to rape her. That had triggered her devastating scream, so that Mym had had a renewed chance to rescue her. It was possible that the demons had been stupid and had given away to their lusts prematurely—but Satan had merely stood and watched. Satan had not started organizing the pursuit until it was too late. Satan was no fool; therefore his lack of initiative must have been deliberate. He had wanted Ligeia to scream, so as to enable Mym to rejoin her.

That scream—that was a most remarkable thing. Others might consider it an ugly thing. But Mym, who had a problem with his own voice, was in a position to understand a liability like that. He felt some empathy. He wasn't stuttering now, but he was in Hell, where Satan's power eliminated it; his consciousness of it remained. Ligeia was a fellow sufferer—and Satan had wanted him to see that. Naturally a man who had suffered because of a problem with his voice would be attracted to a woman with another type of voice problem. A cunning trap indeed!

"You are silent," Ligeia said. "Now you understand. I thank you for being the man you are and now I shall do what I must do and leave you." She started to move toward the cave entrance.

Mym held her back. "I am not leaving without you," he said.

"But I *told* you why that can't be! You have a responsibility on Earth!"

"I came to Hell to rescue you—and rescue you I shall," Mym said. "This has nothing to do with love, but with what is right. If I should fall in love with you in the process, perhaps you will agree to be with me after you have had your hearing and are free of Hell. If not—I still mean to do what I know to be right."

"You're a fool!" she said.

"I'm a man."

"A prince," she said, more gently.

"An Incarnation."

"I could—get very pleased with that kind of a fool," she confessed. "But I can't let you do it. I am only one soul; your work affects millions. So—" She got up again.

He hauled her back, held her down, and kissed her.

She sighed. "You know you really aren't being fair about this," she said. Then she kissed him back.

"Let's get to know each other," he said.

"You already know my curse. When I get excited—"

"I know about curses. I'm a stutterer."

She laughed. "Not that I've noticed!"

"In life. Here in Hell I am spared it. I think it's Satan's way of subverting me. He offered me a demon concubine and free speech, but I prefer to make my own way."

"But if your curse is gone in Hell, why does mine remain?" she asked plaintively.

"Perhaps because Satan isn't trying to subvert you. He's trying to degrade you. He probably would not bother to abate my stuttering if I weren't an Incarnation."

"The Incarnation of War," she agreed. "You rate special treatment."

"So if stuttering bothers you, you will not want to associate with me, once we get out of Hell."

"When I saw you, there in the Palace of Ice, you looked so bold and handsome, really like a prince coming to rescue me," she said. "I knew it was a trap and I tried to warn you away. But you wouldn't go, and now the trap is sprung, and maybe the second one too, because you still won't go. I suppose it's academic, because I'll never get out of Hell, but if I were out, and you got me out, I'd always know that it was the stutterer who did it and I wouldn't care what you looked like or sounded like; I'd want to be with you. But you really didn't come to the Palace of Ice just to pick up a woman, did you? Not when you had a demoness at your beck?"

So Mym told her about Orb, about Rapture, and his desire for a woman of that level, rather than a protean demoness whose ultimate loyalty was to Satan. "Though Lila did shed a tear," he said at the end. "I don't know why a demoness would do that."

"Because it was her business to corrupt you or to send you to Hell; either way, she knew you would be doomed. Demons do have some little emotion, otherwise they couldn't enjoy the base desires. They can't animate the human form without picking up a bit of human nature, so as to act well enough to fool real people. She probably liked you a trifle, or maybe liked her assignment in Purgatory, which is a better place than Hell, so was sorry when she knew it was over. Her will is subservient to Satan, but, when it doesn't conflict with her assignment, she can afford some emotion. Especially if showing it might cause you to react in a manner helpful to her mission."

"You seem to know a lot about demons," Mym said ruefully.

"I have had recent experience." Then she told him how she had come to Hell.

Ligeia had been a European princess. When she came of age and was versed in the things needful for her role, her father the King had begun shopping about for a suitable match for her. "These things are seldom left to individual choice, you know," she said.

"I know," Mym agreed.

Part of that shopping entailed showing the wares. Contemporary monarchs had become canny, as their sons acquired modernistic notions of independence, and facilitated cooperation by seeking brides who were not only advantageously connected, but who were personally attractive. In fact, it was often possible to use a young prince's idealistic notions to keep him in line, because, once he was smitten by the beauty of the prospective bride, he paid little heed to anything else until it was too late. He was trapped by love.

"I know," Mym repeated, remembering how well that ploy had worked with Rapture.

"Well, you don't have to agree so readily!" she said.

"I am already blinded by your beauty," he said. He intended it as humor, but realized as he spoke that it was not. Ligeia evidently had a similar realization, for she blushed. It was dark in the cave, but he knew she was blushing because her whole body seemed to radiate heat. The embarrassment of royalty was a more potent thing than that of ordinary folk.

So, she continued after a delicate pause, she was to be shipped to a Mid-East kingdom for a visit, nominally a routine courtesy, actually a demonstration of exactly what her kingdom had to offer. Her father knew there was no princess currently on the market to match her appearance. She was, of course, under strict orders to prevent her liability from being exposed.

But international terrorists had seen their chance to strike. They managed to skyjack the airplane she was on. They demanded a phenomenal ransom for her, even while the plane was still in flight—one billion Eurodollars, release of all political prisoners, a public apology for misgovernment, that sort of thing. If the King paid, they would land the plane in a neutral country and let her go; if not—

The King refused to acknowledge their demands. The money was easy, the release of prisoners problematical, and the apology impossible, of course.

"Of course," Mym agreed, understanding perfectly.

The King approached the matter forthrightly. He put out notice that a reward would be given for the severed heads of the conspirators.

They arranged to show their determination by putting her image on a magic mirror. They set up the mirror, but Ligeia refused to perform; she would not demean herself by begging her father to buy her freedom.

Balked for the moment and running low on fuel, the hijackers decided on a more direct demonstration. They stripped her naked, and one of them prepared to rape her—on camera, as it were. It was evident that they had had some such notion in mind ever since seeing her, for they were men.

"Not all men are like that," Mym protested.

"*You* don't desire my body?" she inquired challengingly.

Mym sighed. There was no respectable answer he could give to that.

Seeing that practically all was lost, and with the fell pirate almost upon her, Ligeia had screamed. After all, submission to public rape was no more possible for a princess than a public apology was for a king. In private, a different standard obtained. After a princess got married, both rape and apology were likely, perhaps even necessary.

But not desirable, Mym remarked.

Every other person aboard the plane had lost consciousness. Ligeia, of course, did not know how to pilot it. So the plane crashed, and all aboard were killed, including her.

"And so I found myself in Hell," she concluded.

"But you did nothing worthy of damnation!" Mym protested.

"That is my claim," she agreed. "Technically I did commit suicide—but it was to protect my virtue. And I was responsible for many deaths—but it was self-defense, and they were evil men. I feel that if I could only get a fair hearing, the powers who be should agree that I should go to Heaven. But it seems that my scroll was charged with both murder and suicide, and so I was damned. Of course I would have been damned had I submitted, too."

"Damned if you do and damned if you don't," Mym agreed.

"And then Satan had the temerity to force me to—I tried to warn you away, but—"

"The thing to do," Mym said firmly, "is to turn Satan's trap against him. To get out of Hell. That would serve him right."

"But I keep telling you, that can't be done!" she protested. "Only you alone can win free, if you know how. I can only do it if I get my hearing, and Satan will never allow that."

"How can he prevent it?" Mym asked, nettled. "Doesn't God have anything to say about it?"

"God doesn't interfere in the affairs of mortals or with the Incarnations," she said despairingly.

"Well, I am under no such restriction," Mym said. "I shall get you out."

"That is exactly what Satan wants you to try," she reminded him.

"I am disinclined to disappoint him." Mym considered. "Do you think Satan is listening to us now?"

"Well, we're hiding from him—"

"It is in my mind that Satan permitted us to reach this place," he said. "He surely can tune in on us. This is, after all, his domain."

"I hadn't thought of that," she confessed. "But Hell is a very big region. I'm sure he can't devote his attention to every little detail all the time. Once he knew we were together, he probably went on to other business."

"Probably," Mym agreed. "So we can consider our conversation private."

She shrugged. "I suppose so. But it doesn't matter. I can't get out and, as long as I prevent you from getting out, I am serving his purpose. I don't like that, though I do like being with you."

She was probably correct, Mym thought. She had served as the lure to bring him in, and now served as the chain to keep him here. Satan had no need to watch them.

Yet it was hardly unpleasant, being here with Ligeia. She was a nice girl, with compatible values, and extraordinarily pretty, and he had always been fascinated by that type.

He changed his position, as the stone was not really comfortable. His eye fell on the snake.

The snake was watching him.

Mym completed his adjustment as if he had not noticed, but his mind was suddenly awhirl. Surely it was true that Satan had worse things to do than watch two people get acquainted. But Mym was an Incarnation, and, though Satan could penetrate the veil of invisibility Mym had invoked, he probably couldn't do it from any distance. One Incarnation could not interfere with another from a distance. So Satan probably wasn't tuning in on them directly.

But Satan would not want to let an Incarnation move about Hell unsupervised. He would have to have some way to keep track. And what better way would there be than to assign a lesser minion?

The snake was that minion. It would report on Mym's location at all times and on any important activity Mym indulged in. That would certainly be a convenient way to keep track.

He could touch the snake, phase in with it, and learn for sure. But that might alert Satan that he, Mym, had caught on. Better to seem not to have caught on.

But how could he tell Ligeia, without the snake hearing? And how could he get away from the snake, without alerting it and Satan?

Well, he could phase in to Ligeia and plant a thought in her mind. But at this point he preferred not to do that, because it would be an invasion of what little privacy she might have, and because she was, indeed, a young woman he was quite ready to like and perhaps love. Too great an intimacy could spoil such a relationship.

Or was he afraid that if he phased in to Ligeia he would discover that she was merely another agent of Satan's? It was a possibility he had to consider. If she was, not only would he be disappointed, but his verification of her could betray his suspicion to Satan himself. That would leave him with nothing.

He considered some more and decided that he would have to keep whatever escape plan he might have to himself.

For, abruptly, he realized that he did have a plan—a bold, wild one that only he had any chance of implementing. If he could implement it successfully, not only would he rescue Ligeia, he would be able to rescue many other unfairly damned souls. In addition, it would amply repay Satan for his audacity in trying to trap another Incarnation in Hell and force him to do Satan's will.

It wasn't the nice way and certainly it wasn't the easy way. But Mym was Mars and he felt that the honor of his office was at stake. He wanted to teach Satan a lesson about interfering with Mars.

– 15 –

RIVER

When night fell in Hell, they were satisfied that the pursuit had ended. They had talked and slept and now were eager to get out of the cramped cave.

"I believe there is some way out of Hell," Mym said. "I intend to find it. Do you have any idea where it might be?"

Ligeia considered. "For you, many ways. For me—"

"For us both. Maybe you could not use the exit by yourself, but I could enable you to use it."

She brightened. "Maybe—oh, dare I hope?"

"It is better to hope than to have no hope."

"I have hoped many times and always had my hope dashed."

"There's always hope that this time your hope won't be dashed."

She smiled. "For you, I will entertain that hope. But I really don't know where an exit would be. The River Styx circles all of Hell, and only the ferryman Charon can take a soul across. That he will not do, except by the order of Satan."

"But Hell is three dimensional!" Mym protested. "How can one river surround it all?"

"I don't know," she said, surprised.

"And we came down from above, so there must be a route there," he persisted.

"Yes, there must be," she agreed. "Funny that I never thought of that. But I still don't know how to use such an exit."

It occurred to Mym that if Hell were like Purgatory, its apparent three dimensionality could be an actual two dimensions, so that one river could indeed enclose it all. The descending capsule could have carried them right through the River Styx, charmed by Satan's order. But he saw no point in bring up such morbid speculation. "What we need to do is inquire," he said. "There is sure to be someone who knows and will tell us. But we can't question the damned souls openly, or Satan will shut off any exit that we find."

"We could use the back route," she said. "The demons don't go there, because—"

"Back route?"

"There are roads and things for the front route, but the demons use those, so anyone who doesn't belong would be challenged and caught very soon. Of course, if we were invisible, it might work—but we'd have to become visible to talk with anyone, and then the demons might see. But the back route is through the wilderness—the marshes around the rivers, mainly. But though there aren't demons, there are other things, like monsters and natural hazards. I don't know whether—"

"What happens to a person caught by a monster or a natural hazard?"

"A lot of discomfort or pain, mainly," she said. "We really can't die here, but it would hurt a lot to be chomped up and eaten by a monster, and then you'd be in its belly. I really wouldn't enjoy that."

That was something to think about. Could a monster consume Mars? Probably not. But it could consume Ligeia. Could he protect her from such threats? Perhaps he could, by keeping her in contact with him.

"I think I can guard you from that. Are you willing to risk it?"

"At this point it can be no worse that what Satan would do to me, if—" She didn't finish, and Mym knew why. If she failed her assignment of trapping him in Hell, for all that she had never agreed to do it, she would be punished in Hell's worst fashion. There were indeed fates worse than death, and Hell was the place where these were suffered.

"I have a tentative plan of escape," Mym said carefully. "I can't tell you exactly what it is, because news might reach Satan." He flicked his eyes toward the snake without moving his head, hoping that she would understand the signal while the snake missed it. "But it requires that I meet with the various leaders of the souls of Hell—not the ones doing Satan's business, but the ones who are genuinely interested in human welfare. I presume that, though these souls are damned, they are not totally evil. Can the back route get me to these souls, and can you guide me there?"

Her eyes also flicked toward the snake. "Yes."

How comprehensive an answer was that? Whatever it was, he had to accept it.

They climbed down out of the cave and to the ledge, and the snake slithered after them. That was fine with Mym; he did not want to get rid of the snake, because then Satan would have to assign some other creature to snoop, and that one might be more effective. Also, the snake served as the pretext for him not to speak his true plan aloud, so that he did not have to share it with Ligeia. He disliked having to distrust her, but she *was* serving as an agent of Satan, and he could not be quite, quite certain of her ultimate loyalty.

It was nervy business, walking down the narrow ledge in the dark, but necessary. They proceeded slowly for hours, winding around the mountain, and finally, as dawn was threatening, they reached the base.

They were both tired, so sought a place to rest and sleep. To be tired in the spirit form was no more anomalous than dawn in Hell. Mym's body seemed fully physical to him; it even had natural functions, requiring him to borrow the cover of a bush for a minute. It seemed that if one ate in the Afterlife, one also digested and eliminated; if one labored, one became tired.

They formed a bower—a shelter of boughs—under a leaning tree, making a bed of leaves and fern. They lay down to sleep—and the bugs located them. This was Hell, of course; naturally there were obnoxious vermin.

But Mym simply enfolded Ligeia in his cloak, and the bugs could not get to them. Of course this made it more difficult to sleep, because she was very warm and soft against him. He had sought her because he was in need of a woman, but he wasn't quite sure of her, and of course a princess was not a concubine, so he did not want to move things along too hastily. But that did not mean that he could simply ignore her contact and sleep.

"A penny for your thoughts," she murmured.

"No sale."

"Are you sure you don't desire me?"

"Of course I desire you!" he snapped. "But—"

"That's nice," she said. "But don't worry; I won't corrupt you." And she fell asleep.

How nice for her. Did she, as a pampered princess, even know what male desire signified? She had to, for she had been threatened with rape both as a mortal and as a spirit. But probably she assumed that nice men were different and expressed desire only as an intellectual compliment with no physical component. Well, he would try to honor that notion. Certainly if he had really wanted concubinage without content, he could have had it in Lilith/Lila.

Lilith. Lila. Ligeia. He had not before realized how similar those names were. Could it be that—?

No! That was preposterous. Yet, insidiously, he had to wonder. What a fool Satan would be making of him, if he had been tricked into trapping himself in Hell for the same creature he had renounced in Purgatory! If he was now torturing himself with desire unfulfilled for a damned amoral demoness!

He could phase in to her and learn her identity for certain. He knew that he should. But still he refrained. Suppose Ligeia turned out to be genuine, and his intrusion betrayed his distrust? How would she react to him then? He would not blame her for feeling betrayed.

Was he weighing the risk of his actual betrayal against her mere feeling of betrayal? There could be no question of the appropriate course to take. Yet he could not.

She stirred. "Why are you tense?" she asked.

"Just thinking."

"Are you sure you won't tell me?"

"You would not like it."

"I don't see how your thoughts could be worse than the rest of Hell."

She had a point. "I am wondering whether you are who and what you say you are."

"I am," she said, then reconsidered. "Oh, you mean you doubt? I suppose that's sensible. Who else do you think I might be?"

"Lilith, the demoness."

She became fully alert. "The one who went to the cave with the demons? You think I—?"

"I told you you wouldn't like it."

"I don't! But I suppose you are right to wonder. Demons can assume any form, so she could make herself look just like me. But how can I prove my identity?"

"There is a way," he said reluctantly.

"That's what men always say, isn't it? But I understand that demons are better at it than genuine people are, so—"

"As the Incarnation of War, I have certain powers. One of them is the ability to—"

"To incite violence," she said. "You are doing a fair job of it now!"

This was exactly the kind of entanglement he had wanted to avoid. But now he was in it and had to slog through. "Also to phase in to people, to occupy their bodies and minds and grasp their thoughts."

"Oh." She considered. "I thought you meant another kind of penetration."

"I would not practice either on you without your consent," he said stiffly.

"This phasing in, so you can read my mind—does it mean I can also read yours?"

That notion startled him. "I'm not sure. When I have done it with mortals, they were unaware of my intrusion. But I could project my thoughts to them. I suppose, if one realized what the situation was, he might have read my thoughts on his own."

"Then phase in to me," she said.

"But if you should be a demoness—"

"Then Satan will know all your secrets. But you seek to know mine. Turnabout is fair play, isn't it?"

It did make sense. He had distrusted her; she could distrust him. He wanted to trust her; surely she wanted to trust him. The phasing in would resolve all doubts, one way or the other.

"But do you realize that this can be a more intimate association than any physical one could be?" he asked, still hesitant.

"I would rather be known than unknown," she said simply.

So he phased in. For a moment he had trouble orienting, and was afraid that it wouldn't work when there was no mortal body to anchor to. But then he realized that in the mortal realm he had used the physical body to fix the spiritual essence in place; on this occasion it could be done directly.

He overlapped her—and discovered that not only was it possible to do it without the physical bodies, it was much easier, because there was no flesh to get in the way. Just like that, her thoughts were his.

She was genuine. All that she had told him was true. Her mind was so straightforward, and the merging so complete, that there was absolutely no doubt.

So that's the plan! he thought with surprise.

No, that's not your thought, it's mine, the thought followed immediately. *Ligeia's.*

The rapport was so thorough that he had mistaken her thought for his own! He had never anticipated success like this! Why had she even been concerned about—wait, whose thought was this? His or hers?

Does it matter?

Confused, Mym disengaged. They lay there, both their bodies radiant with the experience, assimilating the enormous impact of the prior few moments. Truly, they had known each other for an instant.

Now Mym discovered that he could recollect greater detail in Ligeia's memories than he had been aware of before. He seemed to have acquired part of her mind.

"It was right to let Rapture go, though you still loved her," Ligeia said.

"You share my memories?" he asked, knowing it was so.

"Your memories become you," she said. "You are a decent man. I can see why you are wary of the demoness; that business with the talking head—"

"I had no idea that the phase would be that complete, Li!"

"I know, Mym, I know," she said.

"How well we know each other so suddenly!"

"It was worth it."

"It was worth it," he repeated.

"I think we shall very soon be in love."

"Very soon," he agreed.

"For the first time in my Afterlife, I am glad I went to Hell."

"I know." He kissed her. The acquaintance that should have taken months had been accomplished in seconds.

Now, secure in their knowledge of each other, they slept.

Ligeia did know her way generally about Hell. She had found a map of it in a book Satan had shown her. The book described the various regions and tortures available; the showing of it had not been any favor to her, but a threat. She had been terrified by the threat, but she had remembered the pretty map.

"The River Lethe originates near the center, and that is where Satan's private retreat is," she said. "So we should discover its source spring near here."

"Lethe—the water of forgetfulness?" he asked. "My mythology is not yours, but I seem to remember that."

"True. If we thirst, we had better not drink that water, for we will not even remember our mission thereafter."

They walked along, and the snake followed, and they found the spring, and thirst smote Mym, but he knew he could not drink. The clear water bubbled up from the white sand below, forming a lovely pool surrounded by rich vegetation. There were several canoes on a rack beside it. This was evidently a wilderness retreat.

"Odd that such a thing should exist in Hell," Mym remarked.

"It's a trap. Unwary souls who flee the work gangs find their way here and choose to boat and swim in the water, and—"

"I see. Satan does love to torture insidiously."

"But we can use a canoe," she said. "It doesn't matter if we get splashed, as long as none of it gets in our mouths. Of course it might not be smart actually to swim in it."

"Not smart at all," he agreed.

"The rivers lead to every major section of Hell. Some of them are pretty nasty. That's why there isn't much traffic on them."

They lifted a canoe and turned it over. It was made of aluminum—or whatever passed for it in the Afterlife—and was light. They set it in the water and climbed carefully in. The snake joined them. There were two aluminum paddles with it, too. It floated very nicely on the water.

"I would hardly need to drink the water to forget," Mym said. "This is such a pleasant place."

"Appearances can be deceptive," she said.

They paddled. Mym had had experience with this sort of thing and had the rear seat; he kept a straight course by sculling, while Ligeia paddled on either side in front.

They guided it to the outlet, where the flow of the river commenced. The water was calm; only the slightest current was felt. The vegetation grew richly up to the shore, and trees overhung, so that the stream seemed to be passing under a green canopy. Small fish swam below, and turtles were at the fringe. It was hard indeed to remember that this was Hell!

But soon the stream entered a marshy region where water plants encroached. The plants seemed innocent—hyacinths—but Mym was cautious. This was, after all, Hell.

Sure enough, as they glided close, he saw little feeler-threads writhing out from the plants, reaching toward the canoe. There seemed to be sap flowing that resembled saliva. Those plants were hungry for more than water.

"Stay clear of those plants," he warned Ligeia.

"The hungrycinths," she agreed. "They will leave nothing but bones, if they get the chance to feed."

Mym wondered how a spirit-person could have bones. But surely he did, here in Hell. He liked this quiet stream less.

They found a channel by the plants, but there were more and more of the things, and soon they could go no farther without forging directly through. "I think we'd better do it rapidly," Mym said. "If we travel swiftly enough, they won't be able to get hold."

They gathered momentum and struck the bank of plants at speed. The drag was immediately felt. The canoe slowed, partly from the sheer clogging mass of plants, and partly from the latching-on of their hairlike tentacles. They continued paddling, but soon became bogged down.

Now the plants seemed to crowd in, extending their thick leaves over the sides of the canoe, reaching in with their feelers. Sap fairly drooled.

Mym lifted his paddle high and brought it down beside the canoe, smashing at the plants. They were crushed down with a sick vegetable squishing sound. He smashed again, at those on the other side, freeing what he could reach of the canoe. "Knock them away!" he called to Ligeia. "Then we can move on through!"

She lifted her paddle and brought it down. But her motion was ineffective and dislodged only a few plants. "Harder!" Mym called. His own plants were crowding in again.

She struck harder—and water splashed up against Mym. He shielded his face instinctively. His right arm was spattered—and where the droplets touched, spots of numbness developed. The water of Lethe was making his very flesh forget!

"Don't splash!" he cried.

"Oops!" She restricted her effort and managed to get most of the plants unclung.

"Now paddle forward," he said. "We can do it."

They both worked hard, and the canoe began to move reluctantly. Now the action of the paddles tended to clear the plants from the sides. But it was a lot of work for excruciatingly slow progress.

At last they forged out of the band of plants and into clear water. But there were more hungrycinths ahead. Mym peered about, trying to spy the route of least resistance, but all looked equally bad. No matter which way they went, there would be a struggle.

They made the struggle, navigating interminable rafts of vegetation, and at last came to a weather-worn landing. "This is our first stop," Ligeia said breathlessly. "Why don't I wait in the canoe while you talk to the man?"

He glanced at her, surprised. He was sure she did not want to be separated from him, here in the hind region of Hell. Then he saw the snake and realized that they could not afford to have it reporting on the true nature of his dialogue with the leader of the damned souls. He trusted Ligeia completely now, and she trusted him—but neither of them trusted the snake. So she was volunteering to keep the snake here, providing him the necessary privacy. This was a brave and good gesture on her part.

"Yes, I can see you are tired," he said. "You stay here and rest, and I will return as soon as I can."

Then Mym went and found the leader of the damned souls, who was engaged in shoveling muck out of a canal-ditch. Naturally the muck seeped back in almost as fast as he got it out; that was the nature of Hell.

Mym introduced himself briefly, then phased in to the skeptical man. The contact, as it had been with Ligeia, was instantly perfect, and the man understood the full nature of Mym's plan and acquiesced. Much sooner than would otherwise have been the case, Mym was back at the canoe.

"We'll have to ask the next," Mym said shortly. That was for the benefit of the snake, who would think that Mym had not gotten what he wanted—news of a secret exit from Hell.

They paddled on downstream, and in due course the River Lethe debouched into a river of an entirely different nature. This one was largely frozen. Ice rimmed its shore and closed in on the center current, leaving only a narrow channel. Icicles hung from the neighboring trees.

"What in Hell is that?" Mym inquired, surprised.

"The River Kokytus," Ligeia informed him. "The waters of lamentation."

"I lament the moment I committed myself to this voyage," Mym muttered. "We'll freeze!"

"Doesn't your cloak protect you?"

"It should. But what about you?"

"I may have to help you paddle from the rear seat."

They nudged the canoe into the frozen Kokytus. Immediately a cutting crosswind developed, shoving the canoe sidewise toward the ice. Ligeia had to put her paddle out to stave off a collision, and Mym did the same. Now the wind tore at the woman, whipping her hair across her face, quickly chilling her.

"Come back here with me!" Mym cried. "Before you freeze."

"But then the ice—"

"You can't endure that cold wind long!"

She had to agree. She made her way back to him, and got under the cover of his cloak.

But now the canoe was weighted down at the back, and lifting out of the water at the front. The wind turned it about so that the front overrode the ice. They were unable to paddle it forward.

"I'll have to go back to my seat," Ligeia said, shivering with the expectation. "It's the only way we can—"

"No! I won't have you freezing!"

"But you have to talk with—"

But Mym had a notion. "Let's see if we can travel on the ice!" he exclaimed.

They tried it. They paddled madly and rammed the canoe up farther on the ice. When it would go no farther, they moved up to the front end, overbalancing it and lifting the rear out of the water. Then some scraping and shoving with the paddles got the remainder onto the ice.

After that it wasn't hard. They simply poled the canoe across the ice, downstream. The liability had become an asset.

But when they came to the landing for the next meeting, the problem of cold resumed. If Ligeia remained with the canoe, she would freeze. But if she did not—

"Actually, that snake's torpid," Mym said. "It's coldest in the bottom of the boat, where it touches the ice."

Ligeia checked. The snake was curled up, trying to husband some warmth, but obviously not succeeding. "The poor thing," she murmured. "I'd better get it to somewhere warmer."

"That reptile is—" Mym started, but couldn't finish, because he didn't want the snake to know he knew.

"Cold," she finished. "I don't care what kind of creature it is, it shouldn't be allowed to freeze." She reached into the canoe and carefully picked up the snake.

Mym was disgusted. He would have been glad to be rid of the snake in a coincidental manner, so that Satan would not catch on. At the same time, he appreciated the softer nature of Ligeia, who, however foolishly, was being caring.

So they walked away from the frozen river, and Ligeia carried the snake along, warming it.

The souls of this region resembled snow monsters as they struggled to carry baskets of snow through the drifts. Obviously they had been assigned this work for the same reason the others had to slop muck endlessly—pointless misery. The demons in charge were in a high tower, evidently warmed by a stove, because smoke issued from its chimney. That meant that the workers were not closely supervised—but it seemed the demons kept track of the deliveries, for as Mym watched, a snow-bomb was lofted from an automatic catapult. It arched through the air and landed on a laggard worker, burying him in snow.

Another worker saw the two of them. "New recruits?" he asked. "Here, I've got an extra coat for the lady." He paused to strip his outer layer, a furred jacket, battered but good.

"But you need that yourself!" Ligeia protested.

"Not as much as you do," the man said, handed her the jacket, and resumed his plodding.

It was a help, for now she was able to walk alone. Mym located the leader and matched his step, speaking briefly to him while Ligeia walked some distance behind. Then Mym phased in with the man, and in a moment the understanding was complete; the man would spread the word, and these people would cooperate. Mym disengaged, walked along for another minute, then broke away, trusting that neither the supervising demon nor the snake Ligeia carried had comprehended the true nature of his contact.

They returned to the canoe. "They don't seem like bad people," Mym remarked as they resumed their skid along the ice.

"They really aren't," she agreed. "Of course I am bringing you to the best groups, the ones who were only marginally evil to begin with and who have probably expiated enough of their sin to qualify for Heaven, except that Satan never does let anyone go, regardless. I understand some of the damned souls in other regions are really bad."

"That man gave you his coat," Mym persisted. "Shouldn't that count on his balance card, a good deed?"

"It should," she agreed. "But he didn't do it for that, because they all know Satan won't let them go anyway."

"Which is the truest positive act—sacrifice without hope of reward."

"I wish we could help these people, somehow," she said.

"If we find our avenue of escape, some of them may use it too," he reminded her.

She now understood exactly what he had in mind. "Yes."

The snake, recovered from its lethargy of cold, perked up. It was now coiled about one of Ligeia's legs, warmed by her body without interfering with her use of the paddle. Mym wondered how it reported to Satan, whether it had to make periodic check-ins, or whether it was telepathic. Probably the former; the latter would have betrayed them already, for it would have read their minds and not have to listen to their words. Perhaps it was a variety of demon that could vaporize at will, zip away to report, and return while they were sleeping. That was what Mym was counting on.

The Kokytus debouched into a broad and quiet river, and the ice gave way to polluted water. This was easier to canoe through, but unpleasant to see and smell. "Which one is this?"

"The Acheron," she replied, removing her jacket, as the air had warmed. "River of Sorrows."

"That figures," he said. "The clear, clean spring water is for-getful. The frozen stream is lamenting. And the polluted one has sorrows."

"What greater sorrow is there than the destruction of what once was lovely?" she asked.

He sighed agreement. "Yet the mortals are doing their best to make all their rivers like this."

"The mortal world is going to Hell. Anybody can see that, from this vantage. But it's sad."

"If only they would understand and change course!" he said. "Maybe if mortal people could only see Hell or hear about how it really is, before . . ."

"But, every mortal person has to die before seeing Hell, and then it's too late."

That was the crux of the problem. It meant that Satan stood a fair chance to prevail, because of the ignorance of mortals.

The river narrowed and the current accelerated. "I hope there aren't rapids!" Mym muttered.

"I don't think there are, but—"

The river forked. "Which way do we go?" Mym asked.

"I don't know. They probably rejoin after a bit, so maybe it doesn't matter."

Mym steered the canoe into the left channel, which seemed to be the more navigable of the two. All went well—until they came up against a fallen tree. It hung slantwise over the water, blocking progress.

"We can duck under it," Mym said.

They coasted up to it, and both squeezed down low, and they passed under the trunk. But as they did, several objects dropped from it into the canoe. Mym thought they were bits of bark, but then he saw them scuttling. They were little crablike things, with pincers. They waved little antennae in the air, then headed purposefully for the nearest delicacy, Ligeia.

"Trouble," Mym said. "Get your legs up!"

She looked back—and screamed. She tried to get her legs up, but got a foot caught under the seat. The first crab reached that foot and took an experimental pinch. Ligeia screamed again.

Mym took his paddle and pounded at the crabs with it. Then he jumped—one had pinched him on the ankle. It hurt terribly.

Then the canoe ran up against a submerged log and stalled.

First things first. Mym got to work cleaning out the crabs. He discovered that he could stun them momentarily with a blow, then use the blade of the paddle to lift them up and dump them out. One by one he pursued them, until all were gone.

Next, he considered their external predicament. He could not see the log, but he could not move the canoe off it. "I'll have to get out and lift it off," he said.

"No, no, don't do that!" Ligeia protested. "Any part that touches this water—the sorrows—"

He didn't need to have sorrows in his feet, legs, and however far up the water extended when he stood in it. Hell could make things uncomfortably literal. He looked for some other way.

"Oh, no!" Ligeia said.

Mym looked. There in the water was an alligator. It looked hungry.

Desperately, he paddled, trying to boost the canoe off the hang-up, but all he succeeded in doing was to shove his end around until the canoe was sideways, being pushed by the current but not getting anywhere.

That gave him a notion. He continued paddling, with a watchful eye on the alligator, until his end swung the rest of the way around. The canoe was now backwards, facing upstream, still stuck. But Mym's end was beyond the barrier. "Come back here with me, and we can budge it," he called.

Ligeia moved back. As her end lightened, they were at last able to shove off the log, just as the alligator closed in. They took off backward, unable to turn around. So Mym stroked backward while Ligeia moved back to position. The alligator watched, disgusted, but did not pursue.

After that, they knew how to get over the submerged logs. They struggled on to the next landing and got out. This time, again, Ligeia remained in the canoe with the snake, letting Mym handle his business alone.

Shortly after they resumed their journey, the river widened and joined a truly horrendous tributary. The water of the other river smelled of oil, and small blue flames played across its surface.

Ligeia pointed to it. "The River Phlegethon," she said.

Mym was appalled. "You mean we have to go up *that*?"

She nodded. "The next good group . . ."

So they stroked up the River of Fire. Mym could feel the heat of the flame on it; when his energetic paddling splashed droplets of water into the canoe, they ignited as they landed. Had the canoe been of wood or bark, it would soon have been ablaze! As it was, it grew hot, and the snake crawled up to the seat beside Ligeia to avoid the discomfort of the metal hull.

Then they came to rapids, and the vapor thrown up by the spuming liquid was burning, making a curtain of fire extending several meters above the surface. "No way we can go through *that*," Mym said. "We'll have to portage."

They guided the craft to the side, found a reasonably firm section of the bank, and got out. Then they hauled the canoe out and picked up each end. It was heavy and clumsy, seeming much more so than it had when they first put it into the water. This was an indication of how they were tiring.

Then their feet started sinking down into the marshy ground. Each time Mym took a step, there was a sucking sound, and muck coated his boots, and an odor reminiscent of overripe eggs wafted up. Ligeia, wearing only delicate slippers, was worse off.

"Maybe I can haul it!" Mym exclaimed. He set down his end, slogged to the front, took hold, and hauled. The canoe moved, reluctantly. He stepped forward and hauled again. It was feasible. This allowed Ligeia to pick her way more carefully, sparing her slippers and feet further degradation.

But the marsh got worse. It started making sucking sounds of its own, and holes appeared that were not caused by feet. They looked like pursed mouths. Mym accidentally put a foot in one; it sank in halfway to his knee, and the mouth-hole closed about it and hung on.

He wrenched, but the boot remained captive and he was in danger of removing his foot without the boot. Meanwhile there was a kind of hissing and steaming in the hole, as if digestive juices were being squirted about. So he reached with difficulty into the canoe, fetched out a paddle, and used it to jam into the hole and wedge out his boot. It was awkward, clumsy business, but at last he got it free, somewhat degraded on the outside.

He resumed the hauling, now being more careful where he set his feet. His breath was short as he labored, and he was sweating, but he made progress. Again he wondered idly about the physiological effects here in the spirit realm; had he not known where he was, he would have had no way to tell that he was not in the mortal realm. To a spirit, the spirit world seemed just as tangible as the physical world did to a mortal.

They came in above the fire-rapids, launched the canoe, and paddled on upstream. In due course they reached the fourth encampment and made the connection. Then all they had to do was proceed on back down the River of Fire.

Dusk was at hand as they reached the foul Acheron again; instead of entering it, they landed the canoe and made camp at the fringe of the fire zone. There was nothing to drink except some of the firewater, and nothing to eat except tubers they were able to scrounge from the scorched soil. But they stuck the tubers on the ends of long sticks and toasted them at the fire on the river; the tubers were edible if not enjoyable. The firewater did not properly slacken their thirst, but it soon caused them to cease to worry about the matter. They talked, laughed, rolled together, and decided it was time to get serious about sex . . . and discovered they could not. The firewater had not only inflamed their desire, it had made one or the other of them impotent. Ligeia found that hilarious, but Mym suspected that in the morning, when he was sober, he would not be laughing. Unrequited lust— trust Hell to be the place for that sort of experience!

Indeed, when the morning came, he was not laughing. His body ached from the exertions of the prior day, and his head felt as if he had soaked it overnight in the stench-water of the Acheron. Ligeia seemed little better off; her beauty was now overlaid by grime and fatigue. "Oh, my clothing!" she fussed. "No one would take me for a princess now!"

"True," Mym muttered. "They would take you for a woman."

She glanced at him. "Are you making fun of me?"

"No. I never really cared for princesses, but I have known some fine women." Actually that was a confusion, perhaps spawned by his hangover. He did care for princesses, and needed one to share his life. But at the moment he really craved a woman of the nature of Orb, who had brought him up when he had been low and loved him without questioning his nature. Ligeia was both princess and woman—but the woman aspect was becoming more important to him.

"Oh." She considered for a moment. "But don't you prefer pretty women?"

"Second only to caring ones."

"You *are* making fun of me!"

"Come read my mind." He took her hand and drew her in to him. She came, making only token resistance. He phased in to her—and discovered a kind of tinder that ignited explosively as it encountered the developing flame of his emotion. There was a dialogue, occurring in an instant; parsed into its components it might have been rendered like this:

"But I'm not ready to love!" she protested.

"You don't need to," he responded. "I'm on the rebound."

"This sort of thing is supposed to take time!"

"We'll give it time."

"Too late! I'm already raging with desire!"

"That's *my* desire!"

"Not any more!"

They disengaged and looked at each other. "I'm not sure we should have done that," Mym said.

"I'm not sure we should be doing this," she replied.

"Be doing what?"

"What we couldn't do last night." She began removing her clothing.

Mym realized that they had no secrets from each other. It did make sense to complete what they had started in their minds. On the prior night it would have been largely wasted in their besotted state, but now they could appreciate it to its full extent with their minds clear.

He removed his own clothing. "Afterwards, we can wash up in firewater," he remarked.

That set her off again, laughing. Her whole body jiggled with her mirth.

There was a sound from the river. Mym looked up—and saw a great fiery shape emerging from the water. "What's that?" he asked, alarmed.

Ligeia looked. "The Fireman!" she shrieked.

"The what?"

"The denizen of the River of Fire! I thought he was a myth! We must flee!"

"I'll fight him!" Mym said, getting to his feet.

"You can't!" she protested. "He burns everything!"

Mym faced the emerging monster and reached for the Red Sword. But of course the Sword was gone, along with the rest of his clothing. Gone? He had never brought it into Hell! He had no weapon.

The Fireman pointed at a small tree. A jet of flame came from his hand, and the tree burst into fire. The Fireman pointed at the river; the jet touched it, and the water boiled into a cloud of vapor. The Fireman pointed at Mym.

Mym snatched up his cloak and dodged to the side. The ground where he had been standing jumped as if struck by a bomb, and smoke roiled up.

"Flee!" Ligeia cried, terrified.

Mym concluded that this was good advice. He grabbed her hand and fled.

They ran to the shore of the Acheron, and the Fireman did not pursue them there. He hovered for a moment where they had camped, then marched back into the Phlegethon.

When they returned to their campsite, they found only slag and ashes. Their clothing and the canoe had been destroyed. The only other survivor was the snake.

They stood there. "Maybe we shouldn't have," Ligeia said.

"We *didn't*." Mym reminded her.

"Well, we were going to."

But now the mood was gone. It would have to wait for another time.

They resumed their trip, walking carefully in their bare feet. Fortunately, Ligeia said, their next and final stop was not far ahead. They proceeded to the juncture of the rivers and walked along the bank of the Acheron; in an hour or so came to the merger with the greatest of all Hell's rivers, the Styx. It was so vast as to seem like an ocean in itself, and its waters were inky black and seemed deep beyond imagination. Out across its somber surface, near the horizon, strange waves developed, as if some massive and sinister creature swam below. Mym would not have wanted to take a canoe out there!

In another hour they reached the encampment of the final group. There were women here—indeed, it seemed to be an Amazon community—and they looked at Mym appraisingly, as if judging whether his flesh would be better for soup or for pot roast. But Ligeia spoke up, telling them that Mym was Mars, the Incarnation of War, and needed to meet with their leader privately. They were impressed, for they were warlike women, and soon Mym was closeted with the head Amazon. He explained in a few words, then phased in with her.

"Lovely!" she exclaimed as they disengaged. "You may count on us."

The Amazons provided them with clothing and a tent to stay in and fed them well. "We shall coordinate the signals," their leader assured Mym. "Give us a day, while you rest."

Then Mym and Ligeia retired to their tent, at last having the chance to do what they wished without intrusion—and found themselves both so tired that they simply flopped on the fragrant straw and slept.

– 16 –

REVOLT

In the morning things were ready. Mym and Ligeia and the snake emerged from the tent to find the Amazons in full combat dress. Each stood tall and proud with her bow and quiver of arrows, her left breast full and perfectly molded, her right breast absent. The right one was, of course, burned off in childhood, so that it never developed and thus could never interfere with the drawing of the bowstring. "But we have two problems," Diana, the Amazon leader, said. "First, we lack efficient means of travel. Only the demons can use the front routes, and the back routes, as you know, are slow and treacherous. Since it is necessary for you to be at all the key sites—"

"What is the second problem?" Mym asked.

"There is a demon spy among us."

"Don't hurt the snake!" Ligeia exclaimed. "It has done us no harm!"

"Except to report of your whereabouts every night," Diana said.

"We knew its mission," Mym said. "We saw to it that it did not know our actual plan."

"Still, now that plan must be revealed, and surprise is of the essence. That demon must be abolished."

"It's not a demon, it's a snake," Ligeia protested. "The soul of an animal."

"How do you know?"

"It got cold. A demon would not have been affected."

Mym glanced at the snake, startled. It was true; demons had no vulnerability to extremes of temperature, as they had to function in all the climes that made souls suffer. Yet, that being the case—

"It must still be a spy," Diana said. "We must hack it to pieces, so that it can not report on our activity."

"But you can't kill a soul," Mym said.

"But we can do the equivalent," she said. "When we do to it what would be the killing of a mortal, it becomes nonfunctional for a day, just as the demons do. That is all the time we need."

"But we can't even be sure it *is* a spy," Ligeia said. "It's just a snake Satan used to gag me, and then it stayed with us. Maybe it had no choice."

"I can settle this," Mym said. "I will phase in to it." He approached the snake and put his hand on its body. The snake did not try to avoid him.

In a moment he knew two things, and one of them astonished him. The snake was a spy for Satan—and the snake did not want to be. It had spied because it knew that Satan would have put it into perpetual torture if it did not cooperate. So it had reported each night to a demon who came to meet it. But it wished there were some other choice. When Ligeia had warmed it, it had been grateful to her, for no other creature had shown it such consideration during its life or its Afterlife. But it had had no way to escape its assignment.

But now you have a way, Mym thought to it. *Join the revolt.*

The snake was amazed. *You would have me?*

The revolt is open to anyone or anything who shares its precepts.

Then I join it.

Will other animals join it? Mym inquired.

If they knew they would be accepted and rewarded as the human souls are.

Mym disengaged. "The snake will join us, if we will accept it. Other animals may do the same. Do you see what this means?"

"The animals—will join us?" Diana asked incredulously. "Even the hellhounds?"

"We can but inquire," Mym said. "It is a risk of betrayal, but if successful—"

"You are the leader, Mars," Diana said. "If you are ready to take that risk—"

"I believe I am. I believe the snake speaks for its kind and perhaps for others. If we offer them the same terms—"

Diana shrugged. "Then we shall not protest."

Mym phased in to the snake again. He thought the terms to it. *Bring those animals who accept this here,* he concluded.

The snake slithered away. "Now we wait," Mym said.

It was a painful process, waiting until the animals responded. But the benefit could be critical. Hours passed.

Then two hellhounds bounded toward the camp. The Amazons raised their bows, arrows nocked. Hellhounds were hard to put out of business, because they were so large and tough, but arrows through the eyes and paws could do it.

The hellhounds slowed and paused, then walked slowly on toward the group, tracked by the arrowheads. When they reached the center, Mym approached. He touched one and phased in.

The animals were willing. They hated Hell as much as the human souls did. Most animals retired at death to their own Afterlives, but some few were caught up in the human system, particularly those who had been pets or associates of man. They wanted to be free of it just as much as the human souls did.

Then we shall include you in the reckoning, on the same basis as the human souls, Mym thought to it. *I, the human Incarnation of War, pledge this.*

I, the representative of the animals, accept this, the hellhound thought back. *How may we serve you?*

We require transportation.

We can provide it.

So the pact was made. The two hellhounds loped away.

In an hour, two wild horses galloped in. Their dark manes flung out and their nostrils snorted steam; they were killer equines, damned for killing men. But for this they were tame.

Ligeia, being a princess, knew how to ride well. She and Mym mounted. "You know what to do," Mym called to Diana as they rode away.

The horses galloped to the nearest ford and crossed the Acheron. People afoot would not have been able to do it, because of the foulness of the water, but these horses were toughened to it. Then they carried Mym and Ligeia to the checkpoint of their region of Hell.

This was simply a guard station at the intersection of several paved roads. A demon guard stood there, holding a flamethrower. It was obvious that any soul who tried to pass this point would get burned. Spiked fences extended from the checkpoint away across the terrain, and Mym knew that those would not be subject to passing, either; Hell surely had ways to make a fence tight. The only interruption of such a fence would be a river, which explained how the canoe had gotten them through.

They rode up on the wild horses and dismounted. The demon's gaze followed them, and its flamethrower was ready. Mym took a step toward the checkpoint, then seemed to hesitate. "I don't think we can go this way," he said to Ligeia.

"Oh, and I did so want to be alone with you," she said, speaking the line they had rehearsed.

They started to turn away. "Halt!" the demon cried.

They paused. The thing had taken the bait! "Oh, don't let that demon get me!" Ligeia cried.

"Where were you going?" the demon demanded.

Ligeia turned, evincing a fright that was not wholly feigned. "I just—nowhere," she said, trembling.

The demon's red eyes glowed more brightly as he surveyed her body. Drool dribbled from a tusk. Demons might be incapable of such human emotions as love, but they could compass lust, and Ligeia's figure incited that. "You can be alone with me, wench, and I don't care who watches!"

"No!" she cried.

The demon aimed the flamethrower. "Come here, wench—or fry!"

Reluctantly, Ligeia approached the demon. Then, just as it was about to grab her, she screamed.

The demon dropped like a clod of manure. Mym hurried in and hauled it out of the box. Then he took the flamethrower and fired it, playing the flame over the demon's body. Foul smoke went up as the body burned and vaporized. In a moment, nothing was left.

Mym waved his arm in a signal across the field. Immediately the hidden Amazons rose up, running toward the checkpoint.

A demon was coming down the road, evidently off duty from some mission of malice. "Hey, get back to work, you sluts!" it cried. But the Amazons charged right at it and, in a moment, had overwhelmed it and hacked it to pieces. The revolt was on!

Diana arrived at the checkpoint. "Take over," Mym told her, presenting the flamethrower.

"No demon shall pass, Mars!" she said, thumping her chest on the flat right side with her fist. "We'll mop up those remaining in this sector, never fear!"

They led the wild horses through, and Mym and Ligeia remounted on the other side of the checkpoint. They galloped toward the next one.

Mym was pleased. This first mission had gone smoothly, and the upper echelon of Hell had not been warned. If they could take out the other four as readily, the revolt would succeed before Satan even knew it was in progress.

For it was no secret exit from Hell that Mym had sought. He knew there was none. He had acquainted the leaders of the major sections with his plan for an organized rebellion, occurring virtually simultaneously in several regions, so that the demonic forces would be unable to concentrate on any one. There were a thousand damned souls for every demon, and only the tight organization and repressive tactics of the demons kept the souls cowed. As long as the major sections of Hell were sealed off from each other, no revolt could succeed, because the demons would wipe it out by concentrating their force. The other sections would be unable to assist, if they even knew what was going on. Then, of course, there would be a brutal extra ration of torture for all those who had participated in the uprising. The thing about torture in Hell was that there was no necessary end to it; what would cause a mortal to die in agony merely caused the agony here. Those who did the equivalent of dying woke again the following day, for a resumption of the torture. And the demons were adept at easing up just shy of that momentary relief, so that there was no period of unconsciousness. No, it really wasn't worth it, making trouble in Hell!

Of course they could not come at the next checkpoint from the central road; the demons would know immediately that two souls mounted on wild horses did not belong there. They had to cross at the rear and approach from inside. This checkpoint had merely gotten them into the region of fire; it had not given them freedom of Hell's highways. But since they did not have to follow the devious river channel, they did gain time.

The wild horses, out of their territory, were not familiar with this region, but Ligeia had enough of a notion of it to guide them. They skirted the worst of the blazes and found the camp of the damned souls of this region. "It's on!" Mym called as they galloped through. "Prepare the ambush! The Amazons are in control of their sector!"

There was immediately activity in the camp, as the souls moved out. They would remain hidden until Mym and Ligeia did their job, as would the Amazons.

In due course they emerged from a region of smoldering grass to come in sight of the checkpoint. Here the demon had a firehose, for a flamethrower would hardly stop those who were acclimatized to fire. The water that the hose would squirt was poisonous and would cause any flesh it touched to die and rot. This was just as effective in its fashion as the flamethrower at the other site.

At this station there were two female demons. The vulnerable-girl ploy would not work here; demonesses were no less lustful than the males, but their tastes differed. So for this one Mym made himself invisible and walked up alone. He carried a sharp knife that the Amazons had given him, fashioned from a fragment of bone. Again he wondered how there could be bones where there was no mortal flesh and no true dying; he could only conjecture that Hell was stocked with all manner of repulsive things, including bones.

His foot struck a pebble, and the nearer demoness looked up. She opened her mouth—but Mym leaped at her and cut her throat before she could speak.

Mistake! The slash drew no blood. The mouth screamed warning to the other. Mym hacked away at the rest of the neck, severing the head more readily than he would a human head, for demons possessed no bones. But the severed head continued to scream, even as it rolled on the ground, and the arms flailed at him.

The other demoness caught up the water hose and turned on the water. She swept it in an arc, to catch whatever was there. The blast of it caught Mym dead center and knocked him back. But he retained his invisibility. Because he was an Incarnation, he was immune to the poison. He grabbed the decapitated demoness, used her as a shield, and advanced on the other.

Demons were not noted for spooking, but this sight of her beheaded companion advancing purposefully on her caused this one to stare. Then she dived for the alarm signal, to summon help.

Mym let the headless one go and flung himself on the other. She could not see him, but now she could feel him and she fought savagely, scratching at him with her claws and biting at him with her teeth. Tusks were just as dangerous on a female as on a male, but his cloak protected him from injury. He got her down and held her there. "Firefolk!" he yelled. "Here to me!"

In a moment the damned souls closed in and quickly tore apart both the whole and the partial demoness. Another sector had been liberated.

They mounted the wild steeds again and headed for the next. So far there was no general alarm in Hell—but that last had been close.

They proceeded to the next checkpoint. This one had a male and a female demon. Mym and Ligeia approached them together, but before they got close enough to act, the male did a double-take. "Hey, didn't I see you at the mesa?" it demanded. "You were—"

Mym charged. He managed to take out the male, but not before the female had struck the alarm button. Then Mym dispatched her, and the damned souls took over the checkpoint.

But the damage had been done. The alarm had been sounded, and now the demons would be alert. Three sectors in rebel hands were not enough; they needed five, by Mym's judgment. Five would stretch the demon forces out thin enough to resist; four was doubtful, and three insufficient.

"But maybe if we strike where unexpected," Mym said.

They entered the sector of perpetual snows. The demons knew

they would try for its opposite checkpoint next. Therefore they planned to go for the one by the region of forgetfulness instead.

To do this they had to cross the Acheron, the River of Sorrows. The fence went right up to the bank and down into the river, and the horses balked at entering the water. There was no shallow ford here; the fluid was deep and ugly. Mym was sure there would be much sorrow to the horses if they ventured there; the various boundaries of Hell were effective. But there had to be a way to cross; after all, the river was not that broad.

They tracked down the stream and found a region where the water coursed shallowly past a series of projecting stones. The horses stepped across these, practicing inhuman balance, and reached the farther shore. Then they followed it up past the region of the fence—and discovered that it was an island. They had not yet crossed the River of Sorrows.

They walked along the island, trying to find a way to cross the rest. They came upon an old, deserted building. It had a steeple with a cross on it.

"A church!" Ligeia exclaimed, astonished. "What is that doing in Hell?"

Mym, of course, was not a Christian. "I suppose artifacts of any type can be here. If a church happened to be—what do you call it, excommunicated—"

"I suppose so," she said doubtfully. She opened the door and went in, and Mym followed, curious about this anomaly.

Inside it seemed empty—but Mym's sensitivity to minds alerted him. "Something is here," he said.

Ligeia passed along the central aisle, feeling the air above the pews with her hands. "Yes, there is something—ghostlike—some presence—"

"Ghosts—in Hell?" He touched a region she had indicated and felt it. "No, not exactly. These are mere thoughts. Instead of people, or spirits, there are only thoughts here. One thought per person."

"Each thought in lieu of a person," Ligeia repeated. "I wonder why? And why do they stay here, alone and quiet?"

Mym phased in to a thought. It was of suicide.

"I think these are people who committed suicide," he said.

"They aren't quite damned, but Heaven doesn't really favor them, so they are here in limbo."

"But *I* committed—" she said.

"And you were damned for your other crimes—killing the other people in the airplane. Rightly or wrongly. Otherwise you might have found yourself here."

She nodded, agreeing. "It really isn't a bad place. Or a bad situation, being a thought."

"But we can't stay," he reminded her. "We have other business."

"Yes . . ." Almost reluctantly, she followed him out of the church.

They found a fallen tree that spanned the stream. The horses walked up it, employing their uncommon balance, and jumped down at the other shore. They were across the river and through the fence, too.

"The suicides," Ligeia murmured as they rode away. "In a church on an island in the River of Sorrows. I suppose that's fitting, somehow."

"If they had reason to do it, it doesn't seem right to send them to everlasting torture," Mym agreed.

She seemed satisfied with that, but remained pensive as they rode on.

Now they were in the region of forgetfulness, bounded on the other side by the River Lethe. The demons at the checkpoint, true to form for this region, had forgotten to be watchful, and Mym took them out without trouble. The damned souls of this region took over the checkpoint.

Four down; one to go. This one was in the frozen region, bounded by the River of Lamentation, Kokytus. They had no trouble crossing its ice—but they knew they would not have the advantage of surprise this time.

"If we make this one, we shall be successful," Mym said. "If not—"

"I love you, Mym," Ligeia said. "If I never get out of Hell, I will still be better for that."

"I will not leave you in Hell," he said. They leaned over, each riding a wild horse, and kissed.

The final checkpoint was indeed expecting them. Demons were

ranged along the fence on either side of it, standing in the snow, each bearing a flamethrower.

They drew up at a distance, concealed by snow-covered trees, and considered. "No way we can get there unchallenged," Mym said. "If I approached invisibly, my footprints would show in the snow; in any event, I couldn't overcome several hundred demons."

Snowbeard, the leader of the snow movers approached. "You have the other four regions secure?"

"True," Mym agreed. "But without this one, I doubt the revolt can be successful."

"But we're committed anyway, now," the man said. "All the souls in the other sections will be tortured, after the demons crush them one by one, and us too. So we might as well go for broke."

"What are you thinking of?" Mym asked.

"Charging them outright. I know it's crude, but we do outnumber them, and—"

"That checkpoint is protected," Mym said. "You might eliminate every other demon, but you couldn't get close to that one, and you wouldn't have the checkpoint. You would be throwing away your lives for this day without hope of success, and adding to the torture to be heaped upon you in the following days. I would not ask you to do that."

"But if you made yourself invisible, and took out that checkpoint while we distracted the demons by our charge—"

Mym looked at him appreciatively. "When you made your commitment to this effort, you really meant it," he said.

"We all did," Snowbeard agreed.

"Then make your charge," Mym said. "I will go in invisibly and, when I have taken out the key demon, I will manifest and let you know."

"Right, Mars." They shook hands.

The damned souls charged in a mass. The demons waited for them, then fired their flamethrowers when the men came within range. There were screams of anguish as the men were set on fire, but those behind passed by the scorching bodies and continued the charge. These, too, were tagged with the flame—but the third rank continued. As each rank fell, the next surged closer; though the carnage was horrible, soon the remaining men were grappling with the demons, and the flamethrowers were no longer effective.

"If I could have had an army like that when I was a mortal prince . . ." Mym murmured.

But he had a job to do. He turned invisible and ran across the scuffled, partly melted snow toward the checkpoint. His footsteps did not show now, for the snow was no longer clean.

He reached the checkpoint. This was in an elevated tower, more formidable than the others, for this was a major intersection. The main reinforcements of the tyranny of Hell would be passing through this point. Flamethrowers, hoses, and pellet guns were mounted at its embrasures, capable of wiping out any attack on the tower itself and of preventing any soul from passing below.

But Mym was invisible, and protected by his Cloak of War. He approached the tower, unobserved amidst the tumult, and took hold of its nether struts and hauled himself up. Soon he was climbing over the battlement.

A solitary demon was there, holding a gleaming trident. Though Mym was invisible, the demon had a disturbing focus and seemed to be looking right at him.

"So we meet again, Mars," the demon said. "I admit I underestimated you. But I shall settle this now."

That was no demon—that was Satan himself!

Satan advanced on him, the three-pronged spear ready. "Your little devices are useless against Me, naturally," he said. "I knew you would be turning up here in due course. I can not actually slay you, but I can put you out of commission long enough to enable My minions to put down this insubordination you have provoked against Me. After that you might as well depart these My demesnes, for you will never have another opportunity to make mischief here."

Mym knew he was in trouble. He was facing the Lord of Evil in Hell, weaponless. The fate of his program depended on him—but how could he overcome another Incarnation on that Incarnation's own turf?

He dispensed with the invisibility, as it was of no further use. Then he bit his tongue.

"Ah, you desire blood?" Satan inquired. "Perhaps I can accommodate you." He thrust the spear viciously at Mym's body.

Mym dodged aside, and the thrust missed him. He knew that Satan had intended it to miss; like the figure of evil he was, he preferred to play with his prey before destroying it.

But the blood was in Mym's mouth, and his berserker rage was coming upon him. No mortal man could match the reflexes and power of a berserker; the fact that Mym's rage was controlled did not change that.

"Isn't that quaint," Satan said. "He berserks. Perhaps this will be at least minimally entertaining." He thrust with the spear again, and Mym dodged aside again, but the miss was narrow. "Perhaps he will even be able to avoid getting stuck for a few more seconds."

Satan was baiting him, but Mym was immune to that sort of thing. While he waited for the berserk rage to be complete, he surveyed the surroundings. There was a rack of weapons at one side of the open chamber, and among these was a sword.

Satan thrust again, and Mym moved again—but this time with the blinding speed that only his type could manage. He leaped past Satan and to the weapons rack. He took up the sword and whirled to attack. All this was so fast that an ordinary person would have seen nothing more than a blur before the sword lopped off his head.

But Satan smoothly countered the sword with the shaft of his trident, and sparks spun out from the contact. "Little slow, aren't you, Mars?" he inquired. Then he stabbed again with the points; when Mym used the blade of the sword to block it, there was another spray of sparks—and the blade was melted. Satan's weapon was enchanted, of course, and the ordinary ones were not.

"Too bad," Satan said with mock sympathy. "That would not have happened with your Red Sword."

Of course it wouldn't have happened; the Sword of War was invulnerable and irresistible. Mym now appreciated how cunningly Satan had schemed to divest him of it before bringing him in to Hell; had Mym come armed with it, he could have used it to cut apart any entity of Hell, including Satan himself. Mym also would not have had to sneak through the back route to travel about Hell; he could have used the Sword to convey him to the checkpoints directly.

But Gaea had warned him that Satan would not meet him in a neutral arena. Satan had arranged to strip him of much of his power and lure him into Hell—and he had been fool enough to permit it.

Mym leaped to the embrasure where the flamethrower was emplaced. He whipped it about to bear on Satan and fired.

The flame bathed Satan completely, sending up murky roils of smoke. But Satan only stood there and laughed, unaffected, though the wooden wall beyond him caught fire and burned vigorously. "Do you expect Me to be damaged by fire, Mars? I am the ruler of the fiery realm!"

The trident was similarly unaffected. From the voluminous flame it poked out, forcing Mym to jump away.

He circled, and Satan stalked him. Mym realized that the battle outside had abated; the damned souls and the remaining demons were now watching the combat in the tower. And what was he accomplishing? Nothing except his own humiliation!

"Well, I musn't disappoint My fans," Satan said. "This is, after all, My show." And Mym knew that the next thrust of the spear would be for business.

Too bad he couldn't phase in with Satan, the way he could with other creatures, and put a defeatist thought in his head! But of course Satan could not be fooled by anything like that.

What other recourse was available to him? He was on the verge of defeat, and Satan knew it.

In this moment he remembered *Five Rings*. The book had faded from his consciousness during the excitement of his experience in Hell, and that had perhaps been unfortunate. As Musashi had warned, it was easy to stray from the Way. What did the Way of the Sword have to tell him now?

Cut your opponent as he cuts you. To strike as the enemy struck, defeating him even as he thought the victory was his, even as Satan thought at this moment.

To abandon one's own life, to throw away fear—that was necessary for the final confrontation.

To treat one's enemy not as a thing apart, but as an honored guest.

Then Mym recognized his opportunity. He could defeat Satan after all!

Satan thrust. Mym did not attempt to move; he phased out to unsubstantiality, letting the prongs pass through his body harmlessly. "Satan, your weapon can not harm me any more than these others can harm you," Mym said.

"Ah, so he catches on to an aspect of his power," Satan said. "But he can not displace Me here while he remains insubstantial, and therefore this tower remains in My hands."

"For the moment," Mym said. "Until we meet barehanded."

Satan threw aside the trident. "You are not in your bailiwick Mars, but in Mine. You can not overcome Me barehanded." He spread his arms in a grappling motion, smiling.

"I had understood you to be more perceptive," Mym said. "I am not going to grapple with you, Satan. I am going to phase in with you."

"A foolish ploy! You can not govern my mind. I will remain in control while you dance about in futile vacuity. The victory is Mine, Mars, when you but have the wit to perceive it."

"And when I phase in with you, I will instantly know all your secrets," Mym said. "All the bypaths of Hell. All your private techniques. All your embarrassments. All your bluffs. You can not stop me from knowing all that is in your mind. Then, when I disengage, which you also can not prevent, I shall advertise that information in whatever manner pleases me." He smiled. "Now, with that understanding, shall we grapple, Satan? Shall we become one, honored enemy?"

Satan stared at him. "You have been reading that book!"

"It is a good book, Satan. It advises me that proper understanding is much the same as power. Let me understand you, so that there is no further misunderstanding between us."

Satan literally ground his teeth.

Mym advanced. Satan retreated. Mym leaped—and Satan vanished.

Mym had used the one weapon he retained that Satan feared—information. Satan could not tolerate the truth being known, any kind of truth, even in Hell. Especially not in Hell! For Satan was the Father of Lies, and upon lies he had built his realm. The exposure of those lies would result in the inevitable destruction of that nether kingdom. The only way Satan could preserve his lies was to refuse contact with Mym—which he could not do if he remained here, for Mym would stalk him until he could not avoid contact.

Mym walked to the battlement. "The tower is ours!" he cried. "Satan is gone!"

A cheer went up from the damned souls. The demons fled. It was victory.

The damned souls poured out through the checkpoint, and now the souls in charge of the other checkpoints came to join them. Amazons and muckrakers, snow haulers and fireworkers generated a massive celebration. But soon they sobered.

"You know," Diana said, "we aren't out of Hell. We just have a less restricted region of it."

"You knew there was no escape from Hell by violence," Mym reminded her. "But now we have the leverage to bargain—and that was the real object."

"That's right!" Snowbeard exclaimed. "I near forgot! The Hearing Panel!"

A single demon approached, walking toward them along the highway. "That will be the negotiator," Mym said.

The demon came up to Mym. It turned out to be a demoness. "Lila!" Mym exclaimed, recognizing her.

"Satan proffers terms," she said.

"We are reasonable," Mym said. "All we want is what was supposed to be. The hearings on borderline souls, so that they can be judged and reassigned as their merit deserves, beginning with Ligeia, here."

"Ligeia to be heard," Lila agreed, giving the woman a somewhat competitive look. "In return, you, Mars, shall vacate Hell."

"Not so fast!" Mym protested. "There shall be a thousand souls heard each day, until the backlog is caught up."

"Ten souls," Lila said.

"A hundred."

"A hundred," she agreed. "Satan shall institute a board."

"No. The board shall be composed of souls in Purgatory."

She sighed. "And the remaining souls shall vacate the checkpoints and return to their labors."

"And there shall be no reprisals."

"And no reprisals."

This seemed too easy. Where was the catch? "And I shall have free access to Hell to verify that the terms are being honored."

"But you shall not interfere further, having verified that," she said.

Mym looked around. "That seems tight to me," he said. "When I come again, I shall be bearing my Red Sword and riding my palomino steed. I shall know with whom to talk. I can not lighten your normal loads, but I can see that these terms are met." Because Satan would not give Mars any further pretext to make the kind of trouble that was the speciality of the Incarnation of War.

The others nodded. "We shall make nominations from our own groups," Snowbeard said. "And the animals shall have the same privilege. We shall report to you on any violations."

Ligeia approached. "I suppose you have to go now," she said.

Mym embraced her. "I believe I have freed you," he said. "You will go to Heaven."

"I think I would rather be with you, Mym."

Mym sighed. "And I would rather have you with me, Li. But I shall not leave you in Hell and I can not visit you in Heaven. Accept your just reward; I will survive."

"Maybe I could go to Purgatory, and—"

Mym kissed her. "I know you are destined for Heaven. I would not interfere with that if I could."

"I'm sure you wouldn't," she agreed. "Fare well, Mym." She retreated, so that he could make his partings with the others.

Mym kept a smile on his face, but now he felt dead inside. Of course he did not want to deny her Heaven! But he wished her journey there could have somehow been delayed a decade or two. In the few days they had been acquainted, they had come to know each other about as well as two people could, and he knew she was the one for him. If only she hadn't died before he met her!

Lila was watching him. "*I* am not going to Heaven," she murmured.

"The Hell with you," he muttered. But he wondered—was this what he was to be left with? His recent victory over Satan did not seem very wonderful, now.

– 17 –

WAR

There was no problem about leaving Hell; Satan was eager to facilitate his departure. The capsule that had enclosed Ligeia descended from the sky, and Mym stepped into it. The capsule rose swiftly and soon was back in the palace of frozen mist. It came to rest exactly where it had been.

Mym got off the bed and stepped out, finding the ice now pervious. He walked to his unconscious body and phased in.

He found himself cold and stiff, despite the protective cloak. Apparently what he had worn in Hell had been only a spirit cloak. He climbed to his feet and stretched. He looked back at the bed, remembering Ligeia. If only there had been some way . . .

No point in torturing himself. He turned resolutely and walked out through the ice-passages to the broken entrance. He stepped out. Then he touched the Red Sword and willed himself back to the Castle of War.

The personnel of the Castle greeted him as if his absence had been routine, but Mym knew that the mortal world had not halted in place during the past few days. Satan had wanted him out of the mortal picture, had taken trouble to keep him in Hell as long as possible, and perhaps had paid more of a price than intended. What had Satan been up to on Earth?

He knew one way to find out. He turned on the television set. Its news always related to Mars.

"All hell is breaking loose on Earth," the announcer said. "There has never been a period of greater unrest, short of all-out war. The mysterious absence of Mars, the Incarnation of War, has contributed to the general confusion. Exactly who is managing this violence?"

Satan was, surely. But what was his purpose? Certainly increasing violence in the world would not deprive Mars of his power; it would enhance it.

Yet Satan had tried to make a deal with him before to facilitate just such unrest, because it would generate the problems of war, which in turn would generate conditions that would cause increasing suffering among the mortals, and turn more of them to evil. But could that be all?

It seemed to Mym that Satan had gone to an extraordinary amount of trouble to get him out of the way. It hardly seemed worth it, just for a few more souls. Satan might lose as many souls from the hearings as he would gain from the disturbances among the mortals.

The more Mym thought about this, the less he trusted it. When he couldn't properly fathom the nature of the evil Satan did, that was apt to be because he had missed the true point. He was still new at his job, and he suspected he was missing the point now.

But there was one who should be able to give him the answer. He touched the Sword. "Chronos," he murmured.

There was a shimmer, and the Incarnation of Time appeared before him. "Yes, Mars; I caught your signal."

"Your memory is of my future," Mym said. "I need to know what Satan is up to, and I suspect it will show there. If you will tell me—"

"Tell you what? My memory covers a great deal."

"What Satan has done."

Chronos frowned. "You may misunderstand my nature. I remember your future, true—but I remember it only as it happened, not as it might have happened. So if as you say Satan has done something, then this is the way I remember it, and I don't know how it differs from what you feel it ought to be. If you can be more specific—"

Mym remembered that Luna was supposed to play a key role in foiling Satan's major scheme, and that Satan had been trying to get around that before it happened. "Is Luna—does she remain all right?"

"Why, certainly, though her disappointment has been serious."

"Her disappointment?"

"She had hoped to foil Satan; but, of course, that became impossible."

"Impossible? Why? Isn't she active in politics?"

"She was. But that's academic."

"Academic? Why? Doesn't she cast the key vote against Satan, when the time comes?"

Chronos smiled sadly. "How could she? There was no issue to vote on."

This sounded very much like what he was looking for. "At what point did the matter of issues and voting become academic?"

"Very recently, actually. When martial law was declared in America and the civilian government temporarily suspended. Of course there is nothing so permanent as a temporary—"

"Martial law? Whatever for?"

"Because of the unrest. It was simply impossible for a democratic government to cope, so the military had to take over. I viewed this with extreme regret, myself, but I must admit that the alternative would have been worse. There could have been complete anarchy."

"How long ago—for you—did this martial law develop?" Mym asked.

"Only a week ago. But it was inevitable; the violence in the world is already too great to be contained, as I come to perceive it now. The lesser of evils had to be embraced."

"Thank you, Chronos," Mym said. "You have told me what I need to know."

"Any time, Mars," Chronos said. He tilted his Hourglass and vanished.

Mym paced the floor, his head seeming to spin. Here he had been concerned about his own lost love, while the world really was going to Hell! Now he understood Satan's plot—to foment violence in the world to such a degree that the civilian govern-

ments fell by the wayside. Military dictatorships were things
Satan could shape to his own ends—and of course Luna would
have no way to cast her vote against Satan, when there was no
civilian government.

Well, he could put a stop to that. He would quell every battle
before it happened, restoring relative peace.

Mym touched the Sword. "War's minions," he murmured.

They appeared, in their bright capes. "Rich harvests!" Conquest said, rubbing his hands together.

"No," Mym said. "We are going to suppress these. Provide
me with a list of the most serious situations, so I can go to each."

Conquest brought out a scroll and unrolled it. The thing seemed
to be endlessly long.

Mym looked at it. "But there are thousands here!" he
exclaimed.

"Yes," Conquest agreed heartily. "And more developing
every moment. We have never had as potentially rich a harvest."
Slaughter, Famine, and Pestilence nodded.

Mym shook his head. "I can't possibly get to all of these in
time, let alone defuse them!"

"Why try?" Slaughter asked. "This is our chance for greatest
glory!"

Satan's plot was coming clearer. In only a few days, the Incarnation of Evil had sown so much dissent in the world that it
was now virtually impossible to stop. Had Mars been here, he
would have taken note of the interference and cut it off, for this
was his domain. But Satan had distracted him in the infernal region, thus having free rein on Earth, and had really made it count.
No wonder Mym had seen so little of Satan in Hell; Satan had
been very busy elsewhere!

Mym didn't try to answer Slaughter. "I have other business."
He went outside, summoned Werre, and mounted. "No supervision of battles today," he called shortly, and started the horse
moving.

They went to Thanatos' mansion. Mym could have sent out a
call for the Incarnation of Death, but he preferred to have a little
time to think on the way. If Satan had already stirred the world
up to too great a turmoil to be abated before martial law set in,

what could he do? But the time did him no good; he still had no idea.

The door opened as he approached the Mansion of Death. Thanatos met him. "Chronos advised us yesterday of your problem—and ours," Thanatos said. "We are here to try to help."

And they were. Lachesis and Gaea were there—and Luna, brought to Purgatory for this occasion. They all greeted him warmly.

"But I only talked to Chronos an hour ago!" Mym exclaimed. "How could he have told you yesterday, while I was still in Hell?"

"You forget the direction of his life," Lachesis said. "He spoke to us a day after he spoke to you."

Mym nodded. He kept forgetting! "Maybe he can go on back and tell me before I even go to Hell!"

"He is reluctant," Gaea said. "It seems that there can be serious consequences when he acts to change the course of events that are in his past. On occasion he will do this, but he prefers to keep the compass quite limited, so that the result is fully defined."

Mym realized that it would indeed be a hazardous business, changing past events; people, including perhaps some Incarnations, could be eliminated. Certainly there should be no haphazard dabbling.

"In any event," Lachesis said, "this seems to be your problem, Mars. Satan makes things difficult for each new Incarnation at the outset, and it is necessary for that Incarnation to demonstrate that he can prevail. Then Satan knows better than to try again. If Chronos were to rescue you from your dilemma, Satan would merely try another ploy and another, until successful."

"But the whole world is at stake!" Mym protested. "All of you will lose, too!"

"That is why it is so important for you to prevail," Thanatos said. "We must take the risk of letting you oppose Satan alone, even as each of us must, so as to establish that not one of us is a weak spot."

"But I don't see how I can prevail!" Mym cried. "I thought I had won in Hell—only to learn that I had lost in the mortal realm. And according to Chronos, that loss stands."

"Not necessarily," Luna said. "Chronos can report only on the aspect of history he has lived through. If that is changed, he will live a different life, and that will be as valid as the first. Probably his reality is being constantly changed in little ways by the actions of the rest of us, and he is not aware of it."

"That sounds like paradox to me," Mym said.

"Chronos is immune from paradox," Thanatos said. "This may be difficult for the rest of us to understand, but it must be accepted."

"So I can change future reality—if I can only figure out how," Mym said. "I can take Satan's victory away—somehow."

"That is a thing we have to believe," Lachesis said.

"Unless there *is* no way!"

"There must be a way," Thanatos said. "Otherwise Satan would not have attempted to keep you so long in Hell. He knew it was only safe for him if you remained there until after his move on Earth was complete. You won free too soon, so now it must be in your power to prevail."

"Certainly you must seek it," Luna said.

"Certainly I must seek it," he agreed morosely. "The fate of the world, left to one confused stutterer!"

Then he did a double-take. "I'm not stuttering!"

"Fancy that," Gaea murmured.

"But I didn't stutter in Hell, because—I thought—how can this be?" Then he remembered. "Green Mother—you took something from me and did not tell me what it was. You took my stutter!"

"We do have some power over each other—if we agree to it," Gaea said. "I felt you could spare it."

"And I never noticed!"

She shrugged. "Surely you have other powers you haven't noticed. One of them may yet foil Satan."

Shaken, Mym departed. This seemingly minor demonstration of the special power of an Incarnation impressed him more than all the other wonders he had seen. He had agreed to let Nature take something of his. Now the other Incarnations had agreed to let him affect their futures. He had to come through for them!

Yet the way eluded him. He returned preoccupied to the Castle of War and ate and slept fitfully and ate again, remaining confined.

No revelation came. One day passed, and two, and three, and the situation among the mortals intensified, yet he remained helpless. He simply saw no way to do what he knew he had to do.

He found himself walking again in the garden. There, when he reached the nether extremity, was the demoness.

"So nice to see you again, Mars," she said, stretching languidly. She wore another of her semi-exposive gowns, and her breasts moved almost liquidly as her torso shifted.

"Get out of here, slut!" he raged.

"Nuh-uh, Mars," she said, smiling. "This is a neutral zone, remember? You would not have come here if you hadn't wanted to see me, now would you!"

"I came here to figure out how to defeat your foul master!" he snapped.

"That is not easy to do, Mym. Why don't you just bow to the inevitable and relax? Since you have inadvertently served Satan's design, you might as well accept your reward."

"What reward?" he demanded.

"Me, of course." She stretched again, spectacularly. "I really do want to serve you, Mym, and I am very good at what I do. I can return to you what I denied you in Hell."

"What do you mean?" he asked, sure that he would regret the question, but unable to pass it by.

She fuzzed out, slowly changing shape. "Why, the Fireman. Don't you remember?"

"The fire monster in Hell?" he asked blankly.

"You were just about to possess your beloved, and I was jealous, so I sent the monster to break it up. Now it is of course too late; you can never possess her."

"*You—?*" he began, outraged.

Her form firmed. She looked exactly like Ligeia. "What does she have that I can not emulate?" she inquired in Ligeia's dulcet voice.

Mym found the Red Sword in his hand. But he froze, not striking. How could he slay the facsimile of the woman he loved?

"I don't suppose you would believe that one of my kind could truly care for you," she said.

"True," he said between his teeth.

She shifted back to her presumably natural form. "I'm not even one of the damned. I'm just a construct of ether, existing solely at my Master's discretion. I have no reality other than my assignment. My assignment is to please you. If I fail in this, I will have no existence at all. You have but to instruct me in those things you require of the ideal woman, and I will be those things as perfectly and as long as you desire them. Will you deny me my only chance to emulate that state of grace?"

Even with his rage at her, Mym was struck by the seeming sincerity of her words. How could a genuinely soulless creature speak in this fashion? He knew it was foolish, but he found himself beginning to appreciate her position.

He was without a woman. For the third time he had lost his love. Perhaps it was time for a concubine he didn't need to love or make any pretense of loving.

"The ideal woman serves her man absolutely," Mym said. "Whatever he asks of her, she does without question. Any question he has, she answers honestly and to the best of her ability. Loyalty—that is the salient quality I require. Loyalty to me, before all else."

"I would give you that," Lila said.

"Before Satan?"

She moved back as if struck. "Oh, immortal mortal, you know not what you ask!"

"I think I do. Since it is obvious that you can not give me what I require, you might as well leave me alone."

"But then I will have failed to please you, and the penalty—"

"I am familiar with the penalty," he said, remembering the fate of the lovely concubines he had rejected when his father had kept him prisoner. Satan would surely be no more merciful. Those grisly deaths had hurt him; he steeled himself not to be hurt by this one.

He saw the tear at her eye again. There really was no point in artifice at this point; she surely was experiencing whatever emulation of emotion she was capable of. "If I am to perish, then it behooves me to choose the manner of it," she said. "I would rather let my final act be an expression of my true private will than a lie. Therefore I will agree to this."

This set him back. He had expected her to admit defeat. But

of course she could be lying, as she had no concern for truth, only for convenience.

Or *had* she? He had never caught her in a lie. Satan was the Father of Lies, but did that mean that all of his constructs were liars too? It might be that Lila, sent to subvert an honest man, had been fashioned to be honest and would remain so until Satan changed her.

Still, this was suspect. He needed proof of her commitment. He knew of a way to get it—but the problem was that this would require a commitment from him, too.

Yet what did his relationship with one demoness matter, compared to the fate of the world? It would be selfish of him to put his own preference for a woman with a soul before the welfare of the world.

"Give me your absolute loyalty, and I will take you as my concubine," he said. "But you will have to prove it."

"I will prove it," she said.

"Tell me how I may foil Satan's plot and save the world from his dominance."

"That is simple," she said. "Precipitate the holocaust."

Mym's jaw dropped. "What?"

"Götterdämmerung. Ragnarök. Day of Doom. World War Three. The final confrontation between Good and Evil. Whatever it is termed in your mythology."

"But that would destroy mankind!"

"Yes."

"I ask you how to save the world, and you tell me to destroy it!" he exclaimed incredulously.

"You asked me how to save the world from Satan. I have told you how."

Mym shook his head, disgusted. "I should have known that a demoness would not give me any answer I could use!"

"I gave you truth," she said. "I can explain."

"Don't bother!" he said, turning away.

"But you agreed to take me as your concubine if I proved my loyalty!" she cried. "I have proved it! Are you not a man of honor?"

He whirled on her. "You had to know that that is no answer at all! It would only swamp the Afterlife with all the remaining souls of the mortals, in a few savage minutes. To give an answer you know is useless is no signal of loyalty!''

"But it is a good answer!" she protested. "Why won't you hear my explanation?"

"Then give your explanation," Mym said through his teeth. She had betrayed him, but the terms of his agreement required that much of him, that he hear her rationale.

She spoke. Gradually the sense of it penetrated.

"Lila, I apologize," he said. "Now that I understand it, I see that it is a good answer."

"Take me now, Mym," she said. "Because when Satan learns what I have done, he will abolish me."

True, again. She had shown him how to save the world, but she could not save herself. She had given up her existence for the sake of a few hours of acceptance by him.

He took her in his arms. "Now that it is too late, Lila, I regret that I mistrusted you. You shall have my thanks and my passion, while you exist."

"That is all I desire," she said, meeting him with a fierce kiss.

The day before the last civilian governments on Earth were to fall, Mym emerged from the Castle of War. He summoned his lesser Incarnations, and the five of them mounted. "To the Doomsday Clock!" Mym cried.

At that Conquest, Slaughter, Famine, and Pestilence looked askance. But their steeds knew the way, for the Clock was one of the artifacts of Mars. It was the timepiece that marked the incipience of the Final War that would destroy mankind on Earth.

They drew up before it. The Doomsday Clock stood on its mounting, fifty meters tall, and its huge hands were set at three minutes to midnight. This, in the metaphor of eternity, indicated the proximity of that War; it was not far off.

Mym dismounted and drew the Red Sword. "Let there be War," he said.

Power radiated from the Sword. It bathed all the world—and all about the globe the tensions that led to conflict and violence intensified. Nations that had considered war now declared it; armies that had been in position to do battle now began it; individuals who had been bluffing each other down now called their bluffs and entered combat.

For this was the ultimate power of the Red Sword. It could not pacify violence, it could only enhance it. But what it enhanced, no other power could deplete; only the cessation of its own activity could abate the terrible malice of its nature. When allowed to radiate freely, it would amplify the warlike passions of man until they erupted in the greatest conflagration ever to occur—Doomsday.

The four subsidiary Incarnations stood taller and more imposing as the effect of the Red Sword was felt. Their colors brightened, and their steeds paced eagerly. Conquest's white cape commenced a secondary radiation; Slaughter's red became the texture of flowing blood; Famine turned so black that he was no more than a dark blot; and Pestilence's entire body became a brown mass of vermin. They were approaching the moment of their greatest fulfillment.

Mym's Cloak of War, too, was intensifying, the golden hue suffusing the region. Even his horse, Werre, was assuming a preternatural glow of strength.

The hands of the Doomsday Clock were traveling toward midnight at a visible rate. The two minutes became ninety seconds, then sixty.

Satan appeared. "What are you doing, Mars?" the Lord of Evil demanded.

"I am finishing what you started, Satan," Mym replied evenly. "You fomented unrest during my absence; I am bringing it to climax."

"But you will bring on the holocaust!"

"Yes, this will be the moment of my greatest glory," Mym agreed.

The Clock had moved to thirty seconds. "Wait!" Satan cried. "Are you sure you want to do this, Mars?"

Mym lowered the Sword, and the Clock halted at twenty-four seconds to midnight. "You have a consideration, Satan?"

"I merely wish to point out that, once the final earthly reckoning occurs, you will have no further job, because all the mortals will be dead. Is this what you want?"

"Why, I believe it will do," Mym said. "Why should I limp

along piecemeal, when I can accomplish my purpose in one glorious burst? All mortal cares abated in a single effort!"

Now the other Incarnations appeared. Thanatos rode up on his pale steed Mortis, the woman Luna behind him. Chronos, coasted in obliquely, holding his Hourglass, facing away, oddly. No, not oddly; this was his departure, by his backward's reckoning; he would reverse his perception to phase in to mortal time. Fate, in the form of a giant spider, descended a thread from nowhere. And Gaea coalesced from a cloud of vapor. All knew that this was the showdown.

"But you have always tried to preserve the lives of the mortals," Satan reminded him. "To ease the suffering brought about by war."

"That was before I realized the extent of my power," Mym replied. "Now I prefer to exercise it in full measure." He raised the Sword again.

Satan glanced about at the other Incarnations. "You tolerate this?" he asked. "You, who have always sought what was good for mankind?"

"Each Incarnation is supreme in his own bailiwick," Gaea said. "Our preferences do not matter; this is Mars' show."

Satan shrugged. "Well, certainly if none of you are interested in doing what is good, it ill behooves Me to do it for you. I will receive more souls in one batch than ever before."

"And God will receive even more," Mym said. "Since the balance of this world is currently positive—as it will not be after your folk assume political power among the mortals." The hands of the Clock resumed their motion toward midnight.

"You would destroy the world—merely to deny Me a few souls?" Satan asked. "That is very shortsighted."

"Well, the whole matter of war is shortsighted," Mym agreed. The sweep-hand passed fifteen seconds.

"Wait!" Satan cried desperately.

The hand paused. "I wish you wouldn't keep interrupting me with inconsequentials," Mym said. "I'm sure we all want to get this matter expeditiously completed."

"If the world ends now," Satan said, "God will win, for the balance will be in his favor at the Final Reckoning."

"Fancy that," Mym agreed. "Since I have no interest in your

victory, this does seem to be the appropriate time to make my play. Then I can retire from this office and go to Heaven to join my love who is there. Now, if you have no other observations—''

Small flames crackled about Satan's body. He knew that Mym had found the key to victory. The Lord of Evil could not afford to have the world end in holocaust while the overall balance of living souls was in God's favor, however marginally. "How did you learn of this?''

"Does it matter?'' Mym asked. "All that should concern us is that it is true. Now, of course, if you should happen to choose to give up your plans for dictatorships and martial law on Earth—''

"Lila!'' Satan exclaimed. "That demoness betrayed Me!''

Lila appeared. "I no longer serve you, Satan,'' she said.

Satan stared at her, considering. Then he seemed to come to a private conclusion. "There is something that may interest you, Mars,'' he said. "You mentioned joining a certain party in Heaven. Did you know that your companion in Hell did not go to Heaven?''

"She didn't?'' Mym asked, dismayed. "But I know her balance was good! The hearings—''

"She is good—but she declined to go,'' Satan said. "For some reason she wished to return to mortality, though it would seem that she had little to gain and everything to risk by that.''

"But she's already dead!'' Mym protested. "She couldn't—''

"She could—with the help of one of your kind,'' Satan said, glancing meaningfully at Gaea.

"This much is true,'' Gaea said. "The woman wanted to be with you, Mars, so at the hearing she petitioned for a body among the mortals. There are some few soul-dead bodies, so I made one available to her. I did not realize that Satan had an involvement in this. I think she had in mind a surprise for you.''

"I—I never dreamed—'' Mym said, amazed.

"And here she is,'' Satan said, gesturing.

A woman appeared. Her appearance was not that of Ligeia, but she approached Mym as if she knew him. He put out his hand and touched her, and knew immediately that it was her soul. Now the body began to assume some of the traits of her former one, as her personality animated it. She was young and comely, and her love for him was manifest.

"But it seems she did not realize that you had made a deal with the demoness," Satan said.

Ligeia gazed at Mym with hurt questioning.

Satan, with uncanny insight, had brought about the confrontation Mym least desired. To have his lost love abruptly returned to him—after he had made the pact with the demoness! What was he to do now?

"But of course your choice is clear," Satan said. "You did not know that your true love was returning to you. Therefore any arrangement you made with the demoness is null and void. I will take her off your hands." He raised one arm, pointing a finger at Lila.

"No," Mym said.

Satan arched an eyebrow. "No? You intercede for this soulless slut? That does not become you, Mars."

"I accepted her help," Mym said with difficulty. "I agreed to accept her as my concubine. I can not go back on my word."

"And so you reject your true love, who gave up her place in Heaven itself only to be with you?" Satan made a gesture of dismissal. "You would not do that, Mars."

"What are you bargaining for?" Mym demanded.

"All I ask is that you allow the world to stand, Mars. As you can see, if it is destroyed now, your re-mortal girlfriend will have made her gesture for nothing. She will be returned forthwith to Heaven, and you will be left with the demoness. For I do not believe that you will be bound for Heaven after you have treated the mortal realm so."

The notion of losing Ligeia a second time, after her phenomenal sacrifice to be with him, appalled Mym. But if he backed off now, Satan would have his way with Earth.

"And you have no need to be concerned about this bit of nothing," Satan said. "I will eliminate her memory of you and put her to another assignment. That will leave your situation clear."

It was still a sort of betrayal of the creature who had helped him, Mym realized. He had given his word.

"I want nothing from you but your agreement to abate your

plot against the mortal realm,'' Mym said. ''Otherwise I will destroy it. What happens with the women is incidental.''

Satan shrugged. ''You have My agreement,'' he said. ''You have won this showdown, Mars.''

Mym almost gaped. Victory—just like that?

''And I will take care of this minor business for you, as a gesture of amity,'' Satan said. He turned again to Lila.

Ligeia moved suddenly to throw her arms about the demoness. ''Leave her alone!'' she cried.

''Do not be concerned,'' Satan told her. ''This is for your own good. Mars needs no concubine when he has you.''

''You understand nothing about the ways of princes,'' Ligeia said. ''Mym gave his word. She did her part.''

Satan looked at Mym. ''Does this make any sense to you, Mars? Why should the woman you love want competition from a demoness?''

Why, indeed! Mym did not know what to think. He looked at the other Incarnations, but all of them were mute. It seemed that he had a decision to make.

There was something about this that he didn't understand. It was as if this were far more important than just a decision about a demoness whose presence had become an embarrassment. But what was the significance? He had won, hadn't he? Why should he concern himself over such a trifle as the existence of a demoness whom all parties knew had never expected to survive beyond this point?

A trifle? Why, then, was Satan taking the matter so seriously? *Pay attention even to trifles.* So said *Five Rings.*

He focused his whole attention on that question—and, slowly, it came to him.

''You shall not have Lila,'' Mym said firmly.

The demoness turned her head to look at him, surprised. Ligeia remained holding her.

''Because your friend has a soft heart?'' Satan asked. ''That will not change the nature of a demoness! Believe me, you will be better off without the spawn of Hell in your household.''

The Father of Lies could hardly have spoken more direct truth! Therefore Mym rejected it.

Mym turned to the Clock. He raised the Sword. The seconds resumed their tickoff.

"This is crazy!" Satan protested. "You risk the whole world for this damned bit of ether?"

The sweep-hand passed ten seconds to midnight. Now the hint of the wailing of the world could be heard, as the anquish of the dread finale approached. Missiles rose from their silos, ready for launching. Monstrous destructive spells were being chanted.

Satan turned to the other Incarnations. "Can't you see, Mars is crazy!" he cried. "All this, for a creature who is beyond damnation!"

But no one responded. The others had yielded the decision to Mars. Five seconds, four, three. The wailing swelled into the final keening.

Satan vanished. He had defaulted.

The sweep-hand stopped at one second to midnight.

Lila stared at Mym. "But *why?*" she asked. "You did not owe me this! You know my nature and you do not love me. You had already fulfilled your bargain."

Mym lowered the Sword. The hands of the Doomsday Clock resumed their motion—in the other direction. They retreated slowly from midnight, then accelerated as the forces that had incited violence faded. They passed thirty seconds and kept moving.

"I did what I realized I had to do," Mym said.

"My memory has changed," Chronos remarked. "Satan has been defeated. Soon I will forget that alternate reality I knew before; I did not live through it, now."

"But you had your victory!" Lila persisted. "And I was— am—now a liability to you."

"No," Ligeia told her. "As a princess, I know that a prince needs concubines, and it is better to have them known and subservient. He will use you when I am indisposed. And you made it possible for him to find me and for him to find the way to face Satan down. We would not let you be abolished for that. Quite apart from the fact that the word of a prince is inviolate, not to be sullied or compromised, no matter what the cost."

"But to risk the whole world in war—merely because you interceded—"

"No," Mym said.

Now Ligeia was surprised. "No?"

"I love you, Li," Mym said. "And I owe Lila. But I did not do this for either of you, or to sustain my word."

"But that does not make sense, then!" Ligeia protested.

"I'm not sure whether I can explain," Mym said. "The key I perceived is from the book *Five Rings*. It has taught me the Way of Strategy. It advises me that, if I am trying to follow the Way and allow myself to diverge even a little, then this will later become a greater divergence, and I will lose the Way. I feel this is most especially true when dealing with the Incarnation of Evil himself. I must not diverge even the most trifling amount from the Way, lest I lose all. But it is hard to make that plain to those who have not been studying that book."

"I believe I understand," Luna said. "This matter is larger than any single person or any single episode. Satan is an insidious corruptor who never rests and he is most dangerous in seeming defeat, as all of us know. It is his speciality to proffer a large reward for a very small compromise, for his resources are infinite. But he who accepts the first compromise has made a precedent, and it then becomes easier to accept the next, and the next, until at last Satan has after all won. Only by refusing any compromise at all, no matter how grotesquely uneven the stakes seem to be, can a person be proof against the insidious devices of the Master of Evil. Mars has refused that first compromise, and thus shown Satan that he is not to be corrupted. This, more than the threat of the holocaust, is the true measure of his victory."

Mym met Luna's gaze, nodding. She *did* understand! And now *he* understood how it was that she could be at the center of this titanic struggle between Good and Evil. When the time came for the critical decision to be made, Luna would be there, and would understand, and would have the courage to do what had to be done.

AUTHOR'S NOTE

Part I: Technical

Remember, this Note is a somewhat separate entry that need not be read to appreciate the novel. In life, the author's mundane existence tends to influence the fiction he writes; in fantasy, his fiction may influence his mundane existence. In my case, there can be alarming interactions and feedbacks, both ways. As I believe I have remarked before, I have absolutely no belief in the supernatural; therefore it plagues me incessantly, as if trying to force me to change my attitude.

The theme of this novel is war, with its related aspects of violence and distress and wasted effort and sacrifice of life. I do not like war; naturally it fascinates me in the fashion of a snake with its prey. When I wrote of Death, death impinged on my life; when I wrote of Time, time was my problem; when I wrote of Fate I felt obliged to explain how deviously fate had brought me to this pass. Now I am writing of War, and of course I shall now describe the manner that violence touched my life at this time.

But first news of a more technical nature. If you happen to be one who is sick of hearing about how yet another innocent soul has computerized, and his joys and horrors thereof, skip this section and go on to Part II of the Note, because here is more of the same, only worse.

I have been among the last major holdouts against the computer age and have taken a certain pride in writing my manuscripts with a pencil on paper—sometimes on the back of someone else's discarded computer paper, read what delightful irony you will—and typing them on a manual Olympia, and still outperforming the great majority of computerized writers. Fancy machinery does not a writer make. But then they stopped making good manual typewriters, and mine was ten years old, with ten million words on it, about due for replacement. So, perforce, I surveyed the situation. I discovered that they don't make a Dvorak disk for the print-wheel typewriters, and the element typewriters are too limited for my needs. So I decided to go all the way to the twentieth century and computerize.

Of course I had qualms. I tend to trust most that which is least complicated, and a computer is hellishly more complicated than pencil and paper. Could I compose on the machine? I concluded that I probably could, because I was able to compose fiction on the typewriter sixteen years earlier, before my newborn daughter converted me to pencil. (She was hyperactive, so I had to be constantly mobile to keep her out of mischief. The typewriter wasn't mobile. Yes, I was the one who took care of her; my wife was out earning our living, in those days.) After all, it is my mind that generates my fiction, and it matters little by what route that fiction is expressed: verbally, penciled, or typed. The computer is a different creature than the typewriter, but why should my fingers care what happens after they have performed at the keyboard? So I rationalized and hoped.

There was one problem: that modified Dvorak keyboard I use. I converted to Dvorak before the computer industry did, so I use the original version, not the bastardized computer version, and of course I added my lower-case quote marks, making my version unique to me. Several years ago when I surveyed the situation, I found that no computer was able or willing to provide me with this option, though it should have been the easiest thing for them to do. I would have had to do it on my own, and there I ran into the catch-22 that I could not hire a specialist to modify my computer without violating the patent, and the complexities of designing my own conversion program were such that it wasn't worth it.

But by this time, the market for home computers was beginning to get saturated, so that companies were somewhat more interested in accommodating the needs of the buyer; and technology had progressed. Companies like Apple and Wang had Dvorak as an option, but for complex but valid reasons I elected to do business with neither. (I could say ten times as much about computers as I am saying here; let's just say that I did my homework in this as in other things, and the decisions I have made were not frivolous.) A commercial program existed that would make all the keys programmable. That is, with this program I could change *S* to *O* and *D* to *E* and *F* to *U*, and all the other exchanges required for my keyboard. I would be happy to say, "*F* to *U*"; my problem had been solved. I proceeded to look for the most versatile and reliable computer system on the market, because I work hard and do not like to be balked by equipment failure.

I will spare you the story of our search and of the fits and starts once I got my computer; it seems that just about every writer who has ever computerized has written an article on it, and I refer you to any of those articles for that story. I shall just touch on a few aspects that made my experience different from the norm. It seems I don't do much of anything in the normal way, which is one reason you are reading this material. (We understand each other, don't we, you and I?) (The prior parenthetical note does not apply to reviewers.)

For hardware we bought the DEC Rainbow 100+. That's a heavy-duty home system with enough memory (256 Kilobytes) to handle my needs, enough storage (10 MegaBytes) for several novels, and the best designed keyboard on the market. For software we got SmartKey to redefine the keyboard so that I could have it exactly the way I wanted it. And PTP—Professional Text Processor—for the word processing. With twenty-two little macros for my special needs.

Oh, I see I'll have to clarify this a bit. Very well: the hardware is the stuff you can see—the keyboard, monitor, disk drive, printer, cables and such. It has a masculine aspect; you can manhandle it about, with caution. The software is the programming, or the instructions that make the hardware operate so it doesn't just sit there and ignore you. It has a feminine aspect; you can't manhandle it because it will vacate the premises if you do. The firmware is what contains the software, naturally. "I dreamed I ran a computer in my maiden firm ware." In this case, what is called floppy disks. Yes, they are round and firm, and you can use two of them simultaneously, and no, they really don't sag.

The macros are keys that are programmed to do special tasks that would otherwise take a number of keystrokes. For example, it normally requires five keystrokes for me to save my material to the hard disk, where it won't be lost if the power fails and shuts down the system, and twice that many if I want to mark my place and find it again after the save. My macro does it with a single stroke, returning me to my place and setting a little ≫ symbol in the margin so I know it's been done. Also, because I switched over from pencil, I brought my little arrows with me: ––––⟩ to indicate the resumption of my text after a bracket note (you learned about those brackets in *On a Pale Horse*—one reader wrote to tell me that this device had solved his problem with that dread malady, Writer's Block); ––⟩ to indicate the resumption of the main bracket note after a parenthetical interruption (oh, yes, I have notes within notes, as my disorderly ongoing stream-of-consciousness runs the rapids of my creativity); and a vertical down-arrow to show that there is a long interruption in the text, so when editing I can skip down to the next page or so to find the resumption arrow.

The pencil is more versatile in this respect than the typewriter, but the computer is able to keep pace with the pencil, a fact that goes far to endear it to me. That vertical arrow requires twenty-two strokes, several of which are multi-key—two or three fingers striking simultaneously. That's a real pain to assemble by hand, but one stroke of the macro does it all.

But here: to show you how it works in practice, I shall *not* edit out the brackets and arrows of the second and third paragraphs following this one. No, I did not set those brackets up just for you; it happened just the way it is presented. But what I did do was insert this explanation ahead of it (which is one of the con-venient things a computer can do for a writer: insert material without retyping the prior text) because otherwise those inter-ruptions and arrows would be pretty confusing. So *this* paragraph is faked up, but not what follows. (I always try to be fair to my readers, even the unworthy ones.) Several prior bracket-notes relating to mysterious phone calls that interrupted my typing of this Note have been edited out, however.

But there was another problem. The original keyboard had the period and comma on both upper and lower case, as many typewriters do. Some bright character in the hardware division had elected to save effort by having a default on those keys, so that only the lower-case characters got through to the screen. Thus when a capital period or capital comma was typed, the lower-case one was actually represented. Who would ever know the difference?

(Editor's Note: The following two paragraphs are indented to permit setting Author's symbols. Author does not indent, but sets these beyond the margin, but this is not feasible in the case of book margins. This is a purely mechanical device and has no other significance.)

Well, *I* knew the difference. Because [callback at 4:15 saying that they have a major problem with the line and asking me not to use the phone for another day. I told the man I could not distinguish between a legitimate request and a practical joke, so I would phone the company and inquire. He said fine, and he would call back in twenty minutes. So I called— and the operator pointed out (UPS delivery, three parcels—I didn't hear the truck, but heard the dogs barking) that we are served by United Telephone, not Southwestern Bell, so they would not be calling us about any local line problem. She agreed that it sounded like a practical joke. Good enough; I doubt that I will hear from that guy again.] in my changed layout, those keys are where my *W* and *V* are. So when I typed those capitals, I actually got them uncapped. DEC—Digital Equipment Co.—didn't know any solution to that problem, and neither did SmartKey. How can you get around a default when it is built in to the keyboard? (Later we realized the explanation might be simpler: SmartKey simply translates one symbol to another, not caring how the first symbol is generated. Because a capital period is the same as a lower-case period, SmartKey translates both the same way.)

I am an ornery cuss. I refused to take no for an answer. I discussed the matter with my wife, and she did some research in the computer manuals and discovered that the Rainbow is more sophisticated than it seems. It is an international computer, with fifteen different keyboards, so that the needs of foreign languages can be served. [5:15 after horsefeeding, etc. That guy did not phone back, as I thought would be the case. I looked at the Waldenbooks interview transcription and can see how imprecise my speech is; I'm much better as a writer. But the one doing the transcription isn't much, either. When I said "inversely proportional to its merit," it was transcribed as "inversedly fortunal towards marriage."] Any of those foreign keyboards could be set up on our system, merely by going through the proper procedure—and several of them had different symbols on the lower and upper cases of those two keys.

Well, now. Why not change over to a foreign keyboard, then change *that* to Dvorak via SmartKey? It seemed possible, but there was a problem. (There's always a problem!) Those foreign keyboards didn't have all the same letters as the American one. Instead they had things like ¿ and Ø and ñ and £. How could we put our letters in a keyboard that didn't have them all? Well, there was a way; we would have to bring our letters across, exchange them with the foreign ones, and *then* rearrange them into Dvorak. My wife believed she could manage that. She's the computer expert in the family, having once earned our living as a computer programmer, back before home computers existed. (Such recollections tend to make us feel unconscionably old.)

But there was another problem. Some of the foreign keys were set to their own private programs, and could not be changed. Thus we might get our capital *W*s and *V*s, but lose other letters entirely. So I did some research of my own, poring over the representations of the fifteen keyboards, and discovered three whose programmed keys were not in any critical place. I chose the Finnish keyboard, whose special keys were in the upper corners, bracketing the numbers row. We could work around these, as the symbols there were not critical. We would have to move the American +/= key in one space, because that was in the upper right corner and we needed it, and leave the Finnish `/ˆ key in its place. Also, there were two Finnish keyboards: one for the Correspondence Mode and the other for the Data Processing Mode. The one with the symbols I needed was the Data Processing Mode.

Then I went to work compiling an exchange chart for every letter on the keyboard, as capital and lower-case. Ninety-six exchanges in all—about half of the total on the keyboard. It took me hours. Then my wife got into the guts of the reprogramming of the keys and made the changes, and lo! it worked! We had what was probably the first complete Dvorak keyboard on the Rainbow. No longer did I have to head out into the hinterlands of the Function Keys to find where they had put my capitals.

So I am now typing this Note on the Data Processing Mode of the Finnish keyboard, with certain letters imported from the American keyboard, configured to my special version of the Dvorak layout. Naturally I sent a smug letter to SmartKey telling them how to do likewise. I love it when I, an ignoramus, can tell the experts how to do the job that stumped them—and be right. (No, they did not reply. For some reason I can't quite fathom, experts don't seem to like having me show them up. I wonder whether they will give us credit, when they revise their procedure and their manual? Don't be concerned; this self-congratulatory Note will be seen by the folk who count. Namely, you readers.) (Except for that reviewer who fell asleep early in the Note. No, don't jog his elbow; let him suffer. His face is in the book, and the print is transferring itself to his cheek, backwards. You will be able to recognize him by the steam rising from his review of this book.)

One other thing, before the next reader falls asleep. I mentioned power failures. We have them here by the gross, as we are deep in the forest, at the very end of the line, literally. I broke into the computer by typing letters—I have them by the gross, too— and when the power blinked twice in one hour, erasing me both times, my blood-pressure made like Old Faithful. "I can't work this way!" I told my wife, who had been showing me how to work the buttons. So we quit in disgust and retired to the house. A storm was building; evidently lightning strikes farther up the line were responsible. And in the next hour that lightning found the range and struck right by us and sent a devastating surge along the line. It blew out our good color TV set, and a burner of the electric stove, sending a shower of sparks at my daughter Cheryl; and the timer on our water heater (trees overgrow our solar water heating system, and it sprang a leak, so we had to go back to electric, but we turn it on by the timer only two hours a day); and several components of the Atari computer system my daughters use for games and (before the Rainbow and that lightning strike) for word processing; and all the light bulbs that happened to be on. It put splotches of color on the screen of the Atari monitor and another TV set that weren't even turned on. It raced up the two hundred-foot extension to my study and put my two all-wave radios halfway out of circulation (thereafter they would tune in only the closest, loudest stations). At the very, very end of that line was my new, three-day-installed Rainbow system, the obvious target.

And the surge petered out just at that point. Having wastefully expended its energy taking out all the side-pieces, it lacked the strength to do the job it had come for. Ten thousand dollars' worth of computer emerged unscathed. I think. It is true that it tends to garble the recorded size of files, claiming they are bigger than they are, which has caused me some problems in judging the length of novels. But I think that's a software defect.

But the only reason that system had been turned off—for it surely wouldn't have survived if it had been on—was my disgust at getting erased twice in an hour.

I may be a slow learner, but that got through to me. Forthwith we ordered a UPS box—Uninterruptible Power Supply. Not only did that protect us from power failures, by providing ten or more minutes backup power, it also protected us from power surges. And that box has saved us many times since. In fact, now we own three of them. At $500 per, they aren't cheap, but we do need them.

Actually, my computerization isn't as isolated a phenomenon as this may have made it seem. There is a fannish and a social aspect. Back in OctOgre of 1983 I was co-Guest-of-Honor with

Richard Adams (*Horseclans*) at the science fiction convention NECRONOMICON. I receive about one invitation to a convention a month, and I turn them down because I'm busy writing and I don't like to travel; Del Rey Books got me to the ABA convention in Dallas in 1983 by bringing my whole family along, but that Satanish device is unlikely to work again and I think that more or less covers my out-of-state traveling for this decade. NECRONOMICON, however, was in Tampa, where we often go anyway, so I agreed to attend, and I brought my daughters, then aged thirteen and sixteen. Naturally they got hooked on conventions, and thereafter they attended them without me.

Well, the fan GOH was Bill Ritch, an expert in DR WHO, video cassette recorders (VCR's), computers and such. Bill is a huge, harmless, teddybear of a man who likes people. I met him and talked to him about this and that, and evidently my daughters did too, for two months later, the night before Christmas, he showed up for a visit. He was just passing through on his way to Miami. But he had come down from the north—that is to say, Atlanta, Georgia—and naturally he brought the cold weather with him. The temperature dropped steadily and was freezing by the time he got ready to go. He had it in mind to drive overnight in his unheated car.

At this point our parental instincts got the better of us, and we prevailed on him to stay the night and resume travel in the morning. Indeed this was wise, for it dropped to Florida-record levels that night: the coldest December ever, for the state. By morning it was 15°F on our carport. We were comfortable, of course, for we have a good wood stove. As it happened, Bill had a VCR with him that he was taking to his folks in Miami. So he hooked it up to our TV and showed us *Thriller* and *Blade Runner* and such. That was our first direct experience with a VCR. Later Bill sent us literature on the subject, and we bought a Sony 2700 Betamax. Thus it was Bill who got us into video, and that has certainly brightened a number of what otherwise would have been dull TV evenings. More recently we got a video camera, using it to record the talks I give at local schools and such. For the first time I have been able to see myself as others see me, watching myself on our own TV. I'm sort of angular, and my voice seems somewhat nasal; believe me, I come across better in an Author's Note than I do in person. (Sigh.)

Bill showed up periodically thereafter. I told him how I was unable to computerize because of the keyboard problem, and he told me of SmartKey and the Digital computers. Thus he was directly responsible for the manner I obtained my present setup, which I suspect is the best currently available for a serious writer. No, I promised not to go into tedious detail, and please don't deluge me with letters claiming that IBM or Kaypro are better; I was late coming into this equipment, but I knew what I wanted, and my needs are specialized. Computer companies have very little notion of the needs of novelists, which is why it is necessary to pick and choose carefully. Even the reviewers of software are ignorant in this regard. I read one who condemned a program because it defaulted to overstrike. That is, when you want to correct a typo, you can simply strike over the error, anywhere in the text, without messing up anything else. That's vital for a typo-prone writer like me—but you can't readily do it with the type of program that reviewer recommended. My program can readily be changed to a different default, when I want it.

The software program affects the computer the way personality affects a human being. What counts is not merely what is done, but *how* it's done. The term "user-friendly" is no joke; if you think of the computer for a moment as a big dog, the user-friendly program will cause that dog to wag his tail and slurp your hand when he meets you, while the other type of program would cause him to consume your left buttock. Some programs are menu-driven, and some are command-driven. With the former you can't do anything without having to get into the menu, which is a list of available tasks to choose from. That can get annoying when all you want to do is correct a typo you happened to see in the prior sentence. With the latter you can do it directly by typing the correct code—but that means you have to memorize a squintillion complex codes. That, too, is annoying. I suspect the best programs are compromises, with simple commands buttressed by simple menus for the less-frequent tasks. I started out with what came with the system: The DEC-approved Select-86 word processor, menu-driven. I typed my first novel on that, which happened to be *But What of Earth?* that I was restoring to its original condition for republication, together with twenty-five thousand words of comment on the nature of the (abysmal) editing it had received before. I soon discovered what DEC didn't know about the holes in its own program; whoever approved it had never, for example, tried to use the double-spacing setting or tried to follow the written instructions on how to remove a hard-carriage-return. But the same user-friendly DEC man who had put me on to the amber screen monitor—that's the one that doesn't give you eye-strain—put me on to the PTP text processor, and I composed (as opposed to retyping) the first novel, *Golem in the Gears,* with that one. Then we figured out the Finnish-keyboard device, and I composed the first science fiction novel (as opposed to fantasy), *Politician,* with that.

Now I hear some of you clamoring about why should I settle for a text-processing program no one ever heard of, instead of going first-class with WordStar or Word Perfect. Well, here is another thing that the industry has been slow to understand. The ideal word processor is not the one that tries to do all things for all users, in the process becoming monstrously complex and bur-dening most users with complicated peripheral features they sel-dom or never use. That's like selling a Mack truck to a housewife for her weekly shopping. The ideal is the one that does the basics readily, is easy to learn and understand, and allows the individual to program his own specialized functions. PTP is the easiest of all the programs I have considered to learn and use, and its macros enable me to set up just exactly those specialized features, like down-arrows or my bibliography boilerplate, that I want—and no others. Thus it is simple and sophisticated and personalized, exactly as I am. Oh, I admit there are a couple of things it lacks that I would like, such as "windows" (those enable you to call up another file and view it while keeping the current one on a parallel screen, so you can verify whether you said something in a prior chapter that you are about to say here) and the ability to address my full 256K memory (it addresses only half of it). Every so often I bug the maker, and I suspect that in due course he'll come through with improvements. But basically I feel that I have here a setup, hard, soft, and firm, that would be the first choice of any newcomer who could afford it, if he but knew its features. Oldtimers are lost; once a person has taken six months to master

WordStar, he's not about to throw that away and spend two days to master PTP.

Meanwhile Bill Ritch phoned. A store in Atlanta was having a half-price sale on Rainbow 100's. Were we interested? We were. We sent him the money, he bought Rainbows for us and his own projects, and we set up the duplicate system at the house, where it would be warm in winter. Thus the fourth novel, *Red Sword,* is the first on that second system. Thus, within nine months of computerization, I have done three and a half novels (the first being a rework), which is a fair pace even for me, and yes, I am now thoroughly addicted to the computer. But you can see how closely it ties in with personal connections.

One thing I considered for this novel was changing the operating system. You see, there are levels and levels of these things, even in software. The computer system might be likened to a car, with wheels, engine, doors and such. The software can be likened to the controls that direct the progress of that car. But obviously you don't do things directly; there is a series of linkages between your hands and the engine, and between the engine and the wheels. So I think of the word processor as the layout of the steering wheel, gearshift (or automatic shift), ignition key, dials and such, while the operating system is the gearbox below, the steering mechanism, the clutch and such. You can have a similar layout and the same type of engine as another car, but the intermediary linkages may be quite different, and the kind you want for Sunday morning driving might not be suitable for the racetrack. So with computer operating systems; they are largely invisible, but they are important, and some suit particular purposes better than others.

The operating system I use is CP/M, obviously an abbreviation for an old retired naval man called Captain Manager. Captain M supplements his income by renting his house, which is a fine old edifice of some fifteen storeys (as he spells it) and a capacious cellar. Each floor contains six rooms and is provided with all the amenities of the domicile. Because the Captain never saw fit to adjust all the way to civilian life, he calls his boarders "Users" and he assigns them numbers. Thus User 1 occupies the first floor, and when he enters the building he must step into the elevator and punch out the code USER 1, and instantly he is there. Similarly for User 2, and on up to the one on the top floor, User 15. Some of these boarders sublet individual rooms, and these they reach by pausing in the elevator to punch out *A, B, E, F, G*, or *H*, which are the designations the Captain has coded for this building. Now you might suppose that this was an aggravating nuisance, but in fact it is very much to the advantage of the boarders, for each one had absolute privacy within his number and letter. All the furniture is set up exactly as he wants it, and the rooms are completely individualized. It is as if the rest of the building doesn't exist. The elevator has a Directory that can be flashed on a screen by typing the secret code word MAINT, and it will show a complete inventory of everything in the designated room on that floor. There may be hundreds of other items in the various other rooms and floors, but this Directory ignores them; they have their own Directories.

What this means is that the Captain provides the ideal situation for a writer who has a number of projects going simultaneously and wants to keep them all distinct, without accidentally erasing one, but who also has teenage offspring that wish to borrow the machine for word-processing homework. For the House of CP/ M is my computer, as organized by that operating system. I had nightmares of a daughter turning on the computer, touching the wrong button, and erasing my past week's work. So I set us up with the House, and now the cellar (User 0) contains the assorted software programs including the good Captain M himself, while I have reserved floors 1 through 9 for business purposes, and two floors each for wife and daughters. Penny, who likes the view from the heights, has the top two floors, for example, and when she uses the computer she punches in User 14 or User 15 and there she is, with her margins set the way she left them, her macros ready, and all the files she has saved ready for her. When she punches the Macro 7 button she gets whatever she has put on it; when I punch the same button, down on User 1, I get my down-arrow. On User 3 that same button evokes my About-the-Author boilerplate. (A boilerplate is a set passage that can be inserted into a letter or other text without retyping; it can be very handy for answering the same question from different fans.) I would be quite lost on her floors, because I don't know her macros and don't understand the contemporary teengirl way of doing things. And she would not be at home on my floors, should she go to one by accident. And we don't snoop on each other; I visit her floors only by invitation, so she has privacy of correspondence, and of course she's not interested in *my* correspondence. Neither of us can affect anything on the other's floor from our own floor, so accidents are impossible. A family with fifteen or even sixteen Users could give each a floor, and each one could program each of the six rooms (four sections of the hard disk, plus the two floppy disk drives) differently, to allow for an infinite number of variations. Yes, infinite, because there is no limit to the number of floppy disks that can be used in turn in their drives, and the defaults are stored on the disks themselves. If a daughter takes one of my floppies by mistake and uses MAINT to check what's on it, it won't tell her, because it answers only to my User number. So it is as if we have several computers, and it's beautiful. We even have color-coded cases for the disks: Blue for Penny, Green for Cheryl, Red for my wife, and Black and Yellow for me. I suppose what I'm saying is that we have a family computer system in the most compatible way, and we all like it, and visitors (yea, even Bill Ritch) are impressed by our setup. Bill even took home a disk containing my macros, so that he can get little arrows and things, though I can't imagine what he does with them. (I picture him running about Atlanta, poking people with little arrows . . .)

But the Captain is not the only operating system. There is MS-DOS, obviously the abbreviation for a somewhat prim lady of uncertain age and marital status. Ms Dos distrusts apartment buildings, having perhaps had some bad experience there, but she likes to garden. So her layout is in the form of a garden with paths leading to the various entries. When you enter this garden you encounter a Directory with several diverging paths; pick a path, and it leads to another Directory with several more, and each one of those paths leads to its own sub-Directory of files. So each occupant of the garden can have privacy, with his own selection of flowers and such, but by a different mechanism. Our computer is equipped to handle both CP/M and MS-DOS, so I thought I'd try the latter for this novel. But I found that the Captain and the Lady don't get along together all that well; if I want both at once, I have to split my hard disk into two halves, one for each, and the two hardly speak to each other. And it seems that the Lady doesn't have the MAINT feature that puts all my files in alphabetical order and allows me to change titles, delete files or take a quick peek at any file without disturbing it, and gives me the space used by each file and the total space used by them all. Those are housekeeping features I use constantly, for every day's work is a separate file and there may be sixty of them for a novel. PTP has both CP/M and MS-DOS versions, and so does SmartKey, so I can have my keyboard layout and macros and things with either, but the Captain's type of organization just seemed to be better for me. So my apologies to those of you who know and like Ms Dos, and wish I had used her for this novel. Maybe some other time.

Part II: Personal

But enough (more than enough!) of computers; I realize that the relatively gentle rivalry between the Captain and the Lady is not the type of violence you want to see in this Note. You want to know exactly how violence and war struck at me while I was writing *Red Sword*. Well, I started this just after the turn of the year, Jamboree 2, 1985, in the Ogre Calendar. Penny, whom we taught to drive two years ago in *Hourglass*, now drives to school, taking two friends with her, because they have early classes that the schoolbus doesn't catch. You might suppose that there are no hazards of the road, on that twelve-mile trip through the sparsely inhabited countryside. But one day some truck left a tangled mass of metal just over the brink of a hill that Penny encountered—flat tire, phone call, we got out there to rescue her, discovering one of her teachers changing the tire, and I drove her car in to get the tire fixed. Since I had never even been *in* that car before, I had to figure out how to operate it, which was an uncomfortable business, because it has little features that didn't exist in my day. You might say the macros and defaults are all wrong. But that was before; now, in Jamboree, came a more serious call. That's right; there had been an accident, and she was phoning from the hospital.

Periodically in this region, the forestry folk do what they call controlled burns, burning off regions of the state forest in the slack season so that there will not be uncontrolled forest fires at other times. The policy makes sense, but sometimes the burners lack common sense. This winter has been generally dry, and there have been a number of uncontrolled burns. This time they started a burn adjacent to the highway Penny drives to school, and the wind blew it out of control. We passed it in the evening, as we came home from an archæology meeting; the fires raged for a mile or more beside the road, and the region resembled a section of Hell. (I happen to know what Hell looks like.) The next morning was foggy, and the fire was still smoldering. We cautioned Penny about driving through that region. "If there is thick smoke there, you don't dare slow down too much, because the car behind will ram you," I said. But we doubted that it was bad, because there had been no news of smoke, and the road was open. However, it *was* bad, and Penny, driving in to school alone for the first time (the two other girls coincidentally had other business), found herself caught in dense smog. All night, owing to an inversion, that smoke had accumulated by that road. Penny, mindful of my warning, slowed to 25 mph—and rammed into a truck that was moving at walking speed. The truck was hardly damaged, but our little car suffered a $2,600 repair bill. They pushed the car off the road, and Penny, shaken up but not really hurt, thanks to the use of her seat belt (I taught her, remember; I taught her right. Anyone who drives or rides in a car without using the seat belt is a fool; I don't care how educated he may consider himself to be in other respects.), went out to try to flag down other cars before they collided. Her friend, who normally rides in with her, was next to arrive; she recognized Penny and stopped, then started to maneuver to get off the road. And a fourth car came up and crushed the friend's car against the original truck. So there it was, a four-car accident—and it was obvious that had Penny not driven the speed she had, she would have been rear-ended by that fourth car, or crushed between the two. As it was, she was technically at fault—but alive. A person has to consider not only the law, but common sense.

That smoke, all told, accounted for nine cars that morning, and several more that were peripheral. It was the worst traffic situation in the history of the county. An ambulance was dispatched;

when it encountered the smoke, it had a man walk ahead of it to show the way, and then that man had to slow down because the vehicle couldn't keep up with him. The police said that they had never seen worse driving conditions; that visibility was zero. *Now* they closed off the road; why they had not done so before is an unanswered question. Penny's name appeared in the accounts of three newspapers. Our car was out of commission for the rest of the month. Now Penny is afraid to drive in fog, understandably; the day I started typing this Note, we had to drop breakfast and head out to rescue her because she didn't dare drive into it. The fog gets pretty thick some mornings, and we understand. This is what families are for. I got gun-shy about driving after my roll-over, back in 1956, and I still don't really like to drive. One morning when there was light fog, Penny braced herself and drove anyway. Came a phone call: "Daddy, this is Penny, calling from the bank." Oops; where was she caught now? "The bank? *What* bank?" "The fog bank," she replied. She had made it through. Oh, what about the real culprits in this mess, the forestry and highway departments who burned recklessly and never told the public about the hazard? It seems they are immune from fault, and our insurance paid.

That was Jamboree: fire and collision. But this novel required two months to write, even with the computer. I'm not really a fast writer; I'm a steady one. An average of two thousand words a day for two months covers a one hundred twenty thousand word novel. Actually, I work faster, then suffer interruptions. So what violence occurred in FeBlueberry?

I was awakened at 3:40 A.M. by the phone. It was a neighbor— the high school was burning to the ground. Both my daughters go there. As it turned out, only part of the school burned, but that was enough to eliminate normal functioning. So the freshmen and the seniors had to take their classes elsewhere—and we have one of each. It may never be known whether the fire was natural or arson; it seemed to start with an explosion, but whether it was a bomb or a faulty heater can not be ascertained. Classes will be affected the rest of this year and next year, while they see about rebuilding. Unfortunately the library was lost, with all its books, including some of mine. So we donated a thousand dollars to the library fund; after all, it behooves a writer to support both libraries and the school his children attend. I had a thank-you note from a teacher on another matter, and sure enough, the envelope was scorched. Good thing I knew the cause, or I might have feared it was a letter from Hell.

And more news: a local company asked permission to explore the entire state forest that we live against for possible limerock mining. Now this sort of mining is open-pit, and it leaves a landscape reminiscent of that of the Moon. Reclamation is a joke; the trees and animal ecology are gone. We bought land where we did in order to have a guarantee that the natural land could never be denied us. But it seemed that while the state owned the land, the national government retained the mineral rights, which meant it could license the land for strip-mining. (It is said that profits can run as high as a million dollars per acre.) Ah, but *was* there limerock there to mine? Yes, indeed; it was under our own land. Was the acreage we owned to become an island of wilderness next to a wasteland that was once the state forest? If this was not war, it seemed very like it. The outlook was grim. But then, before the battle was joined, new information came to light; the state forest had been designated for public use only, back when it had been set aside, and could not be signed away for private mining. Satan had been balked by a technicality—about the time I wrote the final chapter.

Let's narrow the focus to the more personal aspect. How am *I* doing, these two months of this novel? Well, I can write well enough, unless distracted by other calls on my time, such as letters and manuscripts and research for other projects. What was the story there?

Life continued at its frenetic pace. I made notes on items I might mention here, but the inclusion of all of them would render this Note much longer than anyone would have patience for. So, just the more significant ones, and briefly. My major concern was research for a mainstream novel relating to the situation of the American Indians of this region of Florida at the time Hernando de Soto passed through. Every Sunday we went out to the Indian mound being excavated, where my daughter Cheryl worked. Our involvement is intimate; there will be more on that elsewhere in due course. For now it suffices to say that significant finds are being made and that the matter has been taking up a significant amount of my time. Associated with this, before the turn of the year, our whole family joined an archæological canoe trip, with Cheryl and I sharing one canoe. It was a kind of nightmare. So I enhanced the details and put it into this novel. Those who wonder where I get my ideas may take due note; I do more adaptation from life than most readers realize.

Just about this time, my right shoulder began bothering me chronically. It hurts when I stretch or reach too far. We'll check with the doctor when we have time, but meanwhile it is progressive and worrisome. I have lost partial use of both knees, and it doesn't please me to have the same thing happen to a shoulder. I'm still doing my exercises, such as the chins on the study rafter, but it is now painful to get my grip, and I can't descend all the way. I still do thirty, operating in the restricted range, but, if the shoulder gets worse, that exercise may be denied me. Since I have always felt that the end of my physical exercise program will mark the beginning of the end of my life, this is not a minor matter to me. I now do seventy-five Japanese pushups in under four minutes, sometimes under 3:30; my best time is 3:03, beating the time that evoked the kidney stone in *Pale Horse* by more than a minute. I hate doing them, but I would hate even more to have to give them up. My runs are slowing, too, and I am no longer able to break 21 minutes for three miles, or 22, and usually can't break 23. I am minded of the line from W.B. Yeats: "The hour of the waning of love is upon us." I love my physical fitness, perhaps the final relic of my youth, and I feel the hour of the waning of it. I fear that even the Ping pong will be ended by this particular incapacity. Well, I'm past fifty now; the war against age and death is one that every person is fated to lose. But I am conscious of a significant loss, right at this time.

In one week in this same period, I addressed three different school classes. I don't like taking the time, but I do support education, so I give these local talks when requested. One was to Penny's college-level English class, and Penny took our brand new video camera and recorded me, as I think I mentioned in Part I of this Note. By coincidence, it was in the homeroom of a different teacher (the school fire jumbled these things)—one who had angrily told her classes that "Piers Anthony is wrong." That dated from a prior address I had given, when I had stated

"You no more need to know the names of the parts of speech in order to use the English language correctly than you need to know the names of the muscles and ligaments of the legs in order to walk correctly." I was once an English teacher, you see, and I take exception to much of what is currently being taught. I believe that less effort should be expended on irrelevant material like parts of speech, and more on relevant material like how to balance a checkbook or understand mortgage interest—things a person could use in today's world. So I repeated my statement—and this time received applause for it. Of course the teacher who objects to my attitude was not there; I did take the trouble to greet her when she arrived. I am not, of course, wrong. Another presentation was for a selected group in a different school in the county, the attendees being students who were fans of mine. But the challenge was the third, to a second grade class. The youngest fan I have had a letter from was eight years old; these were in the seven-year-old range, and none of them had read any of my books, but they were interested in writing. They were doing books of their own, as a class project. I wanted to be sure not to overshoot their level of interest, so I told them about how the baby ogre in *Crewel Lye* foiled the dragon and about the monster-under-the-bed, and these were things they related to. Then they had an Author's Reception with refreshments they had prepared, so it became a social occasion. I think it was a success. That, too is on the videotape. Certainly it was an interesting experience. But this sort of thing does take time, and is one of the reasons I failed to complete this novel within the two-month period I had allotted.

And in this period the question of a motion picture option was settled. In 1984, interest in the Xanth series developed, stipulating a payment of $300,000 for each novel made into a movie, with the possibility of using all nine Xanth novels. But there was also interest in Germany for cartoon adaptation for the first three Xanths, for $500,000. Which was the better bet? The American deal might peter out after the first novel, so was not necessarily better, and of course there was no telling what quality of movie might be made. We pondered, and finally gambled on the American deal, and I signed the option contract. Time passed, and finally it was apparent that the option was not going to be exercised. So it goes.

This was also the time of the Sharon/*Time* magazine and West-moreland/CBS libel suits, both resolved somewhat indecisively, as wars often are. Freedom of the press—I believe in it, but it does get abused, and I think it is best that an accounting be made periodically. And on a lighter note, this was the time when the war between men and women erupted on a new front. Ann Landers conducted a survey and reported that 72% of her women would rather be cuddled than have sex. Furor followed. Mike Royko conducted a hilarious counter-survey, getting the men's side of it. I, of course, have a fairminded solution: let the women wear placards bearing the numbers 72 or 28 so that the men can make more informed decisions about dating, marriage, etc. Any man who prefers Cuddles can probably have her. The divorce rate might drop precipitously. Not to mention the marriage rate. (And to think they call me a sexist!)

And Bantam Books ran a five-page promotional ad in various periodicals, showing reproductions of bestseller lists with their books thereon. But Anthony got shown five times in that ad for the Del Rey novels *On a Pale Horse* and *Bearing an Hourglass*, the first two volumes in this series. I'm sure Del Rey joins me in thanking Bantam for the free publicity.

I typed a record 125 letters in the month of Jamboree, and in FeBlueberry I had a manuscript and a book to read and blurb, sent by two publishers with whom I am not doing business, and another expected from a third publisher. No, this is professional courtesy; I do for other writers what other writers did for me when I was in need, though I am a slow reader and it takes me days to get through a book. But about the letters: most of them were cards, as I have become adept at reducing my responses to that length, though each remains individual. Most other writers, I understand, do not bother to answer their mail; certainly I could save a lot of time if I did not. But those are living, feeling people out there, and I feel that they deserve answers, so as long as I can, I am answering. I have no secretary; I bash them out, with typos, strikeovers, and all, on my manual typewriter. (The computer printer can't handle cards.) By going wholesale to the card format, I have managed to keep up.

One day I received fifty letters: forty-four in a package from

Del Rey, six from elsewhere. Next day I typed thirty cards, and the following day twenty mixed cards and letters, and the third day, seven, saving the complicated ones for last. Only then did I get back to work on *Sword*. But you know, I don't suffer from Writer's Block, while many other writers do. I can not prove this, but it is my suspicion that those writers who are callous about social responsibilities, so do not answer letters, also tend to be callous about their business commitments, so suffer Block. Those who take all commitments seriously, including the need to consider the feelings and rights of others, do a better job at meeting those commitments: correspondence *and* books. If this is true, it is poetic justice. At any rate, I believe I write about as many letters *and* as much fiction as anyone in the genre, and I would like to think the two are linked. There are those who have called me naïve about this sort of thing, though.

And you know, those letters can be interesting. Let me give a couple of examples, positive and negative. One letter in that bunch of fifty informed me that a fan had named her prize colt after me: Piers Anthony Jacob. She says he is the prettiest horse alive. That seems only natural to me. I have asked the publisher whether we can run a picture of that horse on the back flap of this book. Might as well improve that aspect of the volume, after all. Another letter, received as I worked on this Note, is anonymous—no name or address, so I can't answer it. I regard anonymous missives as fair game, so I'll quote excerpts here: "It is becoming abundantly clear that your endless, thoroughly boring rants, diatribes and dissertations 'justifying' (through the many scenes you have depicting them) violent, humiliating [undecipherable word here] and soul-destroying sexual assaults against women are just thinly (very!) disguised versions of apologiae of the same sorts of assaults on children of either sex." It contines in similar vein, psychoanalyzing me and concluding that I am trying to expiate guilt for similar things done to me as a child, and finishes: "Do you *really* want the whole world to remember you as 'Piers Anthony, the Battered Child'?" No novel of mine is named; those familiar with my work are free to make their own conjectures about the accuracy of this charge. Yes, I answer this kind of mail too, when able, though I am not as polite as I am to more positive fans. But as you can see, my mail is not boring.

In FeBlueberry it slacked off, with only thirty-nine letters, but the books-to-be-blurbed took up what slack there might have been. Still, by the end of the month I was two days from completing the editing of the novel. The editing consists of reading it through on the screen, printing out my bracket-notes relating to other projects, deleting both bracket notes and marginal symbols (I have special macros to facilitate that, such as one that locates and highlights all the material between the next set of brackets, so I can check it before deleting it), correcting my own typos and spelling errors (yes, we have a spelling-checker program, but it's easier to do it myself), revising awkward sentences, and adding new material where required. This editing replaces the second and submission-draft typings I used to do and takes about a quarter the time. So I knew I would wrap it up just a couple of days into Marsh.

And on Marsh oneth (1th) came a package from Del Rey Books containing eighty-six fan letters dating back to Jamboree and Dismember. I should have known that if I used Ogre Months I'd get ogrish mail! There was nothing to do but read them (which alone took about six hours) and answer them (six days). So by the end of the Seventh I had answered eighty-seven of those eighty-six letters. (Apparently they were starting to reproduce in the package.) Then I got on the letters that had come in separately. As I type this paragraph, which is being inserted in the middle of this text, I have done 102 letters, as of the Ninth. This novel has been delayed that week. I think the pace is about to slack off, maybe, I hope. But this feels very like a war!

Again, I hear someone muttering: why do I bother? Why not call it quits and stick to my paying work? Or perhaps answer only the most serious ones and let the others go. Ah, yes, I hear the siren song of expediency. I understand that only two writers in the genre answer large volumes of mail personally; the other is Isaac Asimov. But again, I know of only two who never suffer Writer's Block, and the other is Isaac Asimov. My Antiblock Theory gains credence.

But let's consider some of these letters individually. Perhaps some are dispensable. Two from this last bunch were from people who are confined long-term by accident or illness and use my books to ease their solitude and pain. It seems that mine have better effect in this respect than those of most other writers. In the past I had letters from a young man who used my books to divert his mind from the unpleasantness of chemotherapy for cancer. Another in the present group is from an oncology (cancer) nurse who thanks me for taking death seriously in *On a Pale Horse*. Ignore these letters? I just can not; they must be answered.

Well, some of the others, then. Yet they evoke startling bits of individual personality. There is the lady who announces that I have stolen her *heart*. The righteously indignant teenager who isn't sending me any *PUNS*. (You see, most of these are in response to *Crewel Lye*, just published, whose brief Note explains that Xanth is no longer in the market for puns. That didn't stop a number of fans from sending me full pages of them.) The mother who thanks Xanth for doing what nothing else did—hooking her learning-disabled son on reading. (I raised an L-D daughter; I understand about this sort of thing.) The coed who was hooked on Xanth by her boyfriend; she gave up the boyfriend but remained addicted to Anthony and, when my novels ran out, she had to get into Donaldson, Eddings, Moorcock, and McCaffrey. (Those other writers may not realize how much of their success is thus owed to me . . .) The man who brings up seeming inconsistencies in my novels, then proffers intelligent explanations for these that I can use to fend off other critics. The one who wishes to convert me to Jesus. (I am apt to refer these well-meaning people to my three-part novel *Tarot*, which is perhaps cruel. The point is, I am not agnostic from ignorance, but from preference; I suspect I have done more research on religion than most.) The young woman who begins: "I'm 19 yrs. old + I don't want to be a writer. I want to be an editor." (That one popped my eyes open! But why not? Editing is a dirty job, but someone has to do it.) The man who met a college professor of mine and relays that professor's regards to me—along with the news that the professor is dead. (I hadn't realized, so this was a jolt. That prof had been my counselor; I remember him with preternatural clarity.) The woman who relates somewhat graphically her experience in being assaulted by a masked male who put a gun to her head, and her thoughts on death and *On a Pale Horse*. And from the interim mail: a "fan" letter in the form of a fan, that opens out to reveal the writing. And an invitation to a convention, that I turned down, as usual. Which of these do I file without answering?

Well, why not cut off the repeats? Answer each fan once, and not again? Two considerations, there. First, I have found that a kind of universal inverse ratio applies, so that only about half of the first-timers respond again, and only half of the second-timers, and so on, so that the correspondence tends to damp out. That enables me to keep it down without actually having to cut people off, and I prefer that method. Second, some of those fans have excellent continuing input, and an arbitrary limit would be unfortunate. Third, (my difficulty in keeping count has been noted before) there are special cases.

I wrote about sixteen letters to one girl in Jamboree, ranging from cards to a six page missive. Yes, this is a very special case, and illustrates as well as any the levels on which wars are fought, the conflict between good and evil, and the difficulty of telling the two apart. This was a suicidal teenager who said she loved me. Now I was at this writing fifty years old, with two daughters older than this girl, so the matter had points of awkwardness.

You see, though I was never a 'battered child' I was a disturbed child, with compulsive mannerisms and comprehensive fear. Another impression I have is that a person does not have to be totally fouled up to be a successful writer, but that it helps. Today I have a life that is about as comfortable as any life gets, with supportive wife and daughters, an income in the top percentile, and success in the one type of work I always wanted to succeed at. I don't crave the adulation of the masses, but I know I could experience it any time I choose to attend a fan convention. I should be deliriously happy. But I am not. I suffer from chronic depression and I think about death on a daily basis, perhaps an hourly basis. (Yesterday I buried our last hen; we had had twelve, and as time progressed they died off individually; the last survivor had been with us a year and a half after the death of the next-to-last. Call me foolish if you will; I grieve for her, as I do for any pet who dies. Death is much larger in my life than in that of most other people.) I am not suicidal and never have been, but every morning I ask myself whether life is really worth it, and I am uncertain. As the day progresses I become more positive, and by evening I am pretty satisfied with life. Since no economic or social reason exists for this depression, and it is cyclical by the day, and stead-fast by the year, I conjecture that it is a fringe benefit of my mild diabetes; my cells are generally slightly hungry for energy, and that chronic discomfort translates into mild depression.

The point is, I do have a basis to understand the situation of a fouled-up child, because of my memory of my own childhood; and I understand also how depression can be. My depression relates to this girl's depression about the way my adult-onset diabetes relates to the savage juvenile-onset form of it. What I have is token; what she has is serious. So while I only wonder whether life is worthwhile, she thinks seriously of suicide. I, being what I am, can not simply tell her to quit bothering me.

Oh, objectively the situation is clear enough. This girl—I will not identify her here, of course, but let's give her an obvious pseudonym. I shall name her after a suicide I have in this novel, Ligeia, though there is no other parallel that I know of between the two. "Ligeia" was not aware of having experienced love in her home and she longed to be a part of a family where love exists. That is to say, my family. She wanted to love and be loved, which is perhaps the deepest human need. She could not simply invoke that love from others, but she could contribute her part of it. Thus she loved me, because she knew me from my novels and Notes, and because I answered her letters seriously, as I do with all letters. I had been treating her in the way I would a daughter and a child, partly because I was conscious that she was not exactly either. My teenage readers may find this confusing, but I trust that my adult readers will understand. This is not a "childish" matter; Ligeia wanted from me a good deal more than I could afford to give on either the fatherly or the man-woman level. I of course explained that, and she of course refused to accept it. Thus I found myself in a kind of ethical war, and it was difficult indeed to distinguish the nuances of right from wrong.

Why didn't I simply tell her that her interest was misplaced, and reject her letters? Two reasons. First, because I try to follow the Golden Rule, treating others as I would have them treat me, with fairness and compassion. Second, because it was possible that she would have died if I cut her off that way. In that sense this was a kind of emotional blackmail. It happens to be a kind I am vulnerable to. If this be a failing, it is hardly my only one.

I have to say that I really would not care to know a person well who was not similarly vulnerable. This does not mean being mush-minded; it just means that the consequence of one's actions should be a concern of every person, on the social as well as the legal level.

Our correspondence began when she wrote a fan letter. It grew more serious with time. Her letters came in envelopes decorated with cute little butterflies, unicorns, rainbows, balloons and hearts, signifying a sweet and happy little girl, but inside they were desperate. She told of slashing her wrists in an attempt to commit suicide, of turning on her heater and closing the windows tight, of similar things. She spoke of feeling lonely and tired, of the foreboding of evil. She felt trapped, like being in a box with the sides closing in, and was afraid that after she died she would be similarly trapped, as if in a shell. All that enabled her to survive was love. The love I could not return. She believed she was going mad, but that there was no need to worry: her death would stop only her body, for she felt she was already dead in the ways that mattered. She said that suicide might be considered a cop-out, but that for her it would only hasten the inevitable. She expressed difficulty relating to an emotion that sprang from her heart instead of her mind. She saw love as a lifeline, while hate was worse than anything.

Another letter was smeared, as by tears. She had had a good day that then became bad. A discussion with a friend about love and sex and politics and religion and feeling—the things this bright girl really liked to explore—had lifted her. Then there had been a singularly bad episode at home that threw her back into the depths. She said she needed love so much, yet it eluded her; she couldn't wait to die wholly. She concluded with the words "I'm so cold," trailing off with a jerky line as if abruptly interrupted, the letter unsigned.

I think it is evident that my objective, sensible statements were largely wasted here. I had a deep sympathy for Ligeia's plight, but I could not call this love. I tried to help her in various ways, putting her in touch with supportive correspondents and even checking with the authorities, but to no sufficient avail. Ligeia could not escape her situation that way. I saw her swirling down and down in the maelstrom, and I could not rescue her from that without going well beyond permissible bounds. So I wrote to her, with the unhappy suspicion that this was a war that was being lost.

Hence the letters of Jamboree. I tried an experiment: in addition to the fewer, longer letters, I sent her a series of light post cards, saying nothing thereon that other eyes could not see. The heart of them was the Ogre Tail, transcribed chapter by chapter, fourteen chapters on separate cards. The first Tail was "The Ugly Unicorn," and I think it is worth reprinting here:

> Chapter One: Once upon a time, there was a little unicorn. She lived in a shell.
>
> Chapter Two: There was a funny thing about this shell. No one else could see it.
>
> Chapter Three: But to her, it was very heavy, as if an elephant were on it.
>
> Chapter Four: Sometimes that shell just seemed to crush all the happiness right out of her.
>
> Chapter Five: Of course, she wasn't really a unicorn, because little unicorns don't live in shells.
>
> Chapter Six: She was really an alicorn, which is a flying unicorn. Her mane was brown.
>
> Chapter Seven: Alicorns live in shells, because they like privacy. When anyone comes near, they close.
>
> Chapter Eight: Of course that means that hardly anyone ever sees an alicorn, which is unfortunate.
>
> Chapter Nine: Because alicorns are really very special creatures, when they come out of their shells.
>
> Chapter Ten: But the little unicorn didn't know she was an alicorn. She wanted to die.
>
> Chapter Eleven: This is because a magical creature who stifles her magic is in deep trouble.
>
> Chapter Twelve: No one else understood about this, because no one else could see the shell.
>
> Chapter Thirteen: Except for maybe one old centaur— but he was too far away to help.
>
> Chapter Fourteen: He hoped the little unicorn would learn to fly, before she learned to die.

Ligeia loved the chapters, and they buoyed her momentarily, but then her depression resumed its hold. She wrote me a letter signed with her blood.

In one of her letters, she described a dream she had had, involving a cemetery where instead of people there were thoughts. She had not intended it as a suggestion, but I liked the notion and put it into this novel; this is the notice of credit.

Of such stuff was my life made, as I wrote this novel and this Note. My humor is obvious, but privately war and death and injustice were much on my mind.

You may wonder why I have used the past tense. That is because the enchantment that links these novels to my life remains; the theme is War, and so war came to the publication of the novel. The publisher took exception to this inordinately long Author's Note, stating that it was in the business of fiction, not nonfiction, and requested the Note's deletion. I refused. This was no minor matter; fundamental rights were at issue. The publisher is not required to publish material it deems to be unsuitable for its imprint—but the author must give permission for any significant changes. I feel that these notes are important to a sizeable segment of my readership and I do care about that readership. Neither side backed off, while the novel remained in limbo, unable to be published.

My agent, caught in the middle, spent many hours trying to negotiate a cease-fire, but for months the war continued. At last we came to a compromise. Part of the publisher's concern was about Ligeia: I had presented poignant excerpts from two of her letters. I had cleared this with her directly, showing her the material and making corrections she asked for. But she was a minor; therefore she lacked the legal capacity to give permission for my use of this material. That had to come from her parents. But she had made plain throughout that her parents did not know the things she told me, and she did not want them to know. It would be a violation of her confidence even to ask them for such permission, as her secret love and death wish would be exposed. Thus I could not obtain permission, and risked a lawsuit for the violation of a living person's privacy if I ran the letters. So, with deep regret, I revised that portion of the Note. I can not even tell you what happened to Ligeia in the intervening year, because that might serve to identify her. Thus do I lose the battle for part of my text, but win the battle for the rest of it by the somewhat heroic measure discussed here, and the war for Ligeia's life grinds on.

As I write this revision, I am midway through the next novel in the series, the one concerning Nature. Yes, the enchantment continues; Nature is making herself felt emphatically. I will cover that in the next Note.

ABOUT THE AUTHOR

Piers Anthony was born in August, 1934, in England, spent a year in Spain, and came to America at age six. He was naturalized American in 1958 while serving in the U.S. Army. He now lives in Florida with his wife Carol and their daughters Penny and Cheryl. His first story was submitted to a magazine in 1954, but he did not make his first story sale until 1962. Similarly, he submitted his first novel, which was also his thesis for his B.A. degree from college, in 1956, but did not sell a novel until 1966. In 1985 his 50th book was published. His first Xanth novel, *A Spell for Chameleon*, won the August Derleth Fantasy award for 1977. His novel *Ogre, Ogre* may have been the first original fantasy paperback ever to make the *New York Times* bestseller list, and all his fantasies since then have been bestsellers. He is currently writing three or four novels and answering seven or eight hundred letters a year. His house is hidden deep in the forest, almost impossible to find, and he now has a computer in the horse pasture.